MW01039546

$3.00

MAMA FELA'S GIRLS

MAMA FELA'S GIRLS

Ana Baca

UNIVERSITY OF NEW MEXICO PRESS

ALBUQUERQUE

This is a work of fiction. Names, characters, places,
and incidents either are the product of the author's imagination
or are used fictitiously, and any resemblance to actual persons,
living or dead, business establishments, events,
or locales is entirely coincidental.

❦

Library of Congress Cataloging-in-Publication Data

Baca, Ana.
Mama Fela's girls / Ana Baca.
p. cm.
ISBN-13: 978-0-8263-4023-8 (cloth : alk. paper)
ISBN-10: 0-8263-4023-7 (cloth : alk. paper)
1. Mexican Americans—New Mexico—Fiction.
2. Mexican American families—Fiction.
3. Depressions—1929—United States—Fiction.
4. Women—New Mexico—Fiction.
5. Domestic fiction. I. Title.
PS3552.A2535M36 2006
813'.6—dc22
                                    2006016778

DESIGN AND COMPOSITION: *Mina Yamashita*

For Mama

How desirable and how distant

is the ideal of the contemplative, artist, or saint—

the inner inviolable core, the single eye.

❧

—Anne Morrow Lindbergh, *Gift from the Sea*, 28–29

Contents

Santa Lucía, New Mexico
1934

CHAPTER ONE

HOME

One August afternoon as the cicadas strummed their summer melody, Mama Fela and her granddaughter Cipriana strolled up the dirt road hand in hand, shaded by a black umbrella. Ambling up the neighbor's fence lining the walk, the sweet pea sleepily displayed its pastel colors, yawning as it climbed. On every porch, geraniums spilled from the coffee cans that nourished them and Mama Fela knew the preferred brand of morning brew in every household. Their path paralleled the trickle of water that was boldly called the Pecos River but that barely gave sustenance to the inches of land that twisted along its crooked shoulder. In the dusty vacant lots that were peppered between the small houses, *yerba de la negrita* grew tall among the prickly pear and the mesquite bushes, for it needed little water to survive.

Mama Fela walked slowly in the lazy afternoon heat, too slowly for six-year-old Cipriana, who began to fidget. Spinning the parasol up into the air, Cipriana skipped ahead to catch it upon its descent. Delighted with her success, she repeated the action, this time higher and a little bit farther.

"Brinca Charcos!" Mama Fela said as sternly as she could muster considering this was her granddaughter. "Stop that foolishness! We're in public now and you never know whose eyes are watching. Besides," she said, squinting into the relentless sun, "I'm going to melt in this heat." Tucking her black purse more solidly beneath her armpit, she reached out her free hand, wiggling her fingers at her granddaughter. "Come, 'jita. I need your arm," she said more kindly to soften the impact of her scolding.

Cipriana broke into a huge smile, offering one arm to Mama Fela and wrapping the other around the entire stem of the umbrella. Mama Fela grasped the crook of her granddaughter's skinny arm and proceeded to walk quietly. The umbrella skimmed the top of her head but she did not say anything, preferring instead to bask in the moment. Cipriana had become good company for Mama Fela. They spent every afternoon together and most weekends too. They would visit Fela's friends to enjoy a cup of coffee and to learn the latest news. Or, they would visit Fela's clients with pincushion in hand to conduct a fitting or to deliver a new dress just completed, wrapped in waxy brown tissue paper. Cipriana made Fela feel like a child again, and it had been a long time since she knew how that felt. She wondered if she had ever known. Despite the heat, Mama Fela slid her hand down Cipriana's small arm and squeezed her granddaughter's hand affectionately, ignoring her sweaty palm.

They turned onto Route 66, where only the occasional local car whizzed by. The traffic was mostly comprised of overflowing Dodge trucks, filled with families and their worldly belongings: pots and pans, tools, furniture, a mattress or two, sometimes chickens and a dog. Or there were beat-up old Fords stopped by the side of the road, burlap sacks empty and hanging sadly from their windows, depleted of their water supply. Steam escaped from the vehicles' overheated engines while mothers shooed their children from the geysers and men in overalls grasped oily cloths with radiator caps hidden between their folds. These people were moving west, Mama Fela learned, away from their own land to work for somebody else. Once, a young man told her he was taking his family to a place where the orange groves were endless and both the food and work were abundant. She thought it sounded too good to be true. She would never leave her home no matter what the place promised. If you worked hard enough, you could make your world bearable for those you loved. There was no such thing as paradise in this life. You had to work hard, pray hard to make your way up to heaven. Then you could rest.

At Main Street, Mama Fela led Cipriana past the bank and Dr. Beford's Drugstore. She rarely stopped at either place, preferring instead to hide the money she and her husband had up on the top shelf of her *armario* or in the bottom of her bulky purse. She earned her money by sewing and she felt fortunate that she enjoyed working with needle and thread as much as she took pleasure in prescribing her herbs. These were her passion and she was often asked to share her remedies, always doing so without hesitation or payment. When she didn't know how to treat an ailment, she would study up on it in her quarterly herbal magazine, though she didn't like anyone to know that she consulted other avenues besides her memory and her god.

Four stores within a two-block diameter competed for the town's business. They were owned by a *judío*, an *árabe*, a *mexicano*, and an *americano* respectively. Mama Fela preferred to buy her groceries, the material for her sewing, and her shoes at Señor Gould's because her sister Quirina had a good job there. The americano's Cash & Carry was the only other store that had a good selection of groceries but she was loyal to El Judío. Besides, he offered credit.

Mama Fela couldn't help but smile at her granddaughter, who seemed to be very intent on the path they followed. Not only were Cipriana's eyes focused on the ground, but Mama Fela noticed that she avoided every rock that stood in her way, which resulted in zigzag hops and skips along the path.

"What are you doing, 'jita?"

"Nothing, Mama Fela."

"Then why won't you step on those rocks?"

Cipriana looked up at Mama Fela with eager eyes. "Well, do you want to play?"

"Play? I'm too old for play, 'jita."

"No you're not, Mama Fela. Look." Cipriana stopped suddenly, pointing at the ground, gasping in alarm.

"What?" Mama Fela stopped too and looked down at her feet.

"You just stepped on George Washington's head, Mama Fela!" Cipriana screeched.

Mama Fela stepped off balance to the side.

"Oh, oh. Now you're crushing Abraham Lincoln."

"Nonsense, 'jita." Mama Fela frowned but slowly began to move forward again, watching her step nervously. Suddenly, she stopped short. "¡Válgame Dios!"

"What? What's the matter, Mama Fela?" Cipriana asked.

"I . . . I think . . ."

"What?"

"Pobrecito. Perdóname San Antonio bendito," Mama Fela declared, gently sliding a rock from her path while breaking into a quiet cadence of laughter and making the sign of the cross. Giggling, she took her granddaughter's arm again and they continued to walk with hesitation, frequently avoiding a step forward and moving from side to side instead while accusing each other of irrevocably transforming the shapes of prominent figures. Mama Fela was not used to acting so silly but she had to admit it felt good.

They meandered past the county superintendent's office, the post office, the five-and-dime store, and finally approached the little movie theater called the Pecos. The sweet smell of sugar and yeast mingled in the air, wafting from Joe's Bakery a few doors down. On the first Tuesday of every month during the summer, Mama Fela invited Cipriana, Cipriana's mama Graciela, and Mama Fela's own daughter Cita to the picture show since Tuesday was coupon day when two could get in for a special price of twenty cents. Not only children, but the *viejas* and everyone in between. And even though Mama Fela didn't wish to admit it, at age sixty-one, she was indeed a vieja. Inside, she didn't feel a day older than when she was thirty, but when she looked at herself in the mirror and on the days when her arthritis acted up, she knew for a fact the time had come to call herself an old woman.

"Mira, 'jita, let's stand in the shade over there before I melt. Your tía and mama are always late. I'm going to die one of these days in this heat, waiting for them."

"Mama Fela, you're not going to die. Not ever."

"Of course I am, 'jita. Everyone dies once they become old."

"Will I die, Mama Fela?"

"Ooh, 'jita, not for the longest time. You're still a baby, mi'jita."

"But you're not old either, Mama Fela. You don't even have a wrinkle."

Mama Fela's thin lips emerged into a grin. "Ooh, 'jita, you're a good girl. A good girl. Now, let's not talk anymore of this dying. Let's buy those tickets. Now what's showing, 'jita?"

Cipriana frowned. "Mama Fela, it's Shirley Temple!"

"I know, 'jita. I'm just teasing," she said, knowing Cipriana had been waiting for this movie about the little girl with curls for the longest time. She stepped toward the ticket kiosk, removing a black cloth coin purse embroidered with tiny white flowers from her handbag. Slipping out four dimes, she placed them on the counter and scooted them toward the attendant with her slightly crooked fingers. *"Bright Eyes,"* she said slowly, unsure of her English pronunciation.

Mama Fela stared at the young man while he was tearing off four tickets for her. "Hmm. You're el hijo del Evaristo García, ¿qué no?"

The boy nodded his head.

"Is this a new job?"

He nodded again.

"And why aren't you working at your father's store?"

This time, the boy shrugged.

Mama Fela was getting annoyed. She hated to see this young generation lose respect for their elders. It was up to the parents to teach them some manners but when you had the likes of Evaristo García for a father, she couldn't blame the boy for being so rude. And where was Señora García? So afraid of Evaristo that she didn't question him about anything. *Ooh, que mamá tan pobre.* With parents like the Garcías, how would the boy know any better?

"Mi'jo," Mama Fela said, placing her hand over his, "I've known your daddy since he was a baby. I helped his mama bring him into this world, taking him from her womb. And I've known your daddy since he was a little mocoso, before he became a big shot. And you know what? You resemble your daddy a lot. I bet you're going to grow up to be just like him."

The boy blushed but instead of smiling as Mama Fela expected, he looked sad.

"What's the matter, mi'jo? Isn't that good news?"

He shrugged once more. This time, Mama Fela lost her patience.

"Mocoso, just like your father. Now answer me. Why don't you want to be like him?"

The boy cleared his throat. When he spoke, he sounded half little girl, half grown man and Mama Fela immediately understood his aversion to speaking out loud. "I want to be in the movies but Papa won't let me go to California," he croaked. "So I work here to be as close to the movies as I can. He says I have to run the store when he gets old."

"And you don't want that?"

"No, I want to be famous."

"And what if you go and you don't like it? Won't you miss your home and your mama?"

The boy shrugged. "Maybe for a little while but I'll be too busy to think about it. I'll be working in the movies."

"In the movies? Mi'jo, how is that possible? I don't think I've ever seen a real mexicano in the movies."

"Me neither. I want to be the first."

Mama Fela chuckled. She inspected the boy's handsome features while she planned what to say. The boy was young and he would learn soon enough that life wasn't as easy as that. She wished him well, though. "You tell your daddy I said to let you go make movies when you're a few years older. You tell him Doña Fela Romero said so."

The boy grinned. "Thank you, Doña Fela. Thank you."

"You're a good boy, mi'jo," she said, patting his hand once more.

Mama Fela stood with her granddaughter in the shade of the building. Her tender bunion was bothering her, so surreptitiously she slipped off one heavy black shoe and rubbed her big toe with the tip of the other shoe, hoping to soothe the dull pain. There was a time when she could walk the streets of Santa Lucía with the energy of a child like Cipriana but that time had come and gone years ago. Despite the aches and pains of old age, Mama Fela didn't wish to be young again. She liked her age; it gave her permission to be cranky whenever she wished and to scold those around her without holding back. Not that she wanted to scold; she was just born with a sassy streak in her, a bossy bone that made her speak her mind, especially when her husband was in the room. When he was absent, she found others to take his place.

Pulling out a handkerchief yellowed with time and memory, Mama

Fela wiped her brow. Hers was a small face with a narrow forehead and a tiny chin. In between, her cheekbones protruded from her face as if to beckon light and sun. Her cheeks, once rosy, had weathered and blended with the rest of her dark complexion, inherited from her Indian ancestry. Her nose was straight but wide with a rounded tip, and she hated this about herself. It made her feel like a pig, though she was too proud to admit this to anyone. Long ago she had confided in her mother, confessing how embarrassed she was by this facial characteristic that she perceived to be a defect. Her mother had thrown her head back and cackled and since then, she never told another soul and never really forgave her mother. After that fateful day, her mother's nickname for her became *cochina*, which had two meanings: literally, it meant pig, but it could also mean dirty like a pig. Ever since she was a little girl, she had made it a point to be as clean as possible so that no one had a reason to refer to her in this derogatory way. It pleased her when she finally realized that her nose had been inherited from her mother.

In the distance she saw Graciela and Cita coming toward her, laughing together. When they recognized her, they increased their pace and hid their smiles. Mama Fela watched them draw near, readying herself for words of reproach. She would address Cita directly because she was her daughter and, in her estimation, still a girl even though she was already twenty-three years old. But Graciela was different. In fact, she was the tiniest bit afraid of Graciela, afraid to offend her daughter-in-law because deep down, there was something about her that incited admiration. It was more than the smooth light skin and the hazel eyes. It was even more than the beautiful hairline and the almost blue-black hair, always neatly combed into a wavy bob. Mama Fela envied Graciela's small ears because her own large ones required masking with strands of hair, but this wasn't what she admired most about Graciela either. Graciela had a quiet way about her. She didn't gossip and she wasn't judgmental. She could not be persuaded to say an unkind word about anyone, and Mama Fela had tried. Graciela had a dignified way about her, both in bearing and in character. Even at twenty-nine, she was more mature than Mama Fela could ever be. Ultimately, Mama Fela was proud to call Graciela her daughter-in-law. But what really drew Mama Fela to Graciela was that she was a hard worker in the extreme who, like Mama Fela, carried a heavier burden than most mothers because of her husband. But there was also something about Graciela that Mama Fela just could not understand. As far as Mama Fela could tell, Graciela did not like to be embraced. The first time she tried to hug Graciela to welcome her into the family, Graciela went stiff and Mama Fela awkwardly withdrew. From then on, she admired her daughter-in-law from a distance. And when there was no other common ground, Mama Fela secretly latched onto the fact that Graciela did not possess a very pretty nose either.

"Don't you two know you're late again? One of these days I'm going to die out here in this heat," Mama Fela said, looking directly at Cita, handing the women their tickets. "And Cita, how many times have I told you that this dress you wear is not very becoming. It makes you look as thin as a broom handle. It's time I fitted you for another one."

"Oh Mamá," Cita said, shaking her head, "I like this dress. It's the first one I bought with my own money at the store."

"And no wonder it's ugly. Store-bought clothes are rags. Just look at these stitches," Mama Fela said, grabbing a handful of material. "Nothing hand sewn. All done by machine. Ooh, que dress tan pobre."

"Mamá! You don't like it just because I do."

"Pues, I might as well not say anything. You don't listen to me anyway."

"That's not true, Mamá. I always listen to you. Just not about what I'm wearing."

"Ooh, what good does it do to have an opinion then? Making clothes is my life. I won't say anything anymore."

"Oh, Mamá . . ."

"Ssh! Nothing more," she said, holding a finger to her lips.

"But, Mamá . . ."

"We're late for the movie. Now let's go," she ordered, ushering Cita, Graciela, and Cipriana into the theater's lobby. When she threw open the door of the darkened theater, she stood back to let her family go first. "Graciela, lead the way and find us a seat," she whispered into her ear. "Go slowly. We don't want Cipriana to trip." In reality, Mama Fela couldn't see a thing in the dark but she didn't wish to admit it. "Come, mi'jita," she said to Cipriana, "give me your hand."

As Mama Fela trailed behind Cipriana along the aisle, she tried to listen intently to the newsreel but she was finding it difficult to concentrate on two things at once. Cipriana was pulling her along faster than she felt comfortable, and maneuvering her sore feet carefully so that she would not trip was proving to be a challenge. The light from the movie screen lit up the theater as they stopped at a row of seats. It was empty except for the aisle seat, where a balding man sat with his long legs sprawled out in front of him, his head tilted back. Graciela whispered a polite "excuse me" in Spanish, loud enough for Mama Fela to hear, but the man did not budge. Graciela repeated it again, bending closer to the man's ear. Finally, she took the man's outstretched legs and gently maneuvered them to the side, where they spilled over into the aisle. She patted the man's arm hesitantly as she moved past him.

Cita too made an effort to nudge the man awake by gently patting his cheek but when he failed to respond, she reached over Cipriana and poked her mother. "May I borrow a nickel, Mamá?" she whispered.

"¿Qué?" Mama Fela could barely hear her daughter over the noise of the movie reel.

"A nickel, Mama Fela," Cipriana interceded. "Cita wants to borrow a nickel."

Mama Fela was perturbed. All she wanted right now was to sit down and rest her tired feet. She blindly dug into her coin purse and drew out what felt like a nickel. "¡Ándale pues!" she said, pressing the coin into Cita's outstretched palm. "The people can't see with us in the way."

Cita took the money, gave it to Cipriana, and whispered in her ear. Following Cita's instructions, Cipriana slipped the coin into the shirt pocket of the sleeping man and both sidled on past.

Mama Fela thought she must be seeing things. Had Cita really just given this man her hard-earned money? By this time, Mama Fela was close enough to recognize the sleeping face of Don Rutilio, the good-for-nothing husband of Doña Celestina. Poor woman, bringing up her three daughters by herself while her husband wasted away all day drunk and jobless. Like Mama Fela's sister, Celestina earned a living at Gould's Mercantile as their in-house seamstress. With her nimble young fingers, she was much better than Mama Fela but Mama Fela had never begrudged her the business. Celestina needed it more.

For Mama Fela, the day that Prohibition ended was a sad day. She believed in a little liquor for medicinal purposes for the mind and the body but she had seen it ravage too many men in her community. She believed in temperance whether or not it was mandated by law. Mama Fela refused to sit by a man who smelled sour and was a disgrace to his wife. When she moved past him, she slipped her fingers into his shirt pocket and retrieved her coin. She squeezed his shoulder, hoping the pressure would wake him. When it didn't, she slapped the man's cheeks, then pinched them until she could make out a slight twitching of his black mustache. His eyes rolled open and Mama Fela blew air into his face. "Ándale, hombre . . . ," she said mischievously, urging him out of his seat. "It's late and your wife's waiting for you to get home." The man bolted up out of his seat and plunged into the aisle, racing unsteadily toward the exit. The patrons close enough to hear the commotion clapped and said, "¡Ándale, Doña Fela!"

Mama Fela smiled to herself as she settled into her seat, releasing both feet from their tortured but proper existence.

❧

CHAPTER TWO

CANDY

Cipriana could pinpoint the day when her mother first started hating her father. She remembered it precisely because in twenty days she was going to be seven years old. Her Mama Fela had taught her how to count to one thousand that summer and she had been keeping a running count ever since. She remembered it because it was the day that her mother had finally received the letter she had been waiting for all summer and it was the first time ever that her mother bought her an entire bag of penny candy, even chocolate.

Candy was new to Cipriana; the post office wasn't. At the beginning of the summer, she went to the post office every Thursday to ask Doña Sulema if her mother had received any mail. By the middle of the summer, her mother was accompanying her on her weekly jaunt. Toward the end of the summer, they both frequented the post office daily, sometimes twice a day, inquiring about Graciela's mail.

That day, Cipriana's mother had finally received a piece of correspondence that seemed to please her. Cipriana listened intently as her mother read the letter, half aloud, half to herself, offering her a teaching post once again this coming school year in Puerta de Luna. The moment Graciela finished reading it, she pressed the stark piece of white paper to her lips and kissed it. Not just once, but over and over again. This surprised Cipriana, who secretly wished it had been she whom her mother kissed so warmly and emphatically.

Cipriana watched as her mother tucked the letter into her pocket, picked up Cipriana's brother, Pablito, and resumed their walk home. When they got to the steps of the mercantile, Cipriana peered into the window, tapping her finger against the pane, pointing in the general direction of the candy counter.

"Mama, can I get an O'Henry just this once? Ple-ea-se," she said, looking back at her mother. "Mary Jane Beford eats them all the time."

Cipriana's mother didn't respond. Instead, she stepped up to the window alongside Cipriana and gazed into the dark glass, shading her eyes with one hand from the glare, transferring Pablito's weight to one hip.

Cipriana knew the answer to expect but she couldn't resist asking anyway. She remembered her mother's words the last time she had asked her: "Sorry, mi'jita, it's just too much. Some other time." And she knew it would be the same answer today. Instead of giving her mother time to say no again, she asked, "How come we're not rich like Mary Jane, Mama? Daddy says we're regular people and a depression hit our kind the hardest so we can't go around eating sweets when we barely have enough beans in our stomachs. Is that true, Mama?"

Graciela continued to peer into the store window.

"Huh, Mama? Is that true?" Cipriana tugged at her mother's dress, staring up at her intently. She watched as her mother released Pablito to the ground, still clinging to his little hand and squatting just in front of Cipriana.

"Hold onto your brother for a moment, 'jita," she said, snapping open her purse. Cipriana watched her mother's every movement. This reaction was very different from what she had experienced in the past and she did not know what would come next. Her mother carefully unfolded a white handkerchief embroidered with delicate lavender flowers. Cipriana held her breath in anticipation. From the center of the handkerchief, her mother picked out not only one but two nickels and pressed them into Cipriana's hand. "Go on now, Cipriana. Buy yourself some candy."

"Really, Mama?" Cipriana asked incredulously.

"Really, 'jita," Graciela said, smiling, taking Pablito back into her arms.

With the coins secured firmly in her tight little fist, Cipriana pulled open the screen door with her free hand and a string of tiny bells greeted her cheerfully. She ran to the candy counter with visions of caramel and chocolate running through her head. Maybe her daddy was wrong. Maybe they were rich after all. Just like Mary Jane Beford.

"What can I get for you today, young lady?" asked Señor Gould.

"Well, I thought I wanted an O'Henry . . ."

"But . . . ?"

"But I think I've changed my mind. There are so many other kinds of candy, aren't there?"

"Why sure there are. We have licorice and jawbreakers and peppermint sticks and saltwater taffy . . ."

"And how about chocolate?"

"Why of course. We have Walnettos and little Babe Ruths and Butterfingers and Three Musketeers." Señor Gould's voice sounded just like the tinkle of the welcoming bells to Cipriana. So sweet to her ears. She placed her money on top of the counter and said, "Help me pick out the best candy, Mr. Gould. I want to try them all." While she stared into the glass case, mesmerized by all the choices, she responded to each of Señor Gould's descriptions with a nod or a shake of her head. Soon the tiny bag was filled with penny candy. While the storekeeper added up her purchases, Cipriana turned to look outside. Standing there, framed by the window, her mother was grinning wide, wearing a smile that was even larger than her own. Cipriana felt giddy with happiness. The jingle of the tiny bells reflected her mood as she exited the store.

With both hands, Cipriana offered up the candy to her mother, who took a peppermint stick and held it for Pablito as he took a lick. Cipriana chose a piece of pink taffy, deciding to save the chocolate candies until later. As they started for home, Cipriana unwrapped the taffy and stretched it as far as it would go in every direction. Maybe it would last longer this way.

"Watch where you're going, 'jita," Graciela said.

Looking ahead, Cipriana bit into the taffy, stretching it even longer before she bit the piece off. Without a word along the way, she chewed and pulled until they approached their house. Cipriana could smell her father's cooking immediately. "Fried potatoes, Mama! Daddy's home. Race you," she challenged, stuffing the last bit of taffy into her mouth.

"You go on, 'jita. I'll be there in a minute."

Cipriana ran into the house, oblivious to the slam of the screen door behind her. "Daddy, look what Mama got me," she said, holding up her candy bag. Her father turned from the stove, wiped his hands along his pants, and picked Cipriana up effortlessly, throwing her into the air and catching her again upon her descent. Giggling with delight, she snuggled into her father's arms and stuck her nose into his immaculate white shirt. "Mmm, Daddy, you smell good," she said, hoping this would last forever. "Like honeysuckle," she added, as he released her to the floor much too soon. "Or, like the bluing Mama puts in the rinse water," she said, hoping to get his attention once more, pushing her bag toward him again.

"It's only the P&G, 'jita," he said, taking the bag. "What's this?" he asked, peeking inside, rummaging with his index finger. "So much candy for one little girl," he muttered distractedly.

"Yes, Mama gave me ten cents. Ten whole cents. Can you believe it, Daddy?"

At that moment, Graciela entered the house with Pablito in tow. Without a greeting, she went directly to the *platón* and washed Pablito's hands in her own. "Home so soon, Robert?" she asked Cipriana's father without turning.

Cipriana immediately knew something was amiss. Her mother sounded different. Her father didn't say anything. Instead, he watched Cipriana's mother move from the washstand to the door, shutting it tight despite the heat. He watched intently, Cipriana thought, like the wild cats under the house watch the mice before they run after them. Cipriana wondered why neither of her parents spoke. She wondered why her mother didn't tell her father about the letter that had given her so much joy. If she wouldn't tell him, Cipriana would.

"Daddy, did you know Mama got a letter today?" Cipriana asked.

"Cipriana," Graciela said in a warning tone.

"What, Mama? It was a good letter. Daddy would think so too."

"Not now, 'jita. Now's not the time to talk about the letter."

"But, Mama . . ." Cipriana pleaded, not quite understanding her mother's reluctance.

"¡Cállate!" Graciela said sternly.

Cipriana stood stunned at the tone of her mother's voice. Just a moment ago, she had been so cheerful. Puzzled, Cipriana didn't dare say another word. Instead, she turned her attention to her father.

"Daddy, you want me to stir the beans?" she asked.

"Go ahead, 'jita," he said absentmindedly, handing Cipriana the wooden spoon. She whispered in his ear, "Mama got her job."

Instead of smiling as she thought he should, he said nothing, helping Cipriana up onto a stool instead. Cipriana could tell her father's thoughts were far away. He was off in limbo land, the same place her teacher Mrs. Bracket referred to when students stared out the window and didn't pay attention to the lesson. Mimicking her teacher, Cipriana waved her hand playfully at her father, saying, "Yoo-hoo, back to earth, Daddy."

"¡Malcriada!" snapped Cipriana's father, making Cipriana wonder if he was really off in limbo land or not. "Don't you be sassy with me, Cipriana."

"But, I wasn't, Daddy. I was just . . ."

"¡Cállate!"

Hurt, Cipriana turned her attention to the cast-iron skillet, stirring the beans slowly at first, and then, realizing they were burning, faster and faster. But it was too late; they were sticking to the bottom of the pan. She grabbed the handle of the hot skillet to move it off the woodstove, but the pain made her wince and lose hold of it and the skillet toppled to the floor, where all the beans spilled out. Some landed on the patent leather shoes she had just shined up the night before, the only pair of shoes she owned, which would have to last until the following Easter. Cipriana stared down at the mess on her shoes, determined not to cry. Jumping off the stool, she squatted, picking off the beans one by one while her mother's feet approached and her father's receded.

"What are you doing, Cipriana! Your father shouldn't be allowing you to handle these hot skillets," Graciela admonished. "Now the beans are ruined!" she added, kneeling to the floor beside Cipriana, scooping up the food and muttering under her breath.

Cipriana fell onto her backside, shrinking away from her mother. She felt shriveled up inside like a bottle cap squashed by a tire. Her mother cared more about the beans than about her.

When Pablito started to whimper, Cipriana could not take it. She was the one who had a reason to cry. The palm of her hand was beginning to smart just as much as her feelings were. "Shut up!" she yelled at her baby brother.

"Don't you scream at the baby, Cipriana."

"But, he's just a malcriado, Daddy."

"Don't you sass me, malcriada!"

"Shhh. Just hush!" Her mother said authoritatively, ending all back talk at once. The only sound was coming from Pablito, who started to cry again. But Cipriana ignored her brother this time. Instead, it was her mother who had all her attention. Cipriana could feel Graciela's eyes probing her, fixed on her and her brother as if she were anticipating their disappearance at any moment. Finally, Graciela called the children into her arms, hugging them so tight it hurt.

Pablito started crying louder, and Cipriana said, "Mama, stop it! You're hurting me." But Graciela did not let go. Instead, Cipriana could feel her mother trembling, and when she looked into her face, there were tiny tears rolling down her cheeks. As suddenly as she had embraced the children, Cipriana's mother released them, stood, and returned to the washbasin, brushing wisps of hair away from her face.

Cipriana looked at her father with questioning eyes. Perhaps he could explain her mother's behavior. To Cipriana's disappointment, he looked as confounded as she felt, scrutinizing Graciela, his forehead knotted with lines. Cipriana wanted to say something, anything, to her mother but she was too bewildered. She did not want to make her mother cry again. Perhaps it was Cipriana who caused her to cry in the first place. Perhaps she shouldn't have dropped the beans or maybe she shouldn't have gotten so much candy, like her father had said. Her mother's actions scared her; mothers were just not supposed to cry. Baby brothers, yes; children, sometimes; but never mothers. She did not want to see her mother cry ever again.

Eyeing him uncertainly, Cipriana advanced toward her father, who had retreated to the table at the far end of the room. Perhaps he had provoked her mother's tears. He wasn't very nice sometimes, not like a father should be. He was tall like a daddy should be. He was neat and clean most of the time, not a *cochino* who threw *pedos* at the supper table like her friend's daddy. In fact, Cipriana's father referred to that man as a *ranchero mostrenco*, not broken in, like the wild horses tamed by Cipriana's grandfather in the olden days. But at least Lala's daddy was nice all the time, unlike her own father. "Daddy," she said, beckoning him with her finger, "aren't you going to do something?"

He nodded, but he looked flustered. Standing, he stuffed his hands, which had been dusted with flour, deep down into his pockets, staring at Graciela's back. Lightly splashing water was the only audible sound in the room. Finally, he took a few hesitant steps toward Graciela as if he were just learning to walk, like Pablito. Cipriana held her breath. She wanted to hold her father up by the armpits and hurry him along, the same way she helped Pablito get to a destination more quickly. She wanted her father to hurry so that the fight would be over. Before she could take action though, her mother cleared her throat and Cipriana braced herself. Her father ceased to move.

"You walked off another job, didn't you?" Cipriana's mother asked, her voice calm but barely audible. Turning from the washbasin, she moved past her husband without looking at him and sat down at the table to take over where he had left off. She scooped out little balls of dough onto a baking sheet.

The scraping sounds emanating from her mother's direction entranced Cipriana. She strained her ears, thinking she detected another sound that mimicked the first. It was her father tapping his shoe against the floor in perfect time to her mother's spoon taps against the baking sheet. He was looking at the floor and to Cipriana, his eyes seemed glazed over as if he was in limbo land again, his thoughts far away.

Suddenly, Cipriana wondered where her candy had gone. She wished for a piece of taffy so that she could roll it up into a ball, tuck it underneath her tongue, and suck on that creamy goodness until her parents made up. But her father wasn't holding the bag anymore. She scanned the room. And there it lay, next to the hot cooking stove on a chair. She leaped at the crumpled brown bag, grabbed it, and yelled, "Daddy! Look what happened to my candy!" Cipriana's mother and father looked up at the same time. Cipriana held up a couple of pieces of candy, the chocolate oozing from half-opened wrappers, the caramel gooey. She looked from her father to her mother and back to her father again. She couldn't hold back anymore. She just couldn't. She cried right there in front of them both.

Cipriana's mother went over to her and took her face in her hands. She longed for her mother's touch but the dough crusted on her mother's hands made her itch. Cipriana tried to squirm away, but her mother was too quick. Graciela spread a finger full of *masa* on Cipriana's nose, making her laugh despite the sadness she was feeling.

"Why don't we just set out your candy someplace cool, Cipriana," Graciela said. "It'll harden again in no time."

Cipriana nodded, feeling better already. But then her mother turned again to her daddy and before she could intercede between her parents, they were at it again.

"You really didn't want her to have that candy, did you?" Graciela asked in a tone Cipriana hated. She was looking at her husband the way she looked at the kids who made trouble in her classroom.

"What's that supposed to mean, Graciela? It's not as if I left it there to melt on purpose." Snatching the bag of candy from Cipriana, he pulled out a handful of melted candy and piled it on the table. Cipriana anxiously cupped her hands around the mountain of sweets, afraid to lose even one.

"Look," he continued, "wouldn't one or two have done the trick just as well?" When Graciela didn't reply, he shook his head from side to side and threw the rest of the candy down on the table. In an exasperated tone, he said, "You know we can't afford it."

Cipriana's mother stared hard at her father. After a few moments, Cipriana was anxious for her mother to stop. She longed for her mother to say something instead of basking in the silence that was suffocating them.

Finally, Graciela whispered, "And whose fault is that? Robert, don't you see what's happening? You give no thought to Cipriana here when you quit one of those jobs. Only yourself. If you would just think about the children, Robert, you could swallow that pride of yours once in a while."

"You don't think I think about them, Graciela? You don't think I feel guilty quitting?" Cipriana's father asked. Shaking his head, he added, "You just don't understand, Graciela. You just don't know how hard it is."

"No? You don't think I feel like telling that damn school board to go to . . ." Graciela stopped and looked at Cipriana, who knew exactly what was coming: her mother was going to send her off to Mama Fela's. Getting her bag off the table to take with her, she waited, but her mother kept talking and Cipriana kept listening. She wasn't about to go anywhere.

". . . to . . . to go to the devil. Sending me here and there, a different place every school year. And then waiting until the last possible moment to tell me yes I have a job. Of course I feel like nothing, Robert, and I wish I could do something about it, but I can't. Or, I guess I could but then I wouldn't have a job. Like you."

"Thanks a lot, Graciela. You just love making me feel guilty, don't you?"

Graciela was quiet for a minute. She glanced at Cipriana and turned away just as quickly. "Well, you should feel guilty, Robert. Every single time you call one of those bosses a bolillo cabrón and walk off the job, you just hurt yourself. And the children. And me."

Cipriana waited for her father's response, staring at him intently. She had caught his gaze momentarily but he quickly turned his attention to the floor, fiddling with his foot as if he were trying to smash a crumb. Cipriana's attention was diverted when her mother reached out her hand to smooth her hair. Cipriana craved her mother's touch, not like last time where she almost squeezed her into oblivion, but like this, just like this. She savored her mother's gentle caress the way she savored the sweet, smooth taste of chocolate. Neither came around very often.

"There are lots of them who are anti-mexicano," Graciela continued more softly. "You and I both know that, Robert. But every time you quit, they have to find another man. Pretty soon, they're just going to think all nuevomexicanos are irresponsible and next time they hire, they'll think twice about hiring us."

Cipriana's eyes were drawn by the sudden movement made by her father. He was alert, head cocked toward Graciela with an angry knot between his full eyebrows.

"Oh, so that's it," he said. "Now you think I'm irresponsible?"

Cipriana's mother didn't respond. Instead, she shrugged her shoulders and her thin eyebrows rose in an arc while waves of lines appeared on her forehead. Puzzled, Cipriana didn't quite know how to decipher her mother's reaction until she saw the look on her father's face. His mouth twitched as if his words were fighting to escape. His face colored until even the tips of his ears had turned red.

To make matters worse, Cipriana's mother turned her back on Robert, scooping up the pile of candy he had left scattered across the table. Now was not the time for tidiness. Even Cipriana knew that. Cipriana had to think fast and then she knew exactly how she could help. Glancing over her shoulder at her father, she said, "Mama, we could take the candy back, if you want. I've got a stomachache anyhow. And then you and Daddy won't have to fight anymore." Looking at her father expectantly, she lightly touched her mother's skirt with one hand.

For a brief moment, Cipriana thought she had achieved the reaction she wanted. Her mother's face softened as she looked down at Cipriana. Releasing the candy from her grasp, she squatted down to be at eye level with her daughter. Smiling, she took Cipriana's hand in hers and gave it a gentle squeeze. Cipriana held her breath in anticipation. But before she knew it, her mother's focused gaze became a blank stare. Cipriana was sure her mother had left the present for limbo land. "What does it matter anyhow, Robert?" she said in a tone that Cipriana was beginning to recognize. "Nothing I say is going to change your behavior. Nothing is going to change what you have already done to your children."

At that, Cipriana's father exploded. He slammed his hand against the table so hard that Cipriana's candies bounced like Mexican jumping beans. He scowled at Graciela the way the cowboys glare at the Mexicans in the movies. And before Cipriana could react, he turned away, swung open the door, and marched out as if he were racing toward a finish line. Still hanging on to a thread of hope, Cipriana flew out the open door and called after her father. But there was no response. She watched him retreat into the late afternoon sun, his pant legs still dusted with flour.

She scurried into the kitchen again, anxious for reassurance. "Where do you think Daddy went?" she asked her mother, who was busy setting the table.

Graciela ignored the question. "Are you hungry, Cipriana?"

"Not really," Cipriana said, frowning. "Where do you think Daddy went, Mama?" she pressed.

Sitting Pablito down in his high chair, Graciela said, "Not now, Cipriana. It's time to eat."

Cipriana studied her mother as she served them biscuits and potatoes. Her serving hand was quivering.

"I'm sorry about the beans, 'jitos. I would have made a new pot, but there was no time. I'll make some more tomorrow."

Cipriana didn't want to hear about the absence of beans. She wanted to hear about her father. But concluding he would not be a topic for discussion tonight, she let it go.

After supper, Cipriana scraped the dried beans from her shoes and polished them with hair oil.

"Do you want me to polish your shoes, Mama?"

"No, 'jita. I already took care of them. Thank you, though."

Cipriana was relieved. She really didn't want to clean her mother's shoes. She couldn't help feeling that her father's extended absence was her mother's fault. Taking out the dress that Mama Fela had made for her to wear on the first day of school, Cipriana hung it on the doorknob of the armario, staring at it for the longest while. Finally, she pressed it to her nose, breathing in the sweet smells of her grandmother. At first, she could easily detect the licorice aroma of Black Jack gum that escaped from Mama Fela's purse every time she opened it. If she inhaled even deeper, her nostrils were tickled by a hint of lavender, the powder her grandmother brushed on her face every day. Running her hand across its silky softness, Cipriana imagined the way it would feel when she dressed for school. She wanted to put it on immediately, but she knew her mother would not allow such nonsense.

Graciela stood at the ironing table sprinkling and pressing her best dress, the yellow one with tiny daisies and yellow buttons, Cipriana's favorite. Graciela was smiling, the way she always did at the start of a new school year. Cipriana's baby brother was already asleep so she said good night too even though it was still early. She wanted to make sure she got plenty of sleep so that she could wake up early for school.

Her mother turned around and asked, "You're not going to bed, are you? Cipriana, we have to wash your hair so we can make long curls."

Her mother hardly ever made her curls, only for Sundays. She jumped up and down. "Mama, hurry! Should I get the rags ready now?"

Graciela laughed and Cipriana couldn't help but wonder why her mother was in such a good mood after yelling at her father and after crying earlier.

"Let's be a little more quiet, 'jita. Your brother is asleep," she said, putting her finger to her lips. Cipriana's flutter of excitement fled momentarily until she saw her mother replace the iron on the stove and go outside to dip the bucket into the cistern. Cipriana got the rags out of a drawer while her mother heated water. Graciela washed and rinsed Cipriana's hair, running her fingers through it as the warm water made Cipriana sleepy. She wanted this to last forever. Her mother's touch felt so good. Untangling was the hard part, but when it was over, Cipriana's mama wrapped strands of her hair with little rags and catalog paper. When the last piece of hair was rolled and tied, Graciela said, "Cipriana, tomorrow when I get back from Puerta de Luna, we'll go next door to Mr. Woodard's and ask him if we can set out all your candy in his icebox. I'm sure it will harden up again and be good as new."

Cipriana felt so good, as if her mother really loved her. She got into bed, pulling her new dress in with her. Her mother was acting so nice, Cipriana was certain she wouldn't get angry. She wanted to be ready for school early the next morning. She desperately wanted to be the first one there. So right there, under the covers, she slipped on her dress and went to sleep without so much as a thought of her father's absence.

In the morning, Cipriana started to get up out of bed when she felt the wet sheets under her. She touched them again to make sure she wasn't dreaming. She was so mad at herself, she felt like crying. She wasn't about to say anything though because she was going to wear the new dress no matter what, even though she could feel the wetness on her back.

Cipriana's father was there in the kitchen, drinking coffee and reading the newspaper. To Cipriana, he didn't smell clean anymore and his hair was mussed. She didn't like the way he looked.

"Where's Mama, Daddy?"

"Hmm?"

"Where's Mama?"

"I imagine she went to school, 'jita," he said without looking up from his newspaper.

"Oh. Daddy, would you help me take the rags out of my hair?"

"Not right now, 'jita. I'm busy."

"Please, Daddy. Please."

Cipriana's daddy looked up and smiled. He called her over and she leaped into his lap. He took out the rags one by one. "Your curls are as pretty as Shirley Temple's, mi'jita," he said, kissing her on the forehead. Cipriana soaked in his affection for a moment, then just as suddenly, jumped off his lap and rushed to her mother's drawer.

She dug out her mother's special mirror, careful only to touch the handle, not the glass, as her mother had taught her. Squeezing the silver handle between her fingers, Cipriana stared at her reflection and saw that her hair almost did look like Shirley Temple's. She only needed one more thing to make her look pretty like her. She set the mirror down again and looked under Graciela's panties where Cipriana knew her mother kept a little box of shiny jewelry. When she opened the box, she was sure that what she saw inside would make her feel like she was in the movies too. She clipped two gold earrings onto her ears, swallowing the small pain that accompanied them, but it was worth it. When she looked at the mirror again, Cipriana liked what she saw. The jewels made her look pretty, just as she had hoped. She closed the drawer and tiptoed past her baby brother, sleeping in his cradle, and swept past her father, who was still sitting at the table with his nose in the newspaper.

On the way out the door, Cipriana bumped right into her Tía Cita.

"What are these, 'jita?" she asked, fingering Cipriana's earrings.

"Nothing."

"Nothing?" Cita smiled. "Are you sure? Because those nothings sure make you look fancy."

"Tía!" Cipriana said, giggling. Eager to get to school, she hurried off.

Her *tía* called after her. "Cipriana, what do you have in the back of your dress there?"

Cipriana faced Cita again and crossed her arms in back of her. "Nothing, Tía. I better go now 'cause it's the first day of school." Cipriana walked backward but finding it difficult and slow, she turned and ran. Cita called for Cipriana to wait but Cipriana ignored her, adamant that there was no way her tía could make her put on one of her old dresses. Today Cipriana was going to be Shirley Temple. She kept running without turning back until she got to the school.

Lala was there and Gloria and Teodora too. They threw their jump rope down and ran over to Cipriana. "Ooh, what are those, Cipriana? Where did you get 'em?"

"They're earrings. My mama gave them to me . . . for . . . for my birthday."

"But you haven't had a birthday for a long time," Lala said.

Cipriana made a face at her. "Yeah, but it's almost here. Mama gave them to me early."

"Can I try 'em?" Teodora asked her.

"All right, but just for a minute. Be careful, they could break." Cipriana pulled them off and gave them to her friend, glad to rest her pinched ears.

"Ow, they hurt," Teodora said, yanking the earrings off.

"They're supposed to. Here, let me try them," Gloria said.

"Your ears are all red," Lala told Cipriana.

"Really?" Cipriana started to rub them when she heard somebody running up in back of her. All of a sudden, she felt hands like claws on her back, her neck cracked back, and then she fell to the hard dirt. She looked up but the sun was in her eyes. A silhouette of gigantic hair blocked the sun and she saw that it was Esteban.

"Chase. You're it!" he yelled, laughing in Cipriana's face.

She swung her fist at him but missed. He laughed louder and Cipriana felt like she was about to explode. In a rage, she struck out wildly, trying to make contact with her small fist, but he deflected each punch, slithering away just in the nick of time. Taunting her to try again, he jumped in and out of range, breathing hard. Cipriana's knees were hurting now, granules of sand making dimples in her skin. She sat back on her haunches, feeling defeated and about to cry, but she refused to take her eyes off Esteban.

To Cipriana's surprise, suddenly Esteban stopped his bouncing feet and held his hand out. A serious expression descended upon his face as he said, "Here, let me help you." At first, Cipriana was going to take his hand but then she slapped it away, thinking better of her decision. She knew Esteban's tricks all too well. Grinning from ear to ear, he clapped his hands together, threw his head back, and cackled. It was the chance Cipriana had been looking for. She stood quickly, brushing the dirt from her knees.

"Get out of here! Leave Cipriana alone," Lala yelled at Esteban, her hands on her waist. Gloria hooked her arm with Cipriana's and whispered, "Are you all right?" Cipriana nodded, still keeping a watchful eye on Esteban. When Cipriana felt secure, sure that he wouldn't strike again, she turned and shouted, "Run!" She and her friends darted in the same direction toward the school building. She could hear Esteban's panting behind them, close on their heels. Suddenly, his rapid breathing became a burst of laughter that stopped Cipriana in her tracks.

"Look at Cipriana's dress! She made pee pee. Cipriana made pee pee!" Esteban screamed.

"I did not!" Cipriana cried, holding her skirt out in back of her, trying to see and feel if the wet spot from this morning had dried. She didn't feel it wet anymore, but all over her dress was a yellow stain outlined by the hint of a light brown line. Cipriana scrunched up her dress by the handful, ashamed and embarrassed. She hated her grandmother's dress. She hated Mama Fela for making it. She wanted nothing more at this minute than to go home and hide. It was hard not to cry but she knew if she did, everyone would call her a baby. It seemed like the whole school was looking at her, staring at the ugliest dress she had ever worn.

Cipriana glanced around, desperately checking to see where her friends had gone, when she heard the clanging of the bell. All the children stampeded toward the school, but Cipriana found it difficult to run and hide her dress at the same time. Running slowly with her hands in back of her, she felt someone prodding her along with pokes to the back. When she spun around, Esteban was there, jeering at her. "Baby needs a diaper!" he whooped.

"Esteban Mora, you're a big bully and nobody likes you!" Cipriana shrieked. Chasing him, she tried to slap and punch him, but he dodged her blows expertly, taunting her with a wagging tongue. She could feel tears streaming down her cheeks but she wiped them away quickly. When she felt a hand on her shoulder, she flinched. It belonged to a teacher she had never seen who then grabbed Esteban by the scruff of his neck.

"What's going on here, you two?" she asked.

Cipriana tried to talk but she couldn't. Her chest was heaving so hard she couldn't catch her breath. Instead, she started to cry uncontrollably.

"There, there. Calm down now," the teacher said, squeezing Cipriana's shoulder. "Now wait here just a moment."

She walked to the door of Cipriana's new class. Immediately, Cipriana's eyes were drawn to the woman's feet: they were big but her shoes were pretty. They matched her blue dress.

Mrs. O'Riley introduced herself and told the girls to line up on one side, the boys on the other. When Cipriana attempted to follow her instructions, she felt the gentle tug of fingers upon her shoulder and looked up to see Mrs. O'Riley gesture for her to wait. Cipriana fidgeted while she watched her teacher say hello to her classmates, ushering them inside one by one. When Esteban was about to enter, Cipriana glared at him with narrowed eyes but he ignored her, paying close attention instead to Mrs. O'Riley, who was whispering into his ear. Cipriana strained to hear but she could only make out mumbles. She wanted to trip him but it was too late. Esteban went inside without incident, sat down, and put his head on his desk.

"Sit down now. That's it," Mrs. O'Riley told them in a soothing but no-nonsense voice. The room gradually quieted. She pressed her finger to her lips and said, "Now wait very quietly, children. I'll be right back." Cipriana thought her voice sounded like a sweet little birdsong. Before she knew it, Mrs. O'Riley had slipped a soft hand into her own and together, they walked outside.

Cipriana did not want to tell her teacher about her dress because she didn't want her to think that she was a baby. Instead, she told her about Esteban and how mean he was to all the kids. Suddenly, Cipriana looked up at the open doorway and saw Lala at the door. She stared at Cipriana for a moment and then went back inside.

Cipriana soon discovered that Mrs. O'Riley knew all about the stain. But instead of making her feel ashamed, she told Cipriana not to worry. She could go change at lunch. Cipriana hugged her and they walked back to class hand in hand, Cipriana beaming that she had already made a friend. Cipriana was sure that Mrs. O'Riley was the prettiest teacher she had ever had.

Cipriana found her desk and sat down next to a girl with flaming red hair, a color she thought only existed in the funny papers. Immediately, Cipriana noticed the little brown freckles all over the girl's face and arms and wondered what her Mama Fela would have to say about them. When Cipriana turned to look at her classmates, they were staring and giggling and she wondered if it was at the girl or at her. Instinctively, Cipriana reached for her own nose, hiding the trio of spots she knew was there.

Cipriana turned to where Lala was sitting but she had her head down. All of a sudden, Teodora was standing in front of Cipriana's desk, stuffing her earrings into her hand. "Here. I don't wanna wear 'em anymore," Teodora declared, scowling at Cipriana. The golden jewelry in Cipriana's hand wasn't as shiny as before. The earrings were dusted with dirt, making Cipriana wonder what had happened. She watched as Teodora returned to her seat, without so much as a thank you. Lifting the top of her desk, Cipriana dropped the earrings in and turned to smile at her desk mate. The girl, who resembled Orphan Annie, smiled back.

Then Cipriana looked over at Gloria, who waved with her pinkie. "Are you all right?" Gloria whispered.

Cipriana nodded.

"Don't pay attention to them. They're just mean," Gloria said.

Cipriana nodded again, but this time she felt like crying. She blinked back tears, and thought instead about home and her candy. She would go at lunchtime, slip on another dress, and get a piece of candy. Maybe she could even bring one to her new teacher, who wouldn't care if the candy was soft. And oh, she could hardly wait until her mother got home so that they could take the candy to Mr. Woodard's. Then tomorrow, she could share the whole bag with Gloria and the new girl. They could all be friends.

It was finally time to have lunch. Cipriana ran home, still trying to hide her dress in back as best she could, crumpling it into bunches. The door was open and she walked in expecting to see her daddy, but it was her mother who was sitting at the table this time. Cipriana's mama, who had impeccable posture, was slumped over the table. All around her chair, there were wrappers everywhere. Wrappers without candy. Without Cipriana's candy.

"Mama!" Cipriana screamed.

Graciela turned to look at her daughter. She glared at her as if she was one of those kids at school who makes trouble and pedos under their arms.

"You know where he was yesterday? You know where he went?" her mother asked.

"Mama, my candy. Where's all my candy?"

"He was at the superintendent's office. That's where he went."

"You said you'd help me. Help me take my candy to Mr. Woodard's."

"Withdrawing my name. Tearing up my application. Quitting my job."

"Mama! My candy!"

CHAPTER THREE

THE SPEECH

Just before daybreak, Mama Fela stood in front of the washstand with a toothbrush in one hand and her false teeth in the other, listening to the faint rustling sounds outside. She knew her husband was packing his bedroll and his gun, readying himself for a trip out into the *llano* to mope and beat the black mood from his mind. Her husband was *inutil*—at least that's what she called it. Not that he wasn't smart. He was. He just wasn't good at everyday, normal living, and knowing this saddened him. By now, she could predict the onset of one of his spells and knew exactly when to expect his departure. She had become so accustomed to his absence every so often that her own routine was hardly interrupted. It wasn't that she lacked concern for her husband, but she knew she must put his well-being into God's hands.

When she finished washing and powdering her face, she gazed out the window and saw his shadow making its way down the road. As she braided her hair and wrapped it round and round into a tight bun, she watched him and mumbled a little prayer. Slipping on a shawl, she went outside to the cistern, where she warmed her hands with her breath before pulling at the rope for a bucketful of water. Inside, she poured the water into a large kettle kept on top of the stove for use throughout the day. Wood was piled high just outside the kitchen door and she took an armful, nudging the door closed behind her. The fire did not start easily, so she wadded up several sheets from last week's newspaper and tucked them underneath the kindling. This time, the fire took, and she warmed her hands for a moment, staring at the blaze. It was only October, but she could already feel the cold settling in. The ache that cursed her joints told her the plains of New Mexico would see an unforgiving winter this year.

She started a pot of coffee just as the sun began to rise. Her weekly paper, *El Nuevo Mexicano*, hadn't arrived at the post office as of yesterday so she rummaged through the old one, trying to find something she hadn't read. She was able to read the headlines without her spectacles but the small print was a blur. Once the coffee began percolating, she took out a cup and saucer and opened up the *cajón de la provisión* where she had placed the pile of tortillas left over from yesterday's supper. All she found was the muslin towel where they had been wrapped and a few crumbs. She shook her head and rolled her eyes, half amused, half irritated, knowing her husband was the culprit. She quickly forgave him though, knowing he was doing battle now not only with the cold but also with the darkness that invaded his world and paralyzed him. His reality was one she did not understand and deep down, she was grateful for their time apart.

Once the coffee was ready, she poured herself a cup, inhaling its rich aroma. She couldn't make up her mind whether or not to make another batch of tortillas, but she knew she would be hungry later in the day. Taking the time to eat while she was sewing was a luxury she could not afford. It would disturb her concentration and spoil her timeline. Thinking her day through, she decided to quench her appetite now instead of later. She mixed flour, baking powder, salt, and lard with water to make a masa. The *comal* was already on the stove, and she knew it was hot enough by the sizzle it made when she touched a wet finger to its surface. She rolled out each ball without paying much attention to its shape, but managing to create perfectly round tortillas. The mastery she displayed was a direct result of years of experience, not a conscious effort. It used to be that if a tortilla did not meet her expectations, she scrunched it into a ball again and started anew, but she was beyond that now.

When the tortillas were piled high, she sat down, sipping her third cup of black coffee and eating just one tortilla piece by piece, scanning the long table that stretched out before her. She had never been a big eater, because for her it was a greater joy to converse at the table than to eat. Talking never tired her the way it did her husband but she could always tell when it was time for her to swallow her words. When that time came, she quietly put food into her mouth, chewing it deliberately until all the flavor had disappeared, thinking about the things she didn't have a chance to say.

Mama Fela's daughter rushed into the room at that moment, buttoning her green coat with one hand and holding hairpins with the other.

"Cita," Mama Fela said, eagerly, getting up to pour her a cup of coffee.

"No, Mamá. No coffee," Cita mumbled with a couple of hairpins clenched between her front teeth. She dipped her fingers into the basin of water used by Mama Fela earlier and slicked a piece of loose hair back, securing it with one of the pins. She perused the room, asking, "Is Papá gone again?"

Fela nodded. She wanted to explain his departure but Cita's hurried manner persuaded her not to. The explanation would have been more for her own sake than for her daughter's anyway. Her husband and her daughter were two of a kind, and she was sure that Cita understood his moods even more than she did.

Mama Fela stood behind Cita, watching her coif her hair. When she saw a strand of loose hair, she reached up to smooth it, but Cita moved away.

"Mamá!" she said, annoyed.

"Pues, what's the matter?"

Cita turned and grabbed a tortilla. "You don't have to comb my hair. I'm not a little girl."

"Va, 'jita. I only want you to look respectable."

"Oh, Mamá. I am respectable," she said, biting into her breakfast. "Besides, respect doesn't come because you look nice."

"No?"

"No! God, Mamá. Papá would understand. How long will he be gone this time?"

"Three, four days, no sé," she shrugged. "We'll see. ¿Quieres panqueques, Cita?"

"No, Mamá. I'm already late and I have to clean Mrs. Sanders's house this morning."

Mama Fela just nodded, knowing a reprimand would be futile. For years she had fought with Cita, frustrated that she was so disorganized and perpetually tardy. Now, she watched while Cita frantically searched for her satchel. When she could no longer mask her amusement, she called to Cita softly and pointed to her shoulder, where the bag hung.

Ten days later, on Saturday, Mama Fela woke up, wishing her husband were there to start a fire, to get her up out of bed. When he was in good spirits, not only would he light the morning fire, he would also bring her hot coffee to bed, sometimes even a bowl of *chaquegüe*. But now she had to push herself. Instead of making a fresh pot of coffee, she poured herself a cup from yesterday's brew and drank it cold and strong. Now with a bit more energy, she lit a fire and set up her ironing on the kitchen table. When the black iron was heated through, she began pressing the blouses she had starched the day before.

A knock at the door startled her. She wondered who it could be this time of morning. Suddenly, she had a premonition. Placing the iron back on the stove, she jerked open the door, thinking perhaps her husband was back, pretending to be a visitor, trying to surprise her. But there on the step stood her granddaughter, trembling.

"You don't have to knock, 'jita. You know that." Grasping her granddaughter's hand, she gently pulled Cipriana into the house. "Where's your jacket, 'jita? Your hands are freezing," she said, rubbing them between her own. Bending forward so that she was eye level with Cipriana, she realized her granddaughter's eyes and nose were red and swollen. "What's wrong, mi'jita?"

Cipriana burst into tears, trying to speak at the same time, but Mama Fela could not understand her words. They were hidden among giant breaths and sobs as though at any moment, the little girl would choke on her emotion.

" All right now. Cállate, 'jita. No. I said that's enough. That's it. Calm down. You're fine. That's it. Now dry those tears and when you're ready, you can tell me what's wrong." When Cipriana began to cry again, Mama Fela held up a finger. "No, 'jita. I said that was more than enough crying for one day. Come, let's get you something to eat and while you calm yourself," she said, showing Cipriana to the kitchen table, "I'll make you something hot."

From the cabinet, Mama Fela procured a can of milk and two eggs. With a knife, she slit the top of the can and poured the milk into a saucepan. While the milk warmed over the stove, she separated the eggs, and began beating the whites with a fork.

"Mama Fela?"

"Yes, 'jita?"

"All she does is cry anymore."

"Who, 'jita? Your mama?"

Cipriana nodded. "She's mad at Daddy all the time because she lost her job because of him. She says it's not enough that he quits his own jobs; now he quit hers too and all because she called him a flojo and he got mad. Is Daddy a flojo, Mama Fela?"

"Pues, 'jita, that shouldn't concern you."

"But, Mama Fela, Mama doesn't like being home and now she has to. She'd much rather be at school and you know what?"

"What, hijita?"

"I used to want her home all the time but I don't anymore, Mama Fela. I don't because all she does is cry. She can go back to school for all I care."

Looking up from her task, Mama Fela inspected her granddaughter's face. It didn't look the way a child's face should. Her eyelashes were wet with tears, not the ordinary tears of a child throwing a tantrum, but droplets of something deeper, a sign of a childhood betrayed. Stolen. Cipriana was hunched over the table with her head resting on her arms. Her elbows resembled the head of a pin, though not quite as nicely rounded, Mama Fela thought.

"Have you been eating much, 'jita? You're all skin and bones."

Cipriana raised her head and nodded.

"Your mama should be feeding you more so that you can look like that little girl in the pictures, the one with the curls. ¿Cómo se llama?"

"Shirley Temple?" Cipriana perked up.

"That's the one." It felt good to see her granddaughter smile but somehow it was unnatural. Tears and smiles did not go together. Turning again to her task, Mama Fela wondered how she was going to make things better.

To the egg whites, now foamy, Mama Fela added the yolks, beating them together until the foam became creamy yellow. She poured the steaming milk into the bowl, and added sugar and pinches of cinnamon, nutmeg, and ginger at the top. She poured the mixture into two cups, leaving the second cup only half full. "There," she told Cipriana, placing the full cup in front of her. "Un toddy."

"What are you putting in yours, Mama Fela?" Cipriana asked in between sips. Mama Fela screwed the cap back onto a pewter pint and slipped it into her apron pocket. "Oh, nothing, mi'jita, just my medicine," she said, smiling. "Válgame Dios, I almost forgot the tortillas."

She set out a large pile of the flat bread and watched Cipriana beam as she began to eat. Mama Fela had never seen the child wolf her food this way.

"Haven't you eaten this morning, 'jita?"

Cipriana stopped chewing then and looked at Mama Fela. She put down the tortilla slowly and nodded. "A little, Mama Fela."

"No, no, go on. Eat as many as you'd like." Mama Fela unwrapped the kitchen towel from the rest of the tortillas. She sipped her drink slowly, feeling its warmth flow through her body. How was she going to solve her granddaughter's problems? How?

"I've got to do my sewing, 'jita," she said, getting up from the table. "Finish your drink and then come and join me." Mama Fela moved past the washstand and the trunk of provisions to the area she called her sewing room. Even though it also doubled as her bedroom, it was first and foremost her place to sew. To think.

Mama Fela began removing piles of sewing projects from the top of the sewing machine and spreading them carefully on her bed, which she had straightened and covered with a clean starched cotton sheet. To Mama Fela, her bed was sacred ground. It was her cutting table and no one was allowed to touch it when her precious dress materials blanketed the space. She organized the piles into those for which she had a deadline and those she was working on for pleasure: Doña Carlota's lavender dress and a brown silk bodice, begun for Doña Sofia, were at the head of the bed, closest to the sewing machine; two white bridal sleeves ready for lace cuffs were at the foot along with waxy brown tissue paper pinned on top of a square of scarlet material.

A whisper of morning light greeted Mama Fela as she sat down at the sewing machine. Squinting, she inspected her stitch work on Doña Carlota's dress but shook her head in frustration. She turned and called Cipriana. "Bring me my glasses, muchachita. I can't see anything."

Cipriana retrieved the small spectacles from the kitchen table and handed them to Mama Fela, who wrapped the rubber stems around her ears. "Ah, that's better," she mumbled, pulling them farther down upon her nose. "Why don't you look in the armario there, 'jita. In one of those boxes, I'm sure you'll find the perfect dress for that baby doll of yours. ¿Cómo se llama?"

"She doesn't have a name, Mama Fela. I just call her dolly."

"No name! ¿Por qué no, 'jita?"

Cipriana shrugged.

As soon as Cipriana opened the armario, the aroma of mothballs flooded the small room. Mama Fela watched Cipriana rummage through the boxes of scrap, knowing she would be happily occupied for some time. Turning to the task at hand, she smoothed the lavender material in front of her and began vigorously pumping the pedal of the machine. For the rest of the morning, she worked the contraption, stopping at intervals only to smooth the material or to snip a procession of stitches that did not satisfy her.

To Mama Fela, everything had to be exact. She hated living in a world that could not offer perfection but she had always been ready to do what she could to make things right. She wondered if it was within her power now to correct the wrongs committed against her granddaughter. It was easy to blame Cipriana's mother for being selfish and not realizing how her melancholy affected her daughter. And it was even easier to blame Roberto for being the cause of Graciela's unhappiness. His temper had gotten him into trouble before. Deep down, Mama Fela blamed herself. Her son Roberto was a good man but not good enough. The decision, long ago, to allow her own parents, Roberto's grandparents, to raise him was a mistake she would have to live with until her death. It wasn't enough to damn herself; she would be damned by her son, her husband, and finally by God.

Suddenly, Mama Fela slammed down the machine's lid, startling herself and her granddaughter. "Dios mío," Mama Fela sighed. "Sorry, 'jita." She closed the second flap more quietly, stood abruptly, and began folding patterns and dress pieces one by one, placing them neatly on the sewing machine and covering them with the single white sheet. "Bring me my purse, 'jita. I need a smoke. It's there on la cómoda," she said, straightening her bed and indicating the dresser with a lift of her chin.

"Let's sit at the table," she called to Cipriana, who followed with a black flat purse in hand. Snapping it open, Mama Fela rummaged through it until she located a small square tablet of cigarette paper and a tiny pouch of Bull Durham tobacco. Tearing a sheet from the pad, she placed a pinch of the black powder along the length of the paper, rolled it up carefully, and licked the final edge. When the cigarette was lit, she held it securely with her thumb and forefinger, blowing smoke from her nostrils. Sliding her purse over to Cipriana, she said, "Look, 'jita. I must have some chewing gum in there somewhere."

The contents of her satchel were always dusted with the sugary remnants of spearmint or peppermint sticks of gum torn in half on a frugal impulse, and she knew that her granddaughter found delight in it. She knew that the faint smell of licorice would lead Cipriana to her favorite, Black Jack. Fishing out a partial piece of gum with no wrapper, Cipriana sniffed it, licked it, and finally placed it on her tongue as if she were giving herself Communion. She began chewing slowly, a puzzled look on her face. Suddenly, she stopped chewing and began sucking loudly on the wad, her face contorting into displeasure.

"What, 'jita?" Placing her cigarette into a tin, Mama Fela pulled Cipriana toward her and cupped her dark hand under Cipriana's mouth. Spitting the gum out, Cipriana rubbed her tongue against her front teeth. "Yuck. What was that, Mama Fela? It tasted awful."

Mama Fela smiled. She held the sticky wad of gum at her nostril and inhaled once and then a second time. Shaking her head, she laughed quietly, her shoulders and chest moving rhythmically. "Tobacco. That's tobacco, 'jita. Must have rubbed off on that gum." When Cipriana frowned, Mama Fela pulled her to her side and wiped Cipriana's lips with the corner of her apron.

"Mama Fela?"

"Yes, 'jita?" Mama Fela took up her cigarette, holding it between her index finger and her thumb.

Cipriana looked deep into Mama Fela's cloudy eyes. "I don't have a dolly anymore. That's why she doesn't have a name."

"Oh?"

"Daddy broke mine . . . this morning."

Bending over the table, Mama Fela smacked her lips several times against the cigarette and inhaled, avoiding her granddaughter's gaze. Her spectacles lay useless as she sat back in her chair and stared blindly into the swirl of smoke above her. The ashes at the tip of the cigarette grew longer and longer until they threatened to curl and drop into her cupped hand below.

Staring out the window, she wondered where her husband was now. He would know exactly what to say to Cipriana. He could talk to children, that man. Maybe not to women, but to Cipriana, his words were magic.

"All right, 'jita," Mama Fela said breathlessly, suddenly smashing the butt into a plain tin. "Let's go to town."

Mama Fela moved hurriedly to the washstand and let a trickle of water fall from the pitcher into her hand. Reaching for an olive-colored bar of soap, she motioned Cipriana toward her. She dipped a white cloth into the cold water in the basin and began rubbing the soap into the cloth. "Here. Let me clean your face. You're so güera, you get these little brown spots. All you have to do is rub a little lemon juice here and here," she told Cipriana, scouring her face as if it had not been washed for weeks, "and they'll go away."

Cipriana tried to squirm away, but Mama Fela held her firmly in her grasp. "We're going to see your great-grandfather, Cipriana. Be still." When she was satisfied with her granddaughter's appearance, she wet the tips of her own fingers, brushed them together with a little soap, dipped them in the water again, then flicked the drops of excess water from them.

Bending over the basin, she lightly touched her fingers to her smooth skin, massaging droplets of fragrant water onto her face. She patted her skin with a bleached face towel, unscrewed a jar of talc, and applied a puff of powder to her nose, forehead, and chin, sure that it masked her shine.

The little shop was made from lumber and tin and was referred to in polite company as La Carpentería. People tricked themselves into believing that Don Armijo created cabinets and chairs, tables and trunks, not little wooden boxes in which they would one day find themselves supine. Purple bolts of material stood at attention all along the wall, waiting for orders to fill the pine coffins. Some boxes stood upright, others lay open on their backside in between two sawhorses. For Mama Fela, the room held an eerie attraction. It was populated by avid listeners, empty coffins that could absorb both complaint and gossip without censure.

"Papá! Papá, are you here?"

Cipriana was clutching Mama Fela's hand so tightly, her fingers went numb and her pulse weak. "¡Cuidado, muchacha!" she said, prying her hand away and shaking it. "My blood's going to stop if you don't quit. Papá! Where are you?" she asked, annoyed. "Let's go, 'jita. Let's try the barbershop."

"Fela? Is that you?" The voice was a deep monotone, muffled, far away.

Mama Fela laid her hand on her granddaughter's shoulder and when Cipriana jumped so did she.

"Fela!"

"Papá? Is that you? Where are you?"

Neither she nor Cipriana could remove their eyes from the coffins. "Papá? . . . Papá, where are you?"

"Aquí." There was a knock on one of the coffins. "Get me out."

"Where, Papá? Which one?" Mama Fela slid the lid from several until her father's torso emerged from one of them. In his small hand, he held a hammer.

"Hard to breathe in there."

"What were you doing, Papá? What happened?"

"Never mind that now, Fela. Let me get some air."

With one hand, Mama Fela held the lid steady and with the other she tried to guide her father out of the box but he ignored her offer of support. Instead, he clambered out impetuously as if he had been locked in a cell for half a lifetime and was now exulting in newfound freedom. His nimbleness surprised her. Seventy-eight years of life did not stop him from displaying the streak of independence said to run in his bloodline or the youthful exuberance usually reserved for a man thirty years his junior. She loved her father despite his tendency to treat those outside his family better than his own. He could be gruff and cold but she knew that when she needed him, he would be there. But seeing him inside that coffin made her wonder for how long and it frightened her. She had always thought of her father as indispensable. With his ebony hair inherited from his Indian heritage, he looked younger than Fela, who already had a head of gray. For the first time, she realized her father was subject to the same effects of time that she was.

"How did you get stuck, Papá?"

He waved his hand, dismissing the subject. Walking around the coffin, he inspected his work, saying nothing.

Mama Fela could tell he was embarrassed but out of curiosity, she insisted, "What were you doing in the coffin? Can't you work from outside it?"

"No. Gives me a better feel this way. I can see the imperfections. Comes out prettier. What do you need, Fela?"

"Papá . . . ," she began slowly, testing his patience. "Do you still have connections with the school board?"

"Some." Finally he turned to her. "¿Por qué?"

"You know Graciela's out of a job, don't you?"

"Graciela? Yes, I heard."

"She's unhappy, Papá."

"So are a lot of other people. Not much I can do about that."

"Papá, she can't depend on Roberto. You know that. She needs her job back."

"Roberto was your responsibility . . ."

"And yours." Fela's voice was almost a whisper. It took everything she had to meet her father's gaze. "You raised him, Papá."

Papa Armijo was silent, his jaw clenched. "You want me to get her job back?"

Fela nodded.

"What makes you think I can?"

Mama Fela thought for a moment. Was her father testing her? Did he want praise from her? Did he need it?

Just when she was about to answer, her father took up a cloth and began polishing the almond-stained coffin. "I'll see what I can do. Now leave me to my work."

Mama Fela stared at her father, wondering if she should thank him. Behind his mask of stoic indifference, there was a man who did care. She had to believe that. "Cipriana," she said, tearing her granddaughter's fingers from her own, "kiss your Papa Armijo goodbye."

At Gould's, Mama Fela had planned to purchase several yards of black silk to replace her Sunday dress, but while she was examining the bolts of fabric, her youngest sister appeared behind the counter.

"Fela, you said you would come yesterday," Quirina said, almost whining.

"I know. I'm sorry. I had so much to do."

"Well, here," she said, taking a brown package from beneath the counter and unwrapping it, "I already cut eight yards for you."

Mama Fela inspected the silk. "Ay, it's nice, Quirina. It's the one I wanted but . . . I'm afraid I can't get it."

"What do you mean? Fela, I already cut it."

"I know, Quirina. I know." Fela ran her fingers along its sleek surface. Looking up, she scanned the store for Cipriana. "Where's my 'jita?" she asked more to herself than to anyone else.

Quirina tapped Fela's hand. "Mira," she said, pointing out Cipriana's presence at the candy counter.

"Ay que muchacha," Fela mumbled, sighing deeply. Caressing the silk between her fingertips, she said, "It's not that I don't want it, Quirina. I do." Without removing her hands from the cloth, she turned and found

Cipriana still at the same counter. Turning back, she caught Quirina's gaze. "But right now I need the money," she said.

"For what? You've been saving for this dress for months."

Mama Fela nodded. Slowly, she began to survey Quirina's face. No wonder people were surprised when they found out they were sisters. Fela was dark; Quirina light. Fela was thin, both her body and her face; Quirina was slim but more healthy looking, rounded, buxom like the movie stars. And even though Mama Fela felt she was the same person inside as she had been twenty or even thirty years ago, her body had begun to look like that of a vieja. It wasn't that she was wrinkled; her face actually was completely unlined. In fact, Quirina was more wrinkled than she was even though she was ten years younger. But Mama Fela knew where those lines had come from. They told a story that only Mama Fela knew, a tale of pain and shame and abandonment. Mama Fela would never forget the way Quirina looked that day when she found her alone, underneath a nest of blankets, oblivious to her infant's cries, no food in the cupboard, no philandering husband to scold, and no hope. Mama Fela remembered that terrible day and shuddered.

Quirina's eyes met Mama Fela's. For a moment, Quirina's gaze was so intense, Mama Fela felt as if her sister were reading her thoughts.

"It's Graciela. Without her job, they don't have enough to eat," Mama Fela said quietly.

Quirina frowned, looking over at Cipriana. And then she nodded at Mama Fela. "I'm sure someone else can use this silk," she said, wrapping it tightly.

Mama Fela knew that nothing else had to be said. Quirina understood. She followed Quirina across the store to the grocery section while she watched her sister pile flour, potatoes, coffee, macaroni, rice, and beans into a couple of boxes. While Quirina added up her bill, she called to her granddaughter. "'Jita. Come here." Opening up her satchel, she took out a nickel. "Get me a chocolate bar, Cipriana. Hershey's."

"Just one, Mama Fela?"

"Just one, 'jita."

As they left the store, Cipriana carried one box, Mama Fela the other. "You sure it's not too heavy, 'jita?"

"It's not heavy at all. I'm used to helping Mama."

"Bueno, 'jita. Let's stop at the post office then so I can get my newspaper."

When they had made their way down the block, Mama Fela peeked into the tiny window at the post office. "Oh good, Doña Sulema's there," she said. "Here, sit down and watch the groceries. I'll only be a minute." As Mama Fela was about to enter the small building, she turned, digging her hand into her coat pocket and taking out the chocolate bar. "When I bought this I forgot how much trouble my stomach's been giving me. Ay que dolor," she moaned melodramatically, taking a deep breath. "What am I going to do with it, 'jita?"

"You can save it, Mama Fela. Eat it tomorrow or the next day."

"But it could melt, mi'jita. And then I'd have wasted good food." Mama Fela pretended to be worried. She shook her head in frustration, waiting to see what kind of response Cipriana would give.

"Well . . . ," Cipriana said slowly, frowning a little girl's frown. "I could eat it, Mama Fela. If you'd like."

Chuckling, Mama Fela handed Cipriana the candy. "Thank you, 'jita. Thank you," she said, wondering how many years it would take for her granddaughter to see right through her.

Mama Fela had known Sulema from the moment she was born. She had brought her into this world, pulling her from her mother's bloody womb. It was funny, Mama Fela thought, as she stepped up to Sulema's counter, watching these babies grow up, changing from ugly wrinkled things covered in a film of slime to beautiful young women with creamy white skin.

"¿Cómo estás, Sulema?" Mama Fela called out.

Sulema turned. "Doña Fela! I'm sorry I missed you yesterday. José said you came in looking for your paper but it wasn't here yet. I can't imagine why it was a day late."

"No, no, don't worry. It gives me an excuse to leave my sewing for a few hours."

"What are you working on now? How's that wedding dress coming?"

"Shh." Mama Fela put her finger to her lips and looked around the small room. "Where's Don José?" she asked suspiciously.

"He's in the back. Don't worry," she said grinning, "he can't hear."

"Are you sure?" she whispered. "He has big ears and a loose tongue, worse than you or me."

"Doña Fela! Are you saying you and I are mitoteras?"

A slight smile surfaced on Mama Fela's face. It was as if Sulema had given her permission to open her mouth freely to share her latest news. "You know Doña Carlota?"

Sulema nodded.

"I'm making another dress for her. For her funeral."

"Her funeral? I thought she died after dress number five. Which one is this?"

"Let's see . . . number seven, I think. She can't make up her mind which one to wear. This one's lavender."

"Lavender! ¡Dios mío!"

"She's afraid they'll dress her in one of those funeral dresses ripped right down the back. Says she doesn't want to show her nalgas to San Pedro."

"No!" Sulema said, chuckling.

"It's the truth," Mama Fela said, trying to keep her mirth in check. She was starting to feel a tinge of guilt for revealing this knowledge about her friend. She should have held her tongue.

"I heard someone say . . ." Sulema paused, searching the room with her eyes. Lowering her voice, she continued, ". . . that she doesn't talk much these days except to God."

"That's true. She wants to say adios real bad to this world since her Eloy died. I tell her, 'Doña Carlota, but what about your children?' She says, 'Ooh, they've got the way of their father—los americanos. They don't come around. They're off busy with their own lives—too busy to visit their mamá.' She's just praying for God to take her quick."

"Ay que sad."

"Yo sé. But . . . ay Sulema, I've kept you too long," Mama Fela said, looking at the clock on the wall. "I better let you get to your work. Where's that paper of mine?"

Sulema rummaged through a pile of mail. "Here it is and your yerba magazine. You know, come to think of it, Mamá wanted me to ask you what to do for her muscles. They're really hurting."

"Is it los reumos?"

"I think so."

"Does she feel the aches through her bones like they start there and never end?"

Sulema nodded.

"Ooh, Sulema, it's this old age. See what you have to look forward to? Tell her that a little añil tea is the best thing for this rheumatism. That's what I use. I save the leaves in the fall, dry them, and then make the tea for the bath. But you tell your mamá the tea has to be real strong to work and I like to soak until the water starts getting cold. And you get your mamá a tub like the farmers use, long and narrow, not the little round ones where you have to be one of those enanas to fit. But you know," she said, taking up her magazine and flipping through its pages, "I was reading that rubbing a little powdered maravilla mixed with lard works to soothe the tired bones too. Look," she said, tapping the page, "here it is! I'm going to order some, Sulema. Tell your mamá as soon as I try it, if it works, I'll take some to her. But tell her to try the sunflower tea first."

"Where can she get it? The flowers are all dried up by now."

"You tell your mamá I have some extra. I'll drop it by."

"Oh, you don't have to do that, Doña Fela."

Clicking her tongue, Mama Fela said, "Pues, I'm going to anyway and I won't have it any other way." She tucked her reading material underneath her arm and said goodbye to Sulema. "Send my best to your mamá."

The candy bar was a hit with Cipriana as Mama Fela had expected. "Clean your mouth, 'jita. You've got half the chocolate there. Here, let me see."

While Mama Fela worked with a bit of spit and a handkerchief, the door to the post office creaked open once more. "Wait. Doña Fela. There's a letter. I almost forgot a letter came for you."

"A letter?" Mama Fela tensed up. Letters only meant one thing and that was bad news. "From who?"

"I don't know."

"Hmm. Las Vegas." The print was not familiar to Mama Fela and there was no return address.

"Open it, Mama Fela."

"Shh," she scolded, frowning at Cipriana. "We'll wait until we get home."

"But why, Mama Fela? Open it now."

Ignoring Cipriana, Mama Fela slipped the envelope into her coat pocket. Her thoughts suddenly turned to her husband and his absence. Was he hurt? Was the letter his? Where was he? Quickly, she picked up the groceries. "Ándale, 'jita, we have to get home. Sulema," she said, already turning to go, "may God be with you."

Home was her destination. Quickly and without interruption. She felt anxious. Every muscle tensed up and she felt her rheumatism stronger than ever. She walked briskly despite the pain, stiffly, turning at every whisper, every sound to see if it was her husband's voice. Those storefronts along Main Street with a window seat were of particular interest to her. She greeted the men milling about, hoping to see her husband's face among them. Ten days gone was too much. Too long.

"Mama Fela!" Cipriana called, out of breath.

Mama Fela stopped abruptly. "Oh, I'm sorry, 'jita. Is that box too heavy?" she asked.

"I'm tired, Mama Fela."

"We have to get home, 'jita. Here, let me put those things in this one and you carry the beans." One by one, Mama Fela emptied the contents of Cipriana's box into her own, flattened the cardboard, and slid it into the other box. "Vamos," she said, heaving the full load into her arms.

Just yesterday, she had strolled along the dusty alley to her little stone house, admiring the cosmos and the purple wild asters that had survived the mild frost, but now, she barely noticed them because up ahead, she saw a crooked figure in his undershirt and trousers, bent over a basin of water. She squinted, seeing socks and long underwear hanging from the clothesline. Catching her breath, she knew then that her premonition had come true, perhaps a little late, but it had indeed come true: Papa Gilberto was home. "Gracias a Dios," she mumbled. She wanted to call out his name, to run forward and welcome him, but a sense of propriety restrained her.

As she and her granddaughter approached, Mama Fela watched her husband kneeling in the hard dirt, scrubbing the smell of the llano from his clothing, oblivious to their presence. He was rocking back and forth, scraping his clothes across the washboard, when suddenly Cipriana saw him too. "There's Papa Gil," she cried excitedly, grabbing Mama Fela's skirt. "C'mon!"

"You go on, 'jita. Here, give me the beans."

Cipriana ran ahead but Mama Fela approached slowly, burdened by the heavy groceries. Her granddaughter was already hugging Gilberto before he could even stand. He got up slowly then with Cipriana's help, slapping his thighs once he stood erect. "I'm getting too old, mi'jita, for this kind of work. Wish they'd invent some magic to take the stink out of clothes. Press a button and whew," he whistled, snapping his fingers, "they smell cleaner than a summer rain."

Cipriana giggled.

"Where's . . . ?" he began, turning around.

"Mira las pansas de vacas," Mama Fela said with a slight smile, pointing to the wet tattletale gray underwear with her pursed lips.

"Fela, they're supposed to be that color. I bought them special," he said, grinning.

"Gilberto!" she said with mock sternness, studying his face. His smiling blue eyes and his red wind-burnt cheeks told her that the time away had refreshed him. She breathed heavily, chasing her anxiety away. She was glad to see him home.

Taking the box from her, he announced, "I bought a roast. I thought maybe we could have this little girl over for supper." Pulling a strand of hair playfully, he asked Cipriana, "How would you like to be our guest, mi'jita?"

Cipriana nodded. "Are you going to make the meat with potatoes and onions, Papa Gil?"

"And garlic, 'jita. That's the most important ingredient. ¡Ay ay ay!" he moaned, squeezing his eyes tight and slapping his cheek. "I just gave away my secret."

"Papa Gil! That's not a secret. I knew that a long time ago."

Papa Gilberto laughed heartily. "You did? Well, you're way ahead of me since you're such a big girl," he said, pulling her oversized sleeve. "Go home and invite your mama and papa to our celebration. What time do you think we should eat, Fela?"

"It's up to you, Gilberto. When will the roast be ready?" Mama Fela asked.

"Oh, I'd say in a few hours. Let's see, Cipriana. Why don't you come when . . . let's see . . . when the sun hides behind his mother's apron. How's that?"

Grinning, Cipriana turned to go. Mama Fela could tell by her gait that she was as a child should be once again, if only temporarily. She fed her granddaughter with tortillas and chocolate and Gilberto fed her with jokes and fine words and love. He had a way with Cipriana like no one else. He was a good man. Thank God he was home safe and well.

Climbing the steps to the kitchen, Mama Fela sighed. Suddenly, she turned and gasped, "The groceries!"

"I have them," Gilberto said, surprised, trailing up the steps.

"No, they're for Cipriana."

"What?"

"I'll tell you later. Cipriana!" she called, waving her arms.

"Why don't I just take them later?"

"You will?"

"Of course. They're too heavy for Cipriana anyway." Calling to Cipriana, he said, "Right, 'jita?"

"She doesn't know they're for her."

"Oh." He looked from Mama Fela to Cipriana and back again. "Never mind, 'jita. Your abuela can't make up her mind. We'll see you later."

"Wait. What about Mamá and Papá? Shouldn't Cipriana tell Roberto to stop by for them on the way?"

"Not your mamá!" Gilberto groaned.

Mama Fela felt her face go hot. "And why not, hombre?"

"She'll eat all the meat! You know that, Fela," he said, grinning. "And there won't be any left for Cipriana or me!"

Even Mama Fela couldn't help feeling amused. Her mother's slight body could hold nothing more than a few bites of food. Shaking her head, she gave a final wave to Cipriana, trying hard not to smile at her husband.

"Ay, Gilberto, what am I going to do with you?" she asked, holding the door open for her husband. "Saying those things in front of Cipriana."

"What? Nothing wrong with speaking my mind."

"No, but saying those things about Mamá . . ."

Gilberto giggled like a little girl. He put the box of groceries down on the kitchen table. "So what are these for?" he asked, rummaging through the brown paper packages, reading their inscriptions.

Mama Fela stared at her husband, inspecting his face. It was funny how they carried on as if he were never gone. Deep down she wondered where his moods had taken him, to what places he had gone both on foot and in his mind, but she didn't want to pry. When he was ready, he would tell her.

"They're for Cipriana."

"I gathered that much, Fela, but why are they for Cipriana? You're not interfering in something you shouldn't be, are you?"

"Gilberto, why do you always think the worst? Of course I'm interfering, but it's necessary. You should have seen Cipriana this morning. I've never seen a child so hungry."

"What do you mean?" he asked, frowning.

"Now that Graciela's not working, she's not getting enough to eat. I think they don't have enough for groceries."

Gilberto was quiet. He put the packages he had been inspecting back in their box. Slowly, almost meditatively, he made his way to the counter and began picking out potatoes from a basket.

"Are you listening, Gilberto?"

Gilberto nodded, taking a paring knife from a drawer.

"We need to get her job back."

"We!" Gilberto spun around. "Don't go interfering, Fela. You'll be sorry."

"Don't point that knife at me. I already talked to Papá."

Turning to the counter again, with his head bent over his work, Gilberto sighed, shaking his head. "I should have known as much. You work fast, don't you?"

"Someone had to."

"And that someone is you. Always has to be you, right?"

For a moment, Mama Fela paused, digesting every one of her husband's words. His tone was mean, spiteful, unfamiliar. "What's wrong? Didn't you have a good trip?"

"Didn't I have a good trip? Of course I did. But that's not what this is about. You're always interfering."

Mama Fela frowned. "There's something you're not telling me, isn't there?"

"No!" He sliced the first potato.

"What's wrong then?"

"Your father can do no wrong."

"That's right. He can't. What's wrong, Gilberto?"

"I'm always having to live up to him. Your father."

"Live up to him? What do you mean?"

"I'll never be able to provide for you like he did. Never."

"What? You don't have to provide for me. I make my way with the little bit of sewing I do."

"See what I mean? You don't even expect anything from me anymore."

"What? What are you talking about, Gilberto? Didn't you have a good trip?"

"Yes!" Gilberto whirled around. "No! I don't know, Fela." Gilberto looked to the floor as if he would find answers in the linoleum squares. Slowly, he began to explain. "I feel responsible, Fela. I should be the one doing something about this. Roberto's our son. My son. He's the one who loses jobs because of that damn pride of his and then he goes and quits his wife's job too. He was too spoilt, Fela."

"Spoilt! Spoilt? No, Gilberto. No." Suddenly, the urge to cry overwhelmed Fela. She recalled the day she decided to give her son away and the years of guilt afterward. The rumors had been more interesting than the truth. Years later, even her son believed them. "At least he was able to eat, Gilberto. We couldn't have given him even that."

"Exactly! That's what I'm talking about. I couldn't even give him food. We shouldn't have done it, Fela. We shouldn't have given him over for your mamá and papá to raise. It was our job. Our job, Fela. He learned to be irresponsible from us. Can't blame anyone but us." Facing the counter once more, he took the knife to his potatoes.

For the first time in her life, Mama Fela did not know what to say. From across the kitchen, she began placing the ingredients for bread into a bowl. Feeling dazed, she watched as her husband unwrapped a mound of meat from butcher paper. With a paring knife, he began making tiny slits all over the roast, inserting slivers of fresh garlic and slices of onion. He set the roast in a large iron skillet and carefully placed potatoes and onions around it, seasoning everything with salt and pepper. With an iron rod, he stoked the fire. "I'll be outside taking my bath," he said, pulling his potholder from the oven, where his feast was ready to bake.

"Good! You need one, viejo barbón," she said, referring to the growth of white stubble along his jaw. "But take it in here. It's too cold outside, hombre. Anyhow I'll be doing my sewing."

Mama Fela kneaded her bread one more time and quickly divided the dough among several bread pans. She covered the pans with a wet cloth, and retreated to her sewing area, spreading her projects out on the bed. The basting of the red material went slowly but she didn't mind the pace as she listened to Gilberto, pouring cascade after cascade of heated water into his tin tub. It was a good sound.

A few minutes after five o'clock, Mama Fela had just taken a loaf of bread out of the oven when the kitchen door opened and Cipriana walked in.

"Mi'jita. Just in time. You can help me set the table. Be sure and set down all the flatware. Forks, spoons, and knives."

"Why are we using all those, Mama Fela? We never use them all."

"We're having meat, 'jita, and dessert too. We need them all." The moment her words escaped her, Mama Fela had to rethink them. Was it the menu that made her instruct Cipriana to set a formal table or was it because her mother was coming? To this day, Mama Soledad set out fork, spoon, and knife, teacup, and saucer for every meal even when all she had was beans, even when she was alone. It was one of Mama Soledad's rituals still, after all these years, one Fela could never understand. To her, all it meant was more dirty dishes. Out of respect, however, Mama Fela knew without reservation that she would follow her mother's wishes as if she were still a child setting her mother's table.

"Get the cups and saucers too, Cipriana. They're down there. Be careful now," she said, watching Cipriana out of the corner of her eye.

"Well hello, mi'jita!" Papa Gilberto stood in the doorway, his face ruddy and his clothes clean. "Didn't you bring the others?"

"They're coming, Papa Gil. They just don't run as fast as I do."

"I see. Well, Fela, I'm going to borrow Cipriana for a minute."

"Stay close, hombre. There are going to be a lot of people mad at each other tonight. Mostly Graciela and Roberto. And it was your idea to have this, so be ready to interfere."

"Like I said, Fela, I don't interfere. That's your job."

Mama Fela swallowed hard but she knew her husband was joking with her. She had to learn not to take the things he said to heart. "Not this time, Gilberto," she insisted. "It's your turn."

Turning his back, he slipped out the kitchen door, calling, "Mi'jita and I are going outside. We're practicing for something important. We'll be right back."

"Come back here, hombre. What about the roast? Our guests?"

"We'll be right back."

"Ay que hombre," Mama Fela muttered to herself just as Mama Soledad entered through the front door, holding onto Roberto's arm. Papa Armijo and Graciela trailed behind with Pablito in Graciela's arms.

"Mamá! Here, sit over here," Mama Fela said nervously, taking her mother by the hand.

"No. No. I can do it myself," she scolded, slapping Fela's hand away. She was completely blind, the result of untreated cataracts. Sitting down, Mama Soledad ran her hand along several place settings. "Who set this table?" she asked sternly, staring straight ahead.

Timidly, Fela patted her mother's hand. "I did, Mamá. Cipriana and me." Mama Fela was ashamed of her own voice. It sounded scared, like a child's, and here she was a vieja herself. How could her mother's tone still intimidate her? Quickly, she changed the subject.

"Sit down everyone, sit down," she said, indicating the chairs around the kitchen table. When everyone was settled, she asked, "Now what can I get you to drink?"

Mama Fela took their orders and moved back and forth between the stove and the table. The only sound in the room was the clip-clop of her black sturdy shoes thudding back and forth across the linoleum. She tried to make small talk without much success. All her family seemed to be sulking, unhappy to be sitting next to the person near them, unhappy to be called away from the sanctity of their homes. Graciela looked downright ill. Roberto appeared angry. Papa Armijo was indifferent as usual, and Mama Soledad was sitting stoically with her arms crossed at her chest. The anxiety was palpable and the evening had not yet begun. She remembered now why she did not like big family gatherings. It was Gilberto who liked them, but she always ended up taking responsibility for their success. She had to become both mediator and expert conversationalist, and given the tension in the room tonight, she knew she would have to use both skills to the fullest.

Quickly, she called Cipriana's young brother to her side. "Pablito, go give your Papa Gilberto un besito. He and Cipriana are out in back. Tell them we're ready to eat." Mama Fela pointed the way and Pablito waddled away obediently.

"And Papá, can you help me a minute? Gilberto was supposed to slice the roast but who knows what nonsense he and Cipriana are up to."

Papa Armijo nodded and scooted out of his chair. He followed Mama Fela to the counter. She handed him a knife.

As he began to carve the meat, sweat trickled down his forehead. With a sleeve, he wiped it before it fell into his eyes. Mama Fela sliced the bread.

"Fela, I talked with the school board today," Papa Armijo whispered. "Graciela has her job back."

"Papá! Bless you." Mama Fela looked around the room, making sure no one had heard her, especially not Roberto. Unfortunately all of her guests were looking at her.

"What's that all about, Mamá?"

"Never mind, Roberto. It's between your Papa Armijo and me."

"Well, keep it to yourself then, Fela," Mama Soledad scolded. "Don't screech like los niños and expect us to have no curiosity. Have some manners. And get me some more yerba buena."

Mama Fela winced. It was bad enough to be a viejita but a viejita scolded by her own mother was even worse. Swallowing hard, Mama Fela took Mama Soledad's cup and poured more hot tea. She would kill Gilberto for his absence.

At that moment, the door creaked open and Mama Fela looked at it anxiously, taking a deep breath.

"My god! My own house full of people and I wasn't even invited!"

"Cita, watch your language," Mama Soledad scolded.

"And hello to you too, Mama Soledad. So nice to see you."

Mama Fela stared at Cita sternly. "Go bring some more chairs, Cita. They're out in back."

"Well at least I'm good for something."

"Now, Cita. Please." Mama Fela could feel that her voice had also turned stern. It was the same tone her mother often used but she hadn't meant for it to sound so harsh. "Thank you, Cita," she added softly, hoping some of the sting would disappear. Just as Cita began to open the back door, it swung open and Gilberto stumbled in, startled. "Cita, mi'ja."

"Papá! When did you get back?" she asked, wrapping her arms around him. "We missed you."

"I missed you too, 'jita. And you're just in time. Cipriana and I have something to say. Sit down there. Sit down."

"I need to get some chairs, Papá."

"Not now, Cita. This is important. Sit down."

Without a greeting to any of his guests, Papa Gilberto cleared his throat. "I know everybody's hungry, but before we eat, I have something to say. Cipriana's going to help me make un speeche." Swinging her up on a chair, he said, "Cipriana."

When Cipriana cleared her throat too, everyone laughed, including Mama Fela. What was Gilberto up to, she wondered? It was not unusual for him to tell jokes, but speech making was another thing altogether. She sat up straight in her chair, at the edge of her seat. She squeezed her hands together, feeling the sweat of one palm mingle with the other. Gilberto was staring straight at her and she began to feel uncomfortable, knowing all eyes were on her. But as hard as she tried, it was impossible to turn her attention elsewhere. His gaze seemed to cast a spell over her and immediately she knew something was wrong. He was trying to tell her something but she didn't understand. She strained to hear a message in the words he fed Cipriana, whispering in her ear.

"Papa Gil says, 'Ladies and Gentlemen. Señoras y Caballeros.'"

Hurry, 'jita, Mama Fela felt like shouting.

"We have a good man who's running for county treasurer. His name is Serna, Felipe Serna and he's . . ." Mama Fela had heard this before. Gilberto was teaching Cipriana his way of politicking. It was old news as far as she was concerned and she was ready to leave her chair to serve the food when Gilberto called out, "Fela, wait!" and Cipriana echoed him, "Mama Fela, wait!"

"I'll be right here, 'jita. I'm listening. Go on. Go on," she urged, still making her way to the *trastero* where all her dishes were kept.

Suddenly, Cipriana shouted, "Not until you sit back down!"

"'Jita!" Mama Fela whirled around, frowning. "What's gotten into you two?" Looking around the table, she asked incredulously, "Can you believe this pair?"

"Please, Mama Fela, we haven't finished our speech yet."

"Is that you talking, Cipriana, or is that your grandfather?"

"It's me, Mama Fela."

"All right, then. I'll sit, but hurry it up. I'm like a guitarra with no food in my stomach." She looked around the room, happy to see some smiling faces.

"Papa Gil says, 'All of you know how good it is . . . to be proud of what you do, to do a job well.'"

Oh no, Mama Fela thought. *What was coming? Was he going to scold Roberto here in front of everyone?* Mama Fela noticed Gilberto looked straight at their son. Now he was whispering into Cipriana's ear again.

"Papa Gil wants you to know, a man over in Corona has put his trust in him to watch his sheep. It's a good job and he'll get some good money. He'll be watching a flock of sheep like . . . who, Papa Gil?" Cipriana asked. "Like Abraham. In the Bible. He'll be gone while the ground is hard."

In that small moment, Mama Fela's heart sank. "What do you mean 'when the ground is hard,' Gilberto? What does that mean?" She hated his little sayings.

With downcast eyes, Gilberto replied, "Until spring, Fela."

"You'll be gone the entire winter?"

He nodded.

"What will you eat, Papá?" Cita asked.

"I'll manage."

"How much will you be paid?" inquired Papa Armijo.

"Fifty dollars."

"Are you sure that's fair?" Roberto asked. "You're going to be gone all winter."

"Fair enough, I think," Gilberto replied brusquely. "Now then, where are those extra chairs so a man can eat?" he asked, looking around. "Ah, Cita, there you are. Now what about those chairs?"

"Don't forget about me, Papa Gil," Cipriana chimed in. "I'm hungry too."

"Course not, 'jita," he told Cipriana. "You give me a hand with my news. And I give you a hand with your chair. Will the lady sit?" Gilberto bowed ceremoniously as he took a wooden chair from Cita and scooted it closer to the circle of guests. He took Cipriana's hand and motioned her toward the chair. "And for you, Cita," he said, taking his daughter's hand. "Sit down."

His brow was shiny with perspiration, and with a clean sleeve he wiped it dry. "Let's eat," he said, pulling his own chair toward the table.

Mama Fela watched as he served the roast. He filled all the plates, passing them back down the table, until everyone was served. She wondered why her husband had chosen to announce his news in such a public way. It should have been between them. *Damn him*, she thought. He was too much of a coward to face her alone. He had planned it all, the dinner, the speech, knowing she would be angry, hoping her anger would subside by the time the gathering was over.

"Mira tu abuela con ojitos de gallo," he said to Cipriana.

It took every bit of self control for Mama Fela to stop glaring at her husband and to swallow her words of hatred. She wanted so much to retreat into her sewing room but a code of conduct instilled in her from a very young age prevented her from doing so. She remained at the table with her guests despite the urge to let go of all emotion. Avoiding her husband's gaze, she tried desperately to make conversation, but she could not think of anything appropriate to say. Without her full participation, the talk at the table slowed and the deafening silence cut the evening short. Everyone raced through the meal, even the children.

When Graciela got up and started clearing the dishes, Mama Fela did not object. Instead, she pushed her own chair back and followed Graciela. "Will you ask them if they'd like coffee?" she asked her daughter-in-law. She hated to impose on anyone, especially her son's wife, but in this case, it was the only way she could survive the evening. While she spooned *arroz dulce* into small bowls, she called to her daughter without turning. "Cita! Will you help me take the dessert to the table?"

She listened for the squeak of Cita's chair, but when there was none, Mama Fela could not hold it in anymore. "Graciela, will you finish here please?" And to her guests, she said weakly, "Excuse me." Quietly, she slipped out the kitchen door.

Half-blind with tears streaming down her face, she willed herself to the green bench underneath the bare branches of the apple trees. Burying her face in her hands, she cried to herself. No one listened to her. No one valued her. Her children were ingrates. Her husband didn't care. What had she done to deserve this? She would be all alone just like Doña Carlota. Pretty soon, she would be planning her own funeral.

Mama Fela continued to cry softly but when she felt a pair of eyes on her, she looked up startled. Cipriana was staring at her from a distance and when she called her over, Cipriana ran and hugged Mama Fela. "Oh, 'jita. You're the only one who loves me. You're the only one," she said, rocking her back and forth.

Finally, Mama Fela was ready to face her company. As she and Cipriana stood, she noticed Graciela at the back door, observing them. Mama Fela's eyes met Graciela's, who then approached tentatively. After a long moment of silence, Graciela took Mama Fela's hand shyly and squeezed it. It was so unlike her daughter-in-law to make any gesture of affection, much less toward her. She was surprised but only for an instant. With total acceptance and gratitude, she embraced Graciela for the first time.

As soon as Graciela was in her arms, Mama Fela knew everything important about her daughter-in-law. She pushed her away gently and announced jubilantly, "You're with child! You're with child, aren't you, Graciela?"

At first, Graciela said nothing. And then she nodded and Mama Fela saw pain in her eyes.

"You're not happy. Why, Graciela?"

"It's not a good time, Mama Fela. We can't do it. Robert doesn't have a job and . . . I . . ." Graciela took a deep breath. "I don't either."

"Yes you do."

Graciela looked at Mama Fela, puzzled. "No Mama Fela, I lost . . ."

"You've got it back."

"What?"

"It was Papa Armijo. Let's go ask him." Smiling, she took Graciela's hand in her own. "Let's go ask him."

At the doorway, Mama Fela stood side by side with her husband, waving good night to their guests. Smiling at Graciela, she nudged her husband hard with her elbow and said, "Go with them, hombre. Give them some light. Have some manners." In a softer voice she added, "Take the box of food."

When they were gone, she shut the door quickly, falling back against it. At last, the night was over. She breathed heavily, in relief and in dread. The dinner had been a celebration after all for Graciela and Roberto, for

Cipriana and Pablito. But she was exhausted and she still had to face her husband. How would she ever forgive him?

For a brief moment, a wicked thought entered her mind. She surveyed the room for a piece of heavy furniture. Nothing would give her greater pleasure at that moment than to barricade the door. Oh, wouldn't that be a sight? She could just see Gilberto searching for an open window, squeezing himself into the house. Now that would be something to celebrate. That damn man, thinking his departure was cause for celebration.

Her mind was bombarded with a flood of questions. What was she going to do with him gone all winter? Who was going to bring her coffee to bed? Who was going to cheer up Cipriana? How would she get through the winter? How would she eat?

The water in the washbasin was dirty, but she had no energy left to deal with it. Her sponge bath could wait until tomorrow. Tentatively, she splashed the water on her face, knowing her husband would soon be gone and his filthy habits with him. Gilberto didn't care about anyone but himself. He had no manners, no manners at all. He belonged in a stable. He belonged out on the llano by himself. He belonged with the sheep.

Sitting on her bed, Mama Fela brushed out her long graying hair and braided it once again. She removed her teeth and brushed them, placing them in a small porcelain dish on top of her nightstand. As she slipped on a clean nightgown, she heard Gilberto at the door, and quickly she slipped into bed, turned over on her stomach, and closed her eyes. She could not bear to talk to him now.

When he entered the bedroom, he said, "You're mad at me, aren't you?"

Mama Fela refused to answer and kept her breathing steady.

"I know you're not asleep, Fela. Talk to me."

Still, she remained silent.

"Fela, I'm sorry I didn't tell you before supper. To tell you the truth, you scare me, Fela. I didn't know what you would say, what you would do. Fela?" Through the blankets, Mama Fela felt a firm hand on her back.

Mama Fela opened her eyes. Her teeth were on the nightstand and she wondered briefly whether or not she should put them back in. She hated to talk without her teeth. When she clicked them in, she ran her tongue over them while she thought about her answer. She sat up in bed.

"Well?"

"Why now? You came back from your trip in such good spirits."

"But this is why. Shepherding is something I can do. Good. Besides, I'll be out there alone with my moods. I won't bother you or Cita or anyone. It'll be good."

"You'll be gone so long."

He was quiet for a moment. "You know, Fela, there's some money we've put away . . ."

"That's not what I'm worried about!" Mama Fela was defensive. "Gilberto, you're a selfish man. Did you know that? You just go off anytime you feel like it, leaving Cita and me to fend for ourselves. And when you're here, I don't understand you half of the time. But you know what? I don't care anymore. You do what you need to do and I'll do the same. We don't need you here. Go on." Without removing her teeth, she flopped over on her stomach away from him. She felt like a child throwing a tantrum.

"Fela, come on now."

Mama Fela closed her eyes, quietly fighting the tears that made their way down her cheek. She wasn't going to admit what she feared most of all. The reality was she did need Gilberto. She needed him and needing was a terrible thing. It's not that she feared her loneliness; she was quite used to his frequent absences. But, up to now, her small earnings from her sewing had gone toward the purchase of little luxuries like gum and candy and food for others. Now she and Cita would have to make their own way. By themselves. It was selfish of her to think in those terms when she should be thinking of her husband's well-being, but that was the reality.

"Fela." He tried again. "Fela. Please."

She didn't answer. Instead, she clicked out her teeth and reached over to place them in their proper dish. The blankets enveloped her and she closed her eyes. She could hear him removing his boots and preparing his bedroll on the floor at the foot of her bed. For over twenty years, this was the way they had slept, he on the floor and she tucked neatly in between her clean white sheets. Clean bedding was her joy in life and she loved to slip into the sheets after her daily sponge bath. She had never actually asked him to sleep on the floor, but he seemed to know what she preferred.

Papa Gilberto blew out the lamp and was soon snoring. Sleep evaded Mama Fela, though. She tossed and turned until finally, she sat up in bed. From this position, her husband was in full view. When her eyes got used to the darkness, she studied his face. It was the face of a good man, an honest man. What he had said earlier that day was true. He had never really been able to give her the kind of life that her father had. Her father was a successful businessman and a politician; Gilberto was a cowhand and a failed businessman. Mama Fela imagined her husband out on the llano with a flock of sheep. At least now he could go out into the llano, not to escape his inadequacies, but to face them. Maybe he did belong out there. Slowly, her anger subsided as she settled down to sleep.

Suddenly Mama Fela woke up with a start. Her husband was sitting up, coughing into his hand. "You all right?" she asked. He cleared his throat, nodded, and lay back down. He was always waking her up in the dead of night with his coughing spells and yet he refused to keep a glass of water by his side like she had advised him. "You want some water?" she asked.

Still coughing, he shook his head. "No. I'd rather cough than have to leave the house cada ratito to go pee. It's too cold and dark out there."

"Do you think, Gilberto, out there on the llano with your sheep you'll have plumbing like the americanos?" she teased.

"Not even a privado," he replied, chuckling.

The morning came fast. A burst of cold air nudged her awake. She sat up in bed immediately, reached for the kerosene lamp, raised the wick with a twist of her wrist, and lit it with a match. Through the window, she saw Papa Gilberto chopping wood. Jumping from bed, she pulled her skirt over her nightgown and wrapped her shoulders with her winter coat. Just as she was about to open the door, her husband entered with an armload of wood.

"What are you doing? Are you leaving this early?" she asked eagerly, following him into the kitchen.

He cleared his throat and nodded, setting the wood down by the stove.

"Go back to bed, Fela. I was starting some water for your coffee."

"Won't you go to church with me?" she asked, hoping to make amends before he left.

"You know I don't go on Sundays."

Mama Fela knew. He went every day of the week except for Sundays. And he wouldn't sit in the pew they paid for every year but instead in the very last bench at the back of the church. She'd rather go on Sundays because there were so many more people. That's exactly what he didn't like. He belonged by himself. He belonged to the llano.

"What about food?"

"Rabbits," he said, crinkling a page of newspaper.

"Rabbits? Gilberto, you're going to eat rabbit for five months?" She remembered enduring the taste day after day as a newlywed and her stomach turned.

He nodded and cleared his throat again.

"Where's your gun?"

Papa Gilberto struck a match and carefully lit the corners of several wads of paper. He closed the iron door and lifted himself off the floor. "There," he said, pointing to a pile of provisions.

"Let me make you some hot chaquegüe."

"No, Fela. I have to go."

"Without breakfast? Are you so anxious to leave me that you'll go with your stomach empty?"

"Fela," he grumbled, sounding half old man, half little boy. "I can't, Fela. I'm getting a ride. I'm sorry."

Mama Fela eyed him up and down one more time. "You're not going to wear those clothes? Gilberto, they're torn there at the knee. Here, let me fix them," she said, pulling his waistband.

"Fela, I'm going to the llano, not courting."

Mama Fela looked at him in surprise. Then her face softened and she smiled. "Of course."

Slinging his bundle over his shoulder, he turned, picked up his rifle and his bedroll, and opened the door.

"Gilberto?"

Without turning, he waited.

She knew that the time had come to say nothing more. Closing the door softly, she stared at it as if she were memorizing the direction of the wood grain. When she realized she was cold, she sat down in the warm kitchen, straining her ears for a sound, a movement, anything that would betray the reality of her husband's departure. The stillness of the early morning unnerved her. Even the fire felt cold, static, undemonstrative, making her feel chilled, stiff, alone, two steps away from a pine box and a wooden cross. She waited patiently until finally she heard a faint hum. It grew louder and louder until the house reverberated with the rhythm of churning wheels. It was a sound she had blocked out of her consciousness, always deafening, always a threat . . . until now. The call of the coal train, just across Route 66, was no longer an intruder, but instead a welcome friend.

As she placed another log on the fire, her coat fell from her shoulders to the floor. When she bent to pick it up, something white was glowing in the semi-darkness. And then she remembered: the letter. The excitement of Gilberto's homecoming had made her forget all about the white envelope stuck in her pocket. Yesterday, she had feared it was from Gilberto, but now it was even more of a mystery. With anticipation, she tore it open.

❦

CHAPTER FOUR

RESPONSIBILITY

*C*ollier's *Magazine* slipped from Cita's fingers to her chest, then fell to the wooden floor beside her bed. The sound jarred her awake once again. She had fallen into a light sleep after watching from the window as her father escaped into the morning light with all he needed on his back. Like him, she wanted to get away from Santa Lucía, to just get up and go like he had. She could never be what she wanted to be if she stayed.

A gentle knock on the door roused Cita. She opened up the magazine to a random page and called, "Come in."

Mama Fela peeked in the door.

"Mamá, I said you could come in."

Slowly, Mama Fela entered the room. Without a word, she sat at the foot of Cita's bed, fingering an envelope.

"What's that, Mamá?"

Looking up at Cita, she said nothing.

"Who's the letter from?" Cita insisted.

Finally, Mama Fela replied, "It's from your brother, Cita. Solomón."

"Solomón! But we haven't heard from him in years. What does he say? Here, let me see. Let me see the letter," Cita said, reaching for Mama Fela's hand.

Mama Fela held the envelope, placing both her hands on top of it. "Reading it will do you no good, Cita. He's like your daddy that way. Doesn't say much."

"But Mamá, where is he? Why does he write?"

"You can ask him all those questions yourself because he's coming here. Tomorrow."

"Tomorrow? But, Mamá . . ." Cita stepped out of bed, heading toward the window. Blinking into the sunlight, she said, "But that barely gives us enough time to prepare. We have to cook and . . . clean and . . ." Turning to face her mother, she added, "We can't do everything with such short notice. Better tell him he can't come yet."

"Cita. Shame on you. He's your brother. He's welcome in this house anytime. And now that your father's not here, it's a good time."

Sheepishly Cita nodded, inching her way back toward her bed.

"And when have you ever been so eager to clean this house anyway? Never. Look at your room." Mama Fela lifted her chin, indicating the papers on the floor and the clothes strewn about.

"Mamá," Cita said, moving to her knees on the floor to pick up the clothes. "I'm not a child. I was asking simply because I know how you like to have everything spotless and since Solomón is your favorite, I'm sure you wanted to have a feast prepared."

"My favorite! Cita, that's nonsense. I simply came in here to tell you that Solomón needs our help. Berta died and he's left with all these children . . ."

"Died? Mamá, Berta died?"

Fela nodded. "Giving birth."

"Oh, Mamá. I'm sorry. I . . . I didn't know. Is the baby all right?"

Mama Fela nodded. "But Solomón has his hands full. Three small children and a baby. No mamá. He needs our help, Cita."

"What does he want us to do? He hasn't been back in so long. I don't even remember what he looks like."

"Yo sé," Mama Fela agreed. "But we must help him, Cita. We're his family."

Cita nodded, wondering what kind of help Mama Fela meant to give her son who had been absent for over ten years and what kind of help she expected from Cita. It was a wonder Mama Fela could forgive him so easily. She didn't think she ever could. "But he didn't help you and Papá when you needed it. He went off and got married instead."

"He was a man already, Cita. He needed to make his own way."

Cita was silent for a moment. "You mean you'd forgive me that easily if I said I was going off to Albuquerque tomorrow because I was going to get married?"

Mama Fela raised her eyebrows. "¿Tienes novio, Cita?" she asked, surprised.

"No, Mamá. But what if? What if I wanted to leave Santa Lucía so that I could see other places? What if I wanted to meet not just one man but thousands of them so that I could paint their faces? What if I wanted to meet people from around the world?"

"The world? ¡Mentiras, Cita! If you're not going to get married, at least try and become a nun. Try, Cita. Help me with your brother's children. See if you're worthy of serving God."

"What does that have to do with becoming a nun, Mamá? Solomón's not God."

"Cállate, Cita. No es propio."

"But I don't want to be a nun, Mamá, and I don't want to be a mother to Solomón's children!" Cita hated the sound of her own voice for its stinginess and its malice.

"Then what do you want?"

"Mamá . . ." Cita hesitated. She wondered if she should really share her thoughts with her mother. Cita gulped. Now was as good a time as any. "I want to go somewhere else and I want to paint."

Mama Fela was quiet. "Paint what, Cita? Walls? There are plenty of those here."

"No, Mamá. You know—beautiful pictures of people and places. Of flowers and good things to eat . . ."

"Can't you paint those here? Why do you have to go off somewhere?"

"Because I want to paint things I've never seen before. And I do everything but painting here. I take care of Graciela's children and now I'm going to take care of more. I don't have time to paint."

"You mean all you want to do all day is make pictures? Cita, that's foolishness. You're not a child anymore."

"I know, Mamá. But it's not foolishness. There are people who do it and they're famous. And they have families and children and they make money and take care of their families too."

"Even if there were, Cita, todos son americanos."

"No, that's not true."

"And how do you know? How did you come to know these famous ones?"

"The library. Mamá, I read, just like you do. Not newspapers but all sorts of magazines and books this thick. They have pictures of paintings that are kept in famous museums all over the world. I want to paint things that will be in a book someday. Maybe one day you'll be reading about me and you can tell your friends, 'She lives across the ocean now so she can paint her museum pictures.'"

"Across the ocean, Cita! Pues, when will you come and visit me?" A hint of sarcasm was evident in Mama Fela's voice.

"All the time. I'll be rich enough so that I can buy passages across the ocean and ride trains across the country just to visit you."

"Oh, Cita!" Mama Fela chuckled. "You speak of impossible things. Museums. Train rides. Riches. Cita, come on now."

"What, Mamá? Does God only give the americanos these things? Are we only good for having babies and taking care of children and cleaning?"

"Of course not, Cita. But those are the things that we must do. We have certain obligations. We have to be practical, 'jita. You can't go dreaming your fancy dreams when there's so much to be done. We have to live on something besides dreams and pretty colors. Those don't put beans in our stomachs and clothes on our backs."

"They could. If I was rich and famous and people stood in line to buy my pictures."

"Pues, who's going to buy them here, Cita? El doctor? Señor Gould? Who?"

"But that's what I'm saying, Mamá. Maybe I need to go somewhere else so that I can be an artist. I can't do it here. No one even knows what an artist is."

Mama Fela was quiet. Finally, she asked in a wounded voice, "And leave me here, Cita? Alone?"

This time, Cita said nothing. She inspected her mother's face as if it were a history lesson, an imperative for the future. On it, she recognized the years of hard work and the monotony of tradition. Hers was a life without choices, but Cita could imagine a different life and imagining it was the first step toward making it a reality. No matter what her mother said, she was going to continue to dream, but she knew it must be done privately, at night, in the darkness of her soul.

"Mamá, I'm not leaving you." Cita wondered if her mother could detect in her voice the anger that she felt. "I'm not leaving you," she repeated with more reassurance. "But . . ." Cita paused. "I have to know something."

"Pues, sí. Ask me anything."

"Do . . . do you think I'm good?" As soon as it was out, Cita hated herself for asking the question.

Frowning, Mama Fela replied, "Pues, Cita, I don't know much, but the things you draw are very pretty. But . . ."

"What, Mamá?"

"Don't you think it's nonsense . . . I mean for people like us? Don't you ever think of doing something more practical like I do my sewing?"

"Mamá, I hate sewing, you know that."

"Pues, Cita, work is work. I don't always love to sew either. It's hard work."

"I know, but you must like it. You make dresses for Cipriana in your free time. You sew even when you don't have to."

"Yes . . ."

"Well, that's what I want to do. I want to do something that I love, at least a little bit, like you. And I don't love cleaning or taking care of someone else's children."

"But, Cita, you're lucky to have a job. Some people don't have even that. Some people have nothing."

"I know, Mamá. I know."

"At least we have family. Do you ever see a hobo who's mexicano? Never. Todos son americanos because they don't believe in family the way we do. We help family when they need help. We don't let them go and search the world for scraps of food like the americanos, todos roñosos."

Cita nodded.

"Why don't you just make the best of things now, Cita? Besides, you can't leave me here with your papá gone and Solomón coming. Maybe one of these days you can still become a nun or go off and make your pictures. I don't understand it but maybe someday you can. Right now, a lot of people need your help, Cita."

Once again, Cita nodded without saying anything. She watched her mother stand slowly, smoothing the bed linens on which she had sat. For the first time, she noticed how spotted Mama Fela's hands were, like a night sky dotted with stars.

"Get up now, 'jita. It's going to be a long day, getting ready for Solomón. And with your papá gone, I need your help. "

Cita nodded.

Just as Mama Fela was about to close the door, she whispered kindly, "It's good to have hope, Cita. But . . ." She was quiet for a moment. "But don't be too much a dreamer, Cita. It'll get you nowhere." With a click of the doorknob, Mama Fela was gone.

For a moment, Cita leaned against her bed, twirling a strand of her straight black hair between two fingers and staring out the window into the still morning. Inside, she could hear her mother in the kitchen: the crinkle of newspaper, the stomp and shuffle of work boots from the doorway to the woodstove, the creak of the stove's door opening and closing, the rush of water poured from one vessel to another, the steady beat of wooden spoon against bowl, and the clink of the comal against the woodstove. From the sound of it, Cita knew they would be having pancakes and hot coffee before the day's work began.

While Mama Fela worked in the kitchen all day long to create a feast to serve upon Solomón's arrival, Cita removed every piece of furniture from the house in order to give it a thorough spring cleaning. She took down all the organdy curtains, washed them, and hung them on the line to dry. She did the same with all the bed linens. Removing the wool from all the mattresses, Cita washed it in soap and water and laid it out on long pieces of canvas to dry in the sun. She washed all the windows, inside and out. On her hands and knees, she scrubbed the linoleum floors with P&G soap and water. When the floor had dried and with a little less energy, she dragged all the furniture back inside, reassembled what was necessary, and put everything in its place again. When the wool was dry, she and

Mama Fela took long wooden rods and beat the wool until it was fluffy again. She stuffed it back into the mattress covers and made up the beds once again. Finally, she rehung the curtains just as Mama Fela was calling her to supper. Cita had been looking forward to a preview of tomorrow's feast but instead they had fried eggs sprinkled with red chile powder, cold tortillas, and *manzanilla* tea.

That night she was too exhausted and too jittery to sleep. Not even the tea could soothe her aching muscles or lull her to sleep. The brother she hadn't seen in ten years was due to arrive in the morning and she was apprehensive. She didn't know whether to be glad or to be angry. She didn't know whether to embrace him or to hit him. She didn't know whether to love the brother he had once been or to hate the stranger he had become.

There had been a time when Cita had loved her brother dearly and there was a particular moment when she realized it. When she was thirteen, she had persuaded Solomón to accompany her to Dr. Beford's Drugstore. She wouldn't tell him why but he went anyway, having nothing else to do and convinced that he would come home with a comic book or a penny candy for his trouble.

Together, they entered the store and Dr. Beford emerged from the small room at the back in which he saw his patients and kept his overflow stock. "May I help you find something?" he asked from behind the counter.

"Just looking," Cita said, proceeding to browse through the two aisles in the small store. She didn't know exactly how to explain what she was looking for. She would know it when she saw it. Solomón was busy salivating over the comic books.

The doctor promptly turned his attention to a pile of small, square paper on the countertop. From where Cita stood examining the store's small selection of goods, she could hear his urgent scratches with pen on paper. Still, she didn't see what she had come for. After a few moments, the doctor asked in a voice that sounded like it was trained by habit, "You looking for that hemorrhoid ointment for your mother?"

Cita responded with a shake of her head, very intent on her search. To Cita's surprise, the doctor raised his voice, asking, "Huh? Did you hear me, young lady?"

Looking up immediately in alarm, Cita nodded and was about to answer Dr. Beford when Solomón stepped up to the counter and jumped into the fray. "Of course my sister heard you! She's not deaf."

Even though she was grateful to Solomón for coming to her defense, she knew it was impolite to question an authority figure, especially an americano. What would her mother say if she found out? And she was sure to find out. She rushed to the counter and grasped Solomón's muscular arm, maneuvering her slight body in front of his tall one, knowing all too well how his temper could erupt. In the soothing voice of a thirteen-year-old going on thirty, she said, "Yes, Dr. Beford, I heard you. But no, I didn't come for my mamá. I—we, my brother and me, came to see if you had . . . well, to see if you've got any . . ."

"Any what? What do you need, kids? I really don't have all day," the doctor said. He began tapping his fingers against the counter.

"Any . . . well, any color." Cita sighed, relieved that she had finally found the word for what she sought.

"Color? Oh, I see!" Dr. Beford chortled. He eyeballed Cita up and down as he said, "Yes, yes, I guess you're at that age already." And then he hesitated, still staring at Cita, who guessed that he was mentally figuring her age. "Actually," the doctor frowned, "I'm surprised you haven't requested it before."

Shrugging at her brother, Cita followed the doctor, who moved easily through the two aisles of goods. No matter how hard she tried, she couldn't wipe off the grin that was emerging.

Dr. Beford stopped in front of a shelf labeled "women's needs," which Cita thought odd. "Let's see now," he said, scooting his bifocals down upon his nose. "Hmm . . . ah, here we go!" Taking a small box from the shelf and handing it to Cita, he smiled and said, "Coty's finest rouge." And then he said to Solomón, "Now son, you make sure she goes and asks her mama how to apply it, before she goes painting herself up."

Right then, the world collapsed in front of Cita's very eyes. As suddenly as a pair of cymbals clash together, Cita's heart stopped beating at the sight of the little box of "color." She desperately wanted to make Dr. Beford understand that she wanted yellows and greens, blues and purples, not for her cheeks, but for her mind and soul. In her hand, she clutched the few coins she had been saving until she reached the counter and saw through blurring eyes that Dr. Beford's palm lay open. She paid him the money for the little box of red not knowing quite how to articulate her disappointment. She followed Solomón out of the store, ignoring Dr. Beford's goodbye.

"I'm sorry you didn't get your comic book, Solomón," Cita said, trying hard to control her breaking voice.

"Nah, don't worry about it. I'm getting too old for that kid junk anyway," he said.

They walked in silence until Solomón said, "Do you really want that junk?"

"What, this?" Cita asked incredulously, holding out the box of rouge. "Never!"

"Let me have it, then," Solomón said, grasping it in his fingers. "Follow me. There's something I want to show you."

They strode north across Route 66 to Las Botijas, a place where no one wanted to live but many did. Mama Fela had warned them to avoid the area, where bootlegging was common practice and drunken behavior was the immediate result. Beyond the dance hall and the run-down houses, the llano stretched for miles.

"Mamá's not going to like us being here, Solomón," Cita said, beginning to feel tired.

"Mamá doesn't like a lot of things but I think you'll like what I'm about to show you. There," he said, pointing.

Cita's face fell as she scanned the horizon. "What, Solomón?"

"The plants."

"They're weeds, Solomón. You dragged me out here to show me weeds?"

"Not just any weed, Cita. Chamisa," he said, rubbing the crown of the nearest plant between his fingers. On his hand, a yellow powdery substance had accumulated. "It's color, Cita."

It took a moment for her thoughts to register. She snipped off a piece of the plant with her fingernail and squeezed the powder into her palm.

"And I bet you could find millions of colors out here on the llano," Solomón said, interrupting Cita's thoughts. "Look at all those weeds," he kidded. "And who knows plants better than . . ."

In unison, they both exclaimed, "Mamá!"

Giggling, they colored each other's cheeks with yellow stripes and raced back to Route 66. "Watch this, Cita," Solomón said, looking to his left before he stepped onto the road. He placed the box of rouge that he had been carrying on the ground and quickly stepped back up onto the sidewalk as Cita exclaimed, "Hurry, Solomón."

Before they knew it, a pickup truck zoomed past, smashing the box to smithereens. "Good riddance!" Cita bellowed, giving a mock salute to the vanishing truck and hugging her brother.

Cita missed those days. And they hadn't lasted for long. It was soon after that Solomón left for good. He dangled the answers to her dreams in front of her but snatched them away again when he abandoned her. In order to steady her stream of thoughts, Cita reached over to light the lamp. She would read for a little while to try and forget. Rummaging through a pile of Mama Fela's most recent newspapers, Cita's mouth dropped open as she read a headline in bold black letters spanning the page: "Lindbergh Case Cracked Open: Suspect Arrested!"

Cita raced through the article. What a relief it must be to those poor parents: their son's murderer found finally after two long years of waiting. The most famous couple in the world had lost their son years ago. They weren't traveling the world when it happened either; they were in the next room. They must have been devastated, Cita thought, losing their infant son so suddenly—one moment, he was in the next room, and the following moment, he was gone. Just like Solomón.

For years, Cita had been reading about the Lindberghs. How magnificent it must be to travel the world through the air, Cita had thought when she first learned about Charles Lindbergh. To Cita, he was a brave man, but his wife was even more courageous, accompanying her husband on flights across the continent, doing what made her happy despite the criticism for choosing to participate in an endeavor so foreign to everyday living, so different from the life a lady was supposed to lead. Cita admired Mrs. Lindbergh with all her heart. And then, when her baby was kidnapped, she wept for her.

Setting the papers aside, Cita blew out the lamp and scooted into her bed, pulling the fresh linen over her head. Slowly, she inhaled the clean scent, again and again, crying herself to sleep and thinking about the lost child and about mile after mile of blue sky.

The next morning, she was startled awake by the murmur of new voices. She started to slip into her clothes when she heard Mama Fela call in a voice that was giddy with delight.

"Cita! Here's your brother. Come and say hello."

Cita dressed deliberately, pulling on one of the dresses she had picked up from the floor the night before. She was eager to see what her brother looked like, to see how he had changed, but she was afraid that the time gone by might have made him unfamiliar to her. If he was a stranger, she was fearful that his long absence would mean nothing and the years of anger she had harbored and nursed were a waste. She wanted Solomón to feel regret for leaving, and if he didn't already, it was her goal to force it out of him. Tentatively, she entered the kitchen, tucking her uncombed hair behind her ears. As she approached the table, a man with a chest as thick as a slab of salt pork stood up.

"Cita, is that you? My god, what's happened to my baby sister?" he exclaimed, embracing Cita. "You've turned into a beautiful woman."

Feeling herself blush, Cita smiled nervously. She did not know how to address this man, her brother. Finally, she said, "And what about you, Solomón? I thought you were a viejito with that beard and mustache. You look like Papá except his hair is white."

Solomón laughed loudly. "Mamá tells me Papá's out in the llano. Did you scare him away, Cita, with those silly daydreams of yours?"

Cita winced. Her brother had no right to make such a comment. He did not know her and he should not pretend that he did. Ignoring him, she turned her attention to the two girls at the table. She squatted down to meet their gaze. "And who do we have here?" she asked.

Solomón cleared his throat as he sat down at the table. "Sara, Rebeca, stand up. This is Tía Cita. Give her un besito."

The girls, who looked to be about ten and five, were unkempt. When Cita hugged them, she could feel their skinniness through their skimpy clothes. Their faces were maps of sorrow and the streaks amidst the dirt told Cita a trail of tears had been ignored.

"I think you two need some fattening up. After breakfast, we'll go get some ice cream cones. How does that sound?"

Both girls giggled and Cita knew she had made fast friends. "I'm sure your daddy will approve?" Cita asked with a hint of sarcasm aimed at her brother, not caring if he did or didn't.

Solomón nodded. "Do whatever you want. You're a grown woman now."

"That's right, Solomón, I am. And I've been doing whatever I've wanted for a very long time now," Cita said angrily.

"Come now, Cita," Mama Fela said in a stern whisper. "Have more respect for your brother. You'll wake the child, acting as you are." With a large ceramic bowl in her arms, Mama Fela tiptoed to a small cradle not far from the woodstove and peeked in. With her free hand, she nudged the bassinet into a slow rock.

"Oh, is this the baby? Let me see," Cita said, moving past her brother, doing her best to ignore him.

Mama Fela stopped her. "She's sleeping, Cita. You can hold her later."

"I just want to see her," Cita said, slipping past her mother. Crouching by the cradle, she declared, "Oh, she's beautiful."

Solomón went to Cita's side. Looking over her shoulder, he said, "Isn't she? She looks like her mamá."

Cita did not know what to say. She stood slowly, still gazing at the baby. From the corner of her eye, she could see Solomón's face, a face that she had loved at one time but one that had betrayed her. She hated him for leaving so long ago because his absence had made her aloneness that much more palpable. For years, she had so many questions for him, questions that she was never able to ask because he left before she had the chance. And yet she wondered whether or not she could ask them now. Perhaps it was too late. Perhaps she already knew the answers.

Without warning, she felt herself enveloped by her brother's arms. He sobbed quietly into her hair, whispering, "I've lost my wife, Cita. I've lost Berta."

All Cita could do was pat her brother gently but reservedly on the back. For a moment, she wished she could clear her heart of the hatred she still felt for her brother. She wanted to be like a child again with an innocent mind and forgiving heart intact. Cita did not have to look into Solomón's face to see his sorrow. It was enough to stand before him, to touch his shoulder, to feel the pain that he wore on his back like a crippled pack mule. But she would never again be like a child. She knew what pain felt like and now, deep down, she wanted her brother to experience it. She hated herself for resenting his outburst but she wanted to move away from him as quickly as possible. She looked across the small room to her mother for guidance.

Mama Fela moved toward them, touching Cita's hand and placing her hand on Solomón's shoulder as if to move them apart. "Shh now, Solomón. The baby's sleeping. Cita, set the table. The children must be starving. Let's eat, Solomón. Let's eat," she said, guiding him toward the table.

"Why's Daddy crying?" the younger girl asked.

Cita ignored the question, not out of contempt for her brother, but out of sympathy for the children. She could imagine the room ringing with the sounds of sorrow and she wanted to avoid such a scene. Instead, she called the girls to her side. "Help me set the table, girls. The sooner we eat, the sooner we can have ice cream. But Mama Fela won't let us eat ice cream without having a good breakfast first, right Mamá?"

Mama Fela reacted with a slight nod. "This is true. Have your breakfast. Then go and get your ice cream, but wait until you meet the other little one," she said. "Where's Benny, Solomón?"

"I don't know. Where's your brother, Sara?"

"He had to go, Papa."

"Go? Ay, yo sé. That boy has a bladder the size of a dime."

"I do too," Cita said. "I guess I'll have to introduce myself at the privado."

The boy was nowhere to be seen so Cita pulled open the outhouse door, thinking he might be encamped there. He wasn't. As she sat down on the splintery seat, she hooked the door closed when suddenly there was a tremendous thud on the door. "Who's there?" she asked, startled.

The answer to Cita's question was another bang on the door.

"Benny, is that you?"

There was silence for a moment until Cita got up and tried to open the door. "No!" a small voice responded.

"Benny," she said, pushing on the door. "Let me out."

"No!"

"Benny, I'm your tía. Tía Cita. You have to let me out."

"No!"

Cita wondered how a boy with such a tiny voice could have the strength to hold the door closed. "Come on, Benny. I already promised your sisters ice cream and if you don't let me out, we can't get any."

Silence.

"Benny? Did you hear me?" Cita pressed her ear against the rotting wood.

"Can I have ice cream too?"

"If you let me go."

Immediately, Cita heard wood sliding against wood and the door opened, revealing a round-faced boy, dirty head to foot.

"How did you know I'm Benny?"

"Your daddy told me."

"Can I get chocolate?"

"Ice cream?"

"Yeah, ice cream."

"Yes," Cita replied, bending down to tug Benny's ear playfully but enough to sting. "But Benny, that was really mean to lock me in like that. Why ever did you do that?"

Benny shrugged, avoiding Cita's penetrating eyes.

Taking him gently by the shoulders, Cita declared, "Look, Benny, if you want me to be nice, you have to act that way too. I don't take malcriados to get ice cream. Understand?"

"But you said you would, Tía. You said I could get chocolate."

"Yes, and that was because you did such a nice thing by letting me out of the privado. When you do nice things, I do nice things."

"All right, Tía. I'll do nice things all the time."

"She'll soon be married. Don't you think, Mamá?" Solomón directed his question to Mama Fela but his stare toward Cita. He was sitting in his father's place at Mama Fela's urging.

"Mamá . . ." Cita said, ignoring her brother's comment. "How come Solomón's sitting in Papá's chair? That's your place when he's gone."

"Because I'm el hombre," Solomón replied, lowering his voice. "El patrón," he said, grinning.

"Mamá, cuidado. He's going to start beating his fists against his chest."

"Maybe that's why you're not married yet—a beautiful girl like yourself. Maybe you want to sit in Papá's chair and act like the man."

Finally, Cita looked straight at her brother and sighed in exasperation. She realized this man sitting in front of her was her sibling, born of the same parents and raised in the same manner, but she knew him hardly at all. Long ago, she knew him as a boy. Or did she? Perhaps he was never the boy she thought she knew but always the man who stood here before her, a man she disliked, because he left, knowing too much about her; a man who teased and bothered, expecting her to marry just because she was pretty, just because she was female. For a moment, she thought she was glad Solomón had stayed away for so many years.

"She doesn't like what I say. How come, Mamá?" Solomón asked, a silly grin plastered upon his face. "Doesn't she know she's beautiful?"

"¡Cállense! Both of you."

Cita was startled by Mama Fela's outburst. Looking up at her mother, who had stood from the table, Cita recognized Mama Fela's frown directed at her. It was a warning to control her temper.

"Cita, when you go for the ice cream, bring me back some of my ointment. Get some money from my purse and take the children. Ven, Solomón. Let's sit on the porch."

"I have money, Mamá. The hemorrhoid ointment? Is that what you want?"

"Shh. ¡Cállate!" Mama Fela cried, pivoting around as if she were decades younger. "Do you want the neighbors to hear?"

"Sorry, Mamá," Cita said, half amused.

"Ooh, that girl," Cita heard her mother telling Solomón. "She'd have us hanging our paños menores out on the clothesline for the neighbors to see if I didn't stop her."

Together, Cita, Sara, Rebeca, and Benny set off to the drugstore. Cita couldn't help feeling ashamed of the children she led into town but she didn't dare ask their father if she could clean them up. It would have been an insult. As they stood outside of Beford's Drugstore, she took each one of them and wiped their faces with her handkerchief. Sara and Rebeca made no complaint, but Benny fidgeted back and forth until Cita lost her patience.

"Benny! Stop it."

"I'm not dirty, Tía."

"Sara, Rebeca, is Benny's face dirty?"

Both girls nodded.

"See? Benny, don't you want your face to sparkle so that people will say, 'Oh look at that darling little boy with eyes like big brown buttons'?"

"No, Tía. You can't have any fun when you're sparkling," he stated matter-of-factly.

A giggle escaped from Cita's mouth. She was trying to do to Benny what her mother always tried to do to her: make her respectable. Just the other day she had reminded her mother that it wasn't your appearance that made you respectable.

"Fine, Benny, you win. Let's get some ice cream."

With ice cream cones in their hands, they crossed the street to sit on the benches outside the county courthouse. In silence, Cita inspected the children's faces, wondering what they were thinking. Sara and Rebeca sat facing each other, their legs crossed Indian-style, knees touching. Benny sat at the edge of another bench, slowly licking his cone, waiting for a drip to take the next lick.

"Do you like the ice cream, Benny?"

The boy nodded, still staring at his cone. It was as if he was afraid to remove his eyes, afraid it would disappear.

"What kind was yours again, Rebeca? Vanilla?"

"No," Sara answered for her sister. "She likes strawberry."

"So do I," Cita agreed, trying to catch the shy child's eye. "And yours, Sara? I see you like chocolate."

Nodding, Sara said, "Mama used to like chocolate. In the summers before everyone got poor, she'd make Daddy bring home ice cream for all of us. It was always chocolate."

"I see." Cita didn't quite know what to say. This was the first time their mother had been mentioned. She wondered if they knew their mother was dead and that she wouldn't be coming back.

"She used to tell us stories." This time it was Rebeca speaking in barely a whisper.

"She did? Oh, I love stories. I love to hear them and I love to tell them." Cita waited but all the children were looking at her. "What kind, Rebeca?"

Sara answered once again for her sister. Cita gathered it was a habit both girls had gotten used to. "All kinds. Stories about when she was a girl like us and how she worked on the farm and had pigs and chickens and how she was afraid of el viejo barbón."

"El Coco?"

"Yeah, that's what she called him too. El Coco."

"Does El Coco live here, Tía?" asked Benny.

"I don't know, Benny. Do you think he does?"

Benny shrugged, licking his dripping cone. "Mama says he comes around only when kids are bad . . ."

"Mama used to say," Sara interrupted. "She can't say it anymore because she's not here anymore," she stated with authority.

The other children were silent. Suddenly, a troop of Boy Scouts emerged from the courthouse building, marching in a single line. A grown man at the back of the line blew a whistle and the boys scattered, laughing and running across the street to the drugstore. One by one, they emerged with ice cream cones in their hands.

"Tía, I want to be one of them."

"Who, Benny?" Cita looked up.

"Them," Benny said, pointing.

"The Boy Scouts?"

"Yeah. They get to run all over the place and have ice cream and did you see those things on their shirts? Makes 'em looks important like sheriffs or something."

"Are you talking about their badges? Those things sewn on the front of their shirts?"

"Yeah, badges. How come they get 'em?"

"I don't really know, Benny, but I think they earn them."

"Can't we buy some at the store, Tía? I want some on my shirt."

"No, you can't buy badges, Benny. You have to do nice things to earn them."

"Nice things again?" he whined. "How come everyone wants me to be nice all the time?"

Cita chuckled. "I'll tell you what, Benny. If you really want to join the Boy Scouts, I will save a quarter every week for you so that you can get a uniform. And all you have to do is behave yourself."

"You mean be nice?"

Cita nodded.

"Do I have to be nice even after you buy me the uniform?"

"Ay, Benny!" Cita groaned, popping up from her bench and going over to Benny, slapping him playfully on the head. "Let's go home before I take back my promise. And before Mamá's ice cream melts. Come on, girls."

"But Tía, you're really going to buy me one, right?" Climbing up on the bench, Benny laid his sticky hand on Cita's shoulder.

"I said I was."

Before Cita knew it, Benny had leaped into her arms, squeezing her neck so hard it hurt. "I wish I was rich like you, Tía. Then I'd buy you a hundred ice cream cones."

"A hundred? No, Benny," she said, holding him with her one free hand, "you're going to be so rich, you'll be able to buy a thousand ice cream cones." Cita inspected the face of the little boy, hanging on to her with his arms and legs. "A hundred thousand ice cream cones every week." She felt the affectionate pull around her neck again, then relief to her back when he jumped down.

Approaching the porch, Cita saw Mama Fela and Solomón still deep in conversation. "Rebeca, run to your daddy and take him this ice cream."

"No, I want to take it, Tía," Benny pleaded.

"Both of you. Go on before they see us. Surprise them."

"Papa, Papa! Look what we got," Benny called. "It's good. And guess what? Tía's going to get me into Boy Scouts."

"Yeah, and Daddy, look what Tía bought you—ice cream. And guess what? It's chocolate."

Solomón slowly took the container from his daughter's hands. Wrapping his hands around it, he slowly looked up at Cita.

"Ice cream?"

Cita nodded.

Turning the container round and round in his hands, he said, "I used to bring ice cream to Berta and the kids. A long time ago. I don't anymore."

"Solomón . . . ," Mama Fela began.

"No. Excuse me, Mamá," Solomón said, standing up. "I need to find the privado. I don't want this," he said, handing Cita the ice cream, avoiding her eyes.

"What did I do?" Cita asked angrily, watching her brother move swiftly away. "I was only trying to be nice, Mamá."

Mama Fela shook her head slowly back and forth. "I know, Cita. I know. Your brother does too."

"I doubt it. All he can do is feel sorry for himself."

"Come on now, Cita. Pobrecito. He's your brother."

"My brother? Tell me, Mamá, where has he been for ten years?"

"Not now, Cita. Not now."

"You always take his side. Always, ever since I can remember."

"Now who's feeling sorry for whom?"

Cita hated when her mother acted this way, as if she had no faults of her own. Well, Cita knew for a fact, her mother was no saint. "I'm going inside, Mamá. You better eat that ice cream. It was for you anyway."

"Wait. Please, Cita. Talk to Solomón. He wants to talk to you."

"He's waited ten years, Mamá. I'm sure whatever he has to say can wait a few more."

"No, 'jita, it can't."

"Why not?"

"Solomón wants to talk with us but not in front of the children. Mi'jos, go play over there under that tree. Here comes your daddy now and we have some things to talk about. Go on now."

Cita watched the three children move past their father. Benny ran to the tree immediately without the slightest hint of acknowledgment. The two girls, hand in hand, walked toward the bench underneath the tree. Even though Cita could not make out the words, she could see Sara babble on and on, trying to get Rebeca to race. Rebeca's eyes followed her father's every move.

"Solomón, ven p'aca," Mama Fela called, motioning him toward the porch. "Please, now that Cita's here, we can all talk."

"Maybe now's not such a good time, Mamá," Solomón said, glancing at Cita.

"Nonsense, Solomón. We must talk now. Think of your children."

Solomón nodded, looking only at Cita.

"Go ahead, Solomón. Tell Cita what you were telling me."

At first, Cita would not give her brother eye contact. And then, as if out of a dream, she looked up and recognized Solomón's expression from long ago. He was looking at her as if he were frightened. Frightened of her.

"I was asking Mamá . . . ," Solomón started weakly, looking from Cita to Mama Fela.

"It's all right. Go on, 'jito."

"You . . . you can say no, Cita. Mamá says you won't. She didn't. So . . . so I hope you won't."

"What, Solomón?"

"I need your help, Cita."

Cita nodded. *Here it comes*, she thought.

"I'm going to be living in town here but I'd like you and Mamá to help me bring up the children. I'll pay for everything they need. I've set up an account at Señor Gould's so you can get their food and clothes but they need your influence, Mamá's influence—they need a mamá."

"Solomón, I can't be their mamá! I already feel like one, taking care of Graciela's children, but I have other things I need to do. You're supposed to take care of them. You're their daddy and now you have to be their mamá too. That's the way it is. I'm not going to be their mamá, Solomón. And Mama Fela shouldn't have to be either."

"I told you I'd buy their groceries!"

"The groceries? Solomón, that's not enough. Then what, you're going to disappear for years and we'll never see you again until the children are all grown? You'll come back then when they don't need you anymore and you'll brag to them and everyone around saying you raised them right because you bought their groceries."

"Cita!"

"What, Mamá? Don't tell me to be quiet. Have you ever scolded Solomón for leaving? Did you tell him how you cried every night after he left? Or that I cried? Did you even notice how lonely I was after he left? Or how angry I was? Or, what about Daddy? Did you tell Solomón that Papá hasn't even said his own son's name in this house since the day he went off and left us? Did you, Mamá?"

Cita watched Mama Fela shake her head slowly back and forth. She felt like slapping her own mother, but the urge to hit Solomón, who stood staring at her like a bleating lamb about to be butchered, was much greater. He had left them so long ago without the tiniest bit of remorse and here he was begging for their help now. He was pitiful. But so was she, because she knew it was not in her to refuse.

❧

CHAPTER FIVE

LA PRINCESA

Graciela closed the schoolhouse door, locked it, and swung the satchel of papers and books over her shoulder as she did every Friday before leaving town for the weekend. The door of the old black Model T creaked open as she used all her strength to press and pull its handle. Exhausted from the week's work, Graciela dreaded starting the car, but her desire to get home propelled her into action; she tossed her bag to the passenger side, flipped the switch on the dashboard to activate the spark plug, and then, bending to peer under the seat, she grasped the crank from the floor of the vehicle. Standing in front of the hood, she attached it, clutched it with both hands, and turned it sharply five times. The engine roared and, as the jalopy began to roll forward, Graciela quickly pried the crank out, ran awkwardly around to the door, and lifted herself up into the driver's seat.

Because the school in which she taught was located at the edge of Las Aldeas, she had to drive through the small farming community before getting on the main dirt road back to Santa Lucía, fifteen miles away. The vehicle rumbled down the tiny town's main street and despite her weariness, Graciela felt compelled to return the smiles and waves she received from the town's residents. Greeting them from up high in the seat of her Fordingo, the nickname given to the car, she guessed, for the first time, where their appellation for her might have originated. "La Princesa" was what they called her, never directly, but among themselves in private. Doña Leonora Perea, the town's notorious informer, with whom Graciela boarded, had told her this piece of news. It was Graciela's custom not to take anything her kind said seriously, but this tidbit actually flattered her. She knew that as the teacher of the rural village, she was looked upon with more than just respect. Many of the town's inhabitants were in awe of her. Her willingness to help them decipher their letters, fill out Montgomery Ward catalog orders, and bring them their tonics from her own town, raised her status in the community even further. Her services were often rewarded, sometimes ceremoniously and at other times in the form of packages left anonymously on the steps of the schoolhouse. Graciela had only been working in this community for four months and already she had accepted fresh eggs, apple pie, red chile *ristras*, and a freshly butchered rabbit and chicken. She had to admit she enjoyed the respect. And the gifts.

Turning onto the road that would lead her home, she spotted a bald man with a gray patch of fuzz blanketing the back of his head leaving the tiny post office. He looked familiar even from the rear and she wondered where she had seen him before. When he lifted a coffee-colored ten-gallon hat to his head, she realized he was one of the county school board members. Immediately, as if by instinct, Graciela thrust one hand from the steering wheel to her stomach. She remembered how they had called a meeting to discuss her pregnancy with her months earlier, advising her to keep it secret for as long as she could. "It won't set a good example for the teenagers," the spokesman of the group had said. What the man really meant was that she was there on approval and her pregnancy was already one count against her. She knew Papa Armijo had used his connections to get her the job after Robert had lost his temper and resigned her regular position. But Graciela wondered, whom had she displaced? What teacher had lost his job because of her? As quickly as the questions came to mind, she banished them, reminding herself how dangerous it was to feel guilty. Taking this job was a matter of survival.

Some of the men on the school board had been kind to her despite their policy on pregnancy. But Graciela had been puzzled by the surly behavior of the bald man, who sat apart from the others during their meeting with her. He wore shirt sleeves and had huge rings of sweat under his armpits and around his stubby neck. He wouldn't shake her hand nor would he make eye contact. Now, as she passed the man, she raised her hand in greeting, and without waiting to see if he responded, she accelerated, letting her hand drop to release the girdle that hid her bloated belly. Now she felt free. She had dreaded the long drive home, afraid that the fatigue and the cramping she had been experiencing all week would escalate on the road. But leaving the town behind made the journey seem like child's play.

She drove into the dirt lot in front of the small whitewashed house, stopped the car, and was slowly stepping down from it when her daughter ran from the house.

"Mama! Mama! You're home. Finally! Come and look. I'm helping Tía bake bread."

Graciela took her daughter's outstretched hand and squeezed it lightly. "I'm coming, mi'jita. I'm coming."

The door was open and the moment Graciela stepped into the one-room house she was welcomed by warmth and the almost ambrosial aroma of yeast. Cita turned, opened her arms wide, scooted over on her tiptoes, and tweaked Graciela's nose. It was a greeting she knew was coming, but still, Cita's theatrics made her laugh.

"Graciela! You poor thing. You look like you're about to drop. Come on." Graciela felt Cita's rather bony arm around her shoulder and before she knew it, she was planted firmly on a chair in front of the fire.

"Rest your poor nalgas and tell me about La Princesa, princesa."

"Cita!"

Cita grinned. "So . . ." Cita stopped and pulled a chair toward her and straddled it, resting her chin on its back support, staring straight at Graciela. "How was your week?"

Graciela sighed, shaking her head. "Too too long, Cita. Felt more like months."

"I bet. But you don't have much longer to go, do you? A month or two?"

Smiling, Graciela said, "Let's hope not, Cita! If I had that long, I'd be delivering at ten, eleven months. No, Cita, just about two weeks now."

"No!" Cita slapped the table, looking unconvinced. Smoothing the unruly wisps of hair behind her ears, she stared at Graciela. "But you're so tiny, Graciela. I thought you had months and months left. I guess I lost count, but look at you." Inching forward, she touched Graciela's stomach with the tip of her index finger. "My god!"

Graciela smiled, embarrassed. She peered sideways at her daughter, who was busy transporting a large bowl from a stool to the table around which they sat. The weight of the unborn baby didn't make Graciela feel all that small. On the contrary, she felt huge and heavy, like a balloon filled with water. But she knew what people said was true: she had remained fairly flat. The girdle didn't have to work that hard to conceal. And even without it, Cipriana didn't seem to notice anything different. She had never asked questions and that was fine with Graciela.

"But you're so itsy-bitsy," Cita continued. "I thought most mothers got big old bellies and big old nalgas. You know, like María."

Graciela smiled to be polite but because she hated to participate in gossip, she said nothing. Instead, she ran both hands gently over her stomach. "It's a good thing I haven't gained too much weight, Cita. If I had . . . well, you know, they'd make me take a leave of absence or who knows what other nonsense they could come up with."

"See, Mama. See, the bread's rising," Cipriana interrupted, lifting a heavy wet towel from the bowl.

"Yes, Cipriana," Graciela replied, gazing into the round dish in front of her. "Mmmm." She inhaled and exhaled. "Smells delicious, mi'jita."

With a look of delight ascending over her face, Cipriana grinned, covering the bowl again. She climbed up on her mother's lap. "How come you look so sad, Mama?"

"Sad?" Graciela asked, bemused. "I'm not sad, 'jita, just tired." Smiling, she pulled Cipriana's head to her chest and kissed the top of it, surprising herself. She changed her tone of voice immediately, consciously losing the warmth she had just indulged in. Nudging her daughter off her lap, she said, "So, Cita, did Cipriana behave herself this week?"

Cita stood, swiveling her chair around, sat, and scooted forward. "Well . . ." Cita drew in a long breath, holding onto the last two letters as if she were going to break out into song.

Cipriana opened her eyes wide, puzzled, gaping at Cita. She turned and exclaimed, "But I did, Mama. I did!"

Reaching forward, Cita poked Cipriana in the belly. "I'm teasing you, 'jita. I know you did and your mama does too."

"Oh!" The corners of Cipriana's mouth crinkled upward.

Graciela looked down at her daughter's curly brown hair and for a moment, she wished she could reach out and twirl a curl between her fingers. Instead, she said, "Why don't you run out and play, mi'jita. Your tía and I have some things to talk about."

"Like what?"

"Oh, grown-up things."

"What grown-up things, Mama?"

"Cipriana, go on now."

"But, Mama . . ."

"Cipriana. Now."

Graciela watched her daughter slink toward the door. *Poor thing*, she thought. All week without a mother and now she was sending her away again. "Cipriana!" Graciela called suddenly. When Cipriana turned, Graciela cracked a smile. The door closed quietly and Graciela said in a whisper, "I think she's grown since last week, Cita. She seems taller to me, somehow."

"I know. That dress that Mamá made her last Easter barely fits her now. She's shooting up every day. Pretty soon, you'll hardly recognize her."

Graciela's eyes remained fixed on the door. "I know," she said softly.

"Oh, Graciela! I didn't mean . . ."

"It's all right." Graciela put up a hand to stop Cita. "It's true, Cita. I know it's true. I just wish . . ."

"What, Graciela?"

Distracted, Graciela looked around the room. "Where . . . where's Pablito?"

"He's with Mama Fela and Solomón's children. She took them to buy shoes and Pablito wants to go everywhere that Benny goes."

"I hope he took his nap."

"He did."

"You're sure?"

"Of course. He slept about an hour. What's wrong?"

"Nothing, Cita."

"You said you wished for something, Graciela. What is it?"

"Oh, Cita." Graciela shook her head from side to side. "There are so many things I can't even begin to say."

"Don't say that. Come on. Everybody has one wish. One overwhelming wish."

"Do you?"

"Yes. But that's not fair. What's yours first?"

Graciela did not have to think hard but she gazed into Cita's eyes for a moment, wondering if the truth would hurt her feelings. Slowly, she began, "I wish Robert had a steady job . . . one that he would keep. You know, Cita, I love my teaching but I mostly do it because I feel compelled to do it. I can't count on Robert bringing in money regularly. I . . . I just can't rely on him."

Frowning, Cita nodded. She brushed a loose strand of hair behind her ear, asking, "He still hasn't found a job?"

Graciela didn't answer. Instead, she stared at the table. "I'll have to rush back to work after I have the baby because I just can't afford to stay out very long."

"So are you ready?"

Graciela lifted her chin. "For what, Cita?"

"Oh, Graciela, you know." Cita stared at Graciela's belly. "The pain," she whispered.

Stifling a laugh, Graciela nodded. "I'm always ready for a lot of that, Cita. All the work, the laundry, the crying . . ."

"No, Graciela. You know, the pain. The blood and all that." Cita sounded exasperated.

"Oh, that?" Graciela chuckled.

Very seriously, Cita replied, "Graciela, please don't laugh."

Graciela rubbed her hand over her lips, checking her smile. Resting her chin on her fist, she moved her head from side to side. "I'm not. Really, Cita, I'm not. It's just that I'm more concerned with other things. The other kind of pain only lasts a short time. Hopefully." Raising her eyebrows, Graciela snickered softly, concerned immediately that she was treating the subject too casually. Teasing the fates was not a good idea.

"You know, it's because he's Raza."

"What, Cita?"

"Robert can't get a job because he's mexicano."

Graciela nodded matter-of-factly, adjusting her train of thought to follow Cita's. "That's what he says," she replied, knowing Robert's explanation from memory. Sometimes, she wondered if he ever got tired of reciting the same words time after time, lost job after lost job. Fixing her eyes on the table again, she focused on a crumb, moving it round and round with the tip of her index finger.

"But," Cita offered, "you know that Felipe Salas and José Fernández are both working again."

"Oh? Both of them? Since when?"

"This week."

"Really? Are they doing carpentry work?"

Cita nodded. "That's what I heard."

"Where?"

"I don't know but maybe Robert has a chance too."

Graciela shrugged. "I suppose."

"You don't sound very convinced."

"No, I guess I don't. You've seen his temper, Cita. You know what it's like. You know what he thinks of the gringos telling him what to do. He trains them and then all of a sudden they're his supervisors and he stays in the same position."

Cita nodded.

"But why am I telling you this? I'm sure you've heard it as many times as I have." Graciela stood and turned toward the woodstove, rubbing her hands together. She couldn't believe she had just pitched Robert's argument. Did she continue to believe it?

Clearing her throat, she turned around to face her sister-in-law. "I'm sorry, Cita," she said, sitting down again. "I just wish he'd find something. It's too hard by myself."

"I know, Graciela. But maybe he'll find something soon." Cita gently placed her hand over Graciela's. "Maybe he already has."

"Why do you say that?"

"I didn't say anything." Cita squeezed her lips together.

"Cita, you're not telling me something. What do you know that you're not telling me?"

Placing her hands over her mouth, Cita opened her eyes wide and shook her head.

"Cita?" Graciela grabbed hold of her sister-in-law's arms, trying to pry the fingers away from her mouth. Laughing, Graciela begged her, "Please, Cita, tell me."

"I can't. It's got to be a surprise. Don't make me break my promise, Graciela."

"Promise? Did Robert make you promise?"

Cita didn't answer.

She didn't have to. Graciela knew. Embarrassed at her childish behavior, she sighed deeply, calming herself. Smiling at Cita, she gently let her eyelids fall closed. Opening them again, she clasped Cita's hand in her own and said softly, "Thank you. I don't know what we'd do without you."

"But I didn't do anything, Graciela."

"Yes you did, Cita. More than you know."

"Don't tell him we had this conversation, Graciela. Please don't go and say anything."

Graciela nodded. She studied her sister-in-law's face: the roundness, the innocence, the pride, and she recognized herself years before. "Cita, I told you my wish. Now what's yours?"

Cita shrugged. "I don't know."

"Yes you do, Cita. Let's see, do you want to get married . . . ?"

Cita frowned and pulled her hand away from Graciela. "That's odd coming from you," she said with a grimace. "I can expect a question like that from Mama Fela, but from you? You know something else besides being a mother and a wife, but the other women—that's all they think about. It's expected. But it's not all I want to do."

"I'm sorry, Cita. I had no idea."

"I know you didn't. You don't know me at all, Graciela. Neither does Mamá."

The furrow in Graciela's forehead deepened as she fixed her eyes upon Cita. She could relate so well—too well—to what Cita said, but she feared for her—for the disappointments she knew Cita would encounter for having hopes that society did not share.

"To tell you the truth, I just can't bear to stay here any longer. My worst nightmare is that I'll be tied down to this small town."

"Really, Cita?" Graciela could not believe how alike she and Cita were. She had had the exact same thought when she was younger, when the pettiness of the small town seemed as if it would suffocate her.

"Graciela, you're lucky. You're only here on weekends. And every year you're moved to a different school. And you're a teacher. People look up to you. And then you get to leave."

Graciela closed her eyes for a moment and methodically moved her head from side to side. Up to a moment ago, Graciela could understand Cita but when she recalled the long drives to and from school, her children's cries every Sunday afternoon, and the transitions she had to endure once a year, Graciela knew Cita did not understand her. As she opened her eyes once more, Graciela hesitantly asked, "So where would you want to go, Cita?"

"To Albuquerque. Or California. Or, well, maybe even to a convent, like Mama Fela wants. At least I wouldn't have to endure the endless questions about when I'm going to get married. Except Mamá says I need to make up my mind soon because she tells me I'm getting a little old to get God's call." Cita laughed nervously, eyeing Graciela.

Graciela guessed Cita was hoping for the smallest sign of her approval or her encouragement. But she couldn't give it. Not yet. Instead, choosing each word carefully, she said, "Somehow, Cita, I just can't imagine you as a nun."

Cita sat back in her chair, crossing her arms in front of her. "Why not, Graciela? I'm not good enough? Holy enough like you and Mamá? You two go around thinking you're better than everyone else. That's probably why they call you La Princesa. You go around with your chin stuck in the air looking down on everyone, including me."

"That's not fair, Cita. It's not true, either."

"No?"

"No. What makes you say such things? Why are you angry with me?"

A hush settled over the room as Graciela stared into Cita's eyes, hoping they would give her some clue to her behavior. Cita stared back coldly.

"Cita, tell me, have I done something to hurt you?"

For a moment, Cita continued to stare at Graciela without expression. Finally, she looked down, sighing deeply. "No, Graciela, not really. It's not you. It's me. But contrary to what you or Mamá may think, I can be a nun or a teacher or . . . or . . ." Cita mumbled the final word, "an artist."

"A what?"

"Never mind."

"No, Cita, tell me. What did you say?"

"Nothing. All I'm saying is I can be whatever I want. And if I want to be a nun, I can."

"Cita, I'm not saying you can't. I'm just wondering if it's the best thing for you. It seems . . . well . . . you know yourself, you like to do things your own way. I can't imagine you living in such a strict environment."

"Well, Mamá wants me to be a nun."

"Cita, every mother of our generation has wanted her daughters to be nuns. That doesn't mean you have to."

"No?"

"Of course not." Studying Cita's face, Graciela whispered, "Somehow, I don't think becoming a nun is your life's goal."

For a brief moment, silence hung between the two women. Then, suddenly, they both burst into laughter.

Cita shook her head, grinning. "No, no, it isn't, Graciela. But you know what?" she asked, turning serious again. "I don't think I could be a nun even if I wanted to."

"Why not, Cita?"

"I would fight with Mother Superior. I wouldn't take anything I thought was unfair. Just like Robert, Graciela. You know what? That's why he can't keep a job. He's like me in that way."

A look of concern swept over Graciela's face.

"I'm sorry, Graciela. I shouldn't have said that," Cita whispered.

"No, it's true, Cita. You're right. You're absolutely right. I wish you weren't but you are."

Another silence veiled the room. Finally, Cita said, "Do you think dreams are stupid, Graciela?"

"Dreams? No. Why?"

"Mamá says they are. She says people like us have to be practical. She says I shouldn't be dreaming my fancy dreams when there's so much to be done."

Graciela was silent.

"Mamá says dreams don't put beans in our stomachs or clothes on our backs. What do you think, Graciela?"

Graciela sighed. She got up from her chair and turning, she began to stoke the fire. "I don't know anymore, Cita. I really don't know."

Suddenly, Cipriana burst through the front door, holding her father's hand. "Here's Daddy, Mama. Daddy's home."

Graciela turned, grateful for the timely interruption. Now, at least for a moment, she would not have to think about Cita's impossible questions. Years ago, she thought she knew the answers, but today they eluded her completely.

Robert took the poker from Graciela. "Here, let me do that. You should sit down and rest."

Cita quickly rose from her chair. "I better go. I'll see you both on Sunday."

"Where you going, Cita? Have supper with us. After all, you cooked it, right?" Robert winked at his younger sister.

"No, no, I can't," she said distractedly, scanning the room. "I have to see to the children's supper before Solomón picks them up for the weekend. Now, where did I put my things?"

Cipriana went to her parents' bed and picked up a green coat and a pile of blank papers. "Here, Tía. You left them over here."

"Cipriana, what would I do without you? Thanks, mi'jita," she said, taking the items from Cipriana and kissing the top of her head. And then she stopped, flung her arm up into the air, and began moving her hips to an inaudible beat. Smiling at Cipriana, she squeaked, "All right! What do we say?"

In unison, Cipriana and Cita giggled out a radio advertising tune, Cita inching her way backward toward the door. "We are the Rinso gals! We'll always be your pals!" Bowing to Cipriana, Cita waved and closed the door behind her, leaving her niece giddy. Graciela and Robert were staring at each other when the door opened again and Cita peeked in. "Bye bye, pal," she said, winking at Cipriana. "Oh and Graciela," she called, looking up, "I'll bring Pablito by later. Could you finish the bread? Put it in the oven in about . . . half an hour. Oh . . . and . . ." Cita gazed down again, searching the floor. Focusing on Graciela, she added, "All I can say is I'm always here to help. Whenever you and Robert need me, I can be here. All right?" Banging the door shut, Cita disappeared.

"What was that all about?" Robert asked Graciela.

Graciela shrugged.

After the supper dishes were finished, Graciela removed the bread from the oven, sliding each loaf from its pan onto a large white dish towel spread out on the table. She sliced a small piece each for Cipriana and Pablito and poured canned milk into two glasses, taking them to her daughter and son, who were sitting up in bed, listening to Robert, entranced by one of his tales. When the last drop of milk had disappeared, Robert ended his story, only to be beseeched by Cipriana for more. Watching Robert tuck Cipriana into bed, she realized how much she was missing by being away all week. She envied the connection he had with his children, especially with Cipriana, who had a special affection for her father that seemed to be missing with Graciela. And it was so easy for Robert to be demonstrative; it didn't come naturally to her. How she envied her husband.

Graciela went to her own bed and pulled back a layer of covers. With her clothes still on, she slipped into bed, resting against a pile of pillows. She was flipping through the pages of *Ladies' Home Journal* when Robert called out her name. Without looking up, she said, "Yes?"

"Graciela, look."

Graciela slowly peeled her eyes from the magazine. "Yes?" She noticed the children were kneeling up in their bed, eager and alert, not a sleepy bone in them. "What's wrong, 'jitos?"

Robert tossed a small box onto the bed. "Open it."

"What's this?" For a brief second, she felt a flutter of excitement as she held the fancy red box in her hands.

"Open it, Mama! Open it," Cipriana and Pablito cried in unison.

Staring at the box, her thoughts rapidly turned to guilt. Without knowing what the gift was, she instinctively knew it was something expensive. Even the box looked extravagant. She was afraid Robert was spending money they didn't have. If only Robert knew, to her the greatest gift in the world would be for him to have a steady job. "Robert, what did you go and do?"

"Don't worry, Graciela," he said, sitting beside her on the bed. "Just open it. You deserve it."

Slowly, she took a deep breath and lifted the lid off the red box. Inside was an elegant wristwatch with Roman numerals.

"Robert!" she gasped. "What's this?"

Chuckling, he said, "Don't tell me you've never seen a watch! You're a teacher. You're supposed to know everything."

"Robert." She was serious. "But how did you afford it?" Graciela took care of their money. She deposited the checks. She carefully balanced the checkbook every time she made a check, which wasn't very often. She knew how much money they had.

"Don't worry so much, Graciela. Look, Cipriana likes it. What do you say, Pablito?"

"Pretty!"

"See? You're the only one who doesn't like it."

"It's not that, Robert. Not at all." Graciela spoke hesitantly. She was afraid to remind him of his joblessness, given his reaction last time, months before.

"Graciela, I thought it was high time you had one. And besides, I got a job today."

"You what?"

"Yes," he said matter-of-factly. "Twenty dollars a week!"

"What?"

Robert snickered. "Now that's the reaction I expected. But I guess it's not the gold watch that does it."

Later as Graciela and Robert lay side by side, a few feet from where Cipriana and Pablito slept, Robert turned toward Graciela, his movement evoking moans from the steel springs beneath the mattress. Both Graciela and Robert instinctively placed their index fingers at their mouths and giggled quietly. Then, gently placing his hand on Graciela's stomach, Robert asked, "How do you feel?"

Graciela placed her hand over his. "Fine. The baby's almost here. I can feel it. See," she said as she moved his hand to a certain spot on her belly, "can you feel it kicking?"

Robert concentrated, moving his hand sideways along her stomach. He looked at Graciela and shook his head, frowning. Suddenly he started, the bed creaked, and he and Graciela began laughing, taking turns hushing each other then laughing again. Settling back down, Robert exclaimed, "Either that baby just kicked the hell out of me or you're getting ready to throw some pretty powerful pedos." Pinching his nose, Robert lay beside Graciela again, still chuckling.

After moments of silence had passed, Graciela glanced sideways at her husband. "Robert?"

"Yes?"

"Where in the world will you get paid eighty dollars a month?"

"In heaven!"

"No, Robert, really."

For a moment, Robert remained silent.

Graciela turned on her side to face him, propping herself up on her elbow. "Robert?"

Without looking at her, he replied softly, "Las Vegas, Graciela."

"Las Vegas!" Graciela pulled herself up to a sitting position, glancing past her husband to her children's bed to see if her voice had disturbed them.

"I know what you're going to say, Graciela," he said breathlessly, maneuvering himself and his pillow against the headboard. "But before you say it, let me explain. I already talked to Cita and she said that between her and Mama Fela they could take care of the kids during the week. You'll be home on weekends and I'll come on Sundays."

"But we can't put them through that. The children or your family. We can't impose on your family any more than we already have, Robert."

"But Cita said it would be fine."

"I can't do that to Cita, Robert. She's young and my children aren't her responsibility. She already has her hands full with Solomón's children. And besides, she has dreams, Robert."

"Dreams?" he scoffed. "We can't afford to have dreams, Graciela. You think cleaning the houses of los americanos is her dream come true? She's better than that."

"I know she is, Robert. That's exactly why she shouldn't have to watch our children day in and day out. She has better things to do."

"Well, do you or don't you want me to take this job?"

"Of course I want you to take it, Robert, but we have to think of another way."

After several minutes of silence, Robert snapped his fingers. "Graciela, since I'll be making enough money . . ."

"Yes?"

"Why don't you stop working after the baby comes. Take the summer off and start teaching again next fall. Or don't."

"But . . ." Graciela was too excited to know what to say. She was elated with her husband's solution. Perhaps this was the chance she had been waiting for: to spend more time with her children; be the mother they deserved; sew pretty little outfits for Cipriana; teach Pablito how to read; make curtains and cook good, nourishing meals. She had dreamed for a long time of hearing the words Robert had just spoken. Since she was twelve, she had worked at a job outside of the home. So, perhaps now the time had finally come when she could concentrate on being a good mother and wife. Maybe Mama Fela was wrong. Dreams could come true.

Robert left for Las Vegas early Saturday morning. Graciela had washed, rinsed, and wrung out all the family's laundry by the time Cipriana woke up. Cipriana stood at the doorway of the kitchen in her bare feet and watched her mother hang laundry on the clothesline that stretched from one end of the front yard to the other. As soon as Graciela pinned a piece of clothing up, it immediately stiffened in the cold early morning air. Hanging up her husband's last bleached white shirt, she turned and saw Cipriana. Quickly, she went to the door, ushering her daughter back in.

"Cipriana, don't stand here in your bare feet. It's cold outside, mi'jita. Put on shoes and a sweater if you want to be outside," she added, shutting the door behind her.

In just minutes, Cipriana reappeared, wearing all that her mother asked. "Where's Daddy, Mama?"

"He went to work, mi'jita."

"Work?" Cipriana asked in a puzzled tone. "How come? He never goes to work."

"Well, he is now, 'jita." Graciela smiled, pleased with her husband's new job, and amused by her daughter's innocent observation.

Graciela did chores all day. She put Cipriana and Pablito to sleep early and continued to clean and sew until the early hours of Sunday morning when she finally climbed into bed, feeling dizzy and nauseated. She didn't braid her hair as she usually did so it lay scattered across her pillow. She remained wide awake for what seemed like hours, feeling more and more sick as time went on. Her forehead began to shine with perspiration and her breathing became labored.

Slowly, Graciela turned on her side, propped herself up on one elbow, and strained to see the numbers on the small wind-up clock that stood on the nightstand next to the bed. Her new watch would be handy right now but she had tucked it back in its box and placed it in a drawer for safekeeping. Reaching to pick up the clock, she tilted it, trying to catch a trickle of moonlight from the window. Unable to make out the time, she finally guessed it was around three in the morning.

Suddenly, Graciela jerked up in bed, clutching her stomach. "Cipriana!" She waited. "Cipriana!" she called more loudly to her sleeping daughter across the small space that separated them. "Wake up, Cipriana. I'm sick."

Cipriana lifted her head from underneath several quilts. She rubbed her eyes and stared at her mother for a moment. "What? What did you say, Mama?"

"Cipriana, get up. You have to go over to Mama Fela's and tell her I'm sick," Graciela whispered loudly to her daughter, who began to slowly climb out of bed.

"Hurry, 'jita." Graciela fell down upon the pillow, holding her belly with both hands. Beads of perspiration dripped from her forehead. She groaned, barely moved her head to the side, eyed her daughter, and whispered, "Hurry! Take Pabl . . ." Graciela held her breath, trying to muffle the pain of a contraction. Intuitively, she knew that her children would be frightened if she did not control the sounds of pain that she was capable of emitting. She wanted her children out of the room. Quickly.

"Go! 'Jita, go!" she said loudly, trying to accelerate her daughter's movements. "Yes, go with your sister, Pablo. Now!" Finally, she matched the slam of the door with her own perfect scream.

While she waited for the arrival of Mama Fela, she counted the time between each moment of pain, hoping the repetition of numbers would keep thoughts of regret from surfacing. The wait was interminable and so instead of allowing her mind to wander to places she refused to go, she talked to herself aloud, reciting rules of composition she taught to her eighth graders and spelling words her students were to recite on Monday. When the pain came, Graciela tried to internalize it by grinding her teeth and holding her breath, but when it was too much, she let herself be carried away with a groan, sometimes a scream.

When Mama Fela came through the door, followed by Cita, Graciela was in the middle of a contraction. Through watery eyes, she watched Mama Fela come toward her and take her hand. "Squeeze, Graciela. Squeeze my hand as hard as you have to."

When it was over, Graciela asked weakly, "Where are the children?"

"Don't worry, Graciela," Mama Fela said, patting her shoulder. "Quirina's with them. How often do the pains come now?"

Graciela informed her mother-in-law of the frequency of the contractions. She watched with admiration as Mama Fela gave Cita instructions and bustled about the room with purpose, lighting lamps, gathering clean linens, and stoking the fire.

Instead of the contractions becoming more frequent, they stopped. Graciela could tell Mama Fela was concerned. She took Cita aside and whispered something to her. Cita left.

"What was that about, Mama Fela? What's wrong?"

"I think the contractions were fooling you . . ." Mama Fela paused and Graciela could feel her eyes penetrate her soul. Chuckling, Mama Fela added, "I bet you don't think so though. It's what's called a false labor. I'm having Cita call on the doctor just in case. Don't worry, Graciela. It's really nothing to worry about."

"The doctor?"

"You know my ways, Graciela. I always like everything to go smoothly. For the time being, I want you to drink this cardo santo tea. Sit up now. There. Sip it slowly."

It was terribly bitter but somehow Graciela was able to swallow it. "What will this do?"

"If your body's not fooling you and it really is time for labor, it's going to make the baby come faster, but only if it's supposed to."

"How does tea do that?"

"Ay, Graciela, you ask too many questions. All I know is that it works. Come. Rest now. It's going to be a long night."

"Why should the baby come faster, Mama Fela? Isn't that dangerous?"

"This is your third baby, Graciela. It's two weeks early. And if your contractions started at the time you said, the baby should be here by now."

"Is . . ." Graciela did not wish to think of the possibility. "Is something wrong, Mama Fela?"

"No. No. Don't worry, Graciela. I've seen this before and before you know it, you'll be up and ready to eat breakfast with a new child in your arms."

When Graciela finished the tea, she lay flat with her eyes shut. Trying to relax, she reminded herself that her new life was about to start. She would not have to go back to Las Aldeas tomorrow. She would not have to rush through Sunday supper and leave her children behind. Not any of them. And tomorrow there would be one more.

Suddenly, a pain shot through her body and Mama Fela rushed to her side. "Have they started again?"

Graciela nodded.

"Let the pain go, Graciela. Don't hold it in."

When it was over, Mama Fela helped Graciela scoot farther down the bed so that she could prop her feet up on the footboard with her knees bent. Graciela felt a gentle breeze flit over her as Mama Fela snapped a sheet open and laid it across her body. Pain came again swiftly but once it left her body, she followed Mama Fela's movements, recalling the little rituals she performed just before the births of her other children. From a large satchel, Mama Fela removed a prayer book and three candles, which she placed on three chairs, one on each side of the bed and one at the foot. She lit them and knelt down to pray, mumbling words Graciela strained to hear, but could not make out.

Pain came again, and this time Graciela watched as Mama Fela stood, telling her to lift her knees. Taken hostage by the pain that racked her body, Graciela could not focus on the words that spilled from Mama Fela's mouth. Suddenly, she saw other faces—Cita's, Dr. Beford's—and a swirl of activity began that produced sounds and smells familiar to her and at the same time, dreamlike.

Finally, just when she was about to cry in agony, she pushed with all her might and felt a sudden sense of relief. A shrill cry broke the spell she felt she was under and she knew her baby had been born. She heard the snip of scissors, and followed Mama Fela with her eyes as she moved to the basin, a bloody sheet trailing behind her. Trying to ignore the fingers sewing her closed, she shut her eyes, listening to the soft splashes of water and the giggles she knew were Cita's.

"Graciela," Mama Fela said, "here's your baby girl."

With Cita's help, Graciela sat up against a pile of pillows, taking her baby in her arms. She was wrapped snugly in a sheet so Graciela peeled the layers back, eager to see the miracle from God.

"Call Cipriana and Pablito," Graciela said, smiling, without taking her eyes from the newborn.

"They're probably still sleeping, Graciela."

"That's all right. Tell them to come see their baby sister."

"Mrs. Romero, let your children sleep a while longer. It's time I gave your baby the once-over anyhow. How about it?" Dr. Beford asked, extending his arms.

For a moment, Graciela resented the intrusion. She had already inspected every finger, every toe, every nail, and every limb. What did she need the doctor for? Besides, she wanted to hold onto her baby forever.

"Please, Mrs. Romero. It's procedure."

"I'm sorry. Of course," she said coolly, allowing the doctor to take the baby from her arms. Watching his every move as if he were a criminal about to abduct her child, she counted the minutes until he placed her gently back in her arms.

"She's in perfect health, my dear," Dr. Beford announced.

"Thank you, Doctor," she said, elated. "Thank you for helping Mama Fela."

Dr. Beford nodded. "I'll expect to see you and the baby in a few weeks."

"Fine," Graciela replied, smiling politely but eager to see the doctor go. "I'll be there."

When the doctor had left, Mama Fela sat unsmiling next to Graciela's bed.

"What's the matter, Mama Fela? Are you tired?"

"Tired! Psh. I deliver babies all the time."

"I know, Mama Fela, but I just thought . . ."

"I've delivered more than that doctor of yours."

"I'm sure you have."

"He was too pushy. He should have let me do my job. I didn't need his help."

"But you said you did, Mama Fela."

"I changed my mind. He thinks he knows everything. And he can't even speak Spanish. I have to speak his language and when I don't, he thinks I can't deliver babies either. Just like un americano. Just like them."

Later in the morning, Graciela was settled beneath a layer of covers with a pillow propped behind her head, admiring her sleeping baby, when Quirina entered the room with Cipriana and Pablito in tow. She smiled, seeing the children move forward tentatively.

"Hello, Mama," Cipriana said quietly, approaching Graciela's side, unable to remove her eyes from the small bundle at the foot of Graciela's bed. "Did your stomachache go away?" she asked distractedly.

"Yes, Cipriana, it sure did," Graciela laughed, smiling at Mama Fela and Cita. "And how are you this morning, 'jitos?" Graciela asked. "Better go and see what's on the table there." Graciela indicated with her chin. "I think Cita has something for you."

"Oh! Did you get them? Did you get the long johns, Tía?" Cipriana skipped toward the table that divided the bedroom from the kitchen.

Cita patted the seat of the chair next to her and pulled a paper bag from the center of the table to her lap. "Right here, Cipriana. Just like I promised. Don't go and get sick though, or your mama will get mad at me," Cita said, smiling at her niece, who had already grabbed a doughnut and bitten into its cream center.

Cipriana walked toward her mother's bed, an éclair in each hand, and stared again at the pile of blankets at the foot of the bed. "Mama, would you like one?"

"Oh no, thank you, mi'jita." Graciela made a face. "Give one to your brother. I understand you two were very brave last night."

Cipriana smiled at her mother and then looked all around the room. Finally she walked to the edge of Graciela's bed again and poked her sticky hand into the pile of blankets. A baby screamed and Cipriana leaped back. "What's that?"

A flood of laughter filled the room. "It's a baby, Cipriana," Cita giggled. Bounding toward the bed, she picked up the crying child.

"A baby? Who brought it?" Cipriana asked incredulously.

"Dr. Beford," Mama Fela replied resentfully.

Cipriana cautiously stepped toward Cita and stood on tiptoe to see the baby's face. Cita quieted the newborn and bent to show it to her niece.

Cipriana stared at the tiny, flushed, wrinkled face. She couldn't take her eyes off of it. "Mama, it sure is pointy. Dr. Beford's baby has a pointy face just like him."

Graciela chuckled, as did the others around the room. "But 'jita, it doesn't belong to Dr. Beford. It's mine. And your daddy's, of course. She's your sister. Dr. Beford, well, he just brought it to me. You know that black case that he always carries?" Cipriana nodded. "And you know how he says that he has the medicine in there that makes people feel better? Well, that's where he brought the baby. See, and I don't have a stomachache anymore."

"Oh," Cipriana mumbled, puzzled, staring at her new sister's face.

A week later, on Sunday, Graciela sat at the edge of her bed with her back toward Cita, maneuvering her nipple to the baby's mouth. She watched the tiny lips move up and down, greedy for milk. Placing her index finger in the baby's palm, she felt the tiny fingers curl around her own and immediately she felt a sense of identity. This baby was hers and she was the baby's. They belonged to each other for a time, until the baby grew into its own being. The baby still had no name, partly because Graciela knew once she was named, she would belong to the world, not solely to her. And, deep down, Graciela thought it would be best for her husband to have some say in the name when he returned from Las Vegas. They had sent him a telegram of congratulations but he was not expected until today.

Just then, the kitchen door swung open and Robert ran in. "Where's my baby girl?" he called.

"Wait, Robert. Hold on," Graciela cried, hearing her husband's voice. She scrambled to pull the baby from her breast and to cover herself up, half resenting her husband for the intrusion and half eager to see him and to show him their baby. Without the steady stream of warm milk, however, the baby began crying.

Robert took her in his arms anyway and kissed the smooth head. He rocked her for a moment, cooing and clucking his tongue. "There, there now, mi'jita. I know you want your mama's milk, but I haven't seen you yet and I'm your daddy. Come on, now. Come on."

To Graciela's surprise, the baby stopped wailing. She watched Robert bend over the baby, making faces and sounds, delighting the baby and himself. For a long while, she watched and listened to the gurgle of steady gibberish flowing from Robert's mouth. She was in a trance, happy but tired, taking in sound but blocking out meaning. When he mumbled something into the baby's blankets, at first Graciela thought he was still speaking to the baby.

"Did you hear me, Graciela?"

"What?" she asked, startled.

"I said, did you hear me?"

"No. I'm sorry. I'm half asleep. What did you say, Robert?"

"I quit, Graciela."

"What?"

"The job, Graciela. I couldn't take it anymore."

Robert's mouth continued to move but Graciela blocked out all sound. She knew his tirade by heart and if she heard it once more, she would just lie down and die. She shuffled to her bed like a sleepwalker, ignored Cita, slipped into her sheets, and fell asleep, exhausted.

Chapter Six

RUMORS

Graciela abandoned her newborn one week after the birth. She returned to her teaching post, miles away from home, feeling as if her body were a mound of clay that had been stomped on and beat upon until it turned to mud. Sitting now in the empty schoolroom at her small pine desk, she massaged her temple, realizing the screaming headache was not the product of disobedient children or unceasing chatter, but rather the result of worry and guilt. Until she could return home on Friday, she could only wonder how her baby was doing.

She had memorized every detail that defined the infant: the tiny wrinkled face with that funny long chin that even Cipriana had noticed; the baby fingers and toes, each a mystery, each a miracle in its delicate precision; the black beauty mark on the right buttock. Graciela smiled. The vision of her baby heartened her but only for a moment. That word. That awful word was the only one she knew to describe what she had done. Graciela repeated it to herself over and over. Abandoned. Abandoned. Her newest daughter would only know a weekend mother, and she hated herself for it.

The one-room schoolhouse had a small woodstove in the corner but it was not enough to keep Graciela warm. She shivered as she tried to grade a pile of compositions but she could not concentrate on the grammatical errors that marred the papers. Was it her imagination or had the room turned bitterly cold? Despite the temperature, she was thirsty. And her mouth felt hot and sticky. She eyed the water bucket on the window ledge and wondered if there was still a film of ice over it. One of the children had said it did not thaw until the spring. She slapped her red pencil down on her desk and walked to the bucket to see for herself. Sure enough, chunks of ice were floating through the liquid. She swirled the ladle around, finally fishing out a few small ice chips and quickly sticking them in her mouth. The ice was so cold it was hot and it tasted of salt. But it served the purpose.

Graciela slipped a few more pieces of ice onto her tongue. She hoped that the freezing temperatures had killed the germs she knew lived on the surface of the bucket and ladle. Her students were constantly sick with runny noses and nasty coughs and she was careful to avoid catching these. She had read that it was possible to catch pyorrhea by sharing someone's cup or glass. One of her greatest fears was losing her teeth, so she made it a habit never to share the same ladle that her students used. Instead, she customarily brought her own tin cup from home and every weekend she returned it again for its weekly scrubbing. With so much on her mind lately, she had forgotten the cup. But somehow, germs seemed insignificant right now. Her baby was far away.

A knock on the door startled her. She turned and saw a tiny woman dressed in a powder-blue smock. Her black hair was pulled back severely and she carried an envelope in her hand. "Teacher?" she called timidly. "Miss Teacher?"

"Yes." Graciela stood stiffly. A cramp in her leg caused her to wince. "Mm . . . may I help you?"

The woman stepped forward. "I'm . . . Trini says . . . she says you read real good. And, well . . . you read this?"

To Graciela, this woman's statement was more of a command than a request. Taking the envelope, Graciela asked, "You're Trini's mother?"

The woman nodded. "Yes, yes. I'm Trini's mama, yes."

Graciela smiled. "Please sit down. Trini is such joy to teach. She's bright and energetic. She's catching on to reading so fast, she's . . ."

"Read. Yes, read." The woman gestured toward the envelope Graciela held in her hands.

The urgency the woman displayed intrigued Graciela. Sitting down at her chair, she carefully slid the creased page from the envelope and began to unfold it. The woman sat tensely across from Graciela, her nervous hands restricted between her knees.

Graciela then began speaking in Spanish. Immediately, the woman grinned and rapidly responded to Graciela's inquiries and comments. Graciela witnessed the strain in the woman's face subside. Just as Trini's mother was clearly more comfortable speaking in her native tongue, so was

Graciela. Even though she spoke English fluently and also taught it to her students, she still thought in Spanish. All her sentences, in fact, were at first formed in Spanish then translated into English. It was one reason she loved working in these small communities—she could let her guard down and speak to her students' parents as equals. Of course, she was still the teacher, and that brought a certain level of automatic respect, which Graciela had come to appreciate.

"It's a big letter, no?" Trini's mother asked Graciela, reverting to English again.

Graciela nodded absentmindedly and quickly scanned the letter for content. It was actually a very short form letter from the catalog store stating they did not currently carry the merchandise ordered but Graciela knew any letter in English must seem daunting for a Spanish speaker who, more than likely, did not read. "Dear Mrs. Sanchez," she began in English first and then translated it into Spanish.

Placing her hand on her cheek, Trini's mother exclaimed, "Va, mira, me dicen 'dear.' Quizás me quieren mucho."

Amused, Graciela smiled kindly, even though she felt like laughing heartily. She was not absolutely sure if this woman was honestly flattered by the standard salutation or if she was poking fun at it. More than likely, however, she was not used to getting letters, especially in English, and indeed it seemed complimentary to her. Graciela decided to remain cautious to avoid patronizing behavior. She continued reading and translating when suddenly, the door burst open.

"Ven aqui," the intruder called loudly, beckoning Trini's mother. As she excused her husband's lack of manners, Mrs. Sanchez went to him, a look of disapproval descending upon her face. The man whispered in the woman's ear while Graciela looked on. Mrs. Sanchez shook her head vigorously, looking at Graciela. He whispered again. This time, Trini's mother frowned and began walking toward the door, peering over her shoulder at Graciela as her husband led her by the arm.

Puzzled, Graciela focused her eyes on the grains of wood on her desk. Hearing the door creak open, then closed, she wondered what she had just witnessed. Suddenly she remembered the letter in her hands. She waved it in the air and rising to her feet, she called out, "Señora Sanchez!" Opening the door, she called out again, "Señora Sanchez! Your letter." The Sanchez couple had made their way across the dirt road but they both turned when Graciela's voice reached them. Hesitantly, Trini's mother moved forward, and Graciela noticed how hard she was trying to avoid her gaze. Handing the letter over, Graciela asked, "Is there something wrong, Señora?"

Mrs. Sanchez continued to stare at the ground. Slowly, very slowly, her eyes rose to meet Graciela's. Graciela attempted to smile, inspecting Mrs. Sanchez's blank face. "And . . . and you . . ."

"What, Mrs. Sanchez? What's wrong?" Graciela asked as she crossed her arms at her chest, shivering.

". . . you, you who my Trini's teacher."

Graciela nodded slowly, worry lines multiplying upon her forehead. And then she jumped back, startled when a wad of spit landed at her feet.

"Señora!" A feeling of surprise overwhelmed Graciela. She had time to be neither angry nor sad, only shocked at the woman's action.

With shaking fingertips, Trini's mother wiped saliva from the corners of her mouth. At that moment, Graciela thought she saw tears in the woman's eyes, not sorrowful tears but hatred and resentment and disgust obscured by a translucent gaze. Graciela wondered why and she stepped back in retreat. Mrs. Sanchez walked away, muttering words inaudible to Graciela. Stunned, Graciela watched her, watched every footstep, every swish of her skirt, every imprint in the dirt below her until Mrs. Sanchez was a safe distance away.

The desire to reach the steps of the schoolhouse overwhelmed Graciela. Her small pine desk now seemed like a place of safety and comfort and when she reached it, she carefully released herself into its care, bracing her ankles around the feet of the chair. The compositions she had been grading stared up at her and they appeared to be mocking her. The red pencil marks screamed up at her, a reminder of the teacher she tried to be. The woman had spit at her. Actually spit at her. What had she done to incite so much anger?

All afternoon, Graciela mulled over the question again and again but she had no answer. It was late now and she had watched darkness draw its cloak around the town. It was time to return to her room or Doña Leonora would start with her endless questions. One minute late and it was news the next day. Slowly, Graciela managed to rise from her chair. She did not look forward to Leonora's prodding and nonstop chatter, but perhaps the landlady could lend some insight into today's incident and help Graciela decipher the motivations of the townspeople. Indeed, if anyone could help Graciela figure out her role within the town, it was Doña Leonora. With hope on her side, Graciela felt motivated to face the cold and unforgiving night. Wrapping her threadbare camel-colored coat around her, she closed the door behind her and stepped into the windy darkness toward Doña Leonora's home.

Even the main road through town was deserted. Graciela did not normally leave the schoolhouse this late, but she would often take walks after supper and see people moving along the streets, going home after a day's work in the fields or purchasing supplies at the mercantile or socializing with their neighbors. Now the town was eerily empty and she knew it wasn't just the cold weather that kept the inhabitants away. She knew something was wrong and all conceit aside, she had the feeling she had something to do with it. At this moment, Graciela longed to see her baby daughter.

Graciela stood outside, peering into Doña Leonora's dark window. Usually, this woman with whom she boarded kept the house well lit. She was not stingy with kerosene and the very moment twilight descended upon the little house, she lit her lamps, defending herself from gloom. One lamp was reserved solely for Graciela to burn into the night while she graded papers and made lesson plans and it was from this one that Doña Leonora would remove the chimney once a week. She insisted on scrubbing it clean for Graciela and trimming the wick so that she had the purest light by which to do her teacher-work. But tonight, the house appeared dreary and abandoned. Graciela could see only one lamp burning back toward the kitchen. What was going on around this town? Everyone seemed to be taking cover. Graciela breathed deeply and opened the door. She made her way to the kitchen in the back of the house and there, sitting in the dark, was Doña Leonora, her arms crossed, her eyes unblinking, her brow stern. The kitchen was cold. The fire seemed to have burned out hours ago for when Graciela opened the door of the woodstove, no welcoming embers were left. Only cold ashes greeted her. "Doña Leonora?" Graciela whispered. "Doña Leonora," she said again a little more loudly.

Immediately, panic replaced the blood that usually flowed through Graciela's veins. Could her landlady be dead? "Doña Leonora!" Graciela called with urgency, staring into the woman's unblinking eyes. "What's wrong?" she asked, hesitantly touching the woman's knee.

All at once, the rocking chair began to sway. Graciela flinched. Doña Leonora blinked and Graciela knew nothing was wrong with her landlady's health or well-being. But in her heart, she also knew that something indeed was terribly wrong. Graciela was anxious to find out what it was but she recognized the inevitable: it would be a long night before she could discern the truth. She would have to wait until her landlady was good and ready to speak. Graciela had learned early on that Doña Leonora believed in the old adage, "Do not speak until you're spoken to," and in her case, she extended its application beyond children. As Graciela bent to add a handful of kindling to the bed of cold ashes, she could feel Doña Leonora's cold stare follow her every movement.

To Graciela, Doña Leonora deserved respect only because she was her elder and because by the dictate of the directors of Las Aldeas School, she provided room and board. There were no other reasons. In Graciela's opinion, Doña Leonora was bad news pure and simple. She was not old, nor was she young. She had been widowed long ago and had no children, and was in that middle stage of life that often rendered an introspective person conscious of every detail of her life. Actions were up for investigation, words spoken were subject to probing. But Doña Leonora was not a reflective, soul-searching individual and Graciela was disturbed by her total lack of self-examination. Instead, she spent her time chewing on the affairs of others. And that would be fine if she kept this knowledge to herself, but she spread truths and untruths alike, and Graciela respected no one with such repute.

Poking the newly lit fire, urging its flames awake, Graciela stood uncomfortably, her back to Doña Leonora. The sound of the rocking chair's rhythm lulled Graciela into a state of relaxation despite her anxiety. Neither she nor Doña Leonora spoke. Nor did Doña Leonora ask her to sit. They both stared at the fire. Graciela's eyes were growing heavy with sleep.

Suddenly Doña Leonora stood and went to the window in her small kitchen. From the windowsill, she removed a round dish and placed it on the small wooden dining table in the corner of the room. Graciela watched as Doña Leonora filled two small bowls with green Jell-O. "Come," she told Graciela, placing one bowl at each of two table settings. Tapping the table with a spoon, she motioned for Graciela to sit. "Eat," she said, maneuvering herself into her own seat.

Graciela stared at Doña Leonora, puzzled.

Doña Leonora pointed to the bowl. "Go on. Eat."

Seeing no other choice, Graciela sat down slowly in the appointed chair. She picked up her utensil and spooned Jell-O into her mouth obediently, watching Doña Leonora do the same. Even though Jell-O was a rare treat that, under normal circumstances, she would relish with every sweet bite, now she could merely feel herself swallow the slimy mass. She wanted nothing more right at this moment than to listen to Doña Leonora spill out everything she knew of the day's incidents, but the gossipmonger seemed to have something else in mind.

"Have some more," she told Graciela in a tone that Graciela could not ignore. Graciela sat, staring at the hand that required obedience by its very appearance, stern in its boniness, mature in its spottedness, moving back and forth from the Jell-O bowl to Graciela's bowl, filling it with green stuff. When it was full, Doña Leonora sat sideways in her chair to face the fire. Graciela watched Doña Leonora's eyes, which now reflected the flames that had become spirited and healthy. She said nothing to Graciela as she continued to stare at the fire. Finally, she spoke.

"You had a visit, Trini's mama? Yes?"

Graciela stiffened. "Yes. How did you know?"

Doña Leonora waved Graciela's question away. "Señor Sanchez also?" She turned from the fire to Graciela.

Graciela nodded.

"It wasn't nice, no? She spit, here, no?" Leonora pointed at her own face.

"No," Graciela said indignantly. Looking down, she continued more softly, "On the ground. At my feet." When the incident had first occurred, Graciela felt no rancor toward Mrs. Sanchez, only bewilderment, but now she was beginning to see the behavior for what it was: hostile and distressing. Suddenly, Graciela sounded like a child, begging her mother for an explanation after punishment. "But why, Doña Leonora? What did I do?"

"Your baby, whose is she?"

"What?"

"Your husband's?"

"Of course!" Graciela stated defensively, confounded by the question. "Why would you think otherwise? My god!"

"Psh, psh," Doña Leonora said with a snap of her fingers. Crossing herself, she mumbled a prayer in Spanish.

Taking God's name in vain was unforgivable and Graciela realized her mistake as soon as it escaped her mouth. Honestly though, Doña Leonora was a grown woman and surely she could forgive a slip of the tongue when it was clear that Graciela was suffering in anticipation. It used to be that Graciela thought she had won the respect of the townspeople, which was more important to her than friendship or goodwill, but now she wasn't so sure. "They used to call me La Princesa, Doña Leonora."

The landlady nodded. "Ah, yes, La Princesa." The frown Doña Leonora had been wearing all evening softened. Chuckling, she nodded and unfolded her arms. "Who was it—Doña Chela? No, no, Doña Tiles, yes, Doña Tiles said you were La Princesa. You know at first I thought she meant like . . . what's that dicho? You know, 'prosapias de rico, traje de enpelotado.' 'Puttin' on the dog,' as my nephew says." A wicked smile appeared on Doña Leonora's face and she shook with laughter, attempting to conceal her amusement but appearing as if she would boil over if she were a pot of tea.

"Doña Leonora, what happened?" Graciela asked seriously. "Why was Trini's mama so angry at me? Last week, people brought me gifts. Now I'm spit at. Why?"

Doña Leonora smoothed her skirt, avoiding eye contact with Graciela. "She was told your husband wasn't there for the birth. Is this true?"

"Well, yes. But he was working. He got a new job. But Mrs. Sanchez said this? How could she know that?"

"She knows."

"How? That doesn't make sense."

The room was silent except for the crackling of the fire.

"What are you saying, Doña Leonora?"

The landlady was quiet. Looking up at Graciela, she finally said, "Dr. Beford was there, no?"

"Yes."

"He was there for the birth?"

"Yes. He's my doctor."

"Your husband was not there?"

"No! I already said that. He had just gotten a new job and was out working."

"Are you sure?"

"What? What do you mean?"

"He doesn't work, no?"

"What?"

"He was out a lot, no?"

"Out? What do you mean?"

"Out a lot but not working."

Graciela felt like she was being ambushed with small-town innuendo. The details of her life were exposed for the busybodies to pick and prod apart and she resented it. "What are you implying, Doña Leonora?"

"She thinks your baby girl was made from sin. Not your husband's. They say you had a baby with Dr. Beford."

Graciela gasped. Her mouth fell open as she absorbed what Doña Leonora had just said. She inspected Doña Leonora's face to see if it would reveal anything more—perhaps something more rational after such illogical, reckless, absurd statements. Swallowing hard, she moved her head back and forth in disbelief as tiny lines gathered between her thin eyebrows. With a sigh, she closed her eyes, setting her elbows on the table and rubbing her temples with each middle finger, trying to relieve the pressure that was slowly growing there. She felt nothing but shock: not outrage, not disgust, not sadness or resentment, nothing but astonishment. It was all too unbelievable, too outlandish. She would wake up in the morning and it would all be a distant dream.

She slowly opened her eyes again, hoping to find relief from the day's events, but the reality of the situation stung her like a snake bite: Doña Leonora was waiting with eyes wide for Graciela's reaction to the scenario she had put before her, and her demeanor was grim. All Graciela could think about at this very moment was how much she hated this woman with the green Jell-O, this woman who personified small-town pettiness. "Doña Leonora!" Graciela cried. "Shame on you! This is just one of your lies."

"Lies?" Doña Leonora slapped the table. "I don't tell lies," she hissed. With an exasperated sigh, she turned from Graciela to stare at the fire once again.

For several minutes Graciela tried to collect her own thoughts. She was concerned that by departing from her usual restrained and dignified deportment, she had overstepped the bounds of formality and respect. Restrained again, Graciela stood. "Forgive me, Señora," she whispered. "It's been . . ." Graciela gulped, refusing to release the tears that were threatening to flow. "It's been a hard day."

With her eyes, Doña Leonora followed Graciela's movement, then focused again on the fire. She made no effort to respond.

Graciela slowly retired from the room into darkness. She could hear her own footsteps reverberate down the hall.

"Graciela," Doña Leonora called, her voice barely audible.

Graciela stopped immediately. For a moment, she wearily laid her hand against the wall, checking her balance. She waited, cocking her ear toward the room where Doña Leonora sat. She was eager to hear another word, anything kind. She waited. Then she heard Doña Leonora stirring the fire. Graciela pushed on to her room.

The following morning, Graciela looked at herself in the small pocket mirror she carried in her satchel. Her eyes were puffy with dark circles beneath them. Her face, usually smooth and moist, was developing spots of acne. After washing her face with a moist cloth and applying lipstick to her mouth, she finished rolling the last bit of her hair and secured it with a pin. For a moment, she sat down at the edge of her thin bed, feeling chilled and jittery. She couldn't stop thinking of Mrs. Sanchez and her husband. Over and over, she saw Mrs. Sanchez in her mind, wiping the spit from her lips. She remembered the glistening spittle there on the corners of her mouth. How quickly she had moved from La Princesa to sinner in the town's eyes, Graciela thought. How quickly lies spread.

For a moment, Graciela lingered. No, she had to face the day. She had to go to school. She recalled this was the day for the championship spelling bee. She had given her level third and fourth graders one list to study and her level fifth and sixth graders another. So far, the third and fourth graders were beating the older students, and their eyes just shone knowing that fact. During the last few days, both sides had been honing their spelling skills, eager to be the class leaders. Even Alfonso, not the brightest or most motivated child, was learning his spelling words with enthusiasm. And Joaquín had stopped his fighting while Antonieta helped him study.

"Oh, goodness!" Graciela exclaimed. She sat down at her desk and hurriedly began scribbling algebraic equations, remembering the test she had promised Raul and María, who were competing for the highest grade this quarter in all subjects. Two tests to go and they would complete the math portion. When she finished, she stood, determined to make the most of the day.

The rest of the house was quiet. She hadn't heard a peep from Doña Leonora, who on a normal morning would have a fire burning in the stove, coffee brewing, and tortillas made. Today, the kitchen burned only with emptiness and cold.

The morning was bitterness personified. The wind had gained momentum during the night and it ripped through Graciela like a whip on bare skin. She wrapped her thin coat tighter around her body and headed in the direction of the schoolhouse, shielding her face from the blowing dust. The sand blowing against her stockinged legs stung and she wished for wool trousers. A handful of townspeople made their way through the weather also. Rather than stopping and tipping their hats as was the country custom, a group of men in work clothes eyeballed Graciela as they passed. Two women stopped when they spotted Graciela, whispered to each other, and crossed the rural road. No children were in sight and when Graciela reached the school yard, she saw no one—no children teeter-tottering, no boys playing kick-the-can, no girls enjoying hide-and-seek. The school yard was abandoned. Perhaps, she thought, all her students were avoiding the wind and waiting inside where it was warm.

Climbing the steps was painful. The frigid wind had numbed Graciela but her desire to reach shelter propelled her up. The large wooden doors would not budge when she tried to pull them open. The wind acted as suction, clamping the doors tightly shut. Finally, she slipped her gloved hand in and pulled, letting herself through the tiny space. A sudden gust then threw the doors open wide and Graciela had to use all her strength to harness them back in. When she turned around, Graciela's expectations were crushed. All along the wall that separated the actual entrance from the rest of the schoolroom, not one jacket appeared on the coat hooks. The cloakroom was barren.

Slowly, Graciela trudged up the aisle to investigate a foreign object on her lonely pine desk. Graciela was sure she had left her desk completely free from clutter. She was meticulous when it came to her workspace and even when she was grading papers, she kept precisely two stacks at any one time on the table. Everything else was cleared. There, on top, lay a single envelope with one line of proper penmanship. Without touching the piece, Graciela read her name. She read it again, mouthing each syllable as if she were teaching herself to spell. She decided to reach for the document and then she stopped, guessing the letter's contents. Her hand began to shake. The skin was beginning to show the signs of winter: it was cracked and dry, the spaces between her knuckles bearing marks of dry blood. Both hands suddenly disappeared into her coat pockets and staring at the white item in front of her, she waited: waited for the envelope to vanish, for the children to reappear, and for yesterday to be erased. Closing her eyes was as futile as wishing for a warm summer day on this March morning. When she reopened her eyes, the envelope sat in the same spot, indifferent and final. After several moments, Graciela picked it up and slid her pinky under the seal. Quickly, she tore the letter open, unfolded it, and began to read. The words she read over and over could not be for her. She checked the envelope to see that it was her name written there. It was.

Leaving the schoolhouse, Graciela walked toward Doña Leonora's home, the wind now propelling her in that direction as if it drew her up within its breath and carried her away. She hardly felt her feet touch the ground, and all that passed her was a blur. She had to get home. She had to see her babies. She had to leave this place.

Instead of going inside to pack up the rest of her belongings, Graciela prepared her vehicle for a start and wound it up. Quickly, she jumped into the car as it began to roll down the drive. At that moment, Graciela thought she saw the curtains move inside Doña Leonora's window. Accelerating, she drove off.

The streets were not friendly. The townspeople walking along the streets did not acknowledge her. When they looked up to see the jalopy running past, instead of smiling and waving as they had always done, they turned their focus to each other, inventing, Graciela suspected, new lies about her.

Graciela drove as fast as the old vehicle would let her. The dirt roads were a menace and the high-speed winds that made the car sway were beginning to make her feel quite queasy. She slowed down just long enough to settle her stomach but because she was so determined to get home, she speeded up again, deciding it was better to deal with nausea than what seemed like an interminable wait.

When at last she drove into the lot facing her home, she slid down from the high seat, gathering her skirt around her, and ran inside, eager to see her baby and to tell her story to someone, anyone. She slammed the whitewashed door behind her but the house was empty. Immediately, Graciela panicked. Where were Cita and the baby? Was the baby sick? Yes, she must be. She had to be. Graciela threw open the door and ran outside. She ran and ran, not really knowing where she was running. Yes, she did. She was running to the doctor. To Dr. Beford's. In mid-sprint, Graciela stopped. Stopped cold. She couldn't go there. She couldn't go see Dr. Beford. Even if her child were sick, she could not go see the doctor. Doing so would give those rumors credibility.

Graciela had always despised gossip because usually it was all lies created by people who were jealous, hateful, or bored, sometimes all three. She also knew Doña Leonora was the worst kind of *mitotera*, although she had believed her gossip was the innocuous kind, discussed at baptisms and funerals, over a bowl of hot posole or a plate of tamales, not the kind that could ruin a life. But Graciela knew better now that she felt the full effect of Doña Leonora's poison—lies spread around like a communicable disease.

But at this moment, Graciela was more disgusted with herself than with Doña Leonora. To think that her reputation was more important than her child. What kind of mother was she? What if her baby were dying? At once, Graciela continued in the direction of downtown, calmer now but just as determined. And there, walking toward her, was Cita, without a coat, carrying Graciela's baby daughter wrapped in a single blanket.

Graciela rushed forward. When Cita recognized her, she opened her mouth wide, and happily exclaimed, "Graciela!"

Instead of greeting her warmly, Graciela scolded her. "Cita, my god, you're so stupid, sometimes! Here, let me take her."

"What, what did I do?"

"It's freezing out here, Cita. The baby's going to catch its death, don't you realize that? Let's get her home. The poor child," Graciela said, seizing the baby from Cita's care and tucking her within her coat. The child began to cry and Graciela rocked her in her arms and caressed her face and chest, but to no avail. What was the matter with her? Graciela asked herself. Did she have a fever? She felt the baby's face with the back of her hand, but it did not feel warm; in fact, it felt wind-blown like hers, cold and fresh but not chilled, and least of all feverish.

Graciela stopped walking when she realized Cita had left her side. Attempting to quiet the baby still and failing, she turned to solicit Cita's help. As much as she hated to admit it, her sister-in-law must know the baby's temperament: the things that frightened her, the things that soothed her and lulled her back into sleep. "Come on, Cita. Let's get home. Let's get the baby home."

"She's scared."

"No, she's cold. Scared? Scared of what?"

"You. She doesn't know who you are."

Graciela looked into the face of her screaming infant. It was true then. As much as Graciela wanted her baby girl to know instinctively she was the woman who had given her life, she was a frightening stranger to her own daughter. It wasn't the cold that was disturbing the child's peace; it was her mother.

Graciela gestured for Cita to take the baby. "Here, Cita, get her please. Maybe you can calm her." It was a heartbreaking admission to make but Graciela acknowledged the likelihood that Cita did know her baby a little better than she did. But of course, it made sense. It was Cita who had been caring for the baby day and night for the last several days, not Graciela. It was Cita who fed her and put her to bed. It was Cita who got up with her during the night. It was Cita who put her arms around her to comfort her in the night. But now Graciela wanted, needed to do all these things.

Falling behind several paces, Graciela stuffed her hands deep into the wool pockets of her coat. She watched Cita's gait. She listened to the sounds of her baby, resonating loudly, drowning out the sounds of the wind. Gradually, the squawking subsided to a slight whine, then to a mere whisper. A deep sigh emerged from Graciela. Now she would have plenty of time to get to know her daughter. But it wasn't supposed to have happened this way. It was supposed to have happened because Robert got a job. It was supposed to have happened because he was a responsible father and husband. It was supposed to have happened because he loved her.

Running up behind Cita, Graciela took off her coat and wrapped it around the baby, who was haphazardly held by Cita. Graciela gently took Cita's arm and hesitated briefly, gazing at her, requesting her permission with wide-open eyes and a questioning nod. Without expression, Cita nodded in response and Graciela moved Cita's arm snugly under the baby. A slight sound of contentment emerged from the baby's lips and Cita and Graciela beamed simultaneously. Graciela resumed her walk a few steps behind Cita. By the time they reached the whitewashed house, the baby was fast asleep.

Watching Cita put the baby to bed, Graciela decided to wait until Robert came home to tell the story of why she had returned before the week was out. She was sure Cita was already wondering and questions were not far away. Graciela managed to avoid the subject by inquiring about her husband. Squatting by the stove and handing Cita pieces of kindling, she asked, "How long has he been gone, Cita? He was supposed to be helping you. Or rather, you're supposed to be helping him. He's supposed to be minding the house." Watching Cita light a match and quickly throw it into the woodstove, Graciela smiled, despite her anxiety. "You still hate to light matches, Cita? Here. Let me do it."

Cita relinquished the box. "He told me he'd be home before lunch."

"Well, where did he go?"

Cita shrugged. "Didn't say."

"Does he always leave you alone to take care of the children?"

"No, not always. He's really good with Cipriana and Pablito and now the baby, Graciela. Solomón's children adore him too. And, he makes the best fried potatoes!"

Graciela couldn't help smiling. She knew it was a fact. He was a better cook than she was. And besides, what was she doing, believing Doña Leonora's lies about her husband? He was a good father, a good man. She was a gossip, the worst kind of woman. Yet, she couldn't help but wonder where her husband was now. She wanted him there immediately—and yet she didn't. She didn't want to have to tell him her news.

Cita's voice startled Graciela.

"What did you say, Cita?"

"I said, are you all right? You look kind of sick."

Graciela took a deep breath. "I'm sorry, Cita," she said, almost inaudibly.

"For what?" Cita asked.

"For not trusting you earlier."

"What do you mean, Graciela?"

"Cita, you know exactly what I mean. The coat and the cold and the baby. You know."

Cita nodded.

"You know I wouldn't trust my baby with anyone else but you, Cita. I was scared though. And jealous. You're becoming my baby's mama before my eyes. She didn't even know me and it scared me."

"Graciela," Cita said matter-of-factly, "somehow, I've become mama to Solomón's children. I don't want to be mama to your baby too."

Frowning slightly, Graciela nodded. "Yes. I know, Cita. I know."

Graciela paused for a moment and then she whispered, "And from now on, you won't have to be."

Later, Graciela sat at the table, her posture perfect and her hands folded in her lap. She looked at neither Cita nor Robert. Her eyelids were heavy with concentration and only occasionally did she look up to gaze cursorily at the two while she relayed the story of Mrs. Sanchez and her husband, the spitting, her conversation with Doña Leonora, and the letter this morning. Throughout Graciela's narrative, Robert sat with one arm across his chest, his eyes focused on his feet, which were spread out before him, and his opposite hand stroking his beard line. The only indication to Graciela that he was disturbed was the frown that grew deeper as the story went on. When she had finished, Robert stood and moved toward the door, declaring, "I'm going to talk with that woman right now to give her a piece of my mind."

Graciela jumped up, blocking his way. "You can't do that, Robert. She'll only tell you more lies."

"Then I want to hear them for myself. At least, I'll have a chance to deny them to her face. Get out of the way, Graciela."

"Then let me come with you."

"Do what you want, Graciela. But with or without you, I'm talking with this Leonora woman."

"I'm coming with you then. Cita, will you . . . ?"

"Don't even ask, Graciela. Go."

They drove in silence but Graciela could tell that Robert's mind was racing. She wished that he would say something to her but she doubted that she could answer his questions to his satisfaction. In fact, she didn't really know the questions or the answers but she could guess what his questions might be. He would never ask them to her face, though, because he believed in her to the core. At times, his confidence in her scared her. She was afraid she wouldn't be able to live up to his expectations. Now, his pending visit with Doña Leonora petrified her. She hated for him to hear the lies that would spew forth from the gossip's lips. She feared what he would think of her afterward. When the moment presented itself, she could not accompany Robert into Doña Leonora's house. She could not bear to listen to the lies again. Instead, she waited in the vehicle.

What was taking him so long? What was going on? Graciela could not wait any longer. She climbed out. Just as she reached the porch, the door opened wide, and her husband was shaking Doña Leonora's hand. "Thank you so much for the tea and pastelitos, Señora. Oh, Graciela, look, she gave us some goodies for the trip."

"Graciela," Doña Leonora acknowledged Graciela with a nod of her head. Graciela did not respond, and instead she turned and made her way back into the car. Her husband stayed a few minutes longer on the steps of the porch, shaking Doña Leonora's hand once more. He turned and to Graciela, he appeared sheepish, looking down at the ground until he met her eyes. She regarded him suspiciously through the dirty windows of the jalopy. Instead of cranking the engine immediately, he mounted the vehicle, shut the door tight, and placed the plate he carried on the seat. At first he said nothing, then he wrapped his hands around the steering wheel tightly and said, "She didn't do it, Graciela. She didn't make up that lie about you."

"What? And you believe her? She's nothing but a low-down, shiftless old lady who has a forked tongue and a . . ."

"She told me who did, Graciela."

"What? Well, then she's lying. She's just trying to blame it all on someone else. And you believed her, Robert? My god, you're just as . . ."

"Graciela! Listen. For once. You know that director Olivas?"

"The bald one? Always sweating, winter or summer?"

Robert nodded. "His wife overheard Tía Quirina in the mercantile the day after you had the baby. Quirina was bragging about Cipriana to some of the ladies, telling them how observant she was. I guess that morning after seeing her baby sister she said something about the baby having a funny chin like Dr. Beford and everyone laughed. Did she say something like that?"

"Yes, and I told her it wasn't Dr. Beford's. It was yours and mine. I just told her Dr. Beford brought the baby."

"Well somehow, this woman, wife to that Olivas character, heard what she wanted to hear. And she went home and told her husband . . ."

" . . . who spread the rumor. But why?"

"His brother needed a job. Your job."

"His brother's a teacher?

"Yes, and he didn't get assigned a post this term. You got his post when Papa Armijo pulled strings to get you a job."

"So he asked his brother to get me dismissed? And you learned all this from Doña Leonora? My god! Well, why didn't she tell me all of this last night?"

Robert shrugged but Graciela didn't pay attention. "What am I going to do now? Make up something about him? Take it to the directors?" Shaking her head back and forth, Graciela was dizzy with options.

"Tell the truth. Go to the directors and tell your story. Leonora said she would go on your behalf."

"Oh, yes, and they're going to believe a town gossip. Sure. Two women, never."

"Or . . ."

"What?"

"Get him, that Olivas character, to come clean with the other directors."

"But how? Robert, it's a men's club. They're all politicos."

Robert nodded. For a moment he turned from Graciela, staring out the windshield. Then suddenly, he slapped his hand against the dashboard. "Damn, Graciela, this is all my fault."

"What? No. What in the world do you mean, Robert?"

"None of this would have happened if my damn pride didn't get in the way of things. I was so mad at you that day when I quit your job for you. I couldn't bear that you called me irresponsible."

"I never said that."

"You didn't have to. I knew you were thinking it."

Graciela felt Robert stare into her eyes as if he were hypnotizing her. Then, suddenly, he took the crank from the floor and opened the door. He went around to the hood and cranked the car up. Before Graciela knew it, he was in the car once again and they were on their way home. With one hand, he unwrapped the plate Doña Leonora had sent, keeping his eyes on the bumpy road. Graciela watched as he stuffed his mouth with one *pastelito* after another. By the time they drove into Santa Lucía, the plate was empty and Graciela never had the chance to taste even one.

The lack of opportunity did not faze Graciela in the least. The rage she felt toward Doña Leonora still simmered; however, it had dulled to righteous indignation.

The next morning, Graciela woke to an anxious gnawing at the pit of her stomach, worried about how she was going to resolve her predicament. She lingered in bed longer than usual, grateful at least to be home for the weekend with time and space to figure out her next move. Today, she would focus on her Saturday morning extension class, postponing her immediate worries in favor of studying early childhood development. She still lacked thirty credit hours for her bachelor's degree but she was determined to earn it even if it took her that many more years. Years ago she had made the commitment to attend weekend and summer extension classes that were taught by faculty who commuted from Highland's University until her goal was met.

In the short run, she would have to be derelict in her duty toward her children but in the long run, she would give them something to aspire to. At least, that's what she told herself to allay the guilt. And she never took a single penny from her children to pay for her schooling. Instead, she wore underwear that was in shreds, wrapped herself with a strip torn from an old sheet to bind her breasts, and consciously ignored the fashions of the day even though she would rather dress well than eat.

She wondered if there would ever be a time when she would feel guilt-free for leaving her children behind—by necessity on weekdays, by choice, on Saturday mornings. She doubted it but at least for now she could make them a hot breakfast before going to class. She nudged her husband awake with her elbow before heading outside to the cistern for a bucketful of fresh water.

When she returned, she expected to see Robert building a fire. Instead, he was gone and Cita was there in his place.

"Well, good morning, Cita. Where did you come from all of a sudden? Where are Benny and the girls?"

Cita cleared the morning grogginess from her throat. "They're with Solomón this weekend."

"And Robert?"

"Yesterday, he asked me to be here by seven so he could do something downtown."

"Oh, really? Did he say when he'd be back? I have class this morning."

"I know, Graciela. I'll watch the children."

"No, no, Cita. You watch them all week. You have things to do too."

"Don't worry, Graciela. I'm sure he'll be back any minute. So tell me what happened yesterday. Robert said it went well, but that's all he would say."

Graciela nodded. "At least we found out who was the source of the gossip, but I still have to figure out whether or not I still have a job."

"Sure you do, Graciela."

"I like your confidence, Cita, but I'm not so sure. I'll have to get Doña Leonora to defend my character. Can you believe that?"

"You'll be fine, Graciela. Don't worry."

Smiling, Graciela asked, "You sure you're fine with watching the children for a little while?"

"Of course, Graciela. Go on now before you're late."

Graciela nodded, slipping her coat on. Gathering her books in her arms, she closed the door behind her and made her way up Route 66. Up ahead, she thought she caught a glimpse of her husband just as he was turning onto Main. She rushed to catch up, now that her curiosity had been piqued. Where would Robert be going on a Saturday morning?

Just as Graciela turned the corner onto Main, she saw her husband entering the little drugstore operated by Dr. Beford several storefronts up the street. Graciela held her breath. Her husband never went into Dr. Beford's store. Never. What was he going to do? Didn't he believe Doña Leonora? Didn't he believe her? Oh, what was he going to do? Graciela looked at her wristwatch. She didn't have time to wait for him. She had to get to class. She crossed the street, making her way toward the two-story stone building that was the county courthouse, where her class was held. Before she entered the building, she turned her head and caught a glimpse of her husband crossing the street, carrying a newspaper under his arm. He sat on a bench at the edge of the courthouse grounds, opened his paper, and began reading. A pang of anger surfaced. Here he was reading the paper at his leisure while his sister was spending her Saturday morning watching his children and his wife was trying to make a future for them.

When she emerged from the building at noon, she was surprised to still see her husband in the same location. Now, he was standing with his foot propped on the bench, his arms crossed, peering across the street at Gould's Mercantile. His hat and newspaper were lying on the bench. Just as she began to approach Robert from behind, he lunged across the street, and called to a man entering the store.

"Are you Olivas? Pedro Olivas?"

"Depends on who's asking."

From where Graciela stood, it seemed for a moment that her husband was extending a friendly hand to the man, but before she could blink again, his left arm swung forward with such force that the next moment Pedro Olivas was lying flat on the cold ground with his hat behind him.

"Don Pedro, hombre cabrón. What kind of man are you, dragging my wife's name through mud? You're not a man, you're a coward. Get up! Get up, hombre sin huevos!"

Even with Robert's boots prodding him, Don Pedro Olivas sat cowering in the middle of the walk. He was trying with all his might to get up but one attempt after the other failed. Sweat glistened on his brow. Watching Graciela's husband closely, he lunged toward his hat, trying to grasp it, but failed. The momentum, however, got him on his feet and he ran, ran with all his might, without turning back.

"You're going to tell the directors the truth and get my wife her job back or you'll have more of this!" Graciela's husband shouted. He walked back across the street and picked up his own hat and his newspaper at the bench. Then he stalked off in the opposite direction, right past Graciela, massaging his left hand with his right. His ears were crimson and his knuckles were bleeding. He did not notice her or any of the passersby who stood gathered around.

Graciela stood for a long while, staring after her husband. On the one hand, she wanted to hide, ashamed of her husband's bravado. On the other, she wanted to go after him, thank him, tell him she trusted him and loved him. She was not used to expressing herself so demonstratively though, and so instead of following him, she headed back toward Route 66. The crowd around her had dispersed by then and as she began to cross the street, she spotted a hat, Don Pedro's hat, lying limp and solitary in the street. She watched as only the feather tucked inside the band fluttered in the breeze. Then, all at once, a gust of wind swept the hat away and it tumbled down the long road.

CHAPTER SEVEN

NEIGHBORS

"Let's go visiting, niña," Mama Fela said to Cipriana while she closed up her sewing machine and hung the white dress from the door of her armario. "Put the buttons away now, 'jita."

"Where are we going today, Mama Fela?" asked Cipriana.

"To Doña Beatríz's."

Cipriana's face lit up. "Do you think she has cherries yet?"

"Shame on you, Cipriana." Mama Fela stopped and frowned at her granddaughter. "We don't go visiting to ask for handouts. From what I hear, Doña Beatríz has been spending all her time in bed since she came back from her brother's farm last week. Probably worked her to death, making pies and canning cherries."

"Sorry, Mama Fela," Cipriana mumbled, looking down at the piles of buttons before her.

For a moment, Mama Fela recognized her mother's sternness in her own voice. Why ever did she scold her granddaughter? She herself was eager to have the first taste of Doña Beatríz's newly harvested cherries, although she would not admit this to anyone. Everyone knew Don Cornelio grew the best cherries this side of the Pecos.

"Mi'jita," Mama Fela said, relenting and lifting Cipriana's chin. "You're right, mi'jita. She has the best cherries, doesn't she?"

Cipriana nodded.

"Pues, we'll go for a visit, see how my comadre is doing. Meanwhile, we'll pray a few Our Fathers that she's feeling better. Then we'll throw in a little prayer on the side to ask that we be rewarded in heaven, but until then, we'll ask God to give us a few cherries while we're still on earth. What do you think?"

Mama Fela hardly waited for Cipriana's answer. She was out the door, pushing open her parasol. Her step quickened and Cipriana had to skip to catch up.

After rapping on the door two times, Mama Fela and Cipriana waited on the doorstep for several minutes. Finally, the door opened a crack and Doña Beatríz peeked out. Even though it had only been two weeks since she last saw her comadre, somehow she seemed older, grayer, more wrinkled. Mama Fela despised seeing these signs of age in her friend because it meant they were happening to her too. Like Mama Fela's, Doña Beatríz's silver hair still boasted patches of black, a reminder, if only to herself, that she was once young. From the waves in her hair and the wooden brush that Beatríz held in her hand, Mama Fela could tell that her friend had been transforming her appearance from night into day.

"Ay, Doña Beatríz. We're here at a bad time."

Beatríz opened the door wide and embraced Mama Fela. "Nonsense, comadre. I didn't know it was you. And Thipriana, ay, 'jita, que linda. Entren. Entren." She kissed the top of Cipriana's head and ushered the two guests into the front room.

Doña Beatríz was the only person Mama Fela knew who had a peculiar way of pronouncing some letters of the alphabet, in particular those in Cipriana's name. If you listened very intently, you could make out those mispronounced words, but who was Mama Fela to judge her comadre? She had plenty of faults of her own, both God-sent and of her own making, and she wasn't about to start looking for the foibles in her friends. She didn't know whether Doña Beatríz had gotten good at concealing her lisp over the years or if Mama Fela had just gotten accustomed to her friend's imperfections as if they were her own.

Doña Beatríz took the parasol from Cipriana and showed her to a chair. She whispered something to Mama Fela and disappeared down the hallway with the long black umbrella trailing behind.

"Where's she going?" Cipriana asked her grandmother.

Mama Fela chuckled. "Our little prayer has been answered," she replied, smiling at her granddaughter, who beamed in response.

Sitting down on a small paisley sofa with her purse in her lap, Mama Fela began to hum, studying the intricate features of the wallpapered room as she did during every visit, never tiring of the details. Doña Beatríz was the only person Mama Fela knew in Santa Lucía, apart from the americanos, who reserved a room just to entertain guests. She knew the americanos called it the parlor, from what Cita had told her, and she enjoyed visiting her comadre just to experience the fancy room. At one time, it might have made her feel uneasy to sit in such a room. She could imagine sensations of unworthiness descending upon her, making her agitated at any fuss made on her behalf. But now she felt that she belonged in the room. Years of hard work entitled her to such a place and she was comfortable in it because it was beginning to bear the same effects of time as she was. The once-starched lace curtains were yellowed with time and frayed at the edges. And even though the wallpaper bore testament to a more affluent time, it was now faded with the western sun.

Cipriana's movement caught Mama Fela's eye. For a moment, Mama Fela watched as Cipriana carefully slid back into the green satin chair, placing her hands on the curved armrests and crossing her thin legs at the ankles. Looking all around the room, Cipriana licked the fingers of one hand and brushed her hair back at her temple. Mama Fela had to look away quickly, holding in the chuckle she felt was about to escape.

Doña Beatríz appeared at the doorway then with a bowl of cherries in her hands and her hair pinned up out of her face.

"I thought you two might like some cherries from Don Cornelio. He picked them yesterday."

Cipriana scooted to the edge of her seat and looked at Mama Fela expectantly.

Mama Fela nodded and immediately, Cipriana jumped to Doña Beatríz's aid. "May I help, Doña Beatríz?"

"Of course, 'jita. Pass them to your Mama Fela," she said, sighing as she sat down in a chair opposite Fela. "I'm so tired."

As Cipriana offered the bowl, Mama Fela scooped up a handful. For a moment, she looked over at Doña Beatríz and drank in every detail of her comadre's face. It was very thin like hers with high cheekbones protruding from the sunken face. Perfect circles of rouge at the cheeks emphasized the boniness and reminded her of the cherry she was about to pop into her mouth. As the juice of the cherry filled Mama Fela's mouth with delight, she proceeded with formalities. "And Don Cornelio?" she asked Beatríz. "Is the farm keeping him busy?"

Doña Beatríz pursed her lips together and wiped the corners of her mouth with index finger and thumb. "Sí, Doña Fela," she said in a monotone. "And me too. Ay, Cornelio worked me to death, comadre. I've been so tired since I got back, I haven't seen the light of day for four days now. I've been una floja."

"Que floja ni floja, comadre," Mama Fela said. "You deserve the rest. Válgame Dios, I can't believe that man worked you so hard. We're not so young like we used to be."

"Yo sé, Doña Fela. Ooh, I made so many pies to sell, I couldn't keep count." Doña Beatríz shifted in her chair. "Even my nalgas are tired."

Mama Fela laughed easily. She could just imagine Don Cornelio working his sister so hard. Shame on him. Didn't he have any sense, that man? Doña Beatríz wasn't young anymore. She was approaching her sixty-fifth year this fall but she was in her youth compared to Cornelio, who was a decade older. He would never admit to getting old, though. He still loved the ladies as he always had, Fela thought half in amusement, half in disgust. She had heard countless stories from her comadres. When they would stop to buy cherries in the summer or apples in the fall, he would very politely give them their change of pennies and nickels while caressing their soft white palms with his farmer's fingers, dirty nails and all. Mama Fela winced at the thought. She wondered why men didn't like to take baths. Even her Gilberto refused to bathe but once a month. By contrast, her favorite time of day was her daily morning sponge bath and Saturdays were a special treat she looked forward to all week when she would get to bathe in a tin tub filled with warm water and her yerbas. For her sixtieth birthday, Gilberto had insisted on buying her one of those long tubs that the horses drank from instead of the little round ones most people squeezed themselves into once in a while. Her arthritis wouldn't let her be as flexible as she once was. Now she could stretch out as she pleased, delighting in the warm bath that soothed her aching joints and calmed her nerves.

"Doña Fela?"

"I'm sorry, what did you say, Doña Beatríz?"

"I said I haven't seen you for two weeks. How's your sewing coming along? How's that special dress you were working on?" Doña Beatríz smiled slyly.

Mama Fela quickly eyed Cipriana. The project Doña Beatríz was talking about was a secret between her comadres and herself. She wanted no one else to know about the dress she was working on—at least not until the right time came to divulge her surprise. Quickly, she changed the subject. "I'm working on a dress for Doña Carlota," she said as a slight smile escaped from her thin lips.

"Doña Carlota? Another dress?" asked Doña Beatríz. "Pobre, mujer con a hundred dresses for death. Does she think she's going to a fiesta?" Beatríz smiled for a moment, attempting to hide her amusement behind a look of genuine empathy. Her brow became a wave of sadness. "Is she ill again?"

"Ill? Psh." Mama Fela couldn't resist making a face and rolling her eyes. "No. She's as healthy as a young girl again. Wanting party dresses. You know what color it is this time? Not white like last time. You know . . ." Mama Fela paused, inspecting her audience, trying to decide if she should reveal her thoughts or not. Of course, this was her friend and she could be as open as she wished. Her comadre wouldn't hold it against her. "Sabes que, she didn't wear white when she was married."

"¡Válgame Dios! No?"

"You remember, Beatríz," Mama Fela said with great emphasis, slightly perturbed that her best comadre for all these years might not have the same memories. For a brief second, she peered sideways at Cipriana, making sure her granddaughter was occupied. Bending forward in her chair, she lifted her eyebrows conspiratorially and whispered, "¡Un escándalo!"

Doña Beatríz nodded fervently, wiping the corners of her mouth. "Yes. Yes. I remember now."

"It was a yellow dress, like Cipriana's here," Mama Fela said, pointing.

"No, comadre. It was red."

"No, Beatríz. No, no, no. Yellow. Like a girl's. I remember it like it was yesterday."

Doña Beatríz was quiet. "Yes," she said, massaging her chin with the tips of her fingers, gazing upward. "Yes. I remember now. It was a creamy yellow, I think."

"Yes. That's right. Remember how in a certain light, it could have passed as white? And remember when Father O'Grady stopped the ceremony and took Carlota aside, telling her he couldn't marry her because she wasn't wearing the white of a virgin . . ."

"No!"

"Yes. And Carlota took him into the vestibule and twirled around, asking him to look at her dress by the light of the stained glass, assuring him it was white. He got down on his hands and knees, looking at the dress, and at that time, I slipped into the church. I thought he was going to scold me for being late but instead, he asked me what color Carlota's dress was. Well I wasn't expecting a question like that but I took one look at Carlota and knew exactly what the answer should be. 'White!' I said."

Doña Beatríz clapped her hands in delight. "Comadre, you didn't!"

"Of course, Beatríz. What else could I do? Poor Carlota, standing there in her finery with all her family and friends waiting to hear if their Carlota was pure all because of the color of dress she chose. Que nonsense ni nonsense. Carlota just likes pretty colors. She always has and she always will."

"But to risk her wedding day? It's a wonder Father let the ceremony go on."

"He had to, Beatríz. And, I'll never forget how he frowned at me as he struggled to stand up. He ushered us all back into the church and as he passed me on his way to the altar, he whispered, 'I'll see you at confession this afternoon.'"

"¡No me digas, comadre!"

Mama Fela could see the whites of Doña Beatríz's eyes. She was enjoying this a little too much.

"Did you go?" Doña Beatríz asked.

Mama Fela grimaced. "Of course not, Beatríz! I had to go to Carlota's reception. And that's where I had my first dance with Gilberto."

Doña Beatríz nodded slowly. "Comadre, you're a lot braver than I could ever be."

"No, Beatríz. Not brave, just foolish."

"But you saved the day for Carlota."

Mama Fela smiled halfheartedly at Beatríz. Suddenly, she felt an invisible cloak draw its dark shadow around her. Her mood changed abruptly. It was like a sickness was overtaking her and she began to think of poor Gilberto. This must be what happened to her husband when he decided it was time to go out into the llano, when his black moods got the better of him.

"Are you sure about that?" Mama Fela asked Doña Beatríz. "I wonder if Carlota feels that way now about her husband."

"Of course! Carlota loved Eloy."

"Yes. But now he's dead and she's planning her own funeral. I wonder if she ever wishes that day so many years ago would have turned out differently. Maybe she wishes she would have never gotten married, never had her children. Maybe she regrets all that. Maybe her life would have been simpler if Father O'Grady had gotten his way and didn't allow her to get married that day."

"Yes, but then Carlota would have been the talk of the town."

Mama Fela winced at Doña Beatríz's choice of words. "She already was. Look, forty years later and here we are still talking about that day."

Doña Beatríz nodded.

"Sometimes I wonder now if I should have married Gilberto. He's not dead yet but he might as well be. He's never here. His true love has called him away again and again. You know Beatríz, I was never the love of his life; the llano was."

"That's not true, comadre. I see the way he looks at you."

"How, comadre? Like a burden that prevents him from doing exactly what he wants when he wants. He never should have gotten married, that man. He belongs out in the llano alone."

"I can't believe that, comadre. Everyone admires you both. Look what good children you have. They're not like Carlota's, who never see to her. They're good children. How is Roberto anyway? Didn't Graciela have her baby?"

A note of panic surged through Mama Fela's blood. "What?"

"She had her baby, no?"

Mama Fela nodded. She turned away from the conversation and began to inspect the furniture of her friend, mentally separating shadow from pure dust, tempted to ask Beatríz for her feather duster. She didn't like these questions.

"It was a girl?" Doña Beatríz asked.

Mama Fela nodded again, wondering what would come next. She studied the brown spots on her hands and the rough skin around her fingernails, pulling at a particularly bothersome hangnail. She felt the way Carlota must have felt all those years ago as she was awaiting the verdict that was dependent on the color of her dress: was she pure or not? Was Mama Fela's daugher-in-law pure or not? Was Mama Fela's honor in question because of the *mitote* about her family or not?

Mama Fela was quite certain she had nothing to fear from her friend, but still she wondered briefly. Was Beatríz capable of participating in all the gossip that had been going around for the past few months? There were many loose tongues in Santa Lucía and they had been flying lately, but she doubted that Beatríz was one of them. They had been friends too long.

Graciela and Roberto had come to tell her all about the rumors. Poor Graciela, telling the news, she had looked as pale as the night she gave birth. Her voice was shaky and she could barely get the words out. Afterward, Fela took Graciela aside and whispered to her, "Te tengo confianza, Graciela." And she meant it. If anyone deserved respect, it was her daughter-in-law.

"And what did Roberto think?" Doña Beatríz interrupted Mama Fela's thoughts.

"What do you mean?" Mama Fela blurted out suddenly. "Just say what you're trying to say and get it over with," Mama Fela said, feeling her temperature rise. "I can't believe you'd be a part of the mitote, comadre."

"Mitote? What mitote, Doña Fela? I don't know what you're talking about."

Mama Fela reached for her purse and nervously dug out her cigarette papers. "Do you mind if I have a smoke?" she asked, not really looking at her friend and not caring if her friend gave her permission or not. She needed a smoke right now.

"Well, comadre . . . ," Doña Beatríz whispered. Fela could barely hear her. "I don't really like smoking in here. Why don't we go out on the porch?" Doña Beatríz started to get up.

But Mama Fela waved her hand at her friend. She stuffed her cigarette paper back into her purse. "Never mind, Beatríz, I don't need a smoke after all. Come, Cipriana we better go." She slipped the thin handle of her purse over her forearm.

"No, no, Fela. Don't go like this. I was only wondering what Roberto thought of his new baby."

Mama Fela paused and swallowed hard. She felt her temperature rise again, but this time from embarrassment. "Ay, comadre. I'm sorry. I should have known better than to think you were trying to dig for mitote. Poor Graciela has had a lot of people talking lately."

"Talking? About her? But why, comadre?"

"Oh, never mind. It's so silly, it's not even worth the time to explain."

Doña Beatríz nodded and Fela knew that if she didn't wish to discuss the matter further, her friend would respect those wishes without another thought. Mama Fela ascended onto arthritic feet. "Come, Cipriana. This time we really must go."

Doña Beatríz stood also. "Wait, comadre! Take some cherry pie." Beatríz touched the top of Cipriana's head and smiled. "Thipriana would love it, no?"

Cipriana looked at her grandmother expectantly. Mama Fela nodded.

"Oh, yes, Doña Beatríz," said Cipriana. "Thank you."

Mama Fela and Cipriana trailed behind Doña Beatríz as she slowly led them into the kitchen, her heavy black shoes clopping against the wood floor. While Doña Beatríz procured a plate and a knife, Mama Fela spotted a round bulge concealed underneath a white towel centered on the kitchen table. The vision of cherry pie was evident even before Beatríz removed its cotton shield. In unison, Mama Fela and Cipriana looked at each other and grinned. Mama Fela was sure that, like herself, Cipriana could already taste the delicacy in her imagination as their hostess sliced through the buttery crust.

Doña Beatríz paused in reflection, pulling at her earlobe, staring down into the pie plate in front of her. Finally, she nodded to herself, wiped the blade clean against her apron, and took the entire pie plate to the trastero. There, she slid open a drawer, removed a clean cloth, and wrapped the entire plate. Walking over to Cipriana, she placed it into the child's eager hands.

At the door, Mama Fela and Doña Beatríz exchanged embraces. Then, Beatríz placed both her hands on top of Cipriana's head and kissed her, saying, "Go with God, Thipriana. Go with God."

Mama Fela took the pie from Cipriana and said, "Thank my comadre, 'jita, for her blessing and for her hospitality."

Cipriana wrapped her arms around Doña Beatríz's middle. Looking up at her elder, Cipriana said, "I love the way you say my name, Doña Beatríz. You make it sound like a storybook character. And I love to come to your house because you're rich and I love to sit in your chairs because they're like thrones!"

"Cipriana, shame on you!" Mama Fela gasped.

Beatríz laughed. "No, no, está bien, comadre. I'm glad she likes to come. You're welcome here anytime, Thipriana."

Mama Fela glanced sideways at her granddaughter, trying as hard as she could to muster a frown. It was too hard so instead, she exchanged smiles with Beatríz. "What children come up with nowadays, comadre!" Fela said, trying to sound exasperated. "Get the umbrella, Cipriana. There, in the corner."

Stepping from the porch, Mama Fela surveyed the midmorning light and squinted, shading her sensitive eyes with a steady hand. "It's going to be a terribly hot summer, comadre. I can feel it in my bones."

"Yo sé," Doña Beatríz said, wiping the corners of her mouth. "And don't forget, tell me how the pie was."

Cipriana licked her lips. Beatríz and Mama Fela laughed. Waving one last time, Mama Fela turned and the door closed softy behind them.

"The umbrella, 'jita. Quickly before I melt in this sun," Mama Fela said to her granddaughter. With nimble fingers, Cipriana released the wings of the umbrella to the rays of sun, placing Mama Fela in its shadow. With one hand, Mama Fela clutched her purse, and with the other, she carried the pie, carefully watching her step. At the end of Doña Beatríz's hard-packed dirt walkway, Mama Fela looked both ways, trying to decide which way to head. Finally, she led Cipriana in the opposite direction of home. Usually, after one visit, they returned to routine, but today, Mama Fela did not wish to go back home yet. Lately, the house was feeling empty without Gilberto. And all this mitote about Graciela was getting to her.

Mama Fela and Cipriana strolled along the path. Who else should they visit today? With whom did she feel like talking? Mama Fela stopped suddenly and nudged Cipriana with her elbow. "Hijita, who's that up ahead?" she asked, squinting into the sun. She watched Cipriana strain her young eyes also, pulling each of her eyelids wide. But she didn't have time for her granddaughter's antics. Finally, she could make out two figures walking toward them; the one in front was at least three steps ahead of the other. The first one was tall and lanky, head and shoulders above the other, whose rounded, buxom figure made up for her lack of height. Mama Fela knew then it could only be the Lavadeux sisters. Just as Cipriana opened her mouth to relate her finding, Mama Fela's own voice rang out. "Doña Adela and Doña Francisquita!"

Mama Fela hurriedly transferred the plate of pie to Cipriana's custody. Brushing past her granddaughter, she rushed forward to meet the pair. "Doña Adela," she said warmly, extending her hand. "And Doña Francisquita," Mama Fela said, embracing her and then holding both of their hands like a little girl set to play Red Rover. "It's so good to see you. I thought you were visiting relatives this month. Come and say hello, Cipriana."

Mama Fela could see that Cipriana was struggling to figure out how to greet her elders with the pie and parasol burdening her hands. Finally, Cipriana simply smiled at the ladies. Mama Fela moved away from her friends and took the items from Cipriana. Frowning, she clucked her tongue at Cipriana and motioned with her eyes and a tilt of her head. "Go and give the Lavadeux sisters a proper greeting," she told Cipriana. "Que smile ni smile."

"Oh, don't be so hard on her, comadre," pleaded Doña Francisquita, whose gray hair was braided in an arc on top of her head. "I know Cipriana has the best manners of any child this side of the Pecos." Doña Francisquita grinned perfectly, displaying a smile only possible with dentures.

"No, Francisca, Fela is right. The children nowadays, ooh, they're bad off. Tell them to do this, they don't. Tell them to give their tía a kiss, they make a face. Tell them to say a rosary and they put it off until Sunday. That's not how it was in my day. No. I'd get a whipping so hard from Papi if I acted the way they do now. Spoilt. Plain spoilt like a bowl of beans three days old."

"Beans don't spoil in three days," said Doña Francisquita. "They go bad sooner, one day even."

"Yes. Yes. That's true. But in three days, beans are really bad. They stink. Like a child."

"Children don't smell, Adela. You say that because you don't know. You've never had any."

"No. Thank goodness."

"Don't say that. There's a child there. You're so hateful, Adela."

"Not as hateful as you when you yell at me."

"What? You started it. You exaggerate and make little Cipriana here feel bad just to impress Fela . . ."

Cipriana and Mama Fela looked at each other. Mama Fela recalled that this was the way a conversation always developed between the Lavadeux sisters. They expressed their varying opinions, sometimes choosing one side of an argument, only to disagree with the other. They could get into polite battles even in front of strangers and it always took a third party to mediate. And Mama Fela knew that Cipriana always acted differently around Doña Adela. Mama Fela knew from observation that not only did Adela speak in riddles, she could also be mean, particularly to children. Cipriana seemed to always hang her head in the company of Adela.

"Won't you come in and visit for a while, Doña Fela?" asked Doña Francisquita.

"No, no. You're on your way into town. I just thought I'd say hello, not stop you from what you were doing."

"Nonsense, comadre. Come over. You too, Cipriana." Francisquita took Fela's arm and guided her toward her house across from the rectory. Adela quickly followed and as Mama Fela knew, Cipriana was sure to stay at least three steps in back of her.

When they came to the steps of the little yellow house, Mama Fela exclaimed, "Pues, where are your flowers?" Adela groaned and Francisquita laughed. "Adela's mad because I told her we wouldn't plant anything if we couldn't compromise on which flowers to plant. She wanted the lilies from last year. They didn't come up this year and I told her it was because she forgot to water."

"No, Francisca, last fall you cut them down to the quick, bulbs and all. And besides, Papi always said never water in the winter or the plants will get a mildew."

"I did not. Well . . . maybe I did get a little carried away." Doña Francisquita looked at Fela. "Well, they looked ugly all dried out."

Mama Fela was struggling to stifle a laugh. "Ay, comadres. Stop it! I have some bulbs I can divide so that you can have your lilies, Adela. And Francisquita, I'll snip off some of my sweet pea. It stays green almost all winter long if you plant it in a protected spot. You two. You're unbelievable," Mama Fela said with a tinge of amusement hidden behind her mask of impatience. Adela looked at Fela sheepishly while Francisquita wore a slight smile.

They entered the house and Mama Fela's nostrils filled with the smell of vinegar. It was a familiar odor because Gilberto loved to pour vinegar on the freshly picked lettuce and tomatoes he grew in his garden in the summer and even in his *frijoles*. But this smell was a hundred times as strong. It made her feel faint.

"I woke up to that smell, too," Adela said. "Francisquita here was washing the windows before the crow had time to wake us up."

"The rooster, Adela. The rooster."

"Whatever, sister. All I'm trying to say is it stunk like a cat in an oven."

"A what?" Doña Francisquita looked to Fela. "Do you get that? I don't understand Adela, sometimes," she said chuckling.

Mama Fela noticed a look pass between the two sisters. She was beginning to think that she and her granddaughter should never have come. They hadn't yet been offered a place to sit and the vinegar fumes were overwhelming. She cleared her throat and said, "Well, comadres, I think it's time to go."

"Nonsense!" Francisquita's voice rang out. She grabbed Mama Fela's and Cipriana's hands and whisked them into the kitchen. "Sit. Let's have some refreshments." Francisquita gently pushed Cipriana into a chair and patted the top of her head. "I just made some biscuits for supper last night and I've been saving a special jar of jelly I just bought from Don Cornelio last fall."

"He has new jelly now," chimed in Cipriana. "We just had cherries at Doña Beatríz's."

"Cipriana!" Mama Fela scolded. "That's not polite."

"No, no, Fela. That's quite all right. Cipriana was just stating a fact. But Cipriana, I have to tell you Don Cornelio told me that this jar was from his best crop yet. You'll have to tell me how this compares to the cherries you ate this morning, all right?"

Cipriana nodded, smiling.

"Excuse me for a moment while I start the coffee. Cipriana, what would you like? Some milk?"

"No thank you, Doña Francisquita. I'd like some coffee, please."

"Coffee! You're drinking coffee now! ¡Dios mío!" Doña Francisquita looked at Mama Fela. "Is that all right, comadre?"

Mama Fela nodded, smiling. "We drink it all the time, Francisquita. I've taught her my bad habits."

Doña Francisquita turned to fetch water for the coffee.

"Francisquita." Mama Fela cleared her throat. "But may I have a glass of water? My mouth is dry." Mama Fela wiped her brow with the sleeve of her dress. "And do you have anything to fan myself with, comadre? It's hot in here, isn't it?" Mama Fela waved her hand in front of her face.

"Ay, Fela, are you all right?"

"Sí, sí. I'm just thirsty."

"You look pale, Fela," Francisquita said, handing her a black fan. "Let's get you outside where there's a little breeze at least." Francisquita waved Adela over. "Adela, help me here. Fela's not feeling well."

Adela took one arm and Francisquita the other. Mama Fela gasped for breath. That vinegar smell was suffocating her. She had to get out of this house, quickly. With the help of her comadres, she made it to the covered porch and dropped her body into a chair that was weather-beaten and faded.

"Quick, Adela. Get Fela some water."

Without a word, Adela slipped into the kitchen. Soon she emerged and handed Mama Fela a glass that felt cool to her touch. Mama Fela sipped it slowly and then she touched her cheeks, one at a time, to the cool glass. Oh, it felt like heaven against her clammy flesh! The fresh air was a godsend. She breathed heavily in and out. The vinegar odor was beginning to dissipate. She exhaled deeply one more time as if she were pushing the poison from her nostrils. And three pairs of eyes were staring at her in anticipation.

Looking up at the Lavadeux sisters, Mama Fela sighed deeply. "I'm all right, comadres. Thank you." Mama Fela breathed in more fresh air. "And Cipriana . . ." Mama Fela took her wide-eyed granddaughter into her lap. "Don't worry, mi'ja, I'm fine now. You're too young to worry so much."

"Mama Fela, what's wrong?"

"I don't really know, 'jita. But I'm fine now."

"What do you say we bring our coffee out here and enjoy the fresh air, Fela?" Francisquita said.

"Ah, yes, comadre. That would be nice. How often do we get to have a picnic outdoors, Cipriana, no? Let Cipriana and me do something." Mama Fela began to lift herself out of the chair.

"Nonsense, comadre. You sit right down there again. Cipriana will help me, won't you, Cipriana?"

Cipriana nodded. "You'll be fine, Mama Fela?"

"Of course, 'jita. Go on, go on," she said, waving her hand impatiently at her granddaughter. Mama Fela could feel her granddaughter's concern but she didn't like people to feel sorry for her. She hated any undue fuss made over her. In fact, she liked to be in the background, always there but very quiet and still, observing and yet unobserved. This chair was perfect for her. Its beauty had faded away long ago but it was there when needed, making her comfortable in her misery.

Just as Francisquita and Cipriana were about to enter the house, Doña Adela was on her way out, holding a pastel yellow oilcloth folded several times over. "Here, Cipriana, why don't you cover the table. We don't want to eat como los trampes, sitting on our haunches, holding a tin plate in our lap."

"What are haunches, Doña Adela?" Cipriana asked.

Adela thought for a moment and then slapped her own buttocks. "Los foonies, Cipriana."

Francisquita gasped. "Adela, you shouldn't be teaching Cipriana those words."

"Why not, sister? Los foonies are los foonies. There's nothing wrong with that."

"You don't say foonies," Francisquita responded. "You say nalgas."

"Francisca, you can say nalgas. I say foonies. What's the difference?"

"The difference is that in polite company, you don't say foonies. Foonies isn't the proper word."

Mama Fela looked from one sister to the other and could not believe what she was hearing. She could not hold it in any longer. Erupting into laughter, she shook her head from side to side. "¡Comadres! Ay, comadres," she breathed in between outbursts of mirth. The two sisters gaped at Mama Fela. Then regarding each other, they too broke into hysterics. Cipriana watched in wonder.

"But . . . but the trampes my daddy feeds don't sit on their haunches! Daddy asks them to eat inside with us."

Mama Fela could feel the air turn cold on this early summer day. She turned from one sister to the other, trying to gauge their reaction, but neither sister returned her gaze. Instead, they were staring at Cipriana.

Finally, Adela broke the silence. "¡Válgame Dios! Your papi lets the trampes inside? But they're dirty. And dangerous. Just the other day I heard of one of those trampes in Las Vegas stabbing a railroad worker to death because he wouldn't let him sleep on the train. Does your mama really allow them inside?"

"Mama isn't there."

"Not there? What do you mean?"

"She works."

"Pues, sí, but who takes care of you then?"

"Daddy and Tía Cita."

"Hmm." Adela looked over at Fela. "Ooh, Fela! Did you bring your son up to let vagrants into his house?"

Mama Fela had to use every bit of self control not to allow the words that were flowing into her mind to escape from her lips. This was the first she had heard that her son was feeding the *trampes*. He was feeding them the food that should have been inside the stomachs of his children. Poor Cipriana, as skinny as *el tasajo de melón* and here was her father giving away the beans and potatoes that should have been hers. Mama Fela had never been so angry. Here was her son, practically un trampe himself, quitting one job after another. Making his wife work to put food on the table. Then giving the food away just like that to the americanos who didn't have anything better to do than to hop on train after train, looking for work. Ooh, she was mad. No, she was fuming. Not only at her son, but at herself.

All she could say to her comadres was, "Pues, sí. I guess I did."

An uncomfortable silence ensued until Francisquita muttered, "It's time we eat, wouldn't you say, comadres?"

Mama Fela nodded. "Good idea, Doña Francisquita," she said with energy animating her voice, grateful for the change in subject matter.

As Mama Fela spread the oilcloth across the rickety table, Francisquita, Adela, and Cipriana bustled in and out of the house, bringing chairs, plates, teacups, knives and spoons, napkins, a basket of biscuits, cream, sugar, a petite jar of preserves, and a pot of freshly brewed coffee to the table.

"Mama Fela, should we eat the pie now?" asked Cipriana.

"Of course, 'jita. Bring it so we can share with the sisters."

"Oh, no comadre," Francisquita said. "You save it to enjoy later. We have the biscuits and jelly now."

"Nonsense, Francisquita. Besides, you and Cipriana have to compare the taste of the cherries. Was last crop better than this one? Go, Cipriana, go get the pie."

Cipriana dashed inside, letting the screen door slam shut behind her.

"Ay, que muchacha," Doña Adela hissed under her breath but Mama Fela ignored her. Instead, she began to act as hostess, pouring everyone's cup full of coffee. Adela passed the biscuits and preserves while Francisquita laid out the utensils at each place setting. When Cipriana returned with the pie in hand, Mama Fela took it from her and began to slice generous portions for each with the butter knife. The crust was so flaky, even air could have sliced through it.

Mama Fela watched Cipriana from the corner of her eye. Whenever they had their coffee together, they followed a ritual, but today she hoped Cipriana would veer from that routine. She wanted her friends to know that she reared children properly. If she couldn't do it with her own children, at least she had a second chance with her granddaughter. As Cipriana placed two heaping teaspoonfuls of sugar and a bit of milk into her cup, then poured it from the cup to the saucer to cool, Mama Fela held her breath. Then, Mama Fela's stomach turned while she witnessed her granddaughter tearing her biscuit into pieces and dipping them into her coffee, spooning the sweet chunks into her mouth. When Cipriana looked up, Mama Fela frowned. In hopes that Cipriana would look to her for guidance as she often did, Fela placed her spoon on the table and her hands in her lap. "Cipriana," she whispered. "Not here. Not like that."

"Let her be, Fela. She's a child," Doña Francisquita said.

"Ooh, if Papi would have seen us do that, eating como los marranos, we would have gotten una patada right where it counts."

"In los foonies?" asked Cipriana expectantly.

There was silence. Mama Fela let her eyes fall to her plate. She couldn't give her dear friends eye contact for fear she would start laughing again. Inside, she shook, desperately holding back her amusement. But she knew Adela was probably ready to pounce on Cipriana.

"Children are supposed to be seen not have any hearing."

Francisquita began to chortle. "You mean *heard*, don't you? 'Children are supposed to be seen and not heard,' como los gringos say."

Mama Fela and Doña Francisquita broke into laughter again. Cipriana looked sheepishly at Adela. Doña Adela placed her napkin on the table and stood.

"I don't have to take this, sister. Excuse me, Doña Fela."

"No, no, no. Siéntese. Por favor, Doña Adela. I'm sorry. It was so funny. We couldn't help ourselves. Please, Adela, have some pie," Mama Fela begged, pushing a plate with the biggest piece toward her.

"Fela, I have had enough of my sister's teasing. If Papi had been here, he wouldn't have allowed it; no, I tell you. I was always Papi's favorite."

"You were not, Adela. I was. You were always complaining. Just like you are now."

Mama Fela sighed. She was growing tired of these arguments between the sisters. You never quite got used to their bickering even if you were as old as Mama Fela and had been their friend for nearly that many years.

Suddenly, as if her granddaughter could read her mind, Cipriana interrupted the squabble. Pointing across the way, she said, "Mama Fela, look, there's Tía Cita."

"Cita! What's she doing here?" Mama Fela strained to turn around.

"No, there. She's going into the rectory. ¡Tía! ¡Tía Cita!" Cipriana called.

"Shh, Cipriana, not so loud. The rectory? Por qué, the rectory?"

"Oh, yes," chimed in Doña Francisquita. "Didn't you know she was working for our Father O'Grady?"

Mama Fela frowned slightly. "No. Since when?"

"Oh, I don't know. Since when, sister? She's been cleaning for at least three months, I think."

"No, more like four or five," added Adela. "Since after Christmas."

Mama Fela fell silent as Cita made her way toward them. She wasn't sure how she felt about her daughter cleaning houses. It was fine to clean Graciela's house because she was family but when all the neighbors knew that her daughter cleaned houses for money and worst of all for the americanos, it didn't make Fela look good. She couldn't put her finger on it precisely, but it wasn't decent, somehow, even if Cita was cleaning for their Father O'Grady.

"Hello, everyone," Cita said with enthusiasm. "How are you, Doña Francisquita and Doña Adela?" she asked, standing in back of Mama Fela.

"Que hello ni hello. That's not a proper greeting, Cita," Mama Fela said without turning to face her daughter. Instead, she stared straight into the eyes of her neighbors. "Not only are these ladies your elders, but they are my friends. And Doña Adela, you're right about the children of today. They are something else."

"Mamá," Cita said, scooting into view of Fela and then squatting on her haunches. She lowered her voice. "I'm not a child."

"No? You're sitting like one—down on the ground, like Benny playing his marbles. Where are they anyway? The children? Did you leave them alone again?"

"Ay, Mamá, can't I ever please you?" Cita asked, standing once again. "What would you have me do—bring them with me to clean houses? You know very well that Solomón has them."

"Children can never please you. They're nothing but heartaches."

"Hmm. You sound like good company today, Mamá."

"Malcriada. Don't talk to me like that, especially in front of my comadres." Now Fela's voice was lowered.

"You started it, Mamá."

"And you never told me you were working for Father O'Grady."

"I didn't? It must have slipped my mind."

"Que slipped your mind ni slipped your mind. What does that mean? You're talking like los americanos now."

"It means I forgot. And besides, I don't have to tell you everything. Like I said, I'm not a child."

"Ooh, says she's no child pero she's not married yet. I was married and had babies of my own by the time I was your age, Cita." Under her breath, she added, "Bless their souls."

"You were different, Mamá. Times were different. We've talked about this before. Why do you have to bring it up here?"

"Pues, I don't know, Cita. Why do you have to work at Father O'Grady's?"

"You know I have to."

"Pues, that's the same reason I have to bring this up now. I can't hold it in anymore. Find a husband so you don't have to work for money like los ladies of the night."

"Now you're comparing me to the prostitutes! My god, Mamá!"

Mama Fela made the sign of the cross. "Don't use God's name in vain, Cita. You'll be punished."

"That's nonsense, Mamá. Besides, I've already been punished enough."

"You don't know real sorrow until you've had children of your own, Cita."

"And that's what you want for me? I don't believe it."

"Maybe, Cita . . . ," Francisquita interrupted, "you could be a nun. Wouldn't that be nice now? The bride of Jesus. You're too precious for any man here on earth anyway. God is the only one good enough for you."

"Thank you, Doña Francisquita. At least you think highly of me, unlike my own mamá."

Just as Mama Fela was about to respond, Adela joined the conversation. "Ooh, Cita, I think you should do whatever feels right for you. People will try to make up your mind for you and believe me many will try. No, as my papi would have said, you've just got to put your foot down. Make up your own mind."

Mama Fela cleared her throat, trying to get control of the conversation once again. She didn't like the direction it was taking; she didn't like her friends' interference. There was a time and place to take the advice of comadres, but concerning this particular topic, their advice was not wanted. In the silence, Mama Fela could hear her own breathing. Finally, she said, "Ay, comadres, I'm sorry you had to hear all this. My daughter and I will save this argument for another time and place."

Mama Fela felt Cita's hand on her shoulder. Slowly, she raised her own to meet Cita's touch. All the while, she smiled at Cipriana, sitting across from her.

"I better get to work," Cita said, slipping away.

"Yes, I think that's a good idea, Cita," Mama Fela said, dismissing her daughter. "Now, let's taste that jelly, comadres." Mama Fela took a biscuit and sliced it open. Slathering a heaping spoonful of jelly over its surface, she bit into it. "Mmm, que sabroso. I have to get your biscuit recipe, Doña Francisquita."

"Ooh, I just add a little of this, a little of that, Fela. Nothing to it really."

"And how's the pie? What did you decide, Cipriana? Last year had the better cherries or this year? Doña Francisquita, what's your opinion?"

Cipriana spooned a generous piece of pie into her mouth. When she was finished chewing, she licked the jelly off her bread. Mama Fela averted her eyes in embarrassment.

"I can't decide. I think I'm going to have to taste another bit of pie," said Francisquita. "What do you think, Cipriana?"

"Oh, I can't make up my mind either. First, I think it's the pie. Then I think the jelly. Mama Fela, may I try one more piece and a little bit more jelly so I can say for sure?"

"But Cipriana, you're going to get a stomach pain with all those sweets."

"No, Mama Fela. I won't. I have a strong stomach."

"Ooh, Fela, in my day, we didn't have enough to eat, much less have a second serving," Adela said. "My papi would have eaten us alive had we asked. No, I don't believe in children getting everything they want."

"Adela, you mean Papi would have skinned you alive, don't you?" Francisquita asked. "I don't think you would have tasted very good, all skin and bones."

"And all he would have had to do was sprinkle a little salt and pepper on you and you would have tasted like a nice plump butt roast. Stuff in a few garlic cloves and mmm, all done."

"Ay, Adela, that's not very nice!" Mama Fela said in amazement. "Come, come you two, we're talking about cherries here."

"Still, comadre, I wouldn't let Cipriana have any more," Adela said. "She's going to have a sweet tooth no one can cure."

"No, Adela," Francisquita replied. "Cipriana's a big girl. Like you said, I think she can make up her own mind when she's had too much. So, Cipriana, which is the better year?" Francisquita asked, ignoring her sister. "The jelly from last year or the pie from this season?"

"I'm not sure, Doña Francisquita. What do you think?"

Francisquita took a bite and swirled it around in her mouth. Mama Fela looked away, feeling her stomach turn. Francisquita took a sip of her coffee and swished it around in her mouth. Fela could faintly hear the sloshing sound back and forth, up and down.

"Ay, Cipriana, I have to say, I think Don Cornelio told a fib. I think this year is even better. That pie is better than good. And I think, I just might need to have another piece."

"Sister! Another piece!"

"Mama Fela, if Doña Francisquita has another, why can't I?"

"Because after a while," Doña Adela chimed in, "you'll be as plump as Francisca. Now is that what you want, Cipriana?"

Cipriana nodded, very sure of herself. "Oh yes. Doña Francisquita has dimples in her elbows and hands just like Shirley Temple."

Doña Adela looked surprised. "Shirley Temple? ¿Pues, quien es Shirley Temple? Do you want your abuela to be able to cook you up if these times get any worse, Cipriana? One of these days, I won't be surprised if Fela invites us over for some of her sweet granddaughter. Ate so much, her abuela had to cook her up because she was eating her out of house and home."

"Adela! That's cruel," Francisquita said, glaring at her sister across the table.

Quietly, Mama Fela said, "Cipriana, it's your pie. Have another slice, if you're not too full."

"Well!" Adela said, standing abruptly, her napkin fluttering to the ground.

This time, Mama Fela made no effort to convince her comadre to stay. She simply smiled at her granddaughter. Adela slammed the screen door behind her as she stormed inside. Francisquita tried to make polite conversation, excusing her sister's actions, but Fela was thinking of other things. She smiled and nodded her head but she comprehended nothing of what Francisquita had to say. Instead, she watched her granddaughter anxiously until she had spooned the last bit of pie into her bulging mouth.

"Pues, it's time we go, comadre." Mama Fela pushed herself up out of the too-comfortable chair. Her leg was asleep, and a pain shot through it when she put her weight down. She had overstayed her welcome this time and allowed her comadres to see a side of her that was reserved for her children only. She was not proud of her behavior and she wanted to forget it as soon as possible.

"The umbrella, 'jita."

"Where is it, Mama Fela?"

Mama Fela paused. She and her granddaughter looked at each other. Cipriana's eyes went wide. And Mama Fela knew they had left it inside— inside where Doña Adela was probably not in good humor. She couldn't send Cipriana into Adela's lair. Not now. She gave her head a little shake to let Cipriana know she was relieved of that responsibility. Cipriana jumped down the stone steps.

"Pues, we'll get it another time, comadre. Thank you for your hospitality," she said, embracing Francisquita. "I'll get you that sweet pea soon."

Cipriana was already skipping ahead. Mama Fela let her go, holding her own hand in front of her eyes to shade them from the rays of the midday sun. Indeed, the summer would be hot. She could feel it in her bones.

❧

CHAPTER EIGHT

R A N C H E R A S

Cipriana didn't hate Sundays anymore, which was a good thing because it meant now she wasn't going to the devil. Doña Adela had told her she would, because it was a sin to hate any day of the week, especially Sundays, when God looked at all His work and smiled with pride. She said if Cipriana didn't like Sundays, she was a *malcriada*, thumbing her nose at all the work God did. But Cipriana never thumbed her nose at anyone, and even if she did, it sure wouldn't be God.

Cipriana used to hate Sundays because it was the day when her mother would go back to school, miles away, leaving Cipriana and her father and brother to fend for themselves. The lingering evidence of Graciela's pretty smell would be covered up with aromas of delicious cooking that were meant to hide her going away: fresh bread just come out of the oven; *cecinitas*, pan-fried until they were toasted; and once, even a golden layer cake speckled with sweet strawberries amid waves of whipped cream frosting. But to Cipriana, the delicious turned rotten once her mother left. Even the day Graciela brought home a chicken for Sunday dinner and fried up the pieces until they were golden and crisp, Cipriana couldn't eat because the smell reminded her that her mother would soon be gone again.

· Cipriana stopped hating Sundays the day that her mother surprised her with the news that, along with her brother and baby sister, she would be accompanying Graciela to her school. Cipriana had already started at her own school just days before, but now that her father was busy working and her Tía Cita had too many kids to take care of, Graciela decided that she was going to be Cipriana's teacher and her mama all in one. They would be going to her new school in Sena.

They left after supper. Cipriana didn't mind saying bye to her father because he would come visit them in a few Saturdays. Her brother threw up all the way, so they had to keep stopping so Cipriana's mother could clean it up. It was funny the way a little sound came out of her brother's mouth like a burp before a puddle of slimy liquid came out of his mouth. It was like melted ice cream only it didn't smell so good. If Cipriana's father had been there, he would have called Pablito a cochino, but her mother just stopped the car, turned around, and wiped it up like nothing had happened. After the first incident, Graciela changed Pablito's shirt and told him to lie down in back with his eyes closed. When it happened again, she told Cipriana to let Pablito sit up in front, where Cipriana longed to sit. It was always her mother's seat when her father drove. Now, Cipriana hated Pablito because he was ruining the trip. Not only was he making the car stink, but he had snatched Cipriana's long-awaited seat. Despite the dust of the road, Cipriana begged to be allowed to roll down the windows.

Graciela placed the baby in back with Cipriana so that Pablo could have lots of room up in front. Cipriana watched as her mother instructed her brother to look straight ahead at the road in front of them, and Cipriana did the same, thinking her mother was showing her brother something special. All Cipriana could see was a long dusty road that seemed to go on forever, swallowing them up as they progressed. Finally, with her eyes closed, Cipriana wished for two things: for her mama to like her better than her brother and to get her seat back. She squeezed her eyes shut and scrunched her hands together until they felt numb, praying to God.

When Pablo vomited all over the front seat again, Cipriana's mother made a retching sound too. Before she attempted to clean him up, she stopped the car, swung open the door, and stuck her legs out. Her hands were on her knees and her head was bent like she was Jesus on the cross. "You all right, Mama?" Cipriana asked, jumping up on top of the seat and leaning over into the front. When her mother nodded without saying anything, Cipriana frowned at her brother like she was his mama and he had just done something terrible. He started to cry like a baby and then Cipriana's baby sister started up too. Graciela turned around then and comforted them like they were the only precious babies in the world, shushing them in a feather-like voice, holding them like they were puppies. Cipriana wanted to shut them both up right then and there.

By the time they got to Sena, it was already dark. Pablo was asleep just like the baby but Cipriana was wide awake, counting the number of hairpins in back of her mother's head and attuned to even the slightest sound. At first a funny noise emanating from her mother's throat seemed to predict an onslaught of vomit but when nothing shot from her mother's mouth, she realized her mother was just clearing her throat. Graciela told Cipriana that she must help find Don Isá's house, the place where they would stay. Her eyes were giving out, she said, and Cipriana was the only one who could help. Cipriana stood up then, watching for the white house with a tin roof and a blue mailbox, the house of Tío's friend.

Cipriana's mother put the baby and Pablo to bed immediately. Cipriana begged to stay up, knowing there would be some leniency tonight because it was the end of a special day, like Christmas. She was sleepy but she had to show her mama that she wasn't a baby anymore like Pablito and her sister. Reminding her mother that her eyes were grown-up eyes because she had found Don Isá's house, she convinced a smiling Graciela to let her follow her to the kitchen table where the grown-ups were gathered.

Don Isá's wife, Doña Maclovia, made coffee and put out a plate of tortillas. Cipriana didn't yet know what to make of their hosts but she knew Mama Fela would approve of Doña Maclovia immediately, if only because she knew how to set a fine table for guests. Doña Maclovia was plump like a *bolillo*, made with care and the best ingredients, allowed to rise for just the right amount of time. She wasn't like a regular biscuit, a *galleta de rebilión*, as her Mama Fela would call it, tasty but with knobs and rough spots, made in a hurry. Her pudginess and her smile made her look just like what Cipriana thought a grandma should look like according to books and movies. Only she wasn't old. She was the age in between mamas and grandmothers, not really old but getting there. One thing Cipriana knew for sure, Doña Maclovia liked to smile and laugh and that alone made her want to stick to Doña Maclovia like gum on a shoe. She didn't know adults could laugh so much.

"Cipriana, would you like a little milk in your coffee?" Doña Maclovia asked.

Cipriana beamed, nodding her head. Doña Maclovia was treating her like an adult, asking her preferences the same way Mama Fela would ask her comadres for theirs when they visited. Cipriana liked Doña Maclovia more and more every minute.

Almost purely by reflex, Graciela blocked Cipriana's cup with her hand and asked quietly, as if she were almost too embarrassed to ask the question, "May I ask if it's canned or fresh, Doña Maclovia?"

"Fresh," Doña Maclovia said with what seemed to Cipriana to be great pride.

"I think Cipriana better have sugar then, Doña Maclovia," Graciela said quietly. "No milk," she added with an almost pained expression on her face.

"Ay, Graciela. Sugar and no milk? Sounds like something I'd feed my neighbor's sick chickies. ¿Por qué?"

Graciela glanced around the table. "I was reading that's how children get el tis," she said slowly. With more confidence, she added, "From fresh cow's milk."

"¿No me digas? From milk?"

Graciela nodded. "Fresh, not canned."

"And all this time, I was buying fresh, thinking I was . . . doing good. Doing the best for him," she said, indicating Don Isá. Sitting down, Doña Maclovia offered Cipriana the sugar bowl.

An opportunity like this didn't come around very often: unlimited permission from her mother and a full sugar bowl. Cipriana dumped three heaping teaspoons of sugar into her coffee before her mother gave her a look of disapproval and she reluctantly passed the bowl back to Doña Maclovia. At home, her mother rarely allowed coffee, much less adulterated with sugar. When Doña Maclovia tore her tortilla into little pieces and dunked them into her coffee, Cipriana turned to her mother and said, "Just like Mama Fela." Graciela smiled but it was only a half smile, Cipriana thought, the kind made when you don't really feel happy but you smile anyway to make other people feel happy. Cipriana started to dip a tortilla into her coffee but Graciela placed a gentle hand over Cipriana's and Cipriana knew her mother was telling her to stop. Graciela smiled.

Don Isá was such a skinny man that he had elbows sticking out of his skin like Cipriana, who wondered if he prayed for pudgy arms with dimples for knuckles like she did. His long beard looked like it needed a thorough washing, especially after he coughed. When he took his handkerchief away from his mouth, there were small drops of spit, some clear and some red. Cipriana went on eating her tortilla but her mother stopped.

In the front room on a mattress that smelled of urine, Cipriana and Graciela tried to sleep without success. They lay on the mattress all night, staring up at the ceiling and listening to all the coughing going on in the next room. Cipriana's brother slept undisturbed as he always did but her baby sister cried all night, keeping Cipriana and her mother up in a futile attempt to comfort her. Pulling the baby from her cradle and playing little games with her had always worked to lull her to sleep. "Lansa, lansa, pica la pansa," they sang in unison, poking the baby's belly button and making her smile. Graciela had never joined in on the ditty. It was usually Cipriana and her father who sang the baby to sleep. But now, Cipriana could tell her mother was trying to cover up Don Isá's terrible sounds with her own pretty voice for the baby's sake and for Cipriana's.

"Mama, why does Don Isá cough so much?"

"He's sick, 'jita," she said.

"Really sick, Mama, or just a little?"

"I don't know, Cipriana."

"What's the red stuff that he gets on his beard when he coughs?"

"Blood, 'jita."

"Blood?"

Cipriana's mother didn't answer. "Mama?"

"Yes, 'jita. Blood."

For the first time that day, Cipriana's stomach turned somersaults. She longed to reach for her mother and to touch her face the same way she used to when she was as small as Pablito but she hesitated, knowing she was much too old for that kind of nonsense.

The next morning, Cipriana's mother looked awful, with dark circles around her eyes because she had hardly slept. Cipriana was particularly obedient, doing everything Graciela told her to do, only twice as fast. It was the first day of school and Cipriana knew how much her mother loved that day. Cipriana wanted to make her mother proud that she brought her children with her. She wanted to show Graciela that they could accompany her to school all the time.

When they left for school, Don Isá was still coughing. His cough seemed to follow Cipriana wherever she went, as persistent as her little brother when she most craved solitude. They had to walk a long way to the schoolhouse along a little dirt road. Even though it was early, the day was already hot because there weren't any trees to provide shade, only boxy piñons with their claw-like needles. Cipriana felt as if the sun and the sky would swallow them up any minute if Don Isá's cough didn't chase them away first.

As they approached the little school, Cipriana could see children out in the yard.

"Mama, where do they all come from? There aren't any houses."

"From the nearby ranches, 'jita."

"But I didn't see any ranches, Mama."

"Not between here and Don Isá's, 'jita. Farther out."

"We didn't see any last night, Mama."

"No, but they're hard to see in the dark, Cipriana. They don't have any lights like some houses do in Santa Lucía."

Just then, a child ran up to them, yelling, "Teacher, teacher! A fight, a fight!"

Graciela placed the baby in Cipriana's arms. "Watch Pablito for me, Cipriana," she called as she ran off with the boy who had alerted her to the activity in the school yard. Cipriana followed as best she could, maneuvering the baby in her arms so that she could see over the swelling blankets and yelling at Pablito to hurry. She wanted to see what was happening before her mother stopped it.

As she arrived on the scene, she heard the crowd of screaming children. Drawing nearer, she could make out distinct voices, rooting for one side or the other. Her mother was fighting her way into the throng, commanding the shrieking children to quiet down and move aside. Even on tiptoes, Cipriana couldn't see anything worth seeing. Suddenly it was dead quiet.

The children parted like the Red Sea and Graciela emerged, grasping the collar of a girl with stringy black hair and a face as white as a ball of masa. The girl's grin seemed out of place, and Cipriana thought she looked scary. With the other hand, Graciela held onto a little boy whose nose was bleeding profusely. Cipriana couldn't help thinking of Don Isá. Graciela spoke in her teacher voice, which was different from her mama voice, and for a minute, Cipriana forgot she was her mother too. Ushering the children inside, she told them she would not tolerate any of this fighting nonsense. Cipriana hoped they would understand her mother's big teacher words, but even if they did not, Cipriana was sure they would understand her teacher eye, a look she herself tried to avoid at all costs.

Cipriana wanted to blend in with the other students to avoid her mother's mood, but she was afraid to go into a classroom that contained that smiling masa girl. Besides, Graciela was more her mother than her teacher at the moment, even though Cipriana longed for her to be both. Following her mother to the water bucket just outside the entrance to the country schoolhouse, Cipriana watched as she cleaned up the little boy and inquired into the circumstances surrounding the fight. In barely a whisper, the boy confided that he was beaten up because he wouldn't get "the big girl" a cup of water. Cipriana had been right. The big girl was someone to avoid.

A chorus of shushing filled the schoolhouse as soon as they entered, and soon it was completely quiet. Distracted by the new faces and the stares, Cipriana had a hard time listening to her mother's whispered instructions to take a seat in back, to lay her sister down, and to give her brother a drink of water. When her mother took her place in front of the classroom, introduced herself, and wrote her name on the blackboard, Cipriana breathed a sigh of relief.

Graciela called attendance while Cipriana observed all the activity. She had never had the chance to be an onlooker before and she liked the feeling it gave her. It was like being a grown-up. The children were all ages, from the tiniest girl picking her nose to the strapping boy who towered over Graciela and seemed out of place in a schoolroom. While her mother grouped the children by their ability to read aloud and do arithmetic rather than by their ages, Cipriana looked after her brother and sister, making sure they didn't bother their mother at work. Cipriana was sure that they only knew Graciela as a mama and not as a teacher like she did, so she took it upon herself to put a stop to their untimely interruptions. Besides, they didn't even know what school was.

By the time recess rolled around, Cipriana was a little tired of her new job. She asked her mother if she could go outside like the other children. Graciela nodded absentmindedly, paying little attention to Cipriana, occupied instead with her attendance sheet. Cipriana asked who would take care of her brother and sister, but Graciela didn't reply. She just nodded her head and waved her hand at Cipriana, studying the papers on her desk. Certain that her mother didn't need her, Cipriana ran out of the little schoolroom, glad to stretch her legs and not have to look after anyone else. Her happiness didn't last for long. She ran right into the big girl who had been in the morning fight.

"What's your name?" the girl asked Cipriana in a friendly voice.

"Cipriana. What's yours?" she asked, hesitating slightly.

"Stella. But I ask the questions around here, Cipriana. You got that?"

Cipriana nodded.

"Your mama's an easy one, isn't she? I know I'm going to be able to get away with a lot with her. She didn't punish me at all this morning."

"She pulled you by the collar."

"Did I say you could talk?"

Cipriana shook her head no.

"Are you smart, teacher's daughter?"

Cipriana nodded.

"Does you mama ever spank you?"

Cipriana shook her head. "But, my daddy . . ."

"Just yes or no."

"No."

"See, I knew it. Your mama's one of those scaredy-cat teachers, and before long, I'll be boss. But, if you tell her that, your face will be bloodied up just like that fregado this morning."

"You speak Spanish?" Cipriana asked.

"Yeah, what's it to you?"

"But, but you're . . ."

"What? Just because I'm not a Mexican . . . hey, did I say you could ask questions?"

"No, but . . ."

"Go on now. I'm tired of talking to you."

Cipriana was quickly tiring of the conversation herself, but she hesitated to say so. Somehow she felt that she wanted to check on her mother right this moment to make sure she was fine. Or maybe she just didn't feel like playing outside anymore. Either way, she started back inside, running right into her mother, who was holding the bell in her hand.

"Mama, can I ask you something?"

"Wait, just a minute, dear."

Cipriana's antennae rose. Her mother called her "dear" instead of "'jita." She was using her English voice now, her teacher voice, and Cipriana was just another one of her students.

"But, Mama . . ."

"Later, dear."

After school, Cipriana craved her mother's full attention. She had been wondering all afternoon how to tell her mother what she had been thinking. As they walked back to Don Isá's, Cipriana struggled with Pablito, trying to make him keep up while she tried to talk to her mother over the baby's erratic cries. Finally, when a moment's peace emerged out of the confusion, Cipriana said, "Mama, I think she needs a spanking."

"Who, dear?"

"Stella. She beat up that little boy pretty bad."

"Yes she did."

"Well, aren't you going to do anything about it?"

"What do you think I should do, 'jita?"

"Spank her. Like I said."

Graciela looked at Cipriana and smiled. "I'll take that into consideration, Cipriana."

"No, Mama," Cipriana pleaded now, turning toward her mother.

"You've got to do it. You've just got to."

Graciela stopped walking then and bent down like she often did in class. "Whatever's gotten into you, Cipriana? Why do you feel so strongly about Stella?"

"I don't like her, Mama."

"That doesn't mean she deserves a spanking, Cipriana."

"But Mama, she's dumb."

"Cipriana!"

"Well, she is. She's a lot older than me and I read way better than she does."

"That may be so, Cipriana, but that doesn't mean she should get a spanking."

"I think she should, Mama. She's dumb and she's mean."

"All right, now. That's enough, Cipriana." Graciela's face was serious again, as if she was double teacher and mother. Cipriana knew her mother had never spanked her or her brother and for a moment, Cipriana thought maybe Stella was right about her mother being a scaredy-cat. But she had never heard of a grown-up being scared of kids. And besides, when Cipriana did something bad, Cipriana knew all too well that her mother's look was a lot worse than if she had just spanked her in the first place.

Cipriana wanted to forget all about Don Isá's cough, so she asked Doña Maclovia if she could help her make tortillas. Doña Maclovia took out a rolling pin for Cipriana, who stood on a chair at the table, helping her as best she could. The ones Cipriana made were never round and they started to get holes in them. Picking the dough up, she showed it to Doña Maclovia. The holes stretched bigger as she held it up.

"I can't do it, Señora. Mine are ugly."

"No, no, 'jita." She took the tortilla from Cipriana and held it to the light. Cipriana dreaded the thought that she was going to scold her for wasting the dough. Instead, she smiled. "Looks to me like my bloomers."

Doña Maclovia's laugh made Cipriana laugh. It wasn't a little giggle. It was more like Cipriana's father's laugh, deep and gurgling like she was gulping down a whole can of Carnation milk. Cipriana made more tortillas then, holding them up after they were rolled out. "Look, Doña Maclovia.

Whose bloomers are these?"

"'Jita," she said after thinking a while. "Now those are no lady's bloomers. Those have to be los b.b.d.s de tu papá."

At first Cipriana couldn't help laughing, mostly because Doña Maclovia's laugh was so contagious. But then she started to wonder if she should be laughing so hard. She wasn't sure if it was right to be thinking about her daddy's underthings.

The next day, Graciela took an old catalog to school. She told Cipriana's group to use their reading and their number skills to make out a catalog order. Leaving them to work independently, Graciela withdrew to check on another group. Not quite understanding the assignment but too embarrassed to ask, Cipriana set about cutting out the catalog's paper ladies instead, and the other children followed her lead. By the time Graciela returned to Cipriana's group, Cipriana had quite a pile accumulated. Looking up and holding her stack in the air, she exclaimed, "Look, Mama, look what we did!"

To Cipriana's surprise, her mother only frowned. "Dear," Graciela said under her breath in a tone that Cipriana had begun to recognize. It was her icy English voice that made her sound far away, like a stranger who didn't recognize her own daughter. "Paper dolls are for recess. You know better than that," she said, clucking her tongue like a castanet. The admonition could only mean one thing: Cipriana knew her mother was ashamed of her, ashamed to be her mother. Graciela turned her back, leaving Cipriana relieved not to have to look at her mother straight in the face. Even if she had wanted to, she wouldn't have been able to.

All the children in Cipriana's group were staring. Cipriana couldn't understand why her mother failed to get angry at them as well. They were as guilty as she was. Cipriana could feel a pair of eyes boring into her. When she turned, Stella, the big girl, flashed a mean look of satisfaction, her mouth hanging open, her teeth huge. Cipriana thought they needed a dip in lye.

Stella mouthed a word Cipriana knew was bad, pointing to Graciela. Once, Cipriana had said the word and her father gave her a whipping so bad, she would never say it again. Even though Cipriana was angry with her mother, she couldn't stand the thought of Stella calling her unmentionable names behind her back. She hated the very sight of Stella. Wouldn't it be nice if Stella's eyes and ears and teeth just disappeared into a blob of masa that Cipriana could roll into anything she wanted her to be? Wouldn't it be nice if she just disappeared totally?

Cipriana snapped out of her fantasy when Graciela clapped her hands, telling everyone to take their seats. Cipriana could tell by her mother's demeanor that she had something important to say so she vowed to listen closely so that Graciela could be proud of her again, knowing that her daughter had learned her lesson and knew how to pay attention.

"Tomorrow, some ladies will be coming to school to visit us," Graciela said. "They're called nurses. Nodrizas. Anyone know what a nurse is?"

"Mama, I know," Cipriana said, raising her hand, eager to please. From out of nowhere, Cipriana heard someone call out, "Lambe!" Knowing it had to be Stella, Cipriana stared her straight in the eye, only to be greeted by a tongue stuck boldly out at her.

"Yes, what are they, Cipriana?" Graciela asked in a voice that told Cipriana that her mother's thoughts were far away.

"They help you when you're sick," Cipriana said with confidence.

"Nadie está enferma," someone shouted in response.

"Ramón is," someone else said, laughing. Everyone looked at the boy whom Stella had beaten up.

Graciela ignored the chatter and said, "The nurses will be doing some tests. Not the usual kind like you're used to in school," she added.

"What kind then, Mrs. Romero?"

"They'll be checking to see that all of us are healthy. That no one has a sickness called tuberculosis."

"Tis?"

"That's right. Some people call it tis."

"Mi tío had it real bad. He died."

"I'm sorry, Elicio. Did your tío live with you?"

"Yes, Mrs. Romero. He died on my mama's bed."

Graciela took out a piece of paper from her desk and wrote something.

She continued to ask questions, writing the responses down until she called recess.

When Cipriana went outside, Stella was waiting by the door.

"I've been waiting for you, teacher's daughter. What's your name again? I forgot."

"Cipriana," she said, wondering what Stella was going to do to her.

"Cipriana, you must be smart, right? Your mama's a teacher."

Cipriana nodded. "You asked me that the other day, Stella," she said softly, afraid she was treading on dangerous ground.

"So? You think I can't ask questions more than once? I can do whatever I want."

Cipriana shrugged and started to go back inside. She would let this girl do whatever she wished.

"Look at the smart girl, too scared to talk to me!"

"I'm not scared," Cipriana said, turning toward her tormentor. "It's just that you're so dumb, I don't like being around you."

"Dumb! Who you calling dumb? I know things you'll never know. You're just a baby."

"I'm not a baby. And you're . . . you're just a big dumb girl who picks on little kids."

"Dumb! Ha! I bet I know why those nurses are coming tomorrow and you don't."

"So? Mama said they're coming to see if we have el tis."

"Do you know what they're going to do?"

"Give us tests, that's what."

"Yeah, that's what your mother said but I know better. Los van a ver la panocha."

"La panocha? What's that?"

Stella laughed. By this time, a bunch of kids had gathered.

"You don't know what la panocha is? You dumb kid. You're so dumb and your mother's the teacher. Boy are we in trouble."

"I do too. I know what it is."

"What is it, then?"

"It's pudding . . . pudding you eat during Lent."

"Ha ha ha ha! Pudding? See, you are a baby. And you're the one who's dumb."

"I am not."

"Aha. So, if you're not dumb, then what else does it mean?"

"I'm not going to tell you. You already know, so why should I tell you?"

"So you can prove you're not a baby. You go tell your mama right now what I said. Tell her why the nurses are coming."

"No. Mama already knows why they're coming. I don't have to tell her. Besides, I don't do everything you say."

"Did you hear that, girls?" she yelled to the children who were making a circle around them. "Cipriana doesn't do what I say. That's not very smart, now, is it? That's not very smart."

"Stella!" It was Cipriana's mother, using her teacher voice and her teacher eye. "Recess is over. Let's all go back inside, children. Now!" Cipriana was never so glad to see the look her mother gave them.

The afternoon went by slowly. The hair on Cipriana's arm seemed to grow faster than time went by. She could almost see each strand bristling upward as she waited for the end of the school day. Every time Cipriana looked up from her arm or her paper, Stella was looking at her and winking. She quickly trained her eyes downward, concentrating on her assignment, but she couldn't figure out how to borrow from the zero. All she could think about was Stella.

That night when they were eating supper, Cipriana blurted out the question she had been waiting all afternoon to ask her mother.

"Mama, ¿que es la panocha?"

"¿La panocha?" Graciela asked. "What do you mean, Cipriana?"

"Well, you said the nurses were coming, right?"

"Yes."

"And Stella said they were coming so they could look at la panocha."

As soon as she said it, Cipriana knew something was wrong. Her mother coughed and closed her eyes like she had done just prior to fights with Cipriana's father. When Graciela opened them, she gave Cipriana her teacher eye, that "I'm not going to spank you even though I should" look. Sitting across from her, Cipriana could see a line growing between her mother's eyebrows. "¡Cállate!" Graciela hissed under her breath.

Don Isá started his coughing too. Cipriana guessed he was playing follow-the-leader with her mother, only it wasn't just one cough. He couldn't stop. It sounded like he was choking, but he was smiling too. His face went red, then purple. Pretty soon, Cipriana figured out the choke was a laugh that went on and on forever. And then he started coughing again but this time he spit up blood. Lots of it. Into his hand and onto his plate. His beans looked like they had red chile on them, except Doña Maclovia hadn't cooked red chile.

Graciela stood up and slapped Don Isá on the back. She gave him a kitchen towel to hold at his mouth. Looking scared, Doña Maclovia didn't move. Her mouth was wide open, wide enough for flies to wander in, probably wide enough even for a mouse to sneak in. Pretty soon, Don Isá put out his hand.

"'Stoy bien," he said. "Estoy bien."

Those words made Doña Maclovia stand up then. With the corner of the kitchen towel, she wiped his eyes.

"You're crying, hombre. ¿Que pasó?"

"No, no," he said, wiping his eyes with the back of his hand. "All that coughing makes me feel weak. I need new shortes. Maybe a bath," he said, trying to stand up.

Cipriana helped him to his feet. She couldn't understand why a man his age could act like a baby, spitting up and wetting his pants just like a child. Grown-ups weren't supposed to act like that.

Doña Maclovia took him to the next room. Trailing behind them, Cipriana and Graciela went too. Whispering, Graciela told Cipriana to go to bed and take her brother and sister along. For once, Cipriana didn't ask any questions.

When morning finally arrived, Cipriana left for school before her mother. She knew she had to tell Stella something and she had to do it before her mother got there. All night long, she had thought about what she was going to tell the big girl today and now she knew. She had heard her father use the word before and she finally convinced herself that because it was not a swear word, she could use it.

When she got to the school yard, she didn't see Stella or anybody else so she sat on the school steps, waiting. A few children arrived in the backs of their daddies' wagons. It seemed like no one had cars around here, so Cipriana felt rich even though their car was old and beat-up. Finally, Stella came, walking alone. Cipriana stood, waiting with nervous anticipation. When Stella saw Cipriana, she grinned. The expression was not a normal smile. Rather, it made Cipriana feel jittery inside, the way she felt when she had a terrible fever. On the outside, she was burning up, but on the inside, she felt like she had been dunked into a tub of ice-cold water in the middle of a winter morning. It took Stella forever to reach Cipriana, who counted the girl's steps. As Stella drew nearer, Cipriana hoped she could avoid peeing in her pants like Don Isá. Finally, Cipriana's mouth went dry at the prospect of fighting with the big girl.

"So, did you tell your mama what I said, baby?"

Cipriana didn't hear what Stella said. All she knew was that she had something to say to her. With a gasp of breath, she blurted, "Ranchera!"

Stella's smile disappeared. "What? What did you call me?"

"I said you're a ranchera." With more confidence, Cipriana added, "Nothing but a ranchera mostrenca."

"Why you . . ."

Before she knew what was happening, Cipriana winced in pain as she felt a fist make contact with her face. And then for a brief moment, she felt grit inside her mouth before her world went black.

The next morning Cipriana walked to school behind her mother, trailing at a safe distance. She was too ashamed to meet her gaze, too afraid of what she would say. Last night Graciela had cleaned Cipriana's cuts for the third time that day. She had taken Cipriana back to Doña Maclovia's and cleaned her up after the fight first occurred, and then again at lunch, and at night. During these sessions, Graciela never smiled. She never said a word to Cipriana, much less take her in her arms to comfort her. It was evident to Cipriana that her mother blamed her rather than Stella. She was a teacher's daughter and should know better.

Suddenly, Cipriana's mother slowed her pace. "¿Qué es esto?" she asked, more to herself than to Cipriana, but Cipriana had heard.

Peeking around Graciela toward the school yard, Cipriana could see two wagons and a shiny car parked by the school. Children were milling about instead of playing their usual morning game of baseball or kick-the-can. Immediately, Cipriana knew this was not going to be an ordinary day.

As the two approached, a child turned and saw them. "Teacher!" he called out, running toward them. "Some men are waiting for you."

At the door, Stella stood waiting. She had her back to the door and one foot up behind her. Cipriana felt like telling her she shouldn't be doing that because for one thing, she would get the door dirty and for another, she could fall back and crack her head open if someone opened it. On second thought, she decided not to say anything.

"My papa wants to talk to you," Stella said, smiling, looking straight at Graciela. "He's called a meeting of the directors and he's the president."

Cipriana felt a sudden urge to whisper a warning to her mother. *Don't go*, she wanted to say. *Stay here with me*, she felt like pleading. But before Cipriana could say anything, her mother was carefully laying the baby's bassinet at her feet and placing Pablito's hand in hers. "Stay here, Cipriana," her mother told her as she entered the school, closing the door behind her.

Quickly busying herself with the baby's blankets, Cipriana tried to avoid Stella's gaze. To her relief, the door opened again as suddenly as it had been shut. Her mother's face reappeared. "Come in but stay in the cloakroom," Graciela said, pulling up the bassinet and guiding Cipriana and Pablito inside. Her mother pressed her index finger to her lips and Cipriana nodded, understanding immediately. With a swish of her skirt, Graciela disappeared around the cloakroom wall. A gaggle of chairs scraped back in unison.

Pablito started asking questions but Cipriana quickly shushed him. She had promised her mother that they would be quiet.

"Señora. How are you?" one man asked.

Cipriana's ears perked up. She could actually hear the conversation in the next room. Sidling up to the wall, she listened even harder.

Some of them called her mother Mrs. Romero. Some called her Señora. One man sounded like a sheep baahing, Cipriana thought.

"How can I help you?" Graciela asked. Her voice sounded softer than it usually was.

"Please sit down, Mrs. Romero."

"That's quite all right. I prefer to stand."

"Well, ma'am, then we'll all stand. This should be short as shortcake anyhoo. Ma'am, I'm Stella's daddy. Green's my name and we came here this morning to chat over what happened yesterday between your girl and mine."

"Mr. Green, I don't think there's anything to talk over. Your daughter hit mine."

"That's not the way Stella tells it. She said your girl called her names."

"Mr. Green, my daughter is several years younger than Stella. Even if she did call her a name, Stella had no business beating her up. Stella's done this before and usually she needs nothing to provoke her."

"Well, ma'am, I just don't buy that. Stella's a fine girl. Maybe she's a little forceful, like me, but in my mind that's good. That's how I've gotten where I am today, ma'am."

"I'm not judging you, Mr. Green. But I do have to be honest with you. Your daughter is a bully, and in my classroom that's unacceptable."

"Unacceptable? Ma'am, I'll tell you what unacceptable is. I understand you've had some problems with school boards in the past."

"What?" Graciela asked, sounding startled. After a pause, she said, "Mr. Green, that matter was cleared up long ago and . . . well, sir, I'm afraid it's none of your business."

"I make everything my business, Mrs. Romero, and I could make things very difficult for you. I could make sure you never get a job in this county . . . no, in this state again."

Cipriana waited for her mother to respond but there was nothing except silence on the other side of the wall. Cipriana was tempted to peek out to see what was happening but then she pulled back when she heard a man's voice again.

"Ma'am, I don't want to be unfair to you, but I would like some things cleared up."

"Sir?"

"Well, for starters, I want your daughter to apologize to my daughter and then I want her out of here. I want your other kids out too, while you're at it. Ma'am, you're the teacher here, not a nursemaid. Having your whole brood here takes away from your teaching my daughter, and I want her to have your full attention."

"Mr. Green, while I agree Stella needs special attention . . ."

"Yes?"

Cipriana's mother cleared her throat. "Fine. I will do as you request, but I also have to have a promise from you."

"You're in no position to bargain, Mrs. Romero."

"No, but unless I have your cooperation on this matter, I cannot do my job effectively. I want your daughter punished every time she beats up a child."

"That's your job, not mine."

"No, sir, it isn't. I do not believe in spanking children, but when they are as out of hand as Stella . . ."

"I beg your pardon, ma'am?"

"I'm sorry you have to hear this from me, Mr. Green, but your daughter needs some discipline and some manners. Her mouth is as dirty as a cowboy's, sir, and unless you agree with me or at least are willing to do something about this, then I'm not needed here and I'll resign immediately. I'll be honest—I need this job desperately, but I can't do it unless I have your cooperation."

Cipriana didn't hear anything other than breathing. She waited. Finally, not able to stand the silence anymore, she peeked out to see what was happening. A big man with a red face diverted his attention momentarily from Graciela to Cipriana and back again to Graciela. Suddenly, Cipriana felt all eyes were on her. Then before she could slip back behind the cloakroom wall, the man nodded and said, "All right, ma'am, we'll give it two months. In the meantime, leave your children at home." The man moved toward Cipriana, fixing his eyes on hers, his heavy boots stomping out all other sounds. Cipriana couldn't move, no matter how much she wanted to hide. When he passed her, she mustered up enough courage to screw her face into what she thought was one of her mama's looks. Quickly, she ran to her mother as the other men dispersed around them.

"Mama, you're not really going to do what he says, are you? We get to stay here with you, right?"

Graciela bent down like she did when helping Cipriana with her spelling. "Cipriana . . . ," she said, taking her hand.

"No, Mama! No!" Cipriana yelled, knowing all too well what her mother was going to say. She ran from her as fast as she could, all the way out of the room. When Cipriana pulled open the door, Stella fell flat on her buttocks. Under ordinary circumstances, Cipriana would have thought this funny, but now she ran right past her enemy.

On Saturday, Cipriana waited for her father to pick her up while sitting outside on Doña Maclovia's steps, cutting out paper dolls from a Sears & Roebuck catalog. From the door, her mother asked if she could help, but Cipriana shook her head. The last thing she wanted right now was to unhate her mother. For the last twenty-four hours, that's all she had been able to focus on: the fact that her mother was sending her home and how much she hated her for it.

Graciela kept a distance, but she joined Cipriana on the porch despite clear indications that she would be ignored. Cipriana could feel her mother's eyes boring into her. She heard Graciela trying to initiate conversation with her but she blocked the words from her consciousness, carrying on instead with her paper dolls and an old sardine can she used as their automobile.

"Cipriana, I wish you could know how much I want to go home. I just can't bear the sound of Don Isá's cough for much longer. But most of all, I want you to know how much I will miss you . . ."

But Cipriana stopped listening then because she knew her mother was lying. She took a pencil in hand and drew an x across all the mouths of the lady dolls. Stuffing them through the cracks of the wood porch, she watched them float down to the ground.

A pickup truck stopped in front of the house and her father emerged. Cipriana ran to him and hugged him like he had been gone forever. "We're going home with you, Daddy," she said eagerly. But his reaction was not what Cipriana had expected. He didn't smile like he was supposed to. He ignored Cipriana altogether, looking at Graciela for answers instead.

"What does she mean, Graciela? I thought they were going to stay here with you."

"No," Cipriana interrupted. "The big man with loud feet and a red face told Mama she had to send us home."

"And why's that, 'jita?" he asked, still looking at Graciela.

"I'll tell you all about it, Robert," Graciela said, taking him by the arm. "Let's go to the little store in Cuervo to buy some groceries for supper. I feel like having deviled eggs."

"Deviled eggs! ¿Como los gringos, Graciela? Just a week with the ranchers and already you're wanting gringo food."

Cipriana's mother smiled. "It brings back good memories, Robert. That's all."

Cipriana winced. Those memories had been made without Cipriana and now her mother was getting ready to make good things to eat once again as preparation for their separation. When Cipriana had turned six, her mother made deviled eggs for her birthday and she gobbled them up ravenously because they were so delicious. But the next day, Graciela left for school and didn't return for many days. Cipriana thought maybe her mother had left because Cipriana had eaten so many of the eggs that were named after devils. Maybe she had turned into one and that's why her mother left. When Cipriana told her mother this and how the name scared her, Graciela only smiled.

"We'll be back in a couple of hours, Cipriana," Graciela called. "Watch your brother for me and we'll take the baby."

"Where's Don Isá, Graciela? I should pay my respects first," Robert said.

"You're right. Come in. I'll be getting mi'jita."

Waiting for her mother and father to drive off, Cipriana went inside and asked Doña Maclovia if she had any eggs. "I'm going to make Mama her special eggs for a surprise," she explained. Cipriana reasoned to herself that since her mother always made food for her family to stay at home, maybe the food she was about to make would somehow send her mother homeward too. To Cipriana's disappointment, Doña Maclovia didn't have any eggs and didn't even know what deviled eggs were. Her plan was doomed.

Dejectedly, Cipriana went outside to sulk. As she tried to retrieve her paper dolls, she stopped in mid-lunge when she heard a rooster crow. Where there were roosters, you were sure to find chickens. Cipriana raced around to the back porch. And sure enough, right there in the yard of Doña Maclovia's nearest neighbor, there were chickens strutting around, pecking at the ground. But Cipriana had to think fast. Asking a stranger for food was practically begging, and she was sure her mother wouldn't approve of that. She had to find Pablito. He was little and didn't know any better. It wouldn't be begging coming from him, she reasoned.

She raced through the little house and finally came across Pablito trailing after Doña Maclovia in the kitchen. "May I borrow my brother for a second, Doña Maclovia? I promise I'll bring him right back."

Before she could answer, Cipriana whisked Pablito outside and gave him instructions. She watched from under the porch, embarrassed to be seen. When her brother knocked on the door, Doña Maclovia's neighbor answered it in an apron. Cipriana couldn't hear the content of the conversation but suddenly the neighbor burst into laughter. Her brother was pointing in her direction and they were both looking her way. Cipriana held her breath, thinking it would help her to remain still, but to no avail. The neighbor waved. Cipriana felt annoyed with her brother. He couldn't do anything right.

To Cipriana's surprise, Pablito followed the neighbor inside. Cipriana crawled out from underneath the porch and stood up. What was he going inside for? He wasn't supposed to do that. He was just supposed to ask her for eggs and come home. He was supposed to hurry. They didn't have much time.

While Cipriana tried to make up her mind whether or not to embarrass herself by hurrying Pablito along, she counted every one of the porch boards three times. When Pablito finally emerged hand in hand with the neighbor, Cipriana dived to the ground so they wouldn't see her. The neighbor led Pablito to the chicken coop, where she gently rolled eggs into Pablito's shirt. He returned smiling, a bizcochito in one hand and the other holding tightly onto his shirt.

"Cookie," he said brightly.

Preoccupied with what she had to do, Cipriana ignored him, grabbing the eggs from Pablito's shirt. Out of the corner of her eye, she saw the neighbor waving and grinning.

With her hands full, Cipriana could not open the door, even using her shoe. "Hurry, Pablito," she said. "Open the door. We've got to hurry."

"Why?"

"Before Mama and Daddy get here."

"How come?"

"Just 'cause. We've got to surprise them."

Once Cipriana unloaded the eggs, she dragged a chair to the stove and looked inside the little silver pot that Doña Maclovia made coffee in. It still had coffee from the morning, enough to boil the eggs in. That's how her father always made their Wednesday morning boiled eggs so he wouldn't be wasteful. Cipriana jumped down from the chair and was starting to poke at the fire when Doña Maclovia came in.

"Do you need any help, Cipriana, with those eggies of yours?" she asked.

Cipriana looked up, giggling. "Eggies?"

"Sí, huevitos. Eggies. Los huevos del demoño."

Suddenly Cipriana turned serious. She didn't like anyone referring to them as eggs of the devil. "No thank you, Doña Maclovia," she said. "I know how to make them all by myself."

·"Well, Cipriana, you're quite the big girl for knowing how to make such a fancy dish."

Cipriana beamed. "You can watch if you'd like, Doña Maclovia. Deviled eggs are just boiled eggs turned inside out. That's what my mama says. And she knows because they're her favorite."

Minutes later, Cipriana scooped the yellow yolk away from the white and began mashing it with a fork. It was hard and didn't mash quite as easily as she remembered when her mother did it.

"What should I do, Doña Maclovia?"

"How about a little mayonnaise, 'jita?"

"That's right! I think that's what Mama uses too but I didn't think you'd have any here since the store is so far away."

Doña Maclovia laughed. "We even have onions way out here in los stickes," she said, smiling. "And ¿sabes que? I bet they would make your devil eggs muy sabrosos."

Cipriana nodded, vaguely recalling that her mother had said onions were the secret ingredient to the best deviled eggs. "I thought you didn't know how to make these eggs, Doña Maclovia?"

Doña Maclovia burst into gurgling laughter as she reached into her cupboard for an onion.

Cipriana was spooning the last of the mashed egg mixture into the last egg half when Doña Maclovia set out two pretty pink plates. "I just got these special, Cipriana. You can use them if you want. "

"Oh, they're so pretty, Doña Maclovia. Just like Mama Fela's. Did you get them from the oatmeal box like Mama Fela does?" she asked.

Doña Maclovia nodded. "Would you like me to make tortillas to go with your eggies?"

Cipriana giggled again. She couldn't help feeling amused by Doña Maclovia's word.

"But do we have time, Doña Maclovia? You know, everything has to be ready when Mama and Daddy come. They'll be hungry."

"Don't worry so much, hijita. You're too little to worry. Pretty soon, you'll have a frown as big as mine."

Cipriana nodded, smiling. And then she asked seriously, "What do you worry about, Doña Maclovia? Is it Don Isá?"

Doña Maclovia stopped smiling then. She bent down and raised Cipriana's chin. "No wonder you worry like a grown-up. I think inside that head of yours, you're three times your age. Come. You can help me make the bloomers."

Just as Cipriana put the plate of freshly made tortillas on the table, her mother and father drove up. "They're here! They're here!" she yelled, almost knocking over her brother, who had joined her at the window. Running to the door and opening it wide, she called, "I made supper, Mama!"

"With what, 'jita? We have the groceries."

"It's a surprise. Close your eyes. You can't look." Taking her mother by the hand, Cipriana led the way to the table. "Come on, Daddy," she said quietly, afraid he was still angry for having to take them home. "You too."

"Where's Don Isá?" Cipriana's father asked Doña Maclovia. "Tell him to join us."

"Y gracias, Roberto, but I can't. He's still napping."

"Napping? Un hombre bruto like Don Isá?"

Cipriana saw her mother poke her father the same way she often poked Cipriana at church to keep her from falling asleep.

"Mama. Your eyes. Close your eyes."

"Yes, Graciela. Close your eyes." Robert snuck up behind Graciela, wrapping his hands over her eyes, marching her to a chair. "You'll join us for supper, though, Doña Maclovia? Please."

"No, no. You enjoy your supper. I'll be in the back."

"Doña Maclovia! You sit right down with us and eat." Robert's voice was joking but Cipriana knew he meant business. He held a chair out next to Graciela's.

Doña Maclovia's face went red. She nodded. "But I must see to Isá first."

"Siéntese, Señora. Siéntese," Robert said. "I'll go get him."

"Don Roberto, please don't wake him if he's sleeping."

Cipriana's father nodded. "I promise."

Cipriana was hoping Don Isá would be fast asleep. She didn't want him to ruin her mother's special meal by joining them at the table. A feeling of hatred toward Don Isá was beginning to creep over Cipriana, not only because he coughed all the time but also because he wasn't like she remembered him. He used to be like her father, young and handsome and nice. But now he had a dirty beard and he smelled. Besides, she had made the eggs for her mother to enjoy. And some for her father, of course, but mostly for her mother. Don Isá would just cough them all up again.

Just as Cipriana was about to show Graciela the eggs, she heard the infamous coughing drawing near. When she looked up, there was her father, in the doorway, hanging onto the arm of Don Isá.

"¿Donde están los frijoles?" Don Isá asked, scooting his chair toward the table.

"No frijoles today, Isá. Cipriana has made a surprise for her mama," Robert said.

Carefully placing the plate of eggs in front of her mother, Cipriana swelled with pride. "Pablo got the eggs," she said. "But I made them. Me and Doña Maclovia," she added, making sure she told the whole truth.

"No, no, 'jita. All I did was keep you company."

Cipriana smiled then because her mother was smiling. A real smile. Suddenly, Cipriana wanted to tell her that she was sorry for acting like a crybaby yesterday. And she wanted her mother to tell her that since Cipriana was so grown-up, she had changed her mind and wanted to go home with them after all. None of this happened, though, because Don Isá had to open up his loud mouth.

"This is gringo food, niña. Never eat the food of the americano. Your stomach will puff out like a marrano empachado."

"¡Isá, cállate!"

"¿Qué?"

"Have some manners, hombre."

"Don't you dare tell me to be quiet, esposa. I'll have manners when I want to. I'm not going to say I like these . . . these . . . I don't even know what they are."

"Eggies, hombre," she whispered. "They call them devil eggies."

"Devil eggies! I'm not eating food of el demoño! I want some beans."

No one said anything. Doña Maclovia started passing the plates of eggs to Cipriana's mother and father. She skipped right over her husband, whose face was puffed and red. He wasn't coughing though. His mouth was shut tight.

Graciela didn't say a word. Neither did Robert. Doña Maclovia did all the talking until everyone had finished eating.

"Is there any coffee?" Robert asked quietly, almost in a whisper.

Doña Maclovia started to get up but Robert sat her right down again. "No, no, I'll get it, Señora. Cipriana here will show me where it is."

"She'll get it," Don Isá said, glaring at his wife.

Doña Maclovia crossed her arms. "Cipriana, 'jita, show your daddy the percolator. Maybe you can make a fresh pot."

Cipriana showed her father the percolator on the stove. "Daddy, they're fighting something awful," she whispered, concerned about the turn of events. She was right. Don Isá was ruining everything.

Robert nodded. "Don't worry, 'jita. Maclovia's just tired. So is Isá. He's tired of being sick."

"When are we going home, Daddy?"

"Tomorrow, Cipriana," he said, opening the lid then shutting it tight again. "Should be enough for all of us," he said. He added a log to the fire and they both sat down again.

Not much talk ensued. Graciela started clearing the plates but Cipriana interrupted, saying, "Please sit down, Mama. This is your special dinner. It's supposed to be like a birthday," she added wistfully.

Graciela smiled but she didn't sit down. Cipriana didn't blame her. The last thing she wanted for her mother was to have to witness Don Isá and Doña Maclovia's bickering. She had enough to deal with, and it would only chase her away faster.

By the time they finished the dishes, Cipriana's father interrupted the silence. "What do you think, 'jita? Is the coffee ready?"

Cipriana nodded even though she wasn't sure. Usually, the pot made a little hissing sound to indicate the coffee was boiling. This time she wasn't paying attention.

Robert rustled up the cups and once Cipriana had poured the coffee, he transported them to the table. When Cipriana sat down, Doña Maclovia took the cup her father had placed in front of Don Isá and pushed it toward Cipriana, who sheepishly avoided eye contact with Don Isá.

Looking right at Cipriana, Don Isá said, "Little girls shouldn't drink coffee."

Doña Maclovia glanced at her husband, then turned toward Cipriana.

"This one likes sopas just like me. She can drink coffee anytime she wants. Like a grown-up," she added. Standing up suddenly, she boomed, "¡Y que hombre tan peseta! Just stop it! Stop acting like a child! Cipriana's over here doing the work of a grown-up. Even Pablito acts older than you. And all you can do is complain."

For a minute, no one said anything. Don Isá didn't even cough. Everyone looked down at their plates.

"Well . . ." Don Isá looked around the table. "I like to be a grown-up too. Can't I have a cup?"

Then all at once, everyone laughed. The tension vanished from the room as even Doña Maclovia joined in the laughter.

Cipriana smiled, dunking a piece of tortilla into her coffee. It emerged with something on it. Inspecting it more closely, she discovered a feather sticking to the tortilla. Gazing around the room, she wondered if anyone had seen what she had seen. Her brother was staring at her quizzically so with her spoon, she quickly submerged the tortilla again. She felt uneasy inside, like she had done something bad.

Once again, she surveyed all the faces around the table but no one said a word. There was no indication that they had observed feathers floating in their coffee. Or, maybe no one minded coffee with caca and feather remnants. Cipriana's stomach turned. She pushed her cup away, hoping the others would follow her lead. Except Don Isá. He could go on drinking his.

"Daddy, I don't think you should drink any more coffee."

"Why not, 'jita?" he asked, taking a sip. "This coffee's nice and strong. I've been craving a cup all day."

Cipriana waited, shutting her eyes tight. She was torn between divulging the truth and hiding her newfound discovery. Finally, she couldn't hold onto the secret anymore. "Daddy, no!" she yelped.

"Cipriana, what's gotten into you?" Graciela asked with concern overshadowing the alarm evident in her voice.

"Mama . . . ," Cipriana began quietly, feeling hot. "I made the eggs in the coffee."

Graciela looked at Cipriana inquisitively. Clearly, she still didn't understand.

"Chicken caca," Cipriana said slowly by way of an explanation.

Cipriana's father put his cup down. Graciela frowned, giving Cipriana one of her teacher looks. Staring at her toes underneath the table, she could already feel them curl from one of her father's spankings. She closed her eyes tightly, gripping the table anxiously, wishing she were somewhere else. The room suddenly rang out in laughter, causing her eyelids to pop open, interrupting her worried reverie.

"But, Daddy, I forgot to tell you to start a new pot of coffee like Doña Maclovia told me."

"No you didn't, 'jita. It was my fault. I insisted on using the cold coffee so it wouldn't go to waste. But, I think . . ." Robert rubbed his teeth. "I think I might have a feather in between my teeth!"

"Daddy!"

"From now on 'jita, you can make deviled eggs anytime, but remind me not to drink coffee when you do!"

It was still dark when Graciela woke Cipriana the next morning. Cipriana thought it might still be night but she could hear the neighbor's rooster singing cock-a-doodle-doo next door.

"Your daddy's ready to go, 'jita," her mother said. "Be good now," she whispered into Cipriana's ear, gently placing her hands on her shoulders. "Last night, you proved to me you are a big girl. You made a delicious supper. You told the truth. You took responsibility for your mistake. And now, I know you're going to be a good big sister to your little brother and baby sister. I'll be home every weekend . . ."

"But, Mama."

"Shush now." Graciela put one finger over her lips and one over Cipriana's who nodded in response. Cipriana wanted desperately to tell her mother how sorry she was for getting her into trouble with Stella's father. She wanted to tell her how much she longed to stay with her now and how much she missed her every time the new week rolled around and snatched her mother away. But Graciela took Cipriana in her arms and squeezed her. Cipriana wondered momentarily if this could really be happening to her. Could this really be her mother, who never hugs, embracing her? Indeed it was, and Cipriana responded in kind.

A honk blasted from the pickup truck outside. Cipriana heard her father shush the man who was at the wheel, reminding him that it was four o'clock in the morning and that he would wake up the entire town. Joining her father outside, Cipriana was just about to climb into the truck when she heard a whistle from the doorway. All Cipriana could see was a shadow. Hoping that it was her mother announcing that she had changed her mind and would be joining their journey home after all, Cipriana ran to the door.

"Niña. Niña linda. Ven p'aca." It was Don Isá. Cipriana was scared but she went over to him anyway. He slipped a coin into her hand and then he coughed into his own.

When they arrived at their house in Santa Lucía, Cipriana helped her father with the baby while he carried Pablito in one arm and their belongings in the other. "Cipriana, why don't you stay home from school today? You're probably tired and anyhow, tomorrow will be soon enough."

"But Daddy, I want to go," Cipriana said, meaning every word.

"I'm sorry, 'jita, but I have to go to work and there's no one else to leave Pablito and the baby with. I'll make arrangements by tomorrow," he promised.

"Don't worry, Daddy. It's all right. I have a lot to do anyway." And Cipriana did. All day long, she tended to her brother and sister like a grown-up. She cleaned the house. She washed the kitchen floor and she waxed it until it shone like a penny. She was on the very last corner when the kitchen door opened and her father walked in. Before she could warn him, his legs slipped out from under him and flew high into the air. Cipriana didn't mean to laugh but it just came tumbling out.

"¡Malcriada niña! Show me some respect," he bellowed, trying to regain his composure. He tried awkwardly to stand, first balancing on all fours and then rising to his feet. "You take a rag to that damn floor until it's rough again, you hear me!"

Cipriana winced at the bad word. She nodded mournfully, regretful that her father's homecoming hadn't been perfect. She had wanted to surprise him by acting like a grown-up, just as her mother had come to expect. Instead of reveling in his praise as she had hoped, Cipriana rubbed the shine out of the floor, wondering what her mother was doing right now, and thinking about how eager she was to return to school tomorrow.

The next morning, Cipriana bought two bags full of doughnuts with Don Isá's quarter. When she got to school, she ran to her old classroom and looked in eagerly. The teacher was sitting at her desk.

"Miss Shute," Cipriana called.

The teacher turned. "Well, Cipriana, isn't it? What brings you back to our school?" she asked in what Cipriana thought was a singsongy voice.

"My mama made us come back," Cipriana said, taking out the first éclair. "Would you like one?" she asked, holding it out in offering.

Miss Shute looked at the pastry with a sidelong glance and shook her head no. Cipriana couldn't imagine why anyone would decline such a generous offer.

"But these are long johns, Miss Shute. My tío's friend gave me money to buy them."

"Well, how thoughtful he is, honey. Now you know there's no food in the classroom so you better hurry and eat those before I ring the bell," she said. "And remember, you must say 'uncle,' not 'tío.'"

Cipriana nodded agreeably before she ran outside to share the doughnuts with her friends. Even though she had acted like everything was fine, she felt hurt that her teacher had refused to take one. She really wanted her to.

Reading was first, and Cipriana relished the subject. Miss Shute called her to read in front of the class and she was proud to do so, feeling confident in her read-aloud skills. But when they switched to arithmetic, Cipriana failed to get the right answers. She could feel Miss Shute standing behind her observing and judging her. Cipriana was so self-conscious, afraid that she would make a mistake at any moment, that she could not think. When Miss Shute placed a hand on her shoulder, Cipriana almost wet her panties. The teacher whispered in Cipriana's ear, instructing her to follow her to another group. That group was David Abernathy's, the dummies of the class. And now Miss Shute thought Cipriana was one too. For the rest of the math period, Cipriana was too preoccupied to answer any of Miss Shute's questions. She was too embarrassed to say anything at all. She had to face the fact that she was in David's group. The dummy group. No matter how hard she tried, Cipriana could not understand how to borrow from the smaller numbers.

That night Cipriana went into the kitchen, where her father was reading the newspaper. She took out her math paper and sat down right beside him. She pretended she was looking at her homework but instead, she was watching to see if he was still angry with her over the slippery floor incident.

Finally, not being able to detect his mood, she said, "Daddy, I'm no good at math."

Her father continued to scrutinize his newspaper. He was still mad at her, she surmised. He wasn't even going to look at her, much less talk to her.

And then, to her surprise, he folded up his newspaper. "Your mama should be here, 'jita. She's the one that's smart, not me."

"Me neither, Daddy. I used to be in the A group in everything but now I'm with the dummies in math."

"The dummies? Who put you with the dummies?"

"The teacher, but it's not her fault, Daddy. I'm just not smart anymore."

"I don't want to ever hear you say that again, 'jita," he said. Cipriana's father set aside his newspaper and scooted his chair close. "Now bring your book here."

✤

CHAPTER NINE

THE APPLE TREE

With a heave, Cita sat Benny atop the newspapers that were piled a foot high on the captain's chair. She dipped her brush in a small bowl of water, flicking the excess into the air. Slowly, she brushed his hair until it was damp, releasing a faint smell of Palmolive soap and dirt. Cipriana, Sara, and Rebeca looked on.

"Tía, the water's cold."

"Cold? Benny, if you're going to be a Boy Scout, you have to be tough."

"But I am tough, Tía. Real tough. See, I have muscles."

"You sure do, Benny. Wow, big ones, too. But I don't mean strong muscles. I mean strong up here," she said tapping her temple.

"Why there, Tía? Why do you need muscles on your head?"

"Not on your head, silly. In. You need a strong mind so you can be smart in school and smart with people. You want your head to be strong so that you do what you want in this life, not what other people tell you to do."

"Yeah. I want to be boss, Tía. I don't want nobody telling me what to do."

"Anybody."

"Yeah, nobody."

"No, Benny. See, that's what I mean, too. You've got to go to school so you can learn how to speak well, just like . . . like Cipriana's mama. Right Cipriana? Your mama knows a lot."

Cipriana nodded. "She's smart, Tía, that's why."

"That's right. And school made her even smarter, right?"

"I guess so, Tía. She likes school a lot. She goes there even on Saturdays and in the summer."

"Ladies don't go to school," Benny chimed in. "Only kids."

"My mama does. Every summer in Las Vegas."

"She's dumb then. I hate school."

"Oh, no, Benny. Why do you hate it?" Cita asked.

Benny looked at the floor.

"I know, Benny. It's hard sometimes but . . ."

"No, it's not that. School's easy but they . . . they say things. That's why I'm always getting into trouble. I fight a lot, Tía."

"Why, Benny? Who says things?"

"The other kids."

"Like what?"

Benny found comfort in the floor again.

"Benny! Like what kinds of things?" Cita insisted.

The boy was still silent, and Cita wasn't sure if she should pry or not. She looked at his sisters, thinking perhaps they might provide a clue.

"Tell Tía, Benny," Sara, the oldest, ordered.

"Why should I?"

"Because I said so."

"You don't know everything, Sara."

Sighing, Sara said, "He means the things they say about Papa."

"Shut up, Sara!" Benny blurted.

"You shut up. I can say whatever I want."

"¡Cállense! What's wrong with you two?" Cita interrupted.

"She's always such a loud mouth. She doesn't have to tell you everything I say, Tía."

"No, she doesn't, but I think she's just trying to be helpful. Isn't that right, Sara?"

Sara nodded, glaring at Benny.

"Now, Benny, tell me. What do they say about your daddy? Maybe I can help."

"Things, Tía. You don't want to hear them. They'll just make you mad like they made me."

"Try me, Benny." Cita wrapped a towel around the boy's shoulders. Tipping his chin upward with a forefinger, she added, "But only if you want to." By now, Cita wasn't sure she even wanted to know what had been said about her brother. She enjoyed hearing gossip but not if it was about her family. When Benny made no response, she took it as a sign that the news was not meant for her ears.

"All right, Benny, let's get this hair cut then so we can get this show on the road. Let's see what we have. Will my assistants step forward, please?"

Giggling, Cipriana and Rebeca moved closer to Cita, holding a pair of scissors and a towel.

"Now then, who has the razor?"

"Razor? Tía, what for?" Benny shouted, scooting forward in his chair.

"I'm kidding, Benny," Cita said laughing, patting his shoulder. "Don't worry." For a moment, Cita stepped back, inspecting her nephew's hair and the shape of his head. She had never cut boy's hair before, only her own and Cipriana's. "Now, how are we going to cut it? Anybody have any ideas?"

The girls were quiet.

"No ideas from my assistants? What are we going to do, girls?"

"Mama used to put a bowl on his head so she wouldn't cut it too short," Sara said.

"No sir," Benny said, frowning at his sister.

"How do you know? You wouldn't remember. You were nothing but a baby, Benny."

"I was not! I remember Mama cutting my hair. She cut it good, too."

"You're a liar, Benny. You were too little to remember that."

"I was not."

"All right now, Benny, Sara. We'll never get it cut if you two go on fighting."

"Tía, why don't you take him to my Tío Juan? He knows how to cut hair."

"Of course he does, Cipriana. But I can't afford to spend a dime on a haircut. Every last one I have is for Benny's uniform."

"You're going to buy it, Tía?" Benny shot up from his chair.

"Of course, Benny. That's why we're getting you all spiffed up."

"Today?"

"Yes, of course today!"

"Oh, Tía, hurry then. Hurry!"

"If you'll sit still, Benny, that's exactly what I'll do." Smiling, Cita took the scissors in hand and with a little more confidence, she snipped piece after piece of Benny's dark hair. His eagerness and excitement was palpable and that made her feel great. She loved to be a part of people's happiness. Especially a child's. And all it took was months and months of saved coins.

When she couldn't bear Benny's wiggling anymore, not from impatience, but from empathy, she put down her scissors and announced, "All right, Benny. We're done." No sooner had she slipped the towel from his shoulders than he jumped down from his perch and was pulling her out the door. The girls ran to catch up.

"Slow down, Benny," Cita cried, out of breath. Her hand was sweaty in his small one and she tried to draw it away for a moment, but he held on. While he tugged, she dragged the chain of giggling girls behind her. Her arms felt ready to rip from her body as they made their way up Route 66 to the mercantile. But nothing could ruin this moment. She felt the excited squeeze of Benny's hand the moment the storefront came into view. That alone made her pain endurable.

Like a rush of wind, together they burst into the store, laughing and chattering. Once inside, Benny released Cita's hand and raced down the wood floor into the clothing section, calling for them to hurry. For once, she did not try to quiet him; today was his day.

"Señor Gould, Señor Gould, do you have my uniform?" Benny asked, running up to the counter.

Folding up a bolt of material, Isaac Gould smiled. "Aha, is that why you're making all that racket? Your aunt ordered it the other day . . . Oh hello, Cita . . . and I think," he said bending down underneath the counter, "I just might have something of the kind right here."

The storekeeper held up a plain box. "Is this what you're looking for?" he asked, pulling out a greenish-tan camp shirt with gold buttons and a red kerchief tied around the collar.

Benny held out his hands. "Oh, Tía, it's exactly like I thought."

"Try it on. Show us what you look like, because in two hours, you have your first Scout meeting."

"Today?"

"Yes, today, silly. Here, take off your shirt. Button up and I'll be right back."

At the counter, Cita loosened the drawstring of her pouch and dumped the contents onto the counter. Slowly, she counted her quarters, nickels, and dimes but had to begin again several times because Señor Gould was staring at her disapprovingly. "Money's money, right, Señor Gould?"

For a moment, Isaac Gould said nothing. Then, shaking his head, he chuckled and began to help Cita organize the coins into piles. Both were intent on the task when a rough hand on Cita's shoulder startled her.

"Solomón!"

In a loud, drowsy voice he said accusingly, "You're getting steke. Eating high off the hog on my penny while I'm over there starving."

"What? Be quiet, Solomón," Cita whispered, feeling the stares of the other customers. "Here, let's talk over here."

"I don't want to talk over there," he yelled, shrugging her arm violently off his.

"Solomón, what's wrong with you?"

"Wrong? You're eating steke; that's what's wrong."

"Steke? What's that, steke?"

"Steke. Steke. Meat this thick. Cooked in a skillet. Expensive."

"You mean steak?"

"That's what I said. You and Mamá are over there eating high off the hog and me? Psh. I'm no longer a man with just these bones on me."

"We are not eating steak. Where did you get that idea?"

"You calling me a liar now? I'm over here working my ass off and then I come to pay the bill and el Isaac shows me you're eating steke. Right there in black and white. Steke."

By now, Cita knew Solomón was drunk. She had never seen him like this before and she wished she hadn't today. She no longer had to wonder what the children's classmates were saying about Solomón. His sour breath and his loud, obnoxious behavior made it abundantly clear.

Her concern at this moment, however, was for the children. She didn't want them to see their father like this.

Softly, she said, "We have not been eating steak, Solomón. I don't know where you got that idea. When you've calmed down, we'll talk about it, but not until then." Turning hesitantly back to the counter, she whispered to Isaac Gould, "Could you finish this, Señor Gould? I have to get the children."

Suddenly, she felt a rush of breath in her hair. Solomón grabbed both of her shoulders, whisked her around, and shoved her back to the counter. She gasped, feeling the air leave her lungs. Long ago, she recalled a similar sensation. The memory was erased momentarily by the rush of running feet.

"Daddy! Leave her alone," Benny yelled.

Benny's voice was a welcome sound. It drowned out the images inside Cita's head. She was sure now she did not know this man, her brother. She was sure. "Sara," she said calmly. "Take Cipriana and your brother and sister home now. Do as I say. Now, please."

"But, Tía . . ."

"Now!"

"But, Tía, the Boy Scouts . . ."

"Benny, do as I say this minute or I'll take that uniform away. Now!"

The children moved slowly, gaping at the scene. Cita wanted to tell them to run, run as fast as they could, away from here, forever, but her tongue was dry and she could not speak. Solomón's voice was loud, though, and it brought her back to the current situation.

"Isaac! Isaac!" Solomón called roughly. "Ven p'acá."

The storekeeper slinked forward.

"Show her. Show her the bill."

Cita watched as Señor Gould stood frozen, his bulk masking the intimidation that she could see in his eyes.

"Now!" Solomón screamed.

Immediately, Isaac Gould fumbled in his trouser pocket for a ring of keys. Cita could see his fingers trembling as he found the right key and slipped it into the keyhole of the metal box kept adjacent to the cash register. Opening it, he licked his finger and thumbed through the stack of receipts. Finally, Señor Gould stopped. Cita's eyes met his, peeking at her over his glasses.

Solomón slapped the counter suddenly. "Where is it? I want to see it now!"

When Señor Gould handed over the piece of paper with a running total of groceries for the past month, Solomón grabbed it and shoved it in front of Cita.

"Look. There it is in black and white. Steke."

Cita inspected the paper while trying to remember any extraordinary purchases. Surely, she would have remembered steak. The closest she had ever come to buying such a cut of meat was when she bought bones to boil for a *caldito*. Shaking her head, she mumbled, "I don't see steak here, Solomón."

Grabbing the paper from her, Solomón groaned, squinting at the list. To Cita, it seemed like eternity while her brother looked it up and down. "Here! Here it is," he said finally, thumping his finger against the page.

"Solomón! That's starch. Corn starch!"

"What? Let me see that," he said, tearing the paper from Cita and staring at it.

"How dare you, Solomón! You're over here accusing us of eating up your money. Maybe you pay for your children's food but what about their clothes? Who do you think pays for those, huh? And what about the time we spend with them? When was the last time you were over to see them? Maybe if you'd eat with them once in a while you wouldn't have to starve. Mamá's always saving a plate for you but you never come. You're a pendejo, Solomón. A pendejo."

Solomón continued to stare at the paper pinched between his fingers. "Starch. I can't believe it. Starch."

"You haven't heard a thing I've said, Solomón!"

"I'm sorry, Cita. I thought it was steak. I'm so sorry."

Falling to his knees, he hung onto Cita's skirt, taking bunches of material into his fists.

"Forgive me, Cita," he pleaded.

Cita was embarrassed. Looking around, she saw customers avert their eyes. She whispered loud enough for her brother to hear over his theatrics, "Solomón, quit it. You're making a fool of yourself. Stop it."

"No, please. Please forgive me, Cita. You're right. I'm a horrible father. I'm a horrible son. I can't see to my children or my mother. And I know I was a terrible brother to you. I know I was, Cita."

Cita felt like slapping her brother. She didn't want him to dredge up old memories, especially here, especially now. She wished he would just go away like he had so many years ago when she needed him. She and Mama Fela could take care of Sara, Rebeca, and Benny. They had already been doing just that. The children would be much better off without their drunken father anyway. Pobres hijos, getting teased at school because of their father's behavior.

"Solomón, I don't want to hear it anymore. You're embarrassing me and your children."

Solomón looked up from Cita's skirt. He wiped his nose across his shoulder, sniffling a few times. "My children? What do you mean, my children?"

"They're being teased at school because of your behavior. Benny especially. And he's getting into fights defending you."

Solomón strained to get up off his knees. "My boy having to defend me? No way. I won't allow that, Cita. No way."

"Then change your behavior, Solomón. You're loud and obnoxious and you smell. Solomón, you've been drinking."

"Drinking! Que drinking ni drinking. Shut up, Cita! You don't know how hard it is being a man in this town. No jobs. No fun. It's the same as it always was. I should never have come back."

"Oh, pobrecito, Solomón. Pobrecito," Cita cooed sarcastically.

Solomón acted like he was about to hit Cita but stopped in mid-strike. Cita stood her ground.

"You're nothing but a bully, Solomón. Something happened to you the day you left here and I haven't liked you since."

Solomón gave Cita a look, one she did not like. She recognized the look from long ago.

"You know exactly what happened. It wasn't just something. You know exactly what it was."

"What do you mean, Solomón? I don't know what you're talking about."

"Yes you do, Cita. You know what happened."

"No, Solomón, I don't!" Cita could feel her voice escalating, her temperature rising.

"Cita, you know why I had to leave, don't you?"

"No, Solomón! I don't. You left me here all alone. I didn't know what to do or say or think. You left me all alone."

"I didn't mean to, Cita. I really didn't. But I . . . I didn't know what to do, how to help."

"You could have helped just by being here. Talking with me. Listening. I've never told anyone about that day."

"Neither have I."

"But why, Solomón? Why haven't we? What are we scared of?"

Solomón said nothing. He turned from Cita's intense gaze.

"Solomón! Listen to me. Look at me!" Cita reached for his arm but he snatched it away. "Don't run away this time. Please, Solomón. Please."

"I can't talk about it, Cita. I'm sorry. I just can't." Solomón dug into his back pocket for his wallet and pulled out a five-dollar bill. "For your troubles, Cita," he said, handing her the money.

"I don't want your money, Solomón."

"Here, take it."

"No. I don't want your money."

Solomón sneered, pulling the money back. He started to tuck it into his shirt pocket, seemed to think better of it, and tossed it on the counter. Turning in a huff, he stumbled out the door.

Cita watched him step by step until her brother made his way across the street. She let out a lungful of air, as if she had been holding her breath for a very long time. At this moment, she felt no compassion for her brother, only scorn. Why had he ever come back? Suddenly aware of customers staring, she quickly acknowledged them with a nod of her head. Señor Gould handed her the box with Benny's old clothes and the pouch in which she had brought her savings. She squeezed it, feeling for any coins left over. The downy material felt even softer when she discovered it held a scattering of miscellaneous coins. Cita smiled at Señor Gould. And then, Solomón's money, still on the counter, caught her eye. It wasn't very often that she would see a five-dollar bill this close. She looked at Señor Gould, and he looked at her.

Grinning, he said, "It's all yours, Señorita."

Cita took it in hand and slipped out the door.

In the distance, she could see Solomón. For a brief moment, she thought of following him, but she wasn't his keeper. She wondered if his thoughts transported him to the same place her thoughts took her. No, she didn't want to think about it. She had blocked it out of her mind once and surely she could do it again. Besides, she had better things to do. Turning in the other direction, she proceeded home to find her nieces and Benny. They had a Scout meeting to go to.

As Cita approached the house, she heard children's voices coming from the apple tree in her backyard. She remembered clambering up into those same branches long ago to forget her own problems. That place of solace hadn't lasted long. When she looked up through the leaves, a memory flashed through her mind, and she had to avert her eyes quickly to drive it away.

With growing impatience, she called, "Benny, Cipriana, Sara, Rebeca! Come down here right this minute."

"Tía! You're back!"

"Why was Papa so angry?"

"Are you all right, Tía?"

Then, as if in slow motion, Cita heard a long rip and down darted Benny through the branches. "Ti-ia!" he screamed. And then he was on the ground in a loud thump, crying. His red kerchief was torn right down the middle.

Cita rushed over to him, falling on her knees. "Oh, Benny, are you all right? Does anything hurt? Is your leg broken, 'jito?"

Benny cried in short bursts, trying to catch his breath in between hiccups of emotion. The girls scrambled down the tree and went to Cita's side. Carefully brushing back Benny's bangs, she smoothed his cheeks, afraid to pick him up for fear anything was broken. Then all at once, Benny climbed into her lap. "Oh, Tía. My uniform's torn. Now I can't be a Boy Scout."

"Oh, Benny, is that all you're worried about? I thought you were hurt," she said, smoothing his face.

"Tía, Mama Fela can fix Benny's shirt."

"You're right, Cipriana. Mama Fela can fix anything," she said, helping Benny to stand. "What do you say we go to a meeting now? I think it's time Benny became a Scout."

"Really, Tía?" Benny asked, wiping his nose across his sleeve.

"Really, Benny."

That afternoon, as Cita and the children emerged from Town Hall, they saw a parade of unusual characters driving in a caravan along Main. All shapes and sizes of people, clearly not those of Santa Lucía, were squeezed and stuffed into old Model Ts and pickup trucks, honking and shouting invitations to their circus carnival.

"Come one, come all! Two days only! Circus animals, trapeze artists, clowns, and for the first time ever, a merry-go-round! See the two-headed lady and the blue-bearded man. Cotton candy and caramel apples! Join in the fun! Just for you, Santa Lucía! Be the first to ride the merry-go-round. See you Saturday! Come one, come all."

"Oh, Tía! Can we go? Can we go?" All four children shouted at once.

Cita couldn't help feeling intrigued as well. She had always wanted to ride on a merry-go-round and she had only ever seen pictures. And now, thanks to Solomón, she had a five-dollar bill in her pocket.

Grinning, she nodded her head. "Race you home!" she shouted, darting out in front of her nieces and Benny, who ran to catch up.

"And, Tía . . . ," Benny shouted, gasping for breath. "Maybe I can even wear my uniform."

On Saturday morning, Cita woke to four pairs of eyes staring at her. She laughed, sitting up as she patted her bed, inviting her nieces and Benny to sit. Leaning back against a pillow, she drew her sheet to her chest.

"You look spiffy this morning, Benny," Cita said, pulling at the mended red kerchief loosely knotted at his neck.

Benny smiled.

"Tía, your eyes are red, white, and blue," Cipriana said.

"Yeah, Tía, just like my mama's," Rebeca quietly chimed in. "Except hers were purple."

"Purple?" asked Sara. "They were not, Rebeca. They were hazel, almost lavender."

"Well, that's kind of purple," Rebeca tried again.

"And you have your mama's pretty eyes, Rebeca," Cita said.

"No she doesn't. I do, Tía," Benny said.

"Boys aren't supposed to have purple eyes. Only brown," Cipriana said.

"No sir, boys can have purple eyes too. Right, Tía?"

"Well, Benny, I think you have beautiful button brown eyes," Cita said."

"But I don't want brown eyes," said Benny.

"Why ever not, Benny?"

Benny shook his head, refusing to answer.

"Because that's the color of Daddy's eyes," Sara said in Benny's defense.

"Is not!" Benny shouted.

"Is too!" Sara shouted back. "And only Mexicans have brown eyes, Tía," Sara added.

"Mexicans? Where did you hear that from, Sara?"

"That's what they call Daddy. A dirty drunk Mexican."

"Who calls him that? The kids?"

Sara nodded. "That's why they don't want Daddy's eyes," she said, indicating her siblings.

"And you?"

Sara shrugged. "I don't have Mama's eyes but I don't have Daddy's either."

"Then whose do you have?"

"My own."

Cita nodded, taking Sara into her arms. "Good for you, 'jita."

"Come on, Tía. The carnival's going to start," Cipriana interrupted, pulling the sheet away from Cita.

"Yeah, Tía, you have to hurry," Benny said. "We've been waiting for you for a billion hours."

"C'mon, Tía. We wanna be the first to go on the merry-go-round," Rebeca added.

Grinning, Cita said, "I know, I know. But it doesn't open until eleven. We have two whole hours, 'jitos. Don't you want to eat breakfast first?"

"Oh, no, Tía, we have to save enough room for the cotton candy," Cipriana said.

"And the popcorn!" added Benny.

"And . . . and everything else," Rebeca said breathlessly.

With a single motion, Cita whipped back the covers so fast that the children's hair whooshed back. Laughing, she jumped out of bed and shooed her nieces and Benny out of the room. "At least let a lady get dressed!"

When Cita emerged, the children were all sitting at Mama Fela's table with long, drawn faces.

"What's happened?" Cita asked. "A minute ago you were all smiles."

"Mama Fela's making us eat breakfast," Cipriana said.

"Yeah," Benny chimed in. "She's mean."

"But, Mamá, we have to save room for all the goodies," Cita said playfully.

"Not you too, Cita. I just heard every reason in the world why they couldn't eat. Some nonsense about a carnival."

"It's true. There's a carnival in town. And I'm taking the children."

"Carnival? Since when?"

Cita shrugged.

"Que carnival ni carnival. Those things cost money."

"And I have it, Mamá."

"Oh? Since when, Cita?"

"Since Solomón."

Mama Fela looked surprised. And then suddenly, as if Solomón himself had entered the room, she perked up. "Good. Good," she said, going about her bustling around the cookstove. "But first the children have to put some food in their stomachs. What would their daddy say if he knew I was letting them out of the house without a proper breakfast?"

"But Mama Fela!" The children groaned.

"I don't want to hear another word about it," Mama Fela said, ignoring them. "We'll have some of your Papa Gilberto's famous panqueques," she said, turning slightly to smile at Cita.

"Mmm!" Cipriana exclaimed. "Benny, you've never tasted Papa Gil's pancakes before. They're delicious."

Benny's face lit up, as did his sisters'.

"Now, Benny, in order for Mama Fela to let you try those famous pancakes, there's something you must do first."

"What, Tía?"

"And you too, Sara and Rebeca."

The girls nodded eagerly.

"You have to set the table. The dishes are down there," Cita said, pointing to the trastero. "Cipriana, you get the Karo syrup."

"I thought you ate pancakes with maple syrup, Tía."

"The güeros do, Sara, but we're not rich like they are."

"But all of you are rich enough to go to the carnival with your tía," Mama Fela said, releasing the first hot batch of pancakes from her spatula. "You're lucky. I've never even been to a carnival."

"Never, Mama Fela?"

"Never, mi'jita."

"Then come with us, Mama Fela!"

"Yeah, Mama Fela, come on."

"Oh, no, 'jitos," Mama Fela said, chuckling. "I'm too old."

"Mama Fela, you are not!"

"Sí, sí mi'jito. I am."

"Please, Mama Fela."

"Shh. I don't want to hear any more about it. You go. Have a good time."

"But Mama Fela . . ."

"I said that's it. Cállate."

To Cita, Benny looked as if Mama Fela had slapped him across the face. She refrained from saying anything because she knew Mama Fela all too well. It was a waste of breath to try and convince her of something she had no intention of doing. She was stubborn to a fault and Cita hated that about her mother.

"Besides, your tía doesn't want me to go."

"Mamá! That's not true. I just know there's no convincing you."

"Pues, what if I said I would go?"

"Then I'd be completely surprised."

"Hmm. I like to surprise my children. I think I'll go."

"Mamá!"

"You heard right, Cita. I'm coming with you. Finish up your panqueques, 'jitos. We're going to a carnival, whatever it is."

Cita stared at her mother in disbelief while the bottle of syrup she was tipping toward her stack of pancakes slowly drained its contents. It was the Romero way to drown their pancakes in syrup but this was overdoing it. Her plate was overflowing with the clear, sticky liquid.

"Tía! Your plate," Cipriana exclaimed.

Quickly, Cita tried to lick up the gooey mess that had started to puddle around her plate onto the oilcloth.

"¡Cochina!" Mama Fela scolded.

As if by instinct, Cita quickly collected her tongue, almost biting it in the process.

"And to think you're wasting good syrup."

"Mamá, I didn't do it on purpose."

Mama Fela held out a larger plate on which Cita placed her plate with the dripping syrup. Mama Fela carried it to the basin and poured out a trickle of water from the large kettle. She dipped the wash rag into the water, squeezed it, and gave it to Cita.

Cita felt like a child. She took the *estropajo* and wiped the oilcloth until the stickiness had disappeared.

"Can we go yet, Tía?"

"In a second, Benny. Let's help Mama Fela clean up."

"No, no, it's too much of a mess. You go without me."

"But Mamá!"

"No, no, Cita, I changed my mind. Someone has to stay with the babies. And besides, there's too much to do in this house. Too many messes to clean up."

"Mamá! That's just mean. I didn't spill the syrup on purpose."

"It's not about the syrup, Cita. Quickly before I put each of you to work."

Mama Fela gave Cita one of her famous looks, one that always instilled her with guilt.

Together, hand in hand, Cita, Cipriana, Sara, Rebeca, and Benny raced from the house and didn't stop until they heard carnival music. The lively accordion sounds broadcast from a tinny loudspeaker made Cita feel like tapping her foot in time to the three-quarter beat. None of the children said a word as they approached the vacant commercial lot that had been transformed overnight into a wonderland. Colorful booths with red, yellow, and blue banners and balloons advertised, "Prizes Every Time Everyone." Darts, a ring toss, and a shooting gallery were housed inside the booths with colorful characters in wigs and makeup shouting to step right up to win. A lady sat caressing a glass ball that sparkled in the sun, her shoulders wrapped in ebony brocade with green and gold stitching. On her table covered in red velvet, a sign written in fancy script read "Fortune Teller. Read your palm 5¢." The smell of popcorn wafted through the air, and Cita inhaled deeply. "Mmm, I smell popcorn."

"Oh, Tía." Cipriana's eyes grew as did her smile. "With lots and lots of butter!"

"And what do you think?" she asked Sara, Rebeca, and Benny.

"Oh, Tía, I've never seen anything like it," said Sara.

Rebeca looked off into the distance, shaking her head and grinning.

Benny grabbed Cita's hand and pulled her to the entrance of the carnival where clowns were dancing and juggling. They wore red and white jodhpurs under multicolored tunics. One wore a green and white polka-dot tie, while another had a flounce lace collar bordered by red stitching. Still another wore a bow tie with red, white, and black stripes. "Step right up," they said, motioning to Cita and the children. "Step right up, kids, and come have a fun fun time at the fun farm." Encircling Cita and the children, the clowns bellowed in unison, "We call it that because . . . young lady, can you tell me why?" The one with the bow tie took Cita's hand. Cita pulled it away.

"Why, I, I don't know," she stammered.

"You, you don't know why?" he asked in alarm. "My dear, you've hurt Bisco's feelings," he exclaimed, pointing at his colleague with the lace collar, whose smile had turned upside down. "Dry your tears, now, Bisco. The young lady didn't mean anything by it. Here's a hanky," he added, giving him a brightly colored cloth from the hem of his sleeve. While Bisco rubbed his eyes in mock fashion, the scarf grew longer and soon the first clown took it and wrapped it around Cita and her entourage. Then, all the clowns joined in until they had the girls and Benny surrounded in a circle. "Get ready for the time of your life because a carnival is fun, fun, fun!" They all honked their noses, released their captives, and pointed to the booth where tickets were sold. "Better hurry, hurry, hurry," the clown with tears exclaimed as he nudged them forward by stepping on their heels with his floppy long feet. "Get your tickets and go visit the merry-go-round over there," he said, taking out five balls to juggle. The third clown whooped, "Have fun!" as he helped the first clown retrieve his immense handkerchief.

Cita untucked the crisp five-dollar bill from the waistband of her skirt. She unfolded it carefully, smoothing each crease. This was the first time she had ever had an entire five-dollar bill to spend frivolously and it would probably be the last, she thought. She wanted to hang onto the thrilling sensation for as long as she could, but the expressions on the children's faces told her she would have to hurry. *This will make them happy*, she thought to herself. *Very happy*. The clerk at the ticket booth stared at Cita, drumming his fingers on the makeshift countertop. Slowly, Cita pushed the money across the wood surface, feeling each potential splinter as she went. This was painful but it was a good kind of pain. Money had that kind of power. Finally, the clerk held one end of Abe Lincoln's face and Cita held the other. The clerk tugged and Cita pulled one last time before letting the money slip from her fingertips.

"Ten tickets, please," she said, calculating one dollar down, four to go. As she scrunched the bills into her hand, Benny yanked her other hand. With Benny leading the way, they all ran to the much-anticipated merry-go-round. All of them stood, staring in wonder at the parade of figures prancing round and round, showing off their wild paints, their exaggerated manes, and their circus eyes.

"This is the merry-go-round?" Cipriana asked excitedly.

"This is a merry-go-round, a real merry-go-round," Cita said dreamily. "And we're going to go on it! C'mon, let's get in line." With Cita in the lead, they all ran to wait for the music to stop. Cita watched with satisfaction as the children's heads moved back and forth in unison, following the figures going round and round.

"Do we get to pick which one we want to ride on?" asked Cipriana.

"Of course!" Cita exclaimed. "Whichever one you want."

"I want that one," Benny said, pointing to a green stallion with a wild black mane and black piercing eyes. "That's the fastest."

"Oh, Tía, I want the one that's smiling," Sara said. "Look, it almost seems like it's jumping."

"Which one do you like, Rebeca?"

"The one with the purple hair, Tía. Do horses really have purple hair?"

"You mean manes, the hair down across their back?"

Rebeca nodded.

"Sure. Some do, Rebeca. The ones in your imagination at least." Turning to her other niece, she inquired, "And you, Cipriana?"

"Oh, Tía, all of them."

"You must have a favorite, Cipriana."

Cipriana quietly watched the merry-go-round go round twice. "There, Tía, that's the one," she said, pointing to a white carriage drawn by two beautiful black stallions with silver manes.

"That is a beauty, Cipriana."

Cita had her eye on a dark-blue horse with fierce yellow eyes and golden hooves. She imagined its muscular legs dancing through the air, never touching the ground, propelled only by sheer fortitude and vision. It went round and round gracefully, carrying its passenger to a magical destination. How she would love to paint this very scene. She took it all in, memorizing every detail for later.

Finally when the music stopped and children of all ages scrambled off,

Cipriana, Sara, and Benny ran to their preferred horses. Rebeca hung back until Cita took her by the hand and pulled her toward the contraption.

"I'm scared, Tía," Rebeca whispered.

"Don't worry, Rebeca, it doesn't go that fast."

"I know, Tía, but I don't want to go."

"C'mon, Rebeca, I'll ride with you. Look, we can sit together on this carriage." Cita pointed to a pink carriage drawn by two white horses with lavender manes and eyes. "What do you say?"

Rebeca nodded hesitantly but Cita noticed just the hint of a smile. Together, she and Rebeca clambered on. And the music started. Cita watched Rebeca's eyes open wide as the machine jolted forward. Gradually, a smile ascended upon Rebeca's face and she slid back comfortably into the carriage.

"Tía, look at me!" Benny called. "No hands."

"Benny!" Cita called, surprised. "Hold on, 'jito."

"But I don't need hands, Tía. And besides, I need my hands to hold the guns. Bam, bam."

Cita feigned a gunshot wound, holding her hand over her left shoulder. "Ay, you got me, Benny."

"What's the matter, Tía?" Rebeca asked.

"Don't worry, 'jita. We're just playing. See, now you have to defend me and try to get Benny. Pretend you're chasing him in your carriage, telling your horses, 'Giddiup, giddiup!' Hurry! Hurry! Before Benny gets away."

"Tía!" Cipriana called from a few horses behind. "Look at me and Sara." The girls sat erect on their horses, one hand holding the pole that connected them to the merry-go-round and the other hand holding each other. Cita noticed that Cipriana was on the horse she had preferred—the navy one with the golden hooves.

"What happened to the carriage you wanted, Cipriana?" Cita called.

Cipriana shrugged. "Somebody else got it first, and besides, this one's better."

Rebeca was twisting in her slippery seat, trying to climb onto her knees to peer over the back of the carriage. Cita lightly rested her hand on her niece's back, making sure she wouldn't fall backward. "Bam, bam. I got you two," Rebeca called, holding out her forefinger and thumb as if she were shooting a gun.

"Ooh, Rebeca, it almost hit me but my horse is so fast, she jumped over the bullet," Cipriana said.

"Na-ah, Cipriana. Horses can't jump over bullets. Can they, Tía?"

"Mine can," Cipriana said. "My horse has magical hooves."

"Really, Cipriana?" Rebeca looked at Cipriana in wonder. "Do you believe her, Sara?"

Sara frowned, letting go of Cipriana's hand. "Of course not, Rebeca, she's just kidding you. There's no such thing as magic hooves."

"Tía, are there?" Rebeca asked.

"It's whatever you want to believe, Rebeca. I'd like to think there are. Just like if you said the magic word, our horses would fly up above this merry-go-round, their lavender manes becoming wings. And they'd fly far, far away from here, leaving Cipriana and Sara and Benny behind."

"What's the magic word, Tía?"

"I don't know, 'jita. That's the trick. We have to figure it out."

"Oh. Can kids figure it out or just grown-ups?"

"Children are best at figuring these things out. You could figure it out if you really thought hard enough."

Rebeca was quiet. She twisted herself around again and sat next to Cita. "But, Tía, that would be scary flying away from here."

"Oh, no, Rebeca. It would be an adventure. Just think what you might find in the place you're going. Maybe all the horses there have lavender manes. And maybe all the people have lavender eyes just like your mama. And maybe all they do all day long is ride in carriages and eat pink cotton candy and have fun. Wouldn't you like that?"

Rebeca nodded. "Oh, yes, Tía. And . . . and maybe even Mama would be there. And maybe besides cotton candy, we'd get to eat strawberry ice cream all the time, whenever we wanted."

"That's the idea, Rebeca. Wouldn't that be a wonderful place and wouldn't you be glad you went there?"

Rebeca nodded just as the merry-go-round music stopped. "What happened, Tía?"

"The ride's over, 'jita. We have to get off now."

"But I want to go again, Tía. Maybe this time, I can ride on top of the horse like Cipriana."

"In a while, Rebeca," Cita said. "Let's go try some cotton candy."

"What's that, Tía?"

"I don't know myself. I've never had it but I've seen it. It's like you're eating a sweet pink cloud."

"You can't eat clouds, Tía," Benny said, jumping off the merry-go-round platform.

"Who says so?" Cita asked, offering her hands to Rebeca and Cipriana. "As long as you can see it inside your head, you can eat it."

"Na-ah, Tía," said Benny. "I see good things to eat inside my head all the time. But I'm still always hungry."

"Benny!" Cita said, playfully swatting him on the head. "Now, I want each of you to sit over there on that bench and close your eyes. Imagine something you've never eaten before but you've always wanted to. No peeking. I'll be right back."

Cita peered over her shoulder to see if her nieces and nephew were obeying her. It was funny to see them all in a row with their eyes closed like baby birds waiting to be fed. Fingering the four dollar bills tucked into her waistband, she felt like the richest person in the world, able to spend her money so frivolously. As she approached the concession stand, the smells of buttery popcorn intermingled with the distinct aroma of sizzling onions. She wondered what the onions were for. Somehow, they seemed out of place at a carnival.

While she waited patiently in line, she read the short menu: popcorn, caramel apple, Coke, cotton candy, hamburger. Oh! How she had always wanted to taste a hamburger. She had only ever heard about them because they sold them at Diego's Bar on Main. The bar had been known for its tequila until Prohibition started. Then its specialty became American burgers. That must be what the onions were for, she guessed. She inhaled deeply, imagining taking a bite of one that was so big she had to hold it in both hands.

A tap on the shoulder startled Cita. Turning around, she recognized the Methodist minister's wife whose house she cleaned every Wednesday. The woman held the hand of her son, who was staring up at Cita. His nose was runny and he had green snot dripping from one of his nostrils. Cita smiled but her stomach turned. She didn't care for this little boy who whined constantly.

"I thought that was you, Cita, but I thought no, Cita couldn't afford to come to a carnival. Then again, I thought, maybe I'm paying her too much." The woman cackled and Cita felt like slapping her. Instead, she smiled politely.

"No, ma'am. Today I brought my nieces and nephew to enjoy the carnival." Cita pointed to the children.

"Hmm. Sure are a lot of children there. But you all always have big families, don't you? Not me, I'm satisfied with my one. He's a handful, that's for sure, but I love him to death. Don't I, Michael?"

The boy stuck his tongue out first at his mother, then at Cita. It wasn't hard to hate this child and Cita did. She wanted to hand him a handkerchief and say "cochino," but she thought better of it. This unlikable child's mother was her employer and Cita couldn't risk a job, even though she was *cusca*, as Cita called her. She always paid less than the other households, but Cita never questioned it. She needed the money no matter the amount.

"And when are you getting married, Cita? It's time, don't you think?"

"I don't really know, Mrs. Johnson."

"What don't you know? Don't you have a sweetheart, Cita? By your age, I was fighting off boys who wanted to marry me. I loved to make them crazy for me but I finally settled on George. He had more prospects than anyone else and besides, he was a religious boy and Mother liked that."

Cita wondered why Mrs. Johnson was so talkative. When Cita cleaned for her, she hardly said two words to her. She always insisted that Cita enter through the back door and once she opened the door for her, she retreated to her bedroom until it was time for Cita to clean it. By then, she was dressed and ready to go grocery shopping. It was the same routine every week.

"Can I help you?" A man's voice from behind the concession stand was a welcome interruption. The drone of Mrs. Johnson's voice together with the intense rays of the afternoon sun were starting to tire Cita. She tried to hold back a yawn without much success.

"You bored, eh?" the man asked Cita.

"No, no, not at all," she said, trying to hide the last of her yawn by cupping her hand over her half-open mouth. "This is wonderful." Cita could feel the man's eyes studying her. She was starting to feel uncomfortable.

Finally, he said, "Hey, aren't you Roberto's sister or cousin?"

Cita nodded. "His sister."

"I thought you looked like I seen you before. I worked with Roberto on a job."

"Really? Which one?"

"El highway."

"Oh, yes." Cita searched her mind for something else to say. "So what are you doing working here now?"

"Pues, it's hard getting a job these days. Roberto knows. But I have one lined up in Las Vegas este January. My tío has some influence over there and I'm going to start working at the University. El Chato working at El University. My mama says, 'Ooh, que suaviters, mi'jito trabajando con los big wigs.'"

Cita laughed easily. "That sounds good, Chato. Really good."

"Yo sé. And once I get some regular money, I want to find myself a wife. But not until then. I gotta treat her right. I gotta be able to buy her whatever she wants." Chato paused and smiled at Cita. "You doing anything tonight? They got those electric lights on the Ferris wheel and they say it's muy pretty, all lit up at night. Want to go?" Chato smiled again at Cita.

Behind her, Cita heard Mrs. Johnson clear her throat loudly. "Excuse me, please, but we've been waiting in line an awfully long time. Could you carry on your conversation another time? My boy's awfully hungry," she said, picking her pouting boy up into her arms.

"Sorry, Mrs. Johnson," Cita said, turning toward her employer and then back to Chato. Raising her eyebrows, she assumed a sour expression and said, "Que mujer tan peseta. Y su hijo siempre tiene mocos verdes."

Chato laughed out loud and Cita grinned conspiratorially.

"What was that, dear?" Mrs. Johnson asked.

Without looking at her employer, Cita said, "Oh, nothing, Mrs. Johnson, I was just telling Chato I'd like one of each of the items on the menu."

Cita felt herself go hot when Chato winked before turning to fill her order. She felt giddy all of a sudden and her cheeks were starting to ache because she just couldn't stop smiling. When Chato handed back the change, his fingertips touched her palm and she flushed with embarrassment. Taking the tray of food, she didn't even stop to count her change.

"Meet you tonight at seven, Cita?" Chato called out.

Without turning back, Cita gave the slightest nod, walking at a determined pace toward her nieces and nephew. She could hear Mrs. Johnson rattling off her order, her voice now fading away.

"Are your eyes still closed?" she asked them.

"Ay, Tía, you took so long. I'm tired," Sara said.

"And I'm hungry," Benny added.

"Me too," Rebeca and Cipriana said in unison. Opening their eyes, they looked at one another and giggled.

"No peeking, girls," Cita said, setting down the tray of food. "Now, I'm going to give each one of you something different and you have to guess what it is, all right? Whoever guesses right gets an extra ride on the Ferris wheel. How does that sound?"

There was a chorus of jubilant "yeses" as Cita passed around the food. To Sara, she gave the hamburger; Benny got the popcorn. Cipriana got the caramel apple, and Rebeca got the cotton candy. Cita kept the Coke. "So, when I say go, I want each of you to take a bite of what you're holding. All right? One, two, three, go."

"Mine's easy, Tía. I got popcorn!" Benny announced happily, licking up the popped kernels with his tongue. His chin was shiny with butter. "Daddy used to make popcorn sometimes when I was little."

Cita laughed. "You're still little, Benny."

"No sir, Tía. Can I open my eyes now?"

"Not yet. Not until everyone's had a chance to guess. What's yours, Sara? I think yours is the hardest."

"It's some kind of meat, Tía," Sara said hesitantly as she chewed.

"That's right, Sara. What else?" Cita asked.

"It has some kind of bread and onions . . ."

"Yes? Go on." Cita was salivating. Her stomach grumbled.

"What was that, Tía?" Cipriana asked, laughing.

Cita patted her stomach. "You all are making me hungry. Now what's another name for a piece of meat inside some bread?"

"A burrito!" Benny called out.

"That's right, but what's the English word? Maybe the rich kids in your class take it to lunch sometimes . . ."

"A chango," Cipriana said excitedly.

"A what, Cipriana?"

"Chango. You know, Tía, a sangwich."

"That's right, Cipriana!"

"Mary Jane Beford takes them to school. Her mama cuts them into little triangles."

"There's a special name for this kind of sandwich though. It has round pieces of bread on either side . . ."

"Tortillas, Tía?" Rebeca asked with a note of pride in her voice.

"That's right, 'jita, just like tortillas, but I think they're called buns."

"Hamburger!" Sara blurted. "I read about them in school."

"Yes, Sara! You're a smart girl. Now what about Cipriana and Rebeca?"

"I can't bite mine, Tía. It's too big," Cipriana said.

"Give it here. Let me start it for you," Cita said, reluctantly, taking a small bite, then spitting it into her hand.

"What's the matter, Tía?" Cipriana asked, opening her eyes. "Don't you like it?"

"Quick, shut your eyes, Cipriana. It's not that I don't like it, 'jita, I just can't eat what it's made of. But you'll like it. I promise you. It's like eating a candy bar." Handing it back to Cipriana, she told her niece, "A big bite now."

Cipriana's face lit up. "Mmm, Tía, this is good," she said in between crunches. "It tastes like an apple or maybe a pear. I had a pear once at Mary

Jane's. But it tastes like it has some sugar on it too." Cipriana took another bite. "And it's chewy just like a Walnetto."

"Mmm, I want yours, Cipriana," Benny chimed in.

"Wait your turn, Benny," Cita said. "We'll pass everything around so everyone gets a taste. Now what's in a Walnetto, Cipriana?"

"Nuts?"

"Yes. What else? What makes it chewy?"

"Caramel!"

"Yes! So what has caramel on an apple?"

"A Walnetto apple."

"Almost, Cipriana. Try again."

"A caramel apple, Tía," Benny interjected.

"Benny!" Cipriana opened her eyes and looked at Cita. "Is Benny right, Tía?"

Cita nodded.

Nudging Benny with her elbow, Cipriana said, "But Tía, Benny ruined it. Do I still get to go on the Ferris wheel?"

"Of course, Cipriana. You had it right too. All right now, Rebeca." Cita took her niece's free hand in hers but tried to release it quickly. "Ooh, sticky, Rebeca. I see you've already been tasting your treat."

Rebeca nodded, smiling. Her mouth was pink. Her eyes were wide open.

"Rebeca's cheating, Tía," Benny said.

Cita ignored her nephew. "Can you guess, Rebeca?"

"It looks like a pink cloud, Tía."

"That's right, Rebeca."

"This is cotton candy, isn't it, Tía?"

Cita beamed. "You got it, Rebeca!" she said, kissing her niece on the top of her head. "Now, let's share so everyone has a taste."

As they were enjoying the goodies and chattering with their mouths open, Cita noticed a woman staring at them through the crowd. At first, Cita didn't recognize her but as she drew closer, Cita noticed that she was the same woman who sat with a crystal ball at the entrance to the carnival. The woman motioned to Cita with a crooked finger, beckoning her forward. Cita looked all around and finally pointed to herself, questioning the woman with her eyes. Was she pointing to her? The woman nodded. Cita hesitated, wondering what the woman wanted with her. Cita gestured toward the children and mouthed the words, "I can't." The woman nodded again, but this time she moved slowly toward Cita, as if she were wading through water. Her fancy cape flowed behind her, sparkling in the sunlight. Cita was curious, but at the same time a wave of fear passed over her. This was no ordinary woman from Santa Lucía.

Without a word, the woman knelt in front of Cita. The children grew quiet as the woman took Cita's hand into her own. With the fingertips of the other hand, the woman began touching Cita's palm lightly, exploring its surface, caressing each groove, tracing each line. Cita was mesmerized. The woman's touch tickled but it also numbed her.

"You have the hand of an artist, my child," the woman whispered in a monotone. Cita had to draw closer to hear her. "Something happened to you when you were a child . . . something very bad." The woman tilted her head just slightly to meet Cita's gaze. The black pupils stared back at Cita. "And this evil forever molded your destiny . . ."

Cita gasped, trying to pull her hand away from the woman's. The woman enveloped Cita's hand with both of hers, not letting go. "You must follow this destiny or you will die," she said, regarding Cita a moment longer. Cita felt her hand go limp as the woman released it, stood slowly, and disappeared back into the crowd. Her cape trailed behind, the gold stitching bouncing a glint of light from its hem before it too was swallowed up.

Cita stared open-mouthed into the crowd. She couldn't describe what had just happened to her. It felt like a dream, but she could see her nieces and nephew surrounding her. All she knew was that at this very moment she had to get the images that were flying through her head onto paper. She stood abruptly and felt as if she were about to faint. When the dizziness passed, she said, "Let's go home, 'jitos." In the background, she could hear their protests, something about the Ferris wheel and "you promised," but none of that was important now. She didn't care. For some unexplainable reason, she had to get to her blank paper. It was something the woman had said.

Cita made her way through the crowd with the children following behind, whining and pleading. She walked briskly past the concession stand, past the merry-go-round, and past the clowns, seeing only the images that were inside her head, smelling only the aromas of that day so long ago, the day that changed her destiny. Once she reached home, she climbed the steps as if she were sleepwalking, walked right past Mama Fela, ignoring her inquiries, and entered her tiny bedroom, closing the door behind her. From underneath her bed, she took out a stack of papers. Some were smudged with black charcoal and others were blank. Cita rummaged through them until she found a clean one. With a pencil and black chalk, she began sketching frantically until the images began to make sense to her.

She remembered years ago how she would sit, hours at a time, up in the apple tree behind the house, gazing down at anyone who passed and listening to conversations held on the green bench below. The leaves hid her from view in the summertime and she stared into the vast blue sky for as long as she wanted, dreaming of places she had only read about. The best times to hide in the tree were during family gatherings, when she learned secrets, gathered information about her family, and avoided the commotion of insincere reunions.

On that day, during the summer when she turned thirteen, Mama Fela found her preserve and infiltrated it. She called Cita down from the tree and told her to come and say hello to her cousin Lala and her family who were visiting from Colorado. Lala's husband, tall and gaunt, bent and planted a thick, wet kiss upon Cita's cheek. She winced at the man's moist touch. He was ugly and skinny. His bones looked like they would pop from his skin at any moment. His head was shiny with perspiration. To Cita, it seemed as if he had walked from Colorado with no food or drink for weeks. When he kissed her, it felt like she was going to be his next meal.

The man, whom she didn't think she had ever met, looked Cita up and down, chortled, and said to her, "Ya es señorita. Ahorita tienes yerno." Cita could not believe his comment. She was not ready to get married. She was still a little girl. Didn't he see that? It was at that moment she decided she never wanted to grow up and she would never marry a man who kissed with *babas*. It was also the day Cita stopped climbing the tree.

Later, after supper, Mama Fela and Lala were inside chatting and doing dishes. Gilberto was slicing wedges of watermelon from his garden for the children and entertaining them with a story. Cita was back in her tree when Lala's husband called her from below. He asked if he could join her in the tree.

Timidly, she answered yes. Her brothers Robert and Solomón climbed the tree with her sometimes but a grown-up had never done so. To Cita, it seemed as if the tree was groaning with each step he took, climbing higher and higher into her space. For a brief moment, she wished he would catch his pantleg on a branch and fall, but he kept coming. Finally, they were face to face, Cita on one limb, he on another. He told her his limb was the better of the two and asked if she would like to see the view from there. She consented even though she did not wish to. She knew every view possible from this tree, her tree. Hers was the best, but you were always supposed to do what your elders said. Mama Fela always said so.

Awkwardly, she scrambled toward him, this man with babas. She expected him to trade places with her but instead he stayed put. When she reached him, he took her into his lap.

"See, it's better, isn't it?" he asked, pointing out the horizon.

Cita nodded, agreeably, not wanting to offend him.

"You're a pretty girl," he whispered into her ear. "Just like your mama."

"Mama pretty?" she asked incredulously.

"Yes," he said, laughing. "When she was young," he added, whispering.

"Why are you whispering?" Cita asked.

Suddenly, Cita felt him running his hand across her stomach, playing with the hem of her dress. "And what a pretty dress this is. I bet your panties aren't as pretty."

"Yes they are," Cita answered emphatically. "They're lace," she added in explanation. Mama Fela always believed in clean, pretty underwear, and she would spend a little more money in order to accent it with lace. She always told Cita that underwear revealed character. Character revealed class. Cita didn't know exactly what that meant but she knew she must wear clean fancy underwear to please Mama Fela.

He lifted her dress, the yellow one, the one she would never wear again, and revealed her panties. He traced the little lace across the top band of her panties but when he slipped his fingers underneath, Cita felt sick to her stomach, ready to retch. As if by instinct, she stood abruptly and elbowed him in the nose with her angular arm. "Get out of my tree," she screamed, turning and stepping to another limb, kicking him in the stomach. He doubled over in pain and then he lost his balance and fell headfirst down through the branches, flailing frantically for a branch to hang onto. A limb caught his leg and he hung there in space while the leaves of the apple tree fluttered in the autumn breeze. For a brief moment, Cita thought of leaving him there until all the blood rushed to his head or he had to scamper down like an animal. Instead, with her foot, she gently nudged his foot from the limb upon which he was caught and down he fell in a whirl of thrashing sounds until he landed with a thud.

She stared down through the leaves of her apple tree, trying to play back in her mind what had just happened. The clean crisp smell of almost-ripe apples peppered the air. The aroma of Mama Fela's warm apple cake sprinkled with a topping of cinnamon and sugar wafted up through the branches of her tree and she vomited.

Suddenly, her name was called out from below. It was Solomón. Cita looked down through the branches with pleading eyes, expecting her brother to help her understand, to climb the tree and take her to safety. Solomón stared up at her with his mouth open. Even from where she stood, she could see confusion in her brother's eyes and disgust in his contorted face. He ran over to the man and started kicking him viciously, screaming expletives in Spanish until Papa Gilberto rushed to the scene with others following close behind. No one could control Solomón until finally, Papa Gilberto stopped him with violent strokes of his belt.

That was the day that Cita threw away her favorite yellow dress and stopped loving her Mama Fela's apple cake. It was the day she stopped climbing the apple tree and the day her childhood melted away. It was the

September that Solomón left and according to the woman at the carnival, it was the year her destiny was born.

Cita sketched the scene frantically, highlighting here, shading there. Scribbles became forms, lines became shadows. Her hands were black from the charcoal dust that she touched, rubbing smudges into meaning. She sketched into the night, ignoring the knocks on her door and the pleas for her to come out. Finally, she fell asleep, her cheek kissing her art, the dance of light and dark images purging her of her memory.

Cita woke to the sound of yelling. For a moment, she wasn't sure if she was dreaming or awake. She lifted herself from the piece of art she had created last night and discovered she had drooled all over it. Panic surged through her until she realized that it had served its purpose. The last thing she wanted to do was to save it. She studied what she had created once more and then tore it into pieces, strip by strip, bit by bit. It was a final farewell.

The voices grew louder as Cita opened her door. There in the kitchen stood Solomón, red in the face, confronting Mama Fela's questions, with Sara, Benny, Cipriana, and Rebeca looking on. Sara was squinting at her father. Benny's hands were clenched at his sides. Cipriana held Rebeca's hand while Rebeca looked at her father with worried eyes. She appeared to be on the verge of tears.

When Cita entered the room, they all looked at her. Cipriana said, "Tía, you're awake. Tío's taking my cousins. They're going away."

"What? What does she mean, Solomón?" Cita asked.

"As I was telling Mamá, I'm going," Solomón said. "That's all there is to it. I'm leaving Santa Lucía and taking the children with me."

"But Solomón, you can't do that. They're happy here," Cita said.

"That's not what you said yesterday. You said I embarrass them."

"Well, that's true too. But we could help you. Help you stop drinking."

"I don't drink."

"Come on, Solomón, think of them. They lost their mother and now they're going to lose us. We're the only mothers they have."

"You're not their mother. You could never be a good mother."

"What do you mean by that, Solomón?"

"You know exactly what I mean."

"No, Solomón. Actually, I don't. You have to say what you mean."

"You're the one who made me leave, Cita. I left because of you. Not Papá. Not because I wanted to. Because of you, Cita."

"What! Damn you, Solomón. What did I do? You abandoned me, not the other way around."

"I didn't abandon you. I left for you. I know what I saw that day and I never wanted Mamá or Papá to find out."

"Did you? Did you really? And it scared you so much, you went away with your tail tucked between your knees, is that it? You cabrón. I'll never forgive you for leaving."

"What are you two talking about?" Mama Fela asked.

"Never mind, Mamá! Solomón, you don't deserve to be a father."

"That's it. Get in the car," Solomón told his children. "Shit, I just can't stand this place," he said, sweeping up his baby roughly into his arms, inciting a flurry of crying.

Mama Fela grabbed his arm. "Don't do this, Solomón. You can't do it to the children, 'jito. It's not fair to them," she said, trying to speak over the baby's cries.

"Que fair ni fair, Mamá. There's no such thing as fair. We have to go."

Benny rammed his head into his father's backside, punching him in the back with his small fists. "I won't go, Daddy. I won't ever go."

"You'll do as I say or I'll give you a whipping so hard, you won't ever forget it. Do you hear me, Benny?" Solomón said, squelching Benny's punches by seizing his fist and pulling him by it. "Get in the car, now!"

Rebeca started to cry as she hung on to Cipriana.

"I'll have none of that!" Solomón yelled. "Rebeca, Sara, get in the car or I'll give you a whipping too. Whippings aren't just for boys, you know."

Sara looked at her father defiantly while Rebeca began to sob.

"No one wants to go, Daddy. Can't we just stay here and you go by yourself?" Sara said with confidence. "We like it here with Tía Cita. She's the best mama or daddy we've ever had."

Solomón shoved Benny into the car and placed the baby down in the front seat. Glaring at Cita, he strode over to Sara and Rebeca and grabbed them by the back of their necks. He pushed them toward the car and into the backseat. All the children were crying as he climbed into the driver's seat and started up the car.

"Wait!" Mama Fela said sternly, slapping the back window with her hand, signaling for the children to open it. The vehicle started rolling away but Mama Fela screeched at Solomón. "Stop! I must give the children la bendición." The car slowed momentarily while Mama Fela caught the three pairs of hands that were thrust at her. Cita ran to her side, reaching in to touch the children one more time. "Que Dios los bendiga," Mama Fela said, barely grazing the heads of the children with her fingers before Solomón raced the engine and drove away.

Cita, Mama Fela, and Cipriana stood side by side in shock, watching the car disappear into a cloud of dust. They could barely make out the tiny hands of the children as they waved one last time.

They stood in silence until a bead of sweat dripped down into Cita's eye. Cipriana started to cry softly and Cita lifted her into her arms, where she began to sob violently. Cita joined in Cipriana's sounds of sorrow, trying to muffle them in the folds of Cipriana's dress.

Mama Fela shushed her granddaughter and her daughter. "¡Cállense!" she said. "You did this, Cita," Mama Fela said. "It was your own doing."

Cita looked up, startled, her eyes bloodshot, her face wet, and her lips swollen. Without saying a word, she handed Cipriana to Mama Fela and went inside. She withdrew to her room once again where she knelt beside her bed. Again, she reached underneath her bed and this time, she pulled out a wooden tray with a tin box of paints and two Folgers coffee cans. One had a handful of paint brushes; the other was filled with murky water from a previous painting session. Cita found a clean piece of paper and, with a pencil, began sketching her nieces and nephew enjoying their first merry-go-round ride at the carnival. Once the sketch was finished, she began to add color. This was her destiny.

CHAPTER TEN

THE BLACKBOARD

On a Thursday afternoon, Graciela walked leisurely along the dirt road, basking in the warmth of the autumn day, listening to the pleasant rustle of the cottonwood leaves, already brushed with gold. The expanse of azure sky never ceased to amaze her. At this time of year, it seemed to rise up and expand, welcoming all with open arms, yet creating a soft intimate light that brought calm and a sense of well-being to everyone who was touched by its beauty.

For once in her teaching career, Graciela loved her new post in Pastura. She looked forward to seeing the woman who boarded her. Mrs. Campos was tiny in stature but her heart was as big as the vast New Mexico sky. She seemed to enjoy sharing her home with Graciela and always had a cheerful fire crackling in the cookstove when Graciela returned from school. Mrs. Campos had turned the front room over to Graciela, with only a curtain dividing the two-room house. Every day, Graciela eagerly anticipated getting home, knowing that no matter how fatiguing the day had been or how raucous the children, the calcimined peach walls, the shiny wood floors, and the windows that were accented by lovely lace curtains would hearten her.

Even before she entered the sunny space, Graciela could smell the sweet, robust aroma of roasting green chile beckoning her to Mrs. Campos's table. When she opened the door, the pungent smells of autumn enveloped her all at once. Memories of autumns gone by were unleashed. Mrs. Campos stood with a fork in hand, turning the blackened chiles.

"Do I hear my very own teacher?" Mrs. Campos sang, still with her back toward Graciela.

"Yes," Graciela replied, amused. "It's me, Mrs. Campos."

"Come and make yourself a little burrito. I just finished chopping the chile."

Graciela set her tote down and washed her hands at the platón. Taking a fresh tortilla from underneath a towel, she spread several spoonfuls of chile onto the bread. Mixed in with the chile were diced tomatoes and miniscule pieces of what Graciela knew could only be garlic.

"Oh, Mrs. Campos," Graciela said with delight, "this is delicious. I used to think Mama Fela made the best chile, but I think you have her beat."

"It's the chile, dear. Over from Puerta de Luna. And my garlic, of course. That's the secret. A lot of garlic. How was school today?"

Graciela finished chewing. "Fine, she said. I had to punish Horacio Gallegos for locking two girls in the outhouse. Ay, that Horacio," she smiled. "He's a handful."

Mrs. Campos laughed heartily. "All the Gallegoses were. Every one of them. You'll wonder what went wrong if a day goes by that you don't have to give him some correction." Mrs. Campos turned. "You had a letter at the post office today." With a lift of her chin, Mrs. Campos gestured toward Graciela's small desk in the corner of the room. "Allá."

Graciela tensed though she knew it was probably from Mama Fela. If it was, this would be the fifth letter from her since she had arrived at Mrs. Campos's. In her letters, Mama Fela had spoken of Cita's melancholy since Solomón's hasty departure. Mama Fela refused to speak of the incident itself but referred to it by way of explaining her concern for Cita. "That girl won't talk to me. Won't eat my food. Plays with it, but doesn't eat it," she had said of Cita. "It hurts me not to see her eat," she added. "Good food gone to waste, that's what. Now I'm feeding los gringos trampes just like your husband. Not because I want to. I have to so God doesn't punish me for throwing away good food. If you ask me, I'd rather give two dimes instead of one every Sunday than have one of those dirty men set foot inside my house. Your husband doesn't seem to mind, though. He invites them in like guests for Sunday dinner. I tell him to be careful because of the children but he goes on doing what he likes. I don't know where he learned to be so good, that son of mine. Not from me, that's the truth. He's more like his father, that one. They know a good thing when they've got it, los trampes. And all of them come now like a trail of ants. They must tell the others where the good food is."

Graciela had replied to Mama Fela each time, assuring her that she would write to Cita. Like Mama Fela, she was worried about her sister-in-law but did not know how to help. In her last letter, she had asked Cita to take a few days to come visit her but she doubted very much that Cita would accept the invitation. It was partly a selfish request, for she wanted Cita to bring her children along since she could not afford the gas to go home. But still she heard no response.

"I'm going to brown a little round steak for supper, Graciela, and you can join me if you'd like," Mrs. Campos said, interrupting Graciela's thoughts. "Mr. Campos butchered a cow just last week."

"Where is Mr. Campos tonight, Señora? He's usually back from the ranch on Thursday evenings, isn't he?"

Mrs. Campos nodded matter-of-factly, a tone of resignation surfacing. "Pues, this time of year, he's busy with the cattle. But he'll be back on Sunday for church," she added optimistically.

Graciela smiled. She liked Mr. Campos as much as she liked Mrs. Campos, even though he rarely joined in their conversation when he was home. He was a shy man, quiet, but he had such a presence about him that no one ever forgot that he was in the room. She and Mrs. Campos carried on the same way as they did during the week, but when he was home, they compassionately refrained from talking about fashion or other frivolous topics. He reminded her of what she thought her father might have been like had he lived past her third birthday. He had been a cattleman too.

"What's got you down, Graciela?" asked Mrs. Campos.

Graciela shook her head, embarrassed that her thoughts might have been transparent.

"Nothing that a little meat and fresh chile couldn't cure now, I hope?"

With a swallow, Graciela escaped from her reverie, compelling herself instead to set Mrs. Campos's table. As Mrs. Campos placed the last of the roasted chiles in a big sturdy bowl and covered it with a kitchen cloth to steam, Graciela asked if she could help with the meat. Mrs. Campos instructed her to retrieve it from the new icebox that Mr. Campos had just bought her.

"This is the first time we'll have meat from an icebox," Mrs. Campos said proudly. "It's usually either freshly butchered or dried. Mr. Campos promises me it will taste so much better than dried. We'll see."

"This looks so fancy and new, Mrs. Campos," Graciela said, opening first the tall wood box, then the metal container inside. "It looks so different from my neighbor's icebox in Santa Lucía. So much bigger, actually."

"Is the meat still cold? That's the important thing."

Graciela took out a package wrapped in coarse brown paper. "I think so. The paper is wet though." She handed the package to Mrs. Campos.

"From the ice, I think," Mrs. Campos said, smelling the package. "Seems fresh enough." Setting a cast-iron skillet on the hot stove, she unwrapped the meat and proceeded to fry it up, sprinkling salt and pepper on top as it began to sizzle in the pan. Graciela inhaled the mouth-watering scent wafting out into the room in a swirl of savory steam. Before she came to stay with Mrs. Campos, meat was a rare treat, though deep in the recesses of her mind she remembered its taste.

Graciela ate ravenously, enjoying the succulent meat complemented by the roasted flavor of the green chile. She wanted to stop after the first serving, guilty that she was eating Mrs. Campos's food, but she could not. Usually, she was extremely disciplined but Mrs. Campos's easy and generous ways made it acceptable to lapse from time to time.

By the time Graciela had parted company with Mrs. Campos and retreated to her own space, it was late, and though she was tired, she wondered what news the letter from Mama Fela brought. Without even so much as a glance at the return address, she slipped a hairpin across the envelope and removed the folded page. Instead of Mama Fela's tight script, a single sentence in thick black charcoal popped out at Graciela. "I'll be there Thursday." It was from Cita.

Just as Graciela's heart danced a beat, she heard the rumble of a car engine outside her window. Jumping up to the front door, she swung it open and bounded down the steps. Cita and Cipriana bounced from the car. "Mama!" Cipriana called, pouncing into Graciela's arms. "I'm in the

A group now! I'm not a dummy anymore."

The impact of Cipriana's body made Graciela lose balance momentarily. Her daughter was growing up and Graciela was not there to witness it. A pang of guilt left Graciela wistful. With a tender hand, she smoothed back Cipriana's hair and said, "Good for you, 'jita. I'm so proud!"

In the meantime, Cita moved around the car and hugged Graciela from behind. Graciela laughed out loud, amused at Cita's old antics.

"I just got your letter," Graciela said, trying to remove herself from the tangle of arms. "I'm so glad you finally came. How have you been, Cita?"

"Oh, you know, Graciela. I'm fine some days. Others are harder. Lucky I have Cipriana here to keep me company." Cita squeezed Cipriana's shoulders, holding her in front of her like a shield, Graciela thought. Another stab of longing coursed through her consciousness.

"How are Pablito and the baby?" Graciela asked.

"Good. I was going to bring them but Mamá convinced me not to. Besides, they're good company for her."

"And Robert?"

"Working, Graciela." Cita smiled and Graciela responded in kind. Nothing more had to be said. Cita understood her, understood what made her heart soar. Now she wanted to try to cheer up Cita.

"You must be hungry," Graciela said, ushering Cita and Cipriana into Mrs. Campos's house as if it were her own. She swelled with pride as she gave them a quick tour of her living quarters, lighting the way with her desk lamp.

"This is nice, Mama. It's nicer than our house. Who's in there?" Cipriana asked, motioning toward the curtain.

"Shh," Graciela whispered gently. "That's Mrs. Campos and she's probably fast asleep by now. Set your things down on my bed over there and I'll warm something up quickly. Take the light," she added, handing over the oil lamp to Cita. In the semi-darkness, she stoked the fire and added more wood. As quietly as she could, she rummaged through the box where she kept her food. Since Saturday was grocery day, all she could find was a can of creamed corn, a box of oatmeal, and a can of peaches. She scraped the corn into a small cast-iron skillet, placing it on top of the woodstove. Methodically, she stirred their supper while the spoon's rhythmic dance, metal against metal, drew her into a trance. In the background of her thoughts, she could hear Cita and Cipriana shushing each other and giggling.

Small footsteps and then the rush of Mrs. Campos's voice calling her catapulted her from her dreamlike state. Graciela's caretaker had swept aside the curtain that separated their quarters and crossed into the kitchen. For a brief moment, Graciela held her breath in dreaded anticipation of a scolding.

Graciela could hear Mrs. Campos's staccato inhalations and in the moonlight, she could see her nostrils slightly flared. Her voice, however, was still kind. "What in heaven's name are you doing, Graciela? Didn't I feed you enough tonight?" she asked.

"I'm sorry, Mrs. Campos, for waking you. My sister-in-law and daughter just arrived and . . ."

"Well, why didn't you say so sooner?" Mrs. Campos interrupted. "Come. Come. I can't see you in the dark and I've heard so much about both of you!"

Cita and Cipriana did as they were bid, moving across the semi-dark space uncertainly toward Mrs. Campos. All at once, she enveloped them in her tiny arms and kissed them both. Beause Cita towered over her, Mrs. Campos only managed to graze Cita's neck, so Cipriana received the greater share of the woman's loving embrace. "You're both welcome here, just like your mamá. So now, what's your mamá feeding you?" she asked, inspecting the contents of the skillet.

Before Graciela had a chance to respond, Mrs. Campos proclaimed, "¡Ave María Purísima! Graciela. Is that all you're feeding them? Creamed corn! Well now, I won't hear of it! Do you hear me? I won't hear of it. They must have a little meat and tortilla too."

"Oh, Mrs. Campos, I couldn't impose," Graciela pleaded. "You've been too generous, already."

"Nonsense! I won't have my schoolteacher's family blowing away in the wind. Not under my watch. Sit, now. Make yourself comfortable," she said, motioning the newcomers toward the table then bustling away toward her icebox. In minutes, she duplicated the meal that she and Graciela had enjoyed earlier, and Graciela watched her daughter and even Cita devour the good food. Graciela beamed with delight, ecstatic that she could share the treasure that was Mrs. Campos with her family. She almost felt as if she were showing her off, like a proud mother would show off a child. In this case, it was a proud adult child showing off her ideal mother. At this moment, Graciela felt perfectly happy.

Three in a row, they squeezed into Graciela's narrow bed, giggling like schoolchildren. Even Graciela let herself relax and be carried away by the momentary bliss. They talked for what seemed like hours until Cipriana showed the first signs of sleepiness. Quietly, Graciela and Cita continued to talk.

"So what do you teach the first few weeks of school, Graciela?"

Graciela thought for a moment. "It depends on the child's age. I try to get a feel for where each child is. I have each of them read aloud and I give them a series of math tests. With the little ones, I have to start with basic things like how to answer when the teacher calls your name or how to get into line."

"Really? That basic?"

"Cita, some of them have never been to school before. Many of them only speak Spanish at first."

"So how do they start to read then?"

"With picture cards. I use their Spanish vocabulary to build their English vocabulary. I show them a picture of a house and they say, 'casa.' Then I introduce the English word. By the end of the year, they're reading in English."

"Wow, Graciela. How do you do that?"

"Well, it's funny, Cita, but I'm not even supposed to allow the children to speak Spanish on the school grounds. But that's just nonsense. It's ironic that their Spanish helps them read in English."

"The rebel!"

Graciela laughed.

"Have you gotten in trouble?"

"No. But the children are reading at grade level or higher by June and that's all that matters to the school board."

"So how do you start teaching them to read full sentences in English?"

"I teach them nursery rhymes."

"Nursery rhymes, really?"

Graciela nodded.

"Like 'Little Bo Peep Lost Her Sheep'?"

"That's right. And 'Humpty Dumpty' and 'Peter Peter Pumpkin Eater.' All of them."

"Do you have a book, Graciela?"

"Sure. Why, Cita?"

"No reason. I just want to refresh my memory. I was never that good of a reader. In Spanish or English!" Cita said mirthfully. "Maybe you can teach me."

"Oh, Cita!" Graciela laughed. She thought Cita was joking but the silence afterward made her wonder. In no time, Cita was fast asleep and Graciela soon followed.

In the morning, Cita was gone. The car was still parked outside so she couldn't have gone far, thought Graciela, peeking out the window. In a moment of self-indulgence, Graciela scooted back down into her covers and propped herself up on one elbow, lovingly surveying her daughter's sleeping features as a ray of sunlight caressed her cheek. How quickly time passed, Graciela thought as she wound one of Cipriana's curls around her little finger. How quickly they grow up. Cipriana would be celebrating another birthday in just two weeks and Graciela would be absent, again. Cipriana's freckles were fading as rapidly as the years were passing. Her hair was growing longer and darker and she was skinnier than ever. Even her tiny nose was taking on more mature proportions. It felt as if it had been years instead of just weeks that she had last seen this little daughter of hers. She was little no more. In fact, Graciela had been the recipient of a few swift kicks in the night. Graciela looked down underneath the covers and spied the culprits. Even Cipriana's feet were stretching out. No wonder her husband had recently nicknamed their daughter Las Patas

Largas, Graciela mused.

Despite her intense desire to linger a while longer, Graciela dragged herself from her daughter's side to groom herself for the day ahead. She would allow Cipriana to sleep until the last possible moment or at least until she prepared breakfast. It felt so good to take on the role of mother again and Graciela savored every moment. She was glad that she could enjoy the privilege alone without having to make conversation with adults. The time with Cipriana would be short and she wanted to make the most of it.

At last, when Graciela had a roaring fire going and the oatmeal was bubbling, she gently woke Cipriana. "Rise and shine, 'jita!" she called cheerfully, opening up the curtains to the day's full glory. Mrs. Campos's sunny perspective was contagious.

"Hi, Mama," Cipriana responded immediately as she rubbed the last remnants of sleep from her eyes. Without protest, Cipriana rose, dressed, and groomed herself very self-sufficiently and joined Graciela at the breakfast table. Graciela was the tiniest bit rueful that Cipriana didn't ask for even a hint of help. She could not blame anyone but herself, though.

After breakfast, they strolled toward school in the morning light while Cipriana chattered on about third grade in Santa Lucía and Graciela absorbed her every word.

"Mama, we're even learning poetry and Miss Shute says we're going to have a recital in the spring."

"That sounds exciting, Cipriana!"

"I know. We even get to wear our best dress because we'll be up in front of an audience, Mama."

"Is your Mama Fela going to make you a new dress?"

"I don't know. I haven't asked her yet."

"Well, you better ask her, Cipriana. Time's a-wasting."

Cipriana laughed easily. "But Mama, it's a long ways off yet. It's not 'til next spring!"

"Spring will be here sooner than you expect, 'jita," Graciela said knowingly. "Now come on. Let's race before your mama's late for school!"

Up ahead, she saw the children already playing in the school yard.

When Graciela reached the schoolhouse, breathless and with a terrible stitch in her side, all she wanted was to tell the children who surrounded her and Cipriana to take their seats. Instead, their boisterous inquiries made it impossible to get their attention.

"Who's that, Mrs. Romero?"

"Can she play with us?"

"There's a strange lady inside."

At the last comment, Graciela's ears perked up. She clutched Cipriana's hand and took the steps into the school building two at a time. Inside, Cita stood at the front of the classroom with her back toward Graciela, very intent upon a corner of the long blackboard that graced the entire wall. Graciela felt her mouth drop open. Cita was creating a world of color and animation, one that she herself recognized and one that was sure to delight the children. The nursery rhymes Graciela would teach her first graders were splashed onto the blackboard with pastel chalk. Jack and Jill, the moon-jumping cow, Jack Sprat and his wife, and Humpty Dumpty all came to life at the hands of Cita.

Graciela stood with her mouth gaping. She could hear the gleeful mumblings of the children as she stood awestruck.

"Say something, Graciela."

Graciela closed her mouth self-consciously, realizing for the first time it had been open. "Oh, Cita," she said finally. "I . . . I didn't realize . . ."

"What? That I could draw?"

"Oh, no, Cita. This isn't drawing." Graciela shook her head slowly from side to side, inspecting the long blackboard at the front of the classroom. "Drawing doesn't seem to go far enough. Cita, this is art."

Cita let out a little laugh, which jolted Graciela from her reverie but delighted her just the same. She stared at Cita but realized she did not recognize this woman who stood before her, wiping her hands on a handkerchief that was soiled with the remnants of color. "Cita, I didn't know." Graciela hesitated. "I didn't know you could do that."

Cita laughed nervously. "Graciela, you act as if I just performed a miracle. It's nothing, really."

Graciela fell into her chair at her desk without taking her eyes from the blackboard. "That's not nothing, Cita. That's really something."

Cita stepped back to inspect her work, distracting Graciela momentarily. Out of the corner of her eye, Graciela thought she saw the hint of a smile.

"Cita, you really need to do something with that."

"Like what, Graciela?"

"Like be paid for it, Cita, instead of cleaning other people's houses. Not that that's not important, Cita, but you have this . . . this talent of making art, and not many people can claim that."

Cita looked on, considering her work. "Thanks, Graciela. Thanks for saying that."

"I'm not exaggerating, Cita. This—this is something else."

Graciela was distracted all morning long. Every once in a while, she just had to give in to the object of her distraction and look at the magnificent blackboard. Finally, she gave in completely and dismissed school before lunch. By that time, she had sent Cita and Cipriana home to retrieve Mrs. Campos with instructions to bring a blanket and to meet her for a picnic lunch back at the school in forty-five minutes.

In honor of Cita, Graciela went to the little corner store and bought Vienna sausages, deviled ham, sweet pickles, an onion, saltines, and four bottles of soda pop. Never before had she splurged on such items, but this was going to be a celebration. She would have to skimp on food until her next paycheck.

Back at her desk in the schoolhouse, Graciela prepared a dainty spread with deviled ham, finely diced sweet pickles, and a bit of onion. She smoothed this onto the saltines and arranged them on the waxy paper that the crackers were wrapped in. She was opening the can of Vienna sausages when she heard the approach of voices. Leaving the lunch, she greeted Mrs. Campos, Cita, and Cipriana at the head of the steps.

"I hear we're going to have a pic-i-nic, dear," said Mrs. Campos.

"That's right, Señora. For once, you have to let me treat you. You've been so kind and generous to me all these weeks."

"Nonsense, Graciela. You're like a daughter to me."

Graciela basked in the compliment though she did not know how to respond. Instead of replying directly, she said, "Mrs. Campos, we're having a celebration."

"Oh? And what are we celebrating?"

Graciela stepped to Mrs. Campos's side and pointed to the blackboard. "Cita made it," she told her.

Mrs. Campos gasped. "My goodness, child."

"See?" Graciela said, looking straight at Cita. Bending to retrieve the pop bottles, Graciela distributed each one. "I would like to make a toast to Cita."

"Graciela!" Cita exclaimed in mock annoyance.

"Ooh, Nehi, Mama. I've never had a Nehi soda pop before."

"Let's listen, 'jita. We're toasting Cita."

"What's that? What's toasting, Mama?"

"A toast is a statement of our support for Cita's incredible talent, 'jita. Now hold your bottles high and together we say, 'To Cita.'"

"To Cita," they said in unison, holding up their Nehi bottles and clanking them together.

Cita giggled nervously, grinning from cheek to cheek. It was the first time that Graciela had seen Cita look embarrassed. When she clinked bottles with Cita, she was overcome with emotion and made a gesture that even surprised herself. She winked and in that wink, Graciela knew their bond was forever sealed.

"You'd like my niece Margarita," Mrs. Campos told Cita. "She paints pictures like you."

"She does?"

"Yes. She's a schoolteacher too."

"Where, Mrs. Campos?"

"Why, over in Las Vegas. She teaches during the week and makes her pictures on weekends."

"Does she sell her work?"

"Pues, no, I don't think so but she was telling me there's talk about El Roosevelte starting a program for artists right there in Las Vegas."

"A program?" Cita asked.

"A federal program?" Graciela interrupted. "Do the artists get paid?" she inquired, raising her eyebrows at Cita as if to say, "Did you hear what I just heard?"

"Pues, I think so. Margarita said it's like the WPA only instead of building bridges, they paint pictures onto walls. Pretty up the government buildings, I think."

"And who can join?" Graciela and Cita both asked at the same time. Looking at each other, they exploded into a joyful titter.

Mrs. Campos smiled. "Why don't I give you Margarita's address and you can ask her yourself. I'm sure she can answer all your questions. Both of yours," she added playfully, nodding at the two women.

Like a child, Cita bounced toward Mrs. Campos and enfolded her in her arms. Kissing the top of Mrs. Campos's head, she whispered, "Thank you."

Mrs. Campos took Cita's hands in hers. Squeezing them, she said, "You're a good girl, Cita. A good girl."

"Now, can we eat, Mama?" Cipriana exclaimed, cutting into the moment.

All the women laughed at once.

"I should say so, 'jita. If there's ever been the right time for a celebration, it's now." Graciela moved toward her desk, handing out one item for each to carry. "Let's take our picnic outside, shall we?"

"But, Mama, I think we should eat here," Cipriana said.

"Here, 'jita? In the classroom?"

Cipriana nodded. "Right here in front of Cita's picture."

"Well?" she asked the others. When they gave their enthusiastic approval, Graciela told her daughter, "I think it's a wonderful idea, 'jita." Taking the blanket from the foot of her desk, she unfolded it and tossed it up and open onto the floor of her classroom with a snap of her wrists. In a swarm, the women and Cipriana descended upon the blanket, extolling the delicacies that Graciela had whipped up.

"What are these little weenies, Graciela? Mmm, they're so good," Mrs. Campos said, stuffing one into her mouth.

"Now this meal has imagination, Graciela. Somehow, I don't think

Mama Fela would approve," Cita said, smirking, taking up another saltine smothered in deviled ham.

Graciela cracked a smile in response but she felt uneasy doing so, as if she were being disloyal to Mama Fela. She didn't always understand the relationship between Cita and her mother and it made her uncomfortable to witness their disagreements. But Graciela did know that she was going to have to help Mama Fela understand Cita's desire to be an artist. She herself didn't quite know what it meant because it was worlds away from her reality. But she did know that it was important to Cita and for that reason alone, she would help. Instinctively, she knew too that it wasn't merely a matter of being important or not. Pursuing her art was a matter of survival. It would mean the difference between fulfillment or stagnation, between a life in bloom or wither. She had seen Cita blossom today with pastel in hand and she wanted to do everything she could to encourage this growth. Like anything though, it would require change. Change in mind-set. Change in routine. Even change in loyalties, and that's what she was most afraid of for Mama Fela's sake. Graciela wondered if she was up to the task.

That afternoon, Graciela sat with Cita, helping her to compose a letter of introduction to Margarita Herrera. After supper, Graciela and Mrs. Campos bid farewell to Cita and Cipriana. Graciela was surprised and disappointed by their short stay. She had guessed that they would visit through the weekend, but Cita informed her that she had a house to clean in the morning. If Graciela could appreciate anything, it was a sense of responsibility. So instead of focusing on their departure, she made Cita promise to let her know the minute she heard back from Mrs. Campos's niece. Graciela assured her daughter that she would be home in two weeks for her birthday, knowing now she would do whatever it took to make the trip. Finally, Graciela and Mrs. Campos stood waving to the retreating car. Graciela crossed her arms, trying to stave off the chill that enveloped her body, though the day was warm. Mrs. Campos put her arm around Graciela's waist. "Come in, dear," she said kindly.

"I'll be just a minute, Mrs. Campos. Thank you."

Mrs. Campos nodded and retired into her house alone. Graciela stood there in silence long after the rumble of the car had disappeared, long after Cipriana's voice had faded with the dust. Despite a tinge of loneliness, Graciela felt excited for the possibilities that lay ahead for Cita. Instead of following Mrs. Campos inside, Graciela made her way in the dark to the schoolhouse. She wanted to see Cita's work one last time before the evening was gone.

By the light of a moonbeam, Graciela examined the world of color Cita had created. She had seen something bloom in Cita that day and didn't want to ever forget it. Silently, she took it all in, as if it were her own breath that she depended upon.

As she turned to leave, she noticed an unusual object on her desk. Picking it up, she turned it this way and that, trying to catch a sliver of light from the window. In a second, a flicker of recognition set in. It was the handkerchief that Cita had used that day to wipe away the smudges of color from her hands. Graciela grasped it, tucking it into the sleeve of her blouse. If she could only preserve this day forever.

❧

CHAPTER ELEVEN

HOLES

Cita closed the door of the brick house behind her, pocketed her week's earnings, and began walking home. The next day was the first day of the new year, but somehow it already seemed old to Cita. Tomorrow she would be doing the same thing she had done today and in her mind's eye, one year from tomorrow would promise the same. She imagined herself thirty years in the future still cleaning houses: wiping other people's dirt off furniture she would never be able to afford, folding the socks of the children she would never have, and scrubbing floors on her hands and knees instead of giving thanks to God in a place of worship, a God whose existence she was beginning to question. At times, Cita thought perhaps she should enter a convent if only to immerse herself in a community of believers. Maybe there she would find evidence of an active God. She wasn't sure to what extent she wanted a divine presence in her life or if it was even possible, but she didn't want emptiness either. And emptiness is what she felt day after day.

Even Mrs. Stevenson and her daughter were going to celebrate the new year by giving a dinner party that evening, though in Cita's eyes, they didn't have much to celebrate. Mrs. Stevenson was a widow of many years, hardly able to maneuver her bulk without the help of a cane. Her daughter, a spinster going on forty or forty-five, was an entire head taller than most men and three times as skinny. They lived in comfort and had money to spare, but otherwise their lives seemed dismal to Cita.

Despite Cita's daily visit to their home, it was messy every morning when she arrived. Dirty dishes filled the sink and crumbs littered the counters. Around midday, once a week when the ladies were finished with their baths, Cita washed the lavatory and the tub and scrubbed the linoleum floor after picking up the dirty clothes that lay strewn about. The house was usually dark, its drapes drawn frequently and doors shut tight against intruders, holding secrets captive in closed-off rooms. Even though her curiosity sometimes forced her to peek through a keyhole or inspect a bathroom cabinet to see what type of soap the ladies of the house used, Cita's intrusions stopped there.

This morning, the younger Miss Stevenson had asked Cita if she could help with the cleanup after the party. Happy for any work she could get, Cita accepted the offer without hesitation, but now she remembered the promise she had made to Cipriana days ago to celebrate the new year by taking her to the new Shirley Temple movie tonight. Cita never broke her promises to Cipriana, and she wasn't about to start now. At the same time, she had made a commitment to her employer. She would have to figure out a way to do both.

Normally, it would probably take her about two hours to clean up a kitchen, she thought, but then again, this was Miss Stevenson who was cooking. Every pot and pan was removed, every bowl and serving spoon used when she cooked. And that was just for pancakes for two on Sunday morning. Tonight would be much worse.

Cutting through the alley, Cita stopped in front of Graciela's house, where Cipriana was removing the laundry from the clothesline. Watching her, she had an idea. She would get Cipriana to help her with the dishes after the dinner party. Together, they could finish the work in no time and then they could enjoy the show free of guilt. Cita's conscience would be clear, having fulfilled both promises. Positive of her plan, Cita called out excitedly, waving her free arm, "Cipriana!"

Cipriana turned and the sheet she was taking from the line fell to the ground. "Tía! Where've you been? I've missed you."

Cita giggled, hugging her niece. "You must like having your mama home for a few days now that school's out for Christmas vacation."

"Uh-huh! And you know that tomorrow we're going to have fried chicken! We never eat that and then Mama's even going to make orange Jell-O with fruit cocktail. Oh, Tía, can't you come for supper?"

"Sounds delicious, Cipriana. I'd love to. It's fine with your mama, though?"

"'Course, Tía."

"Don't you think you should ask first?"

Cipriana shook her head. "Mama says you're always welcome here. Always, Tía."

"That's nice of your mama, Cipriana, but ask anyway, all right? I'd feel better. In fact, if you promise me you'll ask, I'll be over here tomorrow ready to eat until I'm blue in the face or I can't button my skirt, whichever comes first. How's that?"

Cipriana beamed.

"But right now, I have a question for you."

"What, Tía?" Cipriana sounded excited.

"Tonight we're going to the picture show, right?"

Cipriana nodded enthusiastically.

"But first, I need your help."

"Sure, Tía," Cipriana responded. "What do you want me to do?"

"I have a job to do before the show, washing dishes at the Stevensons', and I thought you might want to help."

"All right, Tía. I'm good at that."

"Then, Miss Stevenson will pay us fifty cents, we can go to the movies, and you can keep the dime that we'll have left."

"Are you sure, Tía? The whole dime? I'm going to be rich in one night," Cipriana said, grinning.

"And you can spend it any way you like, Cipriana. The movie is my treat tonight. How does that sound?"

Cipriana's eyes lit up as she nodded again and again.

"I'll pick you up at about six."

Cleaning other people's houses was a way to make money but Cita didn't want to do it for the rest of her life. She realized she wasn't really very good at it because instead of scrubbing the floor until it shone, she imagined how it would look after painting a picture of it on her canvas at home. It would not have a speck of dirt on it, it would be waxed until it was as slippery as ice, and it would even be a different color or pattern, an idea she had gotten while flipping through ladies' magazines. In her mind's eye, she would redecorate kitchens and living rooms, but she never actually got the room as clean as Mama Fela would have. And knowing that she wasn't the most tidy person in the world made her question her suitability for the job. She wasn't like her mother, from whose floors you could eat. She was more like the Stevensons, only she didn't have anyone to pick up after her.

Cita knew they should enter through the kitchen but she wanted to see how it felt to enter a home as a party guest so she led Cipriana to the front porch. "You know your great-grandfather used to own this house."

"No. When?" Cipriana asked.

"Probably twenty years ago or so. At least."

"What happened?"

"He sold it so he could build the stone house where your Mama Soledad lives now."

"Really? But I thought they always lived in that house."

"Not always. They used to live in Las Vegas too." Cita thought for a moment. "But I guess they've always lived there since you've been alive."

Cita looked for a doorbell and pressed it. No sound emerged. She rang it again but realized it didn't work. She should have known the Stevensons wouldn't have a doorbell that worked properly. She rapped on the door lightly and then stood back from the door, her eyes expectant. She looked at Cipriana and then back at the door. No one came. Once again, she took a step forward and this time, with a fist, she knocked loudly. She stood so close, trying to hear movement, her eyelashes could have touched the door. Finally, hearing footsteps approach, she stepped back.

"Cita! What are you doing here?"

"Miss Stevenson," Cita said, cocking her head sideways. "Remember? I'm here to help clean the kitchen."

"Yes, I realize that. But . . ." The hostess turned briefly as if searching out her mother among the guests inhabiting the dining room. Cita could hear the clamor of voices inside. Cita noticed the hesitation and for a brief moment, she wished she had gone through the kitchen. "Well, come in, why don't you. And who's this young miss?"

"Oh, this is my niece, Cipriana. She came to help."

"Well, how do you do?" Miss Stevenson took Cipriana's hand in hers. "That's awfully nice of you to accompany your aunt. Well, come in and

I'm sure Cita will show you the way."

Cita took Cipriana by the hand. Because her palm was sweaty, Cita could tell the situation made her niece nervous. As they walked toward the kitchen, all the guests in the dining room turned around. Some were holding crystal flutes and sipping the pinkish liquid that filled them and some were eating from their forks, dabbing the corners of their mouths with white napkins. The men were dressed in suits and ties. The women wore emerald green and white and even red dresses, not made from the bolts of material found at the mercantile but probably purchased from catalogs like Spiegel or even Neiman Marcus, stores that advertised in *Ladies' Home Journal*. Cita noticed the shimmering necklaces hanging delicately around the swanlike necks of some and heavily around those who wore them only to advertise their wealth. Some of the jewels were so heavy around their necks that the women hunched forward. Cita imagined their mothers nagging them to sit up straight.

One woman waved. "Hello, Cita. Be at my house Tuesday afternoon, right, dear?"

Cita nodded and tried to smile. She quickly ushered Cipriana into the kitchen. As the door swung back and forth, Cita stared at it until it stopped. "Did you see the way they were dressed, Cipriana? My god, I wish I could be like that. Not like the old fat ones with jewelry ready to pop from their turtle necks, but like those other ones. Did you see the one in the red? With that ruby necklace? I bet you she had shoes to match. Didn't she look absolutely elegant? Oh god, I wish I looked like that."

"Like who, Tía?"

"Like the lady in the red gown."

"There wasn't a lady in red, Tía." Cipriana sounded puzzled and Cita wondered if she had imagined it.

"Of course there was. She was sitting next to Mrs. Stevenson."

"Well then who was she, Tía?"

"I don't know. I've never seen her before, but she looked beautiful, whoever she was."

"How do you know it was a ruby, Tía? I thought only princesses wore jewels like that."

"Well, yes, either royalty like queens and princesses or rich people. And she was probably rich."

"What if she was a real queen, Tía?"

Cita grinned. "I doubt there are any queens around Santa Lucía," she said, poking Cipriana in the belly. They both laughed.

"And wasn't that Dr. Beford?" Cita asked.

Cipriana nodded.

"But I didn't see any sign of Mrs. Beford, did you?"

"No, but she probably can't come out."

"What do you mean?"

"She can't walk."

"Well, I know that, Cipriana, but that doesn't mean she can't go anywhere. She has a wheelchair, doesn't she?"

Cipriana shrugged. "All I know is Mary Jane says she's a cripple."

"That's not very nice, Cipriana."

"But that's what Mary Jane says, Tía."

"I believe you, 'jita, but it's still not nice to say 'cripple.' I'm sure Mary Jane doesn't call her mother cripple to her face."

"Well, I don't know. Once when I went home with Mary Jane for lunch, she . . . oh no, Tía. Look!"

Cipriana's abrupt change of subject and demeanor startled Cita. "What, 'jita?" she asked with deep concern, focusing on the object of Cipriana's pointed finger. Cita was not at all surprised by what she saw and couldn't help but be amused by Cipriana's consternation. She knew this could only be the work of Miss Stevenson—no one else. Every pot and pan in the house had been used. Every spice imaginable from curry powder to sage was on the counter, far from the empty spice rack. Not an inch of counter space was clean.

"Tía, we'll never make it in time for the movie," Cipriana whined.

"Guess we better get started then, 'jita. It's a good thing you came to help. I would have been here until Easter without you."

"But I'm hungry, Tía."

"Didn't you eat before you came, Cipriana?"

Cipriana shook her head. "I thought there would be things I've never eaten before. Things that only people like Miss Stevenson and her mama eat."

"You're right, Cipriana. The americanos don't eat like us. No beans and potatoes in these pots," she said wistfully. Inspecting each pot and occasionally sticking a finger in to sample their contents, she said, "From the looks of things, Miss Stevenson must have made a fancy dinner. I would guess right at this moment her guests are feasting on ham with a honey glaze, candied yams made with brown sugar, mashed potatoes with a white gravy and . . ." From her memory, Cita tried to retrieve the dessert recipe from the October issue of *Good Housekeeping*. Each one of Cita's descriptions had elicited a delighted response from Cipriana, so finally Cita beckoned her over. "What do you think, Cipriana? Chocolate or yellow cake for dessert?" Cita guided Cipriana's finger into one of the pots still on the stove. Licking the scoop of goo, Cipriana smacked her lips and purred, "Chocolate."

"With an orange glaze," Cita added, smiling.

"And look, Tía," Cipriana said with reverence in her voice, pointing to the countertop. "A loaf of real white bread, the kind that's already sliced and you buy at the store. Oh, Tía, can't I have just one slice?"

"Just one, Cipriana, but you have to be quick about it." Unwrapping the wax paper, Cita took a slice of the soft white bread and handed it to Cipriana. She felt dishonest even though it was just one slice. She knew the elder Mrs. Stevenson frowned upon Cita helping herself to their food though Miss Stevenson could be quite generous. She was the one who passed on old issues of magazines to Cita, though she had to do it covertly to avoid her mother's disapproval.

Cita waited in anticipation as Cipriana took in a mouthful, eager to hear her reaction but nervous that their mischief might be discovered. Cipriana's mouth was full of chewed bread as she opened it to give Cita her enthusiastic response when a flushed Miss Stevenson flew in, a silver platter balanced in one hand and a serving bowl in the other. Startled, Cita dove to catch the swinging door, brushing past Miss Stevenson and upsetting the platter, which crashed to the floor. Cita fell to her knees, picking up the scattered pieces of meat, furious at herself. "Sorry, Miss Stevenson," she mumbled miserably.

"No, no, don't worry, Cita. You were only trying to help. Now then
. . ." Miss Stevenson paused, looking all around the room. "Where shall I
put this bowl?"

Cita popped up, taking the bowl from her employer. "I'll take care of
it," she said, scanning the countertop for available space. Seeing none, she
made her way to the sink and turned on the running water, hoping to avoid
conversation with Miss Stevenson. She waited for it to warm up, flicking
her finger in and out of the stream, mesmerized by its flow, growing
warmth, and sound. In the background, she heard Miss Stevenson's offer
to Cipriana to help herself to leftovers. She hoped Cipriana would decline
the offer but knew that she wouldn't. Even though ordinarily she didn't
mind doing the dishes for the Stevensons because of their running water,
the evening had already been too long for Cita. It had been a mistake to
bring Cipriana along. Cipriana didn't understand the difference between
being a guest and a hired hand, and Cita was not about to teach her.

From the corner of her eye Cita watched quietly until Miss Stevenson left
the room. Then, she retrieved a plate from the cabinet and absentmindedly
filled it from every pot, nervously listening for Miss Stevenson. "Sit down
and eat, Cipriana, while I get started."

"But, Tía, aren't you going to eat?"

"Not now, 'jita. I'm not hungry," she said even as her stomach grumbled.
In reality, she was so hungry, she could have eaten a tin can. "You tell me
how it is." She watched Cipriana spoon the food into her mouth.

"Delicious, Tía."

"Is it just like I said, Cipriana? Candied yams and glazed ham?"

Cipriana chewed with a thoughtful expression on her face. "No, Tía
. . . I don't think so," she said slowly. "I think it's chicken."

"Chicken!" Cita pulled her hand from the dishwater and shook off
the excess, moving toward Cipriana. "No, not for a New Year's Eve dinner
party, Cipriana! Here, let me have a taste." Cita grabbed the fork from
Cipriana and tasted from every mound. A bitter expression surfaced on
her face. She had expected greater things from the Stevensons. They read
books and subscribed to magazines. They read *Good Housekeeping* and
Ladies' Home Journal and the *Saturday Evening Post*. They had friends who

looked like the ladies out in the dining room. They had running water and electric lights. They were rich! And they served their guests chicken! Chicken! Didn't they have any imagination at all? Chicken was just fine for a special Sunday dinner at Graciela's. In fact, Cita always looked forward to Graciela's fried chicken. No one made better chicken than she did, and there was no doubt that it was hard to come by unless you raised it yourself. But for a dinner party hosted by the Stevensons! Cita couldn't believe it. She didn't want to believe it.

Miss Stevenson bustled into the kitchen at that moment with her hands full of dirty plates. Cita swallowed hard, taking them.

"Now where did I put the coffee?" Miss Stevenson began to rummage through a cabinet, piling boxes of soda crackers and gelatin on top of dirty dishes. "Ah, here it is." Holding the can out in front of her, she said, "Let's see now. Cita, can you read this? I never make coffee anymore and I don't have my glasses. How many spoons for fifteen cups?"

"Miss Stevenson, I don't think you'll be able to make that many cups at a time," she said, setting the plates down. "You'll probably have to do them in batches."

"Yes, I realize that, Cita. I'm only trying to figure out how many teaspoons of coffee I need first.

Cita pretended to read the small print on the can. "Do you want it weak or strong?"

"How about in between?"

Cita took the coffee from her. "I'll take care of it, Miss Stevenson. Go ahead to your guests," she said, smiling politely.

Miss Stevenson patted Cita on the shoulder. "Why, thank you, dear," she said. "I'll be back in to get it in a few minutes." The kitchen door swung back and forth. Cita spooned the requisite number of teaspoons into the aluminum percolator, added water from the faucet, and lit the burner. When a flame appeared, Cita set the pot on top and set out to do the dishes.

In the cabinet underneath the sink, Cita searched for a dishcloth. Nothing. She searched the cabinets near the sink. Rolling up her sleeve, she stuck her hand into the water, maneuvering between dishes, but there was no dishcloth.

Miss Stevenson hurried into the kitchen. "Is the water hot yet?" she asked. She went to the stove and dipped her finger into the pot. "Ouch!" Sticking her finger in her mouth, she said, "It sure is."

Cita helped her prepare the cups with coffee. Miss Stevenson carefully poured hot coffee into each one, spilling some here and there. "Would you pour some milk in here?" she asked Cita, handing her a porcelain creamer with little pink rosebuds along its handle. "And fill the sugar bowl, would you, dear? I'll be right back."

"Oh, Miss Stevenson? I can't find . . ."

"I'll be back. Hold on, Cita."

Cita did as she was told. She smelled the milk before pouring it into the little pitcher just in case. The sugar bowl was filled by the time Miss Stevenson came in for the second tray full of coffee cups.

"Miss Stevenson, I can't find a dishcloth. Where can I get one?"

"A dishcloth? Hmm. Did you look in the water there?"

Cita nodded.

"Did you look . . . ?"

"I looked everywhere," Cita interrupted. "Miss Stevenson," she added quickly.

The hostess gave Cita a look of disapproval. "Well, come here, then. We'll find you one. You better get started. The dishes are piling up faster than you can shout Jehosephat Hallelujah!" An uncharacteristic giggle emerged from her red-lipsticked lips as she tipped the door open. "Whoops, I forgot the coffee," she said, turning around just as the door swung back the other way, hitting the heel of her shoe. Lifting the second tray, she motioned to Cita with her chin. "Follow me," she said.

Slightly embarrassed, Cita stood, watching Miss Stevenson place the tray on the long table. The white lace tablecloth already had a brown coffee stain in the corner. "I'll just be a moment. I have to show the girl where to find a dishcloth." Everyone snickered uncomfortably except the lady with the ruby necklace, who looked straight at her with a pained expression on her face. She smiled then, and Cita, taken by surprise, stared at her until Miss Stevenson took hold of her arm.

Cita followed Miss Stevenson into the hallway where she opened up

· the linen closet. She looked through every shelf, unfolding pillowcases, mussing perfectly creased handkerchiefs. "Damn," she whispered under her breath, still rummaging through the items.

Cita clenched her mouth shut as a snicker bubbled up inside of her. She had never heard either of the Stevensons swear. They were such good Methodists, she had thought.

Finally, Miss Stevenson shut the door. "Wait here. I'll be back." She walked down the hall and entered a room that always had its door closed. She shut the door behind her.

Cita waited, listening to the din of voices in the other part of the house. She couldn't stop thinking about the lady in the red dress. It was as if she felt sorry for Cita, or maybe she just thought the other guests shouldn't have laughed at her. Cita wondered who she was.

Miss Stevenson emerged again and handed Cita something bunched up. "That's all I have, dear," she said almost inaudibly.

Cita began to open her hand, but Miss Stevenson reached over and held it closed. "Wait until you get to the kitchen, would you, Cita?" She smiled nervously, as if she were embarrassed to see it again.

Trailing behind the hostess, Cita was consumed with curiosity. The thing in her hand was soft but perhaps too soft. It certainly didn't feel like a washrag. At the dining room, Miss Stevenson glanced Cita's way, but her eyes gave neither greeting nor goodbye; they merely told Cita to make haste into the kitchen.

Cita let the door between the kitchen and dining room swing shut. Standing in front of it, facing Cipriana, she broke into a huge grin. "You should have heard Miss Stevenson, Cipriana," she whispered, pointing with her thumb at the other room. "She said a bad word and then . . ." Cita stopped and stared at her open hand in disbelief. A smile slowly surfaced. With a flourish, she held up a pair of very large panties with dozens of holes dotting their surface.

Cipriana's eyes opened wide. "Tía!" she exclaimed with glee. "Whose are those?"

Cita tilted her head in the direction of the other room and smirked. "This, Cipriana . . ." she said, flicking her wrists, extending her pinkies, and trying to keep a straight face, "this is our dishcloth."

When a titter bubbled up from Cipriana's throat, Cita pushed her finger to her lips. "Shh!" she exclaimed, ready to burst into laughter herself. Swallowing hard, Cita looked away, trying to suppress her mirth.

"But, but Tía," Cipriana asked incredulously, "are they clean?"

Cita had to turn away from Cipriana, doubling over with laughter. When she finally regained her composure, she turned back toward her niece. With a serious look on her face, she approached Cipriana. Suddenly, she stuffed the panties into Cipriana's face. "Here, you smell them!" she teased.

"No!" Cipriana yelled a little too loudly, peeling them from her face, giggling.

Cita opened her eyes wide. "Shh!" she whispered loudly.

"Girls!" came a stern voice from the adjacent room. It was the elder Mrs. Stevenson. "Is anything wrong, girls?"

Placing a finger at her lips, Cita called out for both of them. "Nothing, Mrs. Stevenson. Sorry."

Even though they giggled sporadically throughout the dishwashing session, both Cita and Cipriana held their raucous laughter in check. Each avoided even glancing at the dishcloth. They washed dish after dish until all the counters were clean, until all of the pots had been washed and dried, until everything was tidy and put in its proper place. Each time Miss Stevenson entered the kitchen, Cita peeked through the doorway to steal a glance at the clock on the mantel in the dining room. When Miss Stevenson retreated, Cita would announce the time to Cipriana and they would both speed up the tempo of the task at hand.

Finally, three hours and ten minutes later, Miss Stevenson gave Cita her two-dollar-and-fifty-cent wage for the week plus an extra fifty-cent piece.

"Happy New Year, girls," Miss Stevenson called out.

"You too, Miss Stevenson," Cita responded, moving at a measured pace, not so fast that she would seem ungrateful and rude, but not so slow that Miss Stevenson would think she was waiting for a holiday bonus. When they were out of hearing range, Cita grabbed Cipriana's hand and said,

"C'mon, we have to hurry if we're going to make it on time." Together, Cita and Cipriana raced from the house through the neighborhood of fancier houses and didn't stop until they reached the movie house on Main Street. Standing in front of the theater trying to catch her breath, Cita said, "We're going to be a little late, Cipriana. Are you sure you don't mind making our way in the dark?"

Cipriana shook her head vehemently. "No, Tía, not at all. I know my way already and you can follow me."

"But we've already missed the beginning," Cita said, teasing.

"Oh, Tía," Cipriana said, pleading. "I can't wait any longer!"

Giggling, Cita pulled her niece toward the box office and handed the fifty-cent piece to the teenager who was doling out the tickets for *Our Little Girl*. No sooner had she given the ten cents change to Cipriana and picked up the tickets than she felt her niece's hand in her own pulling her toward the entrance of the theater. "Whoa, 'jita. Slow down," Cita said, tripping over her own feet to keep up. "We're here and we made it. Now let's catch our breath."

Before Cipriana had time to protest, Cita heard her name called from across the street. Turning around, she saw a man striding toward her. As he drew nearer, she recognized him immediately from the carnival last summer. Cita's eyes darted around for a quick escape route.

"Cita! I would have recognized you anywhere. Do you remember me?"

"Of course. Chato, how are you?"

"Hey, you even remember my name. Pretty good for a girl who doesn't come back to the carnival to meet a vato."

"I'm sorry, Chato. I have a really good excuse and I'll tell you about it one day. It had nothing to do with you."

"Sure. Sure. I've heard it before."

"No, really, Chato. It had nothing to do with you. I wanted to go, believe me."

"Tía! C'mon, we have to hurry. The movie started already."

"I'm sorry, Chato. I promised Cipriana here the movie."

"Don't worry about it."

"Can we meet another time?"

"Naw. I'm leaving for Las Vegas tomorrow morning."

"You are? You're going finally?"

"As soon as I pull my car out of the shop. Too bad, though."

"About what, Chato?"

"You know."

"No." Cita shrugged. "I don't." Feeling uncomfortable with the way Chato was scrutinizing her, she finally blurted, "You're lucky, Chato."

"Lucky? For going to Las Vegas? Naw. I'd be lucky to have you as my lady, though." Chato smiled.

"Your lady! Chato, come on!"

Chato made the sign of the cross. "I'm not lying, Cita. You'd make any man proud to stand beside him. Too bad we didn't meet sooner, eh?"

Sheepishly, Cita smiled. She felt Cipriana tug at her hand. "Well, Chato, we better go now. Good luck in Las Vegas."

"You too."

Cita could feel his eyes on her as they scurried into the theater. She couldn't help feeling a pang of sadness as Cipriana led the way. Together, they slipped into the darkness as the newsreels were ending and the movie was rolling its opening credits. Just as Cita's eyes were starting to adjust, Cipriana pulled her toward a row of seats. Startled, she felt her way blindly into the row, propelled by Cipriana and stepping on a gaggle of toes along the way.

The moment they were seated, Cipriana sat erect at the edge of her seat and stayed that way through the entire movie. At one point, Cita offered to help Cipriana remove her jacket. To Cita, it felt as if she were undressing a doll whose eyes were fixed in space, in this case on the movie screen. Cipriana, in fact, reminded Cita of Shirley Temple: that head of curly hair and that sunny disposition. Like Shirley Temple, Cipriana always seemed to have a confident and happy air for such a little girl, and somehow, Cita knew that Cipriana would make it in this world no matter what. Cita was more like Shirley's father in the movie: she wanted something else out of life but would probably have to settle for her small town after all. That was just the way it was for ordinary people. And even though Graciela thought Cita was special, bless her heart, she was nothing but ordinary. Suddenly, Cita reached over and hugged Cipriana, hoping some of Cipriana's contentment would rub off on her.

As they exited the movie theater hand in hand, Cita looked up into the dark sky. Low puffed clouds were forming and she wondered if it would snow. "Button up, Cipriana," Cita urged. "It's cold out tonight." Cita blew out a puff of breath into the frigid air, watching it disappear as quickly as it came. "You try it, Cipriana. Let's see who can make it last the longest."

"I can, Tía. Watch." Cipriana breathed into the night, and a puff of air hung in the night like a magic cloud. Cita watched in wonder as Cipriana's breath seemed to hover longer than hers had.

"How do you do that, 'jita?"

"What, Tía?"

"Make your breath stick to the air like it wanted to be here."

"What do you mean, Tía?"

Cita laughed. "Oh, nothing Cipriana. Just teasing you. Hey, I liked that thing Shirley Temple did. Pease porridge hot . . . ," Cita's voice rang out with glee.

"Pease porridge cold," Cipriana continued.

Together, their voices merged as they giggled out the rest of the ditty. "Pease porridge in the pot, nine days old!"

As their giggles subsided, Cipriana yawned.

"Tired, 'jita?"

Cipriana nodded. "A little."

"Why don't you just stay with me and Mama Fela tonight, Cipriana? That way you won't wake anybody. It's so late."

Cipriana was quiet for a moment. "But, Tía, I have to get up early tomorrow to make biscuits. Daddy depends on me even on vacation."

Cita laughed. "Can't your mama make them just this once, Cipriana? She's home on break too."

Cipriana frowned, shaking her head with determination. "No, it's my job, Tía."

"Then you can get up early and go straight home in time to make the biscuits." Cita watched her niece stare straight ahead.

After a moment, Cipriana said, "But Mama will worry." This time, she looked at Cita. "Don't you think, Tía?"

"No. She knows you're with me. Besides, you'll be there first thing in the morning." Cita searched her niece's face. "All right?"

Cipriana nodded and took Cita's hand. "I just don't want her to think I ran away."

"Ran away? What do you mean?" Cita asked.

"Like Shirley. In the movie."

"Oh."

"Would you ever run away, Tía?"

"That's an interesting question, 'jita. I'll have to give it some thought. Would you?"

Silence hung in the air like the clouds above them. "Maybe, Tía. If I could get Mama and Daddy to love each other always. And to love me too. Like Shirley did."

Cita stopped. "What do you mean, 'jita? They love you more than you know."

"I don't think so, Tía. Not since I embarrassed Mama at her school."

"That was a long time ago, 'jita."

"Mama's never forgotten."

"Of course she has, 'jita."

Cipriana shook her head. "No, Tía, she hasn't."

"What do you mean, Cipriana?"

"She always goes away. She never likes to stay here with us."

"Oh, 'jita. That's not true. She'd like nothing better than to stay here with you. But she has to work."

"But why, Tía? Why couldn't she just clean houses like you?"

"Oh, Cipriana. Your mama's a smart lady. She's not dumb like me. She's meant to do more in this world than clean the houses of the americanos. She's a role model, 'jita, for me and you. You should really look up to her."

"I look up to you, Tía. I like you better than anybody. I don't care if you clean houses."

"Well, thank you, 'jita," Cita said, laughing, wrapping her arm around Cipriana's shoulder. "That's the nicest thing anyone has ever said to me.

But your mama's a special lady, Cipriana."

"But why can't she teach here? At my school?"

Cita stopped and scooted down until she was eye level with Cipriana. "Believe me, 'jita. If she could, she would. She wants nothing more than to be able to watch you grow up. Every single day."

"Then why doesn't she?"

"It's not that easy, Cipriana. There are forces at work that don't make it easy for her to do what she wants. She'd like to stay home and watch you grow up but she thinks it's more important for you to eat good, nourishing meals and dress nicely and be able to read anything you want. And she'd like to work here in Santa Lucía but none of the teachers are nuevomexicanos like us. Not yet at least."

"Why not, Tía?"

"That's a very good question, 'jita. I guess the people who hire the teachers don't think people like your mama can teach the children of the doctors and the businessmen."

"But Mama's a good teacher, Tía. The best."

"That's right, Cipriana. She is."

"Maybe someday she'll get to teach here, Tía?"

"Someday, Cipriana. Someday, soon."

"Let's go to your house then, Tía. I'll make the biscuits for Mama tomorrow."

"Whatever you want, 'jita." Cita stood again, groaning because her leg had fallen asleep. Hopping on one foot, she said, "Ooh, my foot's tingling, Cipriana. You're going to have to help me home."

Cipriana put her arm around Cita's waist. "Here, Tía. Lean on me."

Cita draped her arm around Cipriana and gave her a tiny squeeze. "What would I do without you, 'jita?"

As soon as Cita opened the door to the house, she knew something was wrong. Dead wrong. Needing only a few hours of sleep, Mama Fela was used to staying up past midnight, kept company by a cozy fire and a bit of whiskey diluted by coffee, cream, and a beaten egg. She would darn socks or knit, needing little light because she was so proficient at the task, letting her nimble fingers act as a guide. Tonight the house was cold and black, so dark both Cita and Cipriana stumbled as they entered the front room. Cipriana giggled but Cita hushed her immediately, calling softly, "Mamá?" There was no answer. "Mamá?" she called again, raising her voice just a notch.

"Where were you?" Mama Fela pronounced every word slowly. Her voice was stern and in very close proximity.

Cita looked around, still blinded by the darkness. "Mamá? Where . . . where are you?"

"I said where were you!" Mama Fela demanded.

"Mamá . . ." Cita paused, still searching the room. Finally, in the corner of the room, she discovered her mother's silhouette. As she moved closer, she noticed a white patch on her mother's eye. "Mamá, what's wrong? What happened?" she asked anxiously, squatting at the foot of the chair and reaching for her mother's face.

Mama Fela slapped her daughter's hand away. "I said where were you!" It was almost a scream.

Cita stood abruptly. "I was at the Stevensons'. You know that. I told you. Look . . ." she dug into her coat pocket. "I got two dollars and fifty cents."

"And after?"

"Then Cipriana and I went to the picture show. You knew that's where we were going."

"I understand you saw a young man there."

"Who? Chato? We spoke for about two seconds. And how did you know? You have your spies following me now?"

"Where did you meet him? Is he from a good family?"

"Mamá! I'm not marrying the man. I met him at the carnival this summer. Then he happened to be by the theater as Cipriana and I were about to go in. I've known him a total of ten minutes."

"¡Vagamunda!"

"Mamá!" Cita was dumbstruck at her mother's accusation. She felt very close to tears. It took every ounce of self-restraint to hold them back. She could barely make eye contact with her mother. Finally, she said more calmly, "I did nothing wrong, Mamá."

"In my day you got married before you talked to a man. Married, Cita. What will people think now seeing you in the street talking to a stranger? What will my comadres think? And now, with my eye, I can't even go visit them to explain. Ay, Cita, you've brought shame on me."

"Mamá . . . !" Cita was going to argue with her mother but knew it was futile. She clenched her mouth shut so nothing she would regret later would escape her mouth. Anyway, her mother was always right. In her mind, Mama Fela had been wronged, shamed, and there was no turning back. No forgiveness. She examined her mother's stern face closely but turned away when she realized that at the moment, she did not have even an ounce of sympathy for her mother's apparent accident. In fact, Mama Fela had probably put the patch on to make Cita feel even more guilty for wandering the town and talking to boys. Cita shook her head from side to side. The whole situation was almost laughable.

"Tía?" Cipriana called in a very small voice. Cita ignored her.

"Tía, I've got to go the bathroom."

"Well, go then!" Cita snapped. "What are you waiting for?"

Cipriana hurried outside, leaving them in silence.

Then Mama Fela cleared her throat. "Los Stevens son americanos," she stated matter-of-factly.

"Yes," Cita replied coldly, not bothering to correct the name.

"You're cleaning for the americanos still?"

"Yes, Mamá," Cita said. A tinge of sarcasm coated her answer. Then, she stared straight into her mother's good eye, baiting her. "You know that's the only way I can earn money. Who else is going to hire me? Your friends? No."

"Ay, que vergüenza." ·

"What's so wrong with it? At least I'm working." Cita paused for a long while, staring at her mother through the darkness. "Mamá, we have to work for people like the Stevensons and Dr. Beford and Mr. Meddles. They're the only ones with money. You know that." A slight hint of pleading was evident in Cita's voice.

Mama Fela remained silent.

Then the kitchen door creaked and Cita turned to find Cipriana entering the house once more. "You all right, Cipriana?" she asked, feeling guilty for her display of impatience earlier.

Cipriana barely nodded, joining Cita at her side. She was breathing heavily.

"What's wrong, 'jita?" Cita asked, alarmed.

Cipriana shook her head. "Nothing, Tía," she barely whispered.

"Really, 'jita?"

Cipriana's nod turned midstream into a shake of the head from side to side. "There were spiders, Tía."

Cita tried not to smile but finally gave in to the urge, averting her attention from Cipriana toward her mother. To Cita's surprise, a hint of a smile emerged on Mama Fela's face as well. A chuckle gurgled its way up out of Cita's throat and soon, she could not control the bursts of joy exploding from her chest. Cita could tell that Mama Fela was also trying to hold her mirth in check. It wasn't working. They both erupted into laughter. The tension of the night disappeared as easily as a cloud of hot breath on a frigid winter's night.

Cipriana looked from Cita to Mama Fela, then back again. Aware that her niece appeared startled, Cita enveloped Cipriana in her arms. In her ear, she heard Cipriana insist, "But there were, Tía. There were lots of them!"

To Cita's relief, Mama Fela's tirade had been squelched. There was no apology and Cita knew there never could be. Instead, Mama Fela changed the subject. She became very talkative, explaining the state of her eye when Cita inquired again. It had been an accident, she told Cita. When she was frying some *empanadas* that evening, a spittle of grease popped into her eye and burned it. She had soothed her eyes with wet compresses and it was feeling better now, but she didn't know if she would ever be able to see again.

"Oh, Mamá, of course you'll see," Cita replied, helping her mother to her feet. "Tomorrow we'll go see Dr. Beford but for now, we better go to sleep."

Cita insisted on helping her mother into bed despite her loud protests. She knew Mama Fela hated to feel dependent on anyone and Cita wanted to believe this was the reason for her invective earlier that evening. She had to be feeling helpless and hated herself for feeling that way, so she took out her anger on whomever she could, anyone within target distance. "Poor Graciela," Cita whispered to herself, wondering if she had been a recipient too.

"What did you say, Cita?"

"Nothing, Mamá." Cita made her way to the other side of the bed and tucked Cipriana in beside Mama Fela, kissing her niece goodnight. Lingering at the foot of the bed, Cita said, "Oh, Mamá you should have seen the Stevensons' party. The ladies were wearing such elegant dresses just like in the movies. Like Carole Lombard in *Now and Forever*. . . . Oh, and this one lady . . ." Cita sat down against her mother's feet. "She had on the most beautiful necklace. It was . . ." Cita sighed heavily and closed her eyes briefly. "It was like heaven, Mamá."

"¿Como el cielo, Cita?" Mama Fela scoffed.

Cita didn't need to have her eyes open to detect the exasperation in Mama Fela's voice. She also felt Cipriana's eyes boring into her. Opening her own at last, Cita asked Cipriana, "What, 'jita?"

"I didn't see a necklace, Tía."

"That's because you were so busy munching on the store-bought bread," Cita replied, unruffled.

Cipriana grinned.

"And on the chicken and the mashed potatoes and the cake . . . Shall I go on, young miss?" Cita asked in a joking tone.

Cipriana shook her head, giggling. "But they were wearing ordinary clothes like us, Tía. They even have holes in their panties!"

"Cipriana!" Mama Fela exclaimed.

"She's not kidding, Mamá. But that's another story for another day, Cipriana," Cita said, winking at her niece. "In my mind, they were all dressed up in elegant clothes and expensive jewels. Mamá . . . ," Cita said dreamily, "I think I'd rather wear diamonds than have enough to eat."

"Cita! ¡Cállate!" Mama Fela made the sign of the cross. "Don't tempt the fates, Cita. You don't know what you're saying. You've never known what it is not to eat."

"Well, neither have you." As soon as the words emerged, Cita regretted them.

Mama Fela sighed deeply. Cita could even see her mother's chest fill with air, then let it go. Mama Fela shook her head back and forth, gazing at Cita with the all-knowing eye.

"Tienes ideas locas," Mama Fela said, closing her eye now.

"But Mamá . . ."

Opening her eye once again, Mama Fela murmured, "You're too much a dreamer, Cita. Remember, as I've told you before, it'll get you nowhere. Now go to sleep and maybe your head will be cleared of all that nonsense tomorrow."

Through the blankets, Cita could feel her mother nudge her off the bed with her toes. Mama Fela reached over to her nightstand and blew out the flame of the oil lamp. The room darkened as Cita heard the click-click of her mother removing her teeth.

Cita said nothing. She was accustomed to her mother's dismissals. For a moment, in the darkness, she studied her mother but she knew she would never understand her. She and her mother were very different. It was the one thing she knew for sure. "Good night," she said finally, standing to leave. Suddenly, the cold seeped through her shoes up through the soles of her feet. And she shivered.

In the darkness, she heard Cipriana's reassuring response. "Happy New Year, Tía!" Despite her niece's optimism, Cita felt anything but happy.

Her own room was very dark and cold. Without removing her day clothes, Cita slipped into bed. She could smell the stale remnants of the dinner, the real one, not the one she had imagined. She could see the jewel on the neck of Miss Stevenson's guest, dim in the shadows. She could see the holes in the panties of the women who paid her to clean up after them. She could see her imagination dulling and her art fading. At the same time, she could hear Cipriana's voice reverberate through her mind: "Happy New Year, Tía." She certainly didn't feel happy and wondered if she ever could here in Santa Lucía.

What her mother said was right. She was a dreamer. She knew it, and she had always been just that. And dreamers didn't belong—anywhere, but especially not in Santa Lucía. Her mother had made that perfectly clear. Even Cipriana thought about running away, and she was the happiest little girl Cita knew, except maybe for Shirley Temple. If Cipriana thought about it, well then, why couldn't she? Cita jumped out of bed and flew to her window. She peered up through the darkness into the old apple tree, remembering the dreams she had had when protected by its leaves. She desperately wanted to get away from Santa Lucía, away from the life she knew she would have to lead if she stayed. She didn't want to be like Mama Fela. And she knew she couldn't be even if she tried. She didn't even want to be like Graciela, whom she admired more than anyone. Even with her education and career, Graciela was trapped in a life that was fraught with endless work and worry. Cita didn't want that. She longed for the freedom of a different time, a new place. What Cipriana said was right and wise. It was a new year, a time for new beginnings. And more than anything, she wanted the new year to keep its promise. She dreamed that it could.

Cita bounded toward her bed and knelt beside it, lacing her hands in prayer. For a moment she looked up at the ceiling, wondering what to say. Instead of beseeching God for the unknown, she fidgeted from side to side until she whispered, "Please help Cipriana and Sara and Rebeca and Benny." Satisfied with her prayer, she groped blindly underneath her bed for the familiar stack of paper and old lard can full of pastels. She pulled them out from the darkness, and at once she felt a sense of comfort drift over her. Leafing through the drawings, she chose three and placed them, along with the colors that had made them, on top of her bed. Standing, she opened up her armario and slid out an ancient suitcase. Snapping open the rusted hinges, she laid it open on her bed. In one motion, she swept the few clothes she owned from their hangers and tossed them into the bag. She grabbed panties and brassieres, staring at them as she placed them on top of her clothes. In amazement, she noticed, not one of them had holes. Mama Fela made sure of that. Finally, she gently placed a box of watercolors and the can of pastels into the case and shut it tight. She sat at the edge of her bed, with the suitcase on her lap, staring out the window into the night sky. The stars were shining brightly.

She waited for the morning light, drifting in and out of sleep, sitting

up in bed. She held the case all night in her lap, lest she change her mind
or lose her nerve. Finally, when she couldn't bear the wait any longer, she
quickly donned her coat and took a magazine from her side table, fanning its
slick pages until she came upon a particular page. There, stuck in the crease
of the magazine, were a few dollar bills folded in half and a letter from
Margarita Herrera. Without hesitation she stuffed them deep into her coat
pocket. She rummaged through the drawings on her bed, contemplating
which ones to leave, which ones to take. Finally, she rolled up two drawings,
tucked them underneath her armpit, and picked up her suitcase. At the
doorway, she glanced back at the single drawing she left lying on her bed.
Even in the semi-darkness of early morning, it exploded with vibrancy.

Stealing into the kitchen, she hesitated, deciding whether to take
a couple of empanadas or biscuits. She chose the biscuits in honor of
Cipriana, tucking them into another pocket. Leaving her belongings in the
kitchen, she paused outside her mother's room, torn between her decision
and her desire to see Mama Fela one more time. She knew her goodbye
would have to be fast if she wanted it to be a silent one without hysterics
and explanations. So quickly, she entered Mama Fela's room. She wanted to
study her face one more time but Mama Fela was totally submerged from
head to foot in a sea of white sheets and blankets. Funny, Cita thought,
these sheets were frayed and a bit tattletale gray, not immaculate like the
ones she kept for her sewing. Despite the quantity of covers, Cita could
make out her mother's petite outline. She saw that Mama Fela was a little
woman, though strong in Cita's eyes. She was reminded once again that
she could never be quite like her.

Cipriana, on the other hand, was completely free of any covers. In fact,
her body was completely reversed, her feet touching the pillow and her
head at the foot of the bed. She appeared fast asleep now but Cita guessed
it had been a restless night. She wanted to pull some of the blankets from
Mama Fela to cover Cipriana but she didn't want to wake either of them.
Instead, she smiled, nodded her head in farewell, and turned to scoot
out the door. For a moment she hesitated. Glancing back for one more
look, she scanned the room as if she were looking for something. There,
on top of the sewing machine, Cita noticed one of Mama Fela's recently

completed sewing projects folded neatly on top: the white wedding dress with lace cuffs, Mama Fela's attempt to make her respectable. Grimacing, Cita sighed. Mamá will never change, she thought, shutting the door softly behind her. The finality of the click reminded her of Mama Fela's dentures the evening before. Her memory of the night propelled her forward.

The morning air was frigid, and she could feel a draft at her throat. Her hands were full, though, so she had no choice but to bear the cold. It didn't matter. It made her feel alive for the first time in a long time. She actually wanted to take in every sound and sight of her town instead of blocking them from her consciousness. Soon they would all be memories anyway.

As she strode through her neighborhood past Graciela's house and onto Route 66, she caught a whiff of the fresh earthy aroma of Folgers coffee. In her mind's eye, she could see Mama Fela sitting at her kitchen table, tearing pieces of tortilla into her heavily sugared coffee. She remembered the days when her father would take coffee to her mother, still fast asleep in bed. Even Gilberto had to leave this place once in a while to refresh himself, to regain his sanity. And her mother always said how similar Cita was to her father.

Cita's thoughts were violently interrupted when a short, round woman in black emerged from a small mud-colored house. She was doubled over as if a terrible pain in her stomach forced her permanently into this position of paralysis. From the stories Cipriana and the other children told, Cita knew immediately who this lady was even though she had never actually seen her before. La Loca, as she was called, began reaching for stones from the ground and hurled them in Cita's direction. "Get away!" she screamed. "Get away!" Frightened, Cita knew now why the children taunted this woman. Her pinched face and her bulk and her words did not make sense to them. All of it scared them. Absolutely certain that she didn't want to remember Santa Lucía like this, Cita hurried away as the woman yelled after her. Most of all, she didn't want to become this woman. La Loca.

Crossing Route 66, she strode into the train station, the new electric lights blinding her. Blinking away tears as her eyes adjusted, she noticed the vacant wood benches lining the walls. Her steps reverberated across the rustic wood floor as she approached the heavyset man behind the ticket counter. His white sleeves were rolled up to his elbows and held in place by rubber bands. He wore a green visor, which Cita had always thought peculiar until she stepped into the bright glare of his world. She recognized him as Mr. Hill, whose wife would be Cipriana's teacher next year. Besides selling train tickets, he also operated the telegraph machine. The brass name plate on the counter confirmed her conjecture.

"Good morning, Mr. Hill," Cita sang.

The man looked up from his magazine. "Up early, ain't you, miss?"

Cita nodded. "And isn't it a beautiful morning?"

"Kind of hazy, if you ask me. Looks like snow."

Cita nodded again.

"Where you headed?"

For a moment, Cita had to think. She knew there could only be one answer. "Las Vegas."

"Nevada or New Mexico?" The man asked matter-of-factly.

Cita squinted. "New Mexico," she said, confused that there might even be a choice.

"That'll be five dollars and seventy cents."

"Five dollars!" Cita said, shocked. She didn't have to take out her money to know she didn't have that much. For a brief moment, a pang of regret made her wish fervently that she could take back every penny spent during last summer's frivolous spree at the carnival. "Isn't there a cheaper fare?"

"That's it."

Cita stared at him in disbelief.

"Well, miss, do you want a ticket or not? It's a little early in the morning to be playing games."

"I'm not playing games. I just didn't realize it would cost so much."

"Rail travel's not cheap. But you wouldn't know that, would you?" Cita felt his eyes move up and down her torso. They fixed on her suitcase. "Not traveled much, have you?"

"No," she said under her breath, embarrassed. Her eyes suddenly felt wet with tears. She could hear the man droning on, asking more questions, but they weren't relevant now. She turned slowly, staring ahead at the deserted station before her, blinking away the tears that magnified the intense lights around her. The light hurt her eyes. She closed them momentarily, wondering what she was going to do now. The sound of the wood floor echoed with each step she took down the length of the room until at last she reached the door. She shivered with dejection.

Before leaving the building, she put her suitcase and her drawings down. She lifted the collar of her coat around her neck, readying herself for the assault of cold air. She took her burdens up again, one in each hand, inhaled deeply, and pushed her way through to meet the gray day. At first, the morning air snapped at her cruelly and she had to fight to catch her breath. Gradually, she was able to breathe easier as she got used to the intensity of the cold. She slowed her pace and began to enjoy the brisk morning, which was helping to clear her muddy thoughts. She began to wander slowly, making her way toward the center of town.

Just a moment ago, she had been ready to give up and go home. That would be too easy, she realized now. She had to fight for her dream. And if she was meant to fulfill a destiny as the woman at the carnival told her, then she had to fight for it. If all it took was money to alter the course of her life, then she would get it. If it took cleaning more houses, then that's what she would do. That's all there was to it. Money was everything. Money was the way out of Santa Lucía, and she would earn it.

Cita began walking faster when she heard a car trailing her and a voice calling out her name.

"Cita, is that you?"

Cita turned and bent to peer inside the old car. At first, she didn't recognize the face looking back at her expectantly. Finally, it registered. "Chato!"

"Yeah, that's me and I thought that was you but I couldn't believe it. I said to myself, 'Hey vato, you know that little lady.' What are you doing out so early?"

"I could ask you the same thing."

"Remember, I'm heading up to Las Vegas today to start my new job."

Cita bolted upright, banging her head on the ceiling of Chato's car. She saw stars.

"You all right, Cita?" Chato called as he jumped from his car and hurried around. "You look like you've seen La Llorona. Here, sit down a second."

While Chato ushered her into the front seat of his car, Cita's mind was racing. Was this her destiny?

"You all right, Cita?" he asked again, squatting by her side.

Cita nodded. Suddenly, she knew she was more than all right. She stuck her head out of the vehicle and pecked Chato on the cheek. "Chato, I'm going with you."

Chato's mouth dropped open. "What!"

"To Las Vegas."

"What!"

"Would that be all right?"

"All right?" Chato stood suddenly, his smile growing by the minute. "¡Que suaviters!" He picked up her suitcase and stuffed it into the backseat, which was already crowded with his belongings. Carefully, he handed her the roll of drawings as if he knew instinctively that they were important to her. He shut the door tight and ran to the driver's side.

The car jerked forward and Cita swallowed hard. This was it. This was the beginning of her new year, her new life. She stared out the window as they passed her old life: the school, the movie theater, the county courthouse, Dr. Beford's Drugstore, Gould's Mercantile. Each place brought back memories, good and bad, but she held on only to the good. They would give her sustenance as she made her way. She remembered the day she promised Benny a Boy Scout uniform, right there in front of the courthouse, and how she fed Sara and Rebeca ice cream and memories of their mother. She recalled her last conversation with Cipriana and how she wished some of her niece's optimism would rub off on her. Well, it must have. She was doing this for them, for the children. And one day, she would return.

From Main Street, they caught Route 66. As they sped up, the town became a blur. She closed her eyes, using her imagination to paint her future. She could envision her new life ahead, a brand new palette of vibrant colors not yet used and a canvas as open and wide as the New Mexico sky. She could imagine her future, and it was filled with color.

CHAPTER TWELVE

CLEANING

The morning was dark for Mama Fela. Sitting on the side of her bed, she took off the eye patch. She covered her good eye and everything went black. She covered it again and her world no longer existed. She shook Cipriana. "Get Cita, mi'jita. Dios mío, get Cita!" While Cipriana jumped out of bed, Mama Fela rummaged through the drawer in her night table, her hands shaking as if they had caught fire. *"Where's my mirror? Where's my mirror?"* she agonized. Newspaper clippings, bottles of ointment, and a rosary fell from the drawer, leaving only the mirror at the bottom. With both hands, she held it up to her face, staring at her reflection. "Cita!" she yelled. "The doctor. Get the doctor!" Quieting herself, she held her eyelid wide open with two fingers and inspected the pupil. "My eye," she whispered. "It's gone."

When Cipriana made a sudden entrance, Mama Fela immediately placed the mirror face down. "Is she coming?" she asked, holding back the fear in her voice.

"She's not here," Cipriana said quietly, still half asleep.

"What?" Mama Fela stood in haste, forgetting the feeling of helplessness that had overcome her.

Cipriana responded with a bit more urgency in her voice. "I looked in her room and outside and in the kitchen, but she's not there, Mama Fela. I even looked in the outhouse," Cipriana said, trying to smile.

Mama Fela did not return the smile. She felt preoccupied, moving at a determined pace to Cita's room. "Ay que muchacha . . . ," she mumbled, ". . . going out on a day of obligation." Opening the door, she was greeted by a barrage of sunlight and quickly she shaded her eyes with her hand. "Close the curtain," she told Cipriana. "Quickly."

The muslin curtain had never been easy to maneuver along the curtain rod. Cita had made the slit too narrow and it never glided across easily.

Mama Fela had told her to do it again, but Cita said she liked it the way it was because it would remind her to never close the curtains. Mama Fela asked her why that was so important and she said so that she wouldn't die of darkness. At the time, Mama Fela was perturbed but now she knew it was just something beyond her understanding. Cita was a hard girl to know and Mama Fela was ashamed to say it, but sometimes, she was even hard for a mother to like.

"Pull it." Mama Fela motioned with her hand to Cipriana but the curtain would not budge. She rushed to the window and tugged. Instead of making it close properly, she heard an unmistakable rip.

Cipriana giggled and immediately Mama Fela shushed her, "¡Cállate!" Feeling anxious and worried, she had no patience for niños malcriados. "Go get your mama. Now!"

Cipriana bolted from the room. Mama Fela waited, staring at Cita's neatly made bed, until she heard the front door shut tight. Then, still in her bed slippers and long cotton nightgown, she moved hurriedly to the kitchen. She peered inside the water pitcher to see what was left from the day before. It was too cold at this time of morning to fetch a clean bucketful from the cistern. Taking the vessel, she poured the last drops of water on her fingers, touching her eyelid with the freezing tips. The icy water felt like it was burning her skin, but after the initial shock, she repeated the action, this time putting the pitcher down and massaging both eyelids. The pressure felt soothing. Finally, after a moment of contemplation, she bent down, taking a washcloth from a drawer in the *petaquía*. This time, she let the water wet the cloth until it was soaked through. She wrung it out, feeling her body shiver at the iciness. With the cloth in hand, she crossed over to her bedroom. Instead of picking up the items that had fallen out of her nightstand, she slid them underneath with her foot. Quickly, she slipped into bed with her slippers still on and pulled the blankets up to her nostrils. She adjusted the wet cloth over her eyes and for a moment, she moved the blanket down a bit to free her mouth. With shallow breaths, she warmed her hands and then quickly pushed them down and tucked them underneath her buttocks. For a moment, she listened to the sound of her breathing and then, from her purplish lips, came a recitation of the first

Sorrowful Mystery. She knew it without thinking, and while the words came to her, she remembered that today, the first day of the new year, was actually a day prescribed by church teaching not for the Sorrowful Mystery but for the Joyful one. Somehow, though, those words escaped her.

Graciela entered the room in bedclothes and boots, breathing hard. Mama Fela pretended she was asleep because she did not want to go to the doctor and she knew Graciela would insist. The question of whether or not she would ever see again was heavy on her mind, but she knew that if God meant her to go blind in one eye, no doctor could stop it.

"Mama Fela? Are you awake?" The inquiry was hesitant.

Mama Fela didn't answer. Instead she breathed harder, conscious that her chest would rise and fall with her breathing, indicating to Graciela she had fallen asleep recently and should not be disturbed.

"Fela? Mama Fela," Graciela called with more confidence, touching her shoulder lightly. "Cipriana said to come right away. What's wrong?"

Mama Fela tried to keep the same tempo of breathing. She wanted to pray again because it helped her to stop thinking about her eye, but she was afraid her lips would move. She could feel Graciela's eyes on her now but she knew the cloth hid her blinking eyes. Suddenly, the cloth was slipped from her eyes and she feared she would be found out. Instead, Graciela's steps retreated from the room and she could hear her call to her daughter. "Cipriana, go and bring in some kindling. I'll start a fire while you get some clean water. Was it this cold last night?" Mama Fela strained her ears but she could no longer make out Graciela's or Cipriana's whispers. All she could hear was the creak of the rusty hinges on the woodstove, which only made her shiver even more.

She lay listening to more comforting sounds emanating from the kitchen: the back door opening and closing, the unmistakable shuffle of Graciela back and forth across the kitchen in her husband's heavy black snow boots, the thud of the cast-iron burners after the fire was stoked, water splashing into a pot and the exclamation, "But isn't that too much, Mama!" and giggling. Giggling! How she loved the voices of children. She missed them. When she and Cita were taking care of her son's children, they had had a full house, and now she missed it. There was nothing like children to bring joy into the house and she often wondered why Cita didn't get married so she could have some babies. Now that she knew she couldn't be a nun, it was time for her to settle down, find a good man. Maybe that way she wouldn't have to go on cleaning for los americanos. As long as she got an ambitious husband. That was the most important thing. A husband like her father, not like her own Gilberto, who went off to the llano anytime he pleased. And she had to stop playing with those silly paints. They were for children. Not for her.

Mama Fela thought she heard the crackling of flames, but she knew her hearing wasn't that good. Even with Cita living with her, it felt so alone sometimes, either because she was gone or because when she was home, she hardly wanted to talk. And when she herself talked, Cita seemed to get bored quickly. She would go to her room and take out those silly paints. How could she prefer that to a good conversation? Mama Fela would never understand.

Mama Fela felt a warm cloth on her eyes. "Cita?" she inquired, confused, trying to wrestle her hands free from underneath her body. Finally, she slipped the wet cloth from her eyes and propped herself up with her elbows. An additional set of blankets had been added to her bed. "Where did you get these?" she asked, eyeing Graciela almost suspiciously. "Where's Cita?"

Graciela shrugged, sitting down beside Mama Fela. "I got here a while ago but you were fast asleep." With her hand on a pillow, she tried to get a glimpse of Mama Fela's eye.

"What are you doing?"

"Looking at your eye. Please, Mama Fela, turn this way."

"It's fine."

"But Cipriana said you wanted me to come."

"Earlier. Not now. I'm fine now."

"But Mama Fela, I've been here. You've been asleep for . . ." Graciela inspected the clock on the nightstand ". . . for about two hours now."

"Two hours! No me digas. Pues, is Cita back then?"

"No, I don't think so. Mama Fela, your eye's . . . all gray! Can you see?"

Mama Fela said nothing. Instead, she looked into Graciela's eyes, allowing her a peek into her own. Getting out of bed then, she began straightening the bed linens. "It was so cold last night. I'm not feeling like myself today."

"Fela. Your eye."

Mama Fela scooted around to the other end of the bed. "The water was like ice. Can you believe it was that cold in here?"

"That's what Cipriana said, but Mama Fela, please sit down here a second." Graciela patted the half-made bed.

"Oh, Graciela. I don't have time. I've got to finish those empanaditas." Mama Fela returned to her side of the bed and, with exaggerated motion, she pulled the blankets taut underneath her daughter-in-law. Tapping Graciela's knee, she said, "Off."

Sheepishly, Graciela stood. After a moment, she frowned, shaking her head as if she were scolding herself, and took Mama Fela by the arm. "Please, Mama Fela, you've got to go to the doctor."

"Sh, sh." Mama Fela shrugged her off. "I've got to make the bed."

"Mama Fela, for god's sake, why don't you want to go?" Graciela stood, two heads taller than Mama Fela, attempting to get a good look at her eye as Mama Fela avoided her gaze. "It's because of what people were saying, isn't it? About the baby having Dr. Beford's chin. You believed them. And now you don't want to go see him."

Spinning around, Mama Fela gasped. "I did not, Graciela! I don't believe all that mitote. What do you think I am?"

Graciela stood unblinking.

Exasperated, Mama Fela put her fists on her hips and frowned at Graciela. "You don't think very much of me, do you?" She fluffed the pillows violently and threw them to the other end of the bed. Tucking in the blankets all around the bed, she felt her face go hot. "I told you before I didn't believe all that mitote but you insist I do, so what am I going to do . . . ?"

"Mama Fela, I didn't mean . . ."

"Yes you did, Graciela. You think that I'm lying to you. I may know all the town news but I'm no mitotera. And you may not know this but Roberto thinks highly of you and maybe so do I."

Graciela's demeanor softened. For the first time in months, Mama Fela saw the hint of a smile on Graciela's face. But just for a moment. Before she knew it, the upturned corner of her mouth descended once again.

"Did you know it's completely gray, Mama Fela? Your eye?"

Mama Fela's fingers immediately shot up to her eye. Sitting down, she nodded, fingering the nubs on her bedspread.

"You can't see out of that eye at all, can you? Mama Fela," Graciela pleaded, "you've got to go see Dr. Beford."

"No, Graciela, I don't."

"Well, then, I'm going to bring him here."

Mama Fela bristled and looked up at Graciela. "You are not. That's final."

"Mama Fela you may never see from that eye again. We're just wasting time. Maybe he can do something."

"It's God's will then."

"What?"

"God's will, if I go blind."

"Oh, Fela, that's nonsense. Not if you can do something to prevent it."

"Only God can."

"You take that too far sometimes."

"What?"

"God can't help with every little detail."

"Little. You call this little? Pues, if I hadn't been making those empanaditas for your dinner today, well, I'd be fine now."

Graciela sat down on the bed, staring at her hands in her lap. Her face showed no emotion. After a moment, she took Mama Fela's hand in her own. "Dr. Beford's a good doctor, Mama Fela. He'll only look at it."

"No doctor."

"But why? He's only going to look at it . . ."

"That's right. That's all he can do. There's not much good in that, is there? No, he's not like Dr. Lewis, who taught me how to deliver the babies. Did you know that?"

Graciela nodded.

"I worked side by side with him until . . . well . . . tenía tis. When he got the t.b. I delivered them all myself. He was a fine man. A good man."

"But Mama Fela, Dr. Beford's a good doctor. You said so yourself. That's why you brought him in for my delivery."

"And that was a mistake, wasn't it?" Mama Fela watched for a reaction from her daughter-in-law but when there was none, she added, "No, Graciela. This doctor of yours treats me like I'm a child."

Without another word, Mama Fela turned away from Graciela and scooted closer to her nightstand. Rummaging through a pile of magazines and newspapers, she said, "I was reading about this eyewash the other day. Dios mío, where is it? I just had it the other day. Ah, here it is . . ." Slipping her glasses on, she began to read the description out loud. As she read, she found her vision passed in and out of blurriness. She hesitated and then began reading again. Suddenly she pulled off her glasses and pressed the magazine into Graciela's hands. "Pues, I can't read it. My eyes are too tired, too old. Go ahead, you read, Graciela," she said.

Graciela took the herb magazine but continued to focus on Mama Fela. Mama Fela didn't like being stared at. Finally, she averted her eyes.

"Please. Do this for me. Do it for yourself, Mama Fela."

All at once Mama Fela knew why Graciela wanted her to see the doctor. Sure, she was concerned for her eye. She probably felt responsible in some way. But her visit would also prove to all those mitoteros out there that she didn't believe the rumors. Fela Romero, a church-going, God-fearing, commandment-following woman, believed her daughter-in-law. She wasn't cheating on her husband. Of course not. This was Graciela they were talking about. It was all a vicious lie. And going to Dr. Befardo or whatever his silly name was would prove it to everybody.

"Bueno, Graciela."

Graciela's eyes met Mama Fela's. "What?"

"I'll go to your Dr. Bófolo."

The smile on Graciela's face was enough to propel Mama Fela into action. "But go and put on some decent shoes. I'm not going anywhere with you unless you take off those horrible things. A woman's got to have some dignity."

The water on top of the stove was warm. She poured enough into the platón to splash her hands with and the rest went into the pitcher. After an unsatisfactory inspection of her teeth, she clicked forward both pieces and put them in the white porcelain dish kept just for this purpose. She wet her toothbrush and sprinkled some baking powder on it. Brushing thoroughly for about three minutes, she finally rinsed off the teeth, inspecting them one more time. After they were back in place, she washed and powdered her face, braided her hair, and twirled the thick braid into a bun, securing it with two large hairpins, a gift from Gilberto for their fortieth wedding anniversary. Except for the fact that they were made from real bone, they were really quite ordinary. Still, she wore them only on holidays. By the time she had slipped on her dress, Graciela and Cipriana were waiting for her in the front room, coats in hand.

Fela slipped into the worn, woolen coat Graciela held open for her. The gesture made her feel like an old woman and at the same time like a child who needed help dressing herself. As quickly as she could, she buttoned herself up while Graciela and Cipriana readied themselves for the cold January air. She felt as if she were racing against time, fumbling with the difficult buttons that had become harder and harder to manage, especially on the days when her arthritis was acting up. Today they were even more of a challenge, not only because her fingers were stiff, but also because she had trouble seeing them clearly with her blurred vision. Looking up, she saw that Graciela and Cipriana were ready, waiting for her once again. Without finishing the buttons, she drew her lavender scarf out of her pocket and tied it around her head. "Vámonos," she said, leading her daughter-in-law and her granddaughter out the door. *God, deliver me from old age*, she thought. *Don't let me be a burden.*

Mama Fela's stride could be rapid if need be. When she was younger, she and Gilberto would take evening walks during the summer and she often enjoyed challenging him to a race or two. She found she had to do this in order to get them home at a reasonable time before dark. Otherwise, with his predilection for exploring new routes and his habit of meandering, they probably would not have arrived home until the roosters bellowed out their morning song.

Now, she felt she had to prove to Graciela and Cipriana that she was as strong as ever. She knew the route to town by memory, so the fact that she could only see out of one eye didn't bother her. She could lead the way blindfolded if she had to. Feeling Graciela and Cipriana trailing behind at her heels, sometimes running to catch up, made her feel like God was on her side.

"Wait, Mama Fela!" Cipriana called.

Ordinarily, Mama Fela would have turned around immediately at the sound of her granddaughter's voice. She slowed her pace but just for a moment. Racing on, she knew she had to prove something, if only to herself.

And then suddenly, Mama Fela lost her footing and tripped. Before she knew it she was on the ground, Graciela and Cipriana fussing around her. Her hands were scraped and her wrist felt twisted, but mostly her pride suffered. Now she really felt like a vieja. She wanted to cry but that would never do, not in public. That would confirm her pitiful state. Not only half blind, now she was a clumsy fool too. And it hurt all over.

Graciela and Cipriana both tried to help her up but she didn't want their help. "¡Quítense!" she scolded them, slapping their hands away. She could feel her body complain as she used all her strength to push herself up. What a creaky old body she had become. In no time, it seemed.

Trying to regain her composure, Mama Fela dusted herself off. She began to finger her buttons and, upon closer inspection, she noticed one was missing. "¡Ave María Purísima!" she exclaimed. "I lost a button." Examining the ground all around, she gestured toward Cipriana, "Come, 'jita. I need your young eyes. See if you can find it." Out of the corner of her good eye, she saw Cipriana look up at her mother. Graciela nodded and they all proceeded to scrutinize the ground. After several minutes, Mama Fela sighed. She envisioned the tin canister at home overflowing with all manner of sizes and colors of pretty buttons. She would find another one. Drawing her coat tighter around herself, Mama Fela said, "It's cold, the wind, no? Let's go."

Mama Fela had only seen Dr. Beford twice before and it wasn't for illness. The first time was when Graciela was having the baby and he would not let her assist. The second time, she had come to find out what the rumors were all about and when he showed no sign of knowing what she was referring to, she scolded him like a little boy, guilty or not. He quickly ushered her to the door and she had never seen him again. Never had to and never wanted to. Later, she was embarrassed that she hadn't thought her actions through. What would Graciela think if she knew Fela had done what she did? She would never forgive her, especially after she told Graciela she trusted her. But she did trust Graciela. That was the truth. Who she didn't trust was that americano. El Dr. Beford.

She was nervous now as Graciela reached for the doorknob to Dr. Beford's office. Mama Fela placed her hand on Graciela's forearm. "Remember, Graciela," she said, looking up at her daughter-in-law. "We have to go to Mass. We already missed the one at ten so we'll have to go at noon. We don't have much time."

Nodding, Graciela turned the doorknob as Mama Fela looked on. "It's locked," Graciela said, and Mama Fela let out the breath she had been holding. She was ready to go when Cipriana, who was standing at the window, called out, "But Dr. Beford's there, Mama Fela. He's sitting right there behind the counter." And before Fela or Graciela could protest, Cipriana was rapping on the window and waving.

With each footstep echoing closer toward the door, Mama Fela shuddered. Dr. Beford appeared at the door and opened it wide. "Sorry, ladies," he said, peeking over his wire-rimmed spectacles. "I'm closed today. It's a holiday."

"But Doctor, my mother-in-law here had an accident yesterday," Graciela said, squeezing Mama Fela's hand. "She burnt her eye."

Mama Fela gave the doctor no eye contact but she nodded, acknowledging both his presence and the truth of her accident. Even though she felt like a child when Graciela spoke on her behalf, it was preferable to speaking herself. Once she opened her mouth in English and her heavy accent became evident, these americanos would lose all respect for her. This had become apparent during the birth of Graciela's child when her dignity had been compromised and her competence questioned.

Very briefly, she felt Dr. Beford's gaze upon her, but instead of speaking directly to her, he turned his attention back to Graciela.

"Describe what happened."

Mama Fela took Graciela's arm and whispered into her ear. "Can't he do this inside?"

Graciela nodded. "Dr. Beford, please, Mama Fela's very cold. Can't you see us just for a moment?"

Dr. Beford looked at the ground. And then he nodded. "But just for a minute." After holding the door open for them, he locked it again and led the way to the examination room at the back of the store.

Leaning toward Graciela, but loud enough for the doctor to hear, Mama Fela said in her best English, "He's not like Dr. Lewis. Not at all."

Dr. Beford turned and produced what Mama Fela believed to be a false smile. "No, I'm not. Mrs. Romero, is it? If I remember correctly, we've met on one or two occasions."

Without expression, Mama Fela nodded, more with her eyelids than with her head. She held up two fingers.

Dr. Beford chuckled. "Ah, Mrs. Romero is right. We have met on two separate occasions. You have a good memory, Mrs. Romero."

"No." Mama Fela cleared her throat. Still avoiding the doctor's glance, Mama Fela directed her comments to Graciela. "I'm getting too old to remember anything. Even my breakfast. Graciela, you know I didn't eat this morning. Not even coffee."

"Mrs. Romero, that's not good for any of us," Dr. Beford said, taking Fela's arm and helping her up to the examination table. "Now, tell me what happened," he said, turning his attention back to Graciela.

"I think Mama Fela can tell you a more accurate story. I wasn't there."

"Fine. Mrs. Romero, I'll let you do the honors."

Fela didn't know exactly what he meant by "the honors" but she would speak for herself if she had to. Without looking directly at Dr. Beford, she told him the details of the accident, annunciating each word with a razor edge and a brisk delivery. She didn't like the hard consonants and cold vowels of the doctor's language, but she persisted. When she couldn't remember the exact pronunciation of a word, she asked Graciela before she uttered it herself.

He examined her eye while she talked.

Finally, he said, "Your vision is fine in the normal eye, but because the other may have been damaged, it's causing you to see cross-eyed. This is what's causing the blurry vision in both eyes. Do you understand, Mrs. Romero?"

Mama Fela squinted, staring straight at Dr. Beford. She nodded once with exaggeration.

"I'm going to put a patch on for a couple of days, Mrs. Romero," Dr. Beford continued, placing a square of white gauze over her eye. "I'm also going to give you this eyewash, which you should put in two times a day. You come back and see me then and we'll see if it's cleared up any." Taping the gauze until it was taut, he said, "I can't tell you for certain whether you'll recover full use of that eye, nor can I be certain that you'll lose total vision. We'll have to wait and see. I can recommend an eye specialist over in Albuquerque but I wouldn't go that route until we're a little surer of what we have here."

Mama Fela frowned. "He's not sure of anything, is he?" she told Graciela in a loud whisper that failed to hide her disgust. "Que doctor tan pobre," she mumbled to herself, scooting her backside off the examination table, now ready to leave. But underneath her disgust, she felt frightened. She had expected the doctor to know, one way or the other, to say either she will or she won't see again and that was it. Waiting was the part she couldn't bear.

"Wait, Mama Fela," Graciela said, putting her hand on her knee. "What about your hands? Don't you want the doctor to put some ointment on them? They're scraped up."

"No, I'm fine. Let's go now."

"But Mama Fela . . ."

"Now. I've had enough of your doctor." And with that, she walked right past Graciela and Cipriana, past Dr. Beford, right out of his office. For more than a few minutes, she waited out in the cold, rubbing her hands together and breathing puffs of warm air into them. Finally, Graciela appeared hand in hand with Cipriana, her face drawn and her eyes menacing. She held out a bottle with an eyedropper and Mama Fela took it, avoiding any and all eye contact with her daughter-in-law. She had never had a confrontation with Graciela and didn't wish to start now.

They walked in silence side by side, staring at the road ahead of them. Even Cipriana was quiet and this made Mama Fela feel somber. Something was wrong with the world when even the children grew silent. It wasn't like Cipriana.

Finally, Graciela mumbled something.

Mama Fela lifted her chin. "¿Qué?" she asked, lost in thought. It seemed that her hearing had gotten worse at about the same time her eyesight had gone awry. Now not only was she *tuerta*, she was also *sorda*. So much for getting old.

"I said you embarrassed me, Mama Fela," Graciela said more loudly.

Mama Fela felt sheepish not only because of her rude exit earlier, but also because Graciela was speaking to her as if she were stupid or deaf. She looked down at the ground again, wondering what to say. Clearing her throat, she said softly, "I'm sorry, Graciela. I didn't mean to. I just couldn't be in that room any longer with that doctor of yours."

After a moment, Graciela said softly, "He's not my doctor, Mama Fela."

Mama Fela nodded then, staring straight into Graciela's face. As something inexplicable passed between the two women, Mama Fela felt Graciela's hand wrap around the crook of her arm. They continued to walk in silence until they reached the wooden steps that led up to Graciela's house.

The few steps that led up to the door had never given Mama Fela trouble before, but now with the patch on her eye, she felt very unsure of herself. Clutching Graciela's arm, she slowly navigated herself up so she wouldn't trip. Her feet felt big and clumsy for their small size. Maybe it was the shoes. She was always having trouble with her feet now. She had become nothing but one big *callo*. Another sign of this old age. Maybe a new pair of shoes would fix her problems.

The house smelled like piñon wood as they entered and she could hear the snap and crackle of the fire. Cipriana dodged around her and ran over to her father, who had just stood up after stoking the fire. The door of the woodstove creaked shut.

"Cipriana! Watch where you're going," Roberto scolded. "You almost knocked down your Mama Fela."

"No, no, I'm fine," Mama Fela said, more to Cipriana than to Roberto. She tried to catch Cipriana's attention but Cipriana averted her eyes.

"What did the doctor say, Mamá?" Roberto asked.

Mama Fela shook her head, slipping off her coat. "Ooh, pues, nothing. Nothing at all," she said, seeing a look pass between her son and Graciela. "Well, he didn't," she insisted, "and you and I both know it, Graciela. He's not certain of this and not certain of that. Just some nonsense about wait and see. Didn't tell me anything I didn't already know."

"But Mama Fela, at least he gave you some medicine for your eyes."

"Ooh, que medicine tan pobre. Sure, it's in an expensive bottle, with an eyedropper even, but I bet I can tell you what's in that bottle. Nothing but a little rosa de castilla crushed up in the molcajete and a little water. I could have saved him the trouble."

"Ay, Mamá, you really don't like Dr. Beford, do you?" Roberto asked, with a slight smile.

"Pues, 'jito, he's no Dr. Lewis, that's all I can say. Now, tell me where's the needle and thread? I need to sew a button."

"But Mama Fela, aren't we going to Mass?" Graciela asked. "It's getting late."

"Of course. But do you expect me to visit my God all shosha? No, I have to be presentable first. Now what about a pretty button?"

As Graciela rummaged through a small jar of buttons, Mama Fela watched her son and her granddaughter as they roasted piñon nuts in a cast-iron skillet, stirring the tiny brown nuts constantly so they wouldn't burn. The sweet woody smell reminded her of Gilberto, who would risk mice and snakes every autumn just to find a few nuts in the nest of piñon branches or on the ground below. He gave away most of them, filling brown paper bags with a pound or so for each of his children and his men friends who put up with him. Then he saved one bag for himself to bring out on Christmas Day. Since he had started going out on the llano with those sheep of his, gone all winter long, the bags had been accumulating. They were probably rancid by now.

"Is that the piñon your papá picked this fall, Roberto?"

Roberto nodded. "Since he's out there on the llano somewhere, I thought I should carry on his tradition."

Mama Fela was quiet for a moment. Her stomach growled loudly. Roberto and Cipriana laughed but Mama Fela only smiled slightly. "But he roasts it on Christmas, Roberto."

"I know, Mamá. But I wanted to make today special."

Mama Fela nodded as Graciela handed her a button. It wasn't one she would have chosen but she smiled, tearing off a piece of navy thread from the spool. She tried to feed the thread into the eye of the needle but she couldn't see straight. Without asking, Graciela took the thread from her and threaded the needle easily, handing it back to her without a word. With nimble fingers, Mama Fela looped the thread around her finger to make a knot. And then another one.

"Cipriana, offer your grandmother some piñon."

"No, Daddy, you do it."

"Cipriana!"

With a pinched expression, Cipriana hesitantly approached Mama Fela. Her eyes looked scared.

Mama Fela set her coat down on her lap and stuck the needle into the heavy material. With outstretched arms, she called Cipriana over. "What's the matter, 'jita? What's gotten into you?"

"Nothing, Mama Fela."

"But, 'jita, you seem scared all of a sudden."

"I'm not, Mama Fela."

"You sure?"

Cipriana nodded.

"Is it my eye?"

Mama Fela could feel Cipriana go stiff in her arms.

"Is it because I fell?"

Finally, Cipriana looked up. "I don't know, Mama Fela. You're different, that's all."

"Different?"

Cipriana nodded.

"You mean I look different?"

Cipriana shrugged.

"What do you mean, 'jita?" Mama Fela persisted, her voice growing impatient.

"Like that, Mama Fela. You never used to do that."

"What, 'jita?"

"Your voice. You have a mean way of saying things sometimes."

Mama Fela was speechless.

"Like to Cita last night. I heard her crying in the middle of the night after you yelled at her."

"Pues, 'jita, I didn't mean anything by it. That's how she and I carry on sometimes. And besides, my eye was hurting. Aren't you cross when you scrape your knee or stub your toe? Or remember that time you stepped on the needle. You screamed at me for dropping it."

"But that was different, Mama Fela."

"Why, 'jita?"

"Because I'm little. And you're my Mama Fela. You're old."

"Old?" Mama Fela asked, startled to hear the word pass her granddaughter's lips. So finally the child had come to believe it too. Mama Fela wondered what had changed. She cleared her throat, trying to regain her composure. "Yes I am, 'jita, and you're right. I should have known better." Smiling tentatively, she gazed into Cipriana's eyes with her one good eye and there she saw her granddaughter's fear begin to dissipate. Gently pushing Cipriana away, Mama Fela said, "Now, let me finish my sewing so we can get to Mass."

"But don't you want to try the piñon, Mama Fela?"

"I can't 'jita. I have to fast until Communion."

"But, it's only a tiny tiny nut. And today's New Year's."

Roberto gently shook the bowl of piñon. "Come on, Mamá," he teased.

"Stop it, you two malcriados!" Mama Fela said, stifling a laugh, trying to be serious. "Ay, and it's a holy day of obligation. Let's get to Mass," she said, tearing off the thread with her teeth and pushing herself up out of the chair.

As they slowly approached the church, Mama Fela wondered for a moment why a crowd was gathered at the doors, staring up at a scroll of paper whose stark glare she could make out even from where she stood, even with her blurred vision. And then she remembered that this was the time of year that Father O'Grady posted the parishioners' monetary contributions from the prior year, family by family, in his own tight script. She didn't have to look to know what she had given. She knew to the penny because she had scrimped and saved every one. She imagined other people knew as well but they studied the list anyway to find out what their neighbors had given. To Mama Fela, this practice was an outrage but what could she do about it? All she knew was that somehow she was able to save the five dollars each year to retain her half pew, fourth from the front of the church, right of the nave. In addition, every Sunday she would drop a dime into the collection box.

Just as they drew near the crowd, Doña Francisquita emerged from the throng of people gathered at the door. "Comadre! What happened to your eye?" she asked, rushing toward Fela, whose hand instinctively shot up to her eye patch. The entire crowd turned then and flocked around her. Some called out, "Señora Romero, ¿qué pasó?" Others, more familiar, called her by her given name. "Are you well? Can we do anything, Fela? What's wrong?" they asked.

Mama Fela was embarrassed but only for a moment. She removed her hand from her patch and immediately launched into a narrative about her accident, embellishing the details just a little. Instead of one batch of empanadas, she had been making ten to give to all her friends. Instead of Dr. Beford saying that time would tell how to treat her eye, she told them he had said she needed surgery. Basking in all the attention, she was glad she had sewn the button on her coat. What would they think of her had she not? Too bad it wasn't one from her own collection, but it would do. She felt like a celebrity. And even better, she felt like she had been responsible for keeping her neighbors from gossiping about who gave how much to the church that year. At least for now.

As the church bells rang, Mama Fela led the townspeople into the church. They filed into their pews one by one and Mass began.

Mama Fela didn't understand a word the priest said but it didn't matter. She came for the ritual, which was mesmerizing to her and allowed her to fall deep into thought and prayer. It also offered her a rest from the day's work. Best of all, she could visit afterward with her comadres. That's what she looked forward to. That's really why she came to Mass week after week. To the contrary, Gilberto never accompanied her to Sunday Mass or even on days of obligation. He said there were too many people. Too many people? There could never be too many people for Fela. She would never understand her husband. And yet, she wanted him to come home.

After Mass, Mama Fela tried to convince Roberto and Graciela to go on ahead of her. "I just want to visit a minute with my comadres and then I'll be right home."

"No, we'll wait, Mamá," Roberto said.

"No, no, you go on ahead. I'll be there shortly, Roberto."

"But Mamá, your eye."

"It's better, 'jito. I can make my own way home," she said, growing weary from the argument.

"No, Mamá, we'll wait. And that's final." Roberto paused, then added softly, "Take your time."

Mama Fela felt exasperated. She hated for her son to treat her like a child. She frowned at him before turning her back to him to join her circle of friends. She resolved to take her own sweet time.

"Show us your eye," Doña Francisquita begged.

"Ay, sister, don't be a tonta," Adela said. "That's rude."

Beatríz reached her hand over to lightly touch Fela's face. Her fingers felt as soft as a child's whisper. "Tell us how you're feeling, comadre," she said. Fela could hear the concern in her voice.

"Estoy bien, comadres. I just can't see as well as I used to. But that's old age for you."

They all nodded.

"Ay, if it's not one thing, it's another," Lupe said.

"Yo sé," Carlota agreed.

"But Sulema here doesn't like hearing about all my aches and pains, no, Sulema?" Lupe said, elbowing her daughter.

"That's not true, Mamá. I've never said that."

"No? You don't have to. Your face tells me everything."

"No, Mamá."

"Ay, these children of ours," Carlota said softly. "Pal quince."

The women laughed, all except Sulema.

"How's Cita anyhow, Doña Fela?" Sulema asked. "On my way to the bakery this morning, I saw her get into a car. I think it was Don Evaristo's but I'm not sure. She had a suitcase. Where's she going?"

Mama Fela was stunned. "Getting in a car?"

Sulema nodded.

"With a suitcase?"

Sulema nodded again. The women grew quiet.

Mama Fela could hear herself swallow. "I thought she was cleaning today."

"But it's a holy day, Doña Fela," Sulema said.

Mama Fela nodded. She felt her vision blur. "But for los americanos—they always make messes. Doesn't matter if it's a holy day or not," she said in a monotone, her thoughts somewhere else. "¿Qué no?" she asked.

All the women nodded, even Sulema.

"I'm sorry, comadres. I have to go. Que les vaya bien," she said absentmindedly, but the words were void of meaning.

Turning to meet her family, Mama Fela felt a chill make its way down her spine. She adjusted her coat, squeezing the collar tighter around her neck. Reaching for her granddaughter with the other hand, she called out, "Take my arm, 'jita. And don't walk so fast. Remember, I'm tuerta."

"What's wrong, Mama Fela?"

"Ssh, not now, 'jita."

"But why . . . ?" Cipriana asked.

"¡Cállate, niña! I need to think."

Mama Fela and Cipriana walked home arm in arm, Roberto and Graciela trailing behind. Mama Fela was deep in thought.

As soon as they got home, Graciela told Mama Fela, "Why don't you take a nap while I prepare supper?"

"I should say not. Even though I'm tuerta doesn't mean I'm not living and breathing. I can help."

"Well all right," Graciela said with concern. "But are you sure you're up to it? It's already been a long day."

"Graciela, I'm not dead and buried, if that's what you think." Mama Fela paused. "And until I am, I'll be helping you with supper. And that's final."

Graciela nodded. Without a word, she ushered Mama Fela to the kitchen table. Silently, they worked side by side, preparing the meal that would begin the new year: fried chicken, mashed potatoes, and red chile. Intent on the task at hand, Mama Fela tried to chase thoughts of Cita from her mind.

When Cipriana had finished cutting out the biscuits with a Folgers coffee can, Mama Fela slid them into the oven to bake. Finally, after several hours of bustling to and from the stove, she sat down at the kitchen table and a heavy sigh escaped from deep inside her.

"What's wrong, Mama Fela?" asked Graciela.

"I want to go home, Graciela."

"But Mama Fela, you have to eat supper. It's New Year's."

"No, I have too much to do."

"Like what?"

"Graciela, did you know Cita was leaving?"

Graciela looked down and began brushing flour into her free hand. She paused before she asked, "Leaving where, Mama Fela?"

Graciela's pause was a little too long, in Mama Fela's opinion. "You knew, didn't you?"

"Knew what, Mama Fela?" Graciela asked, intent on her task.

Mama Fela ignored Graciela. Instead, she stood, gathered her coat, and proceeded to the front door. Mama Fela could hear Graciela call out urgently for her husband as she quietly shut the door behind her.

Suddenly the door popped open again and Roberto and Cipriana ran toward her.

"Mamá, where are you going?"

"Home."

"You can't go home without supper."

"I can do anything I want, 'jito. I'm an old woman. I deserve it."

"You're not an old woman. C'mon, Mamá, stop. Let's talk."

Mama Fela halted in her tracks and turned to face her son. Her feet were hurting. Her focus went in and out. She gazed down at her granddaughter, whose eyes were wide. Looking past Roberto and Cipriana, Mama Fela squinted, seeing Graciela struggle to catch up, the baby in one arm and Pablito in the other, both wrapped in blankets. A sweater was thrown over her shoulders haphazardly, threatening to slip away at any moment. Mama Fela pointed and called out, "See to your wife, Roberto." Turning back around again, she continued to make her way in the semi-darkness.

At last, Fela reached the steps of her home. She stood briefly at the door, reluctant to enter, afraid of what she would find. Then, making the sign of the cross, she pushed open the door. Carefully making her way into Cita's room, she stood a moment in the darkness, allowing her good eye to acclimate. Slowly, she felt her way to Cita's dresser, on which the kerosene lamp was propped. Fumbling for a box of matches, she found one at last. The strike of the match was the only sound audible. She adjusted the brightness as she scanned the room for any signs that what she had heard today was mitote. That morning, she had noticed Cita's nicely made bed but hadn't thought twice about it. In fact, she had felt heartened to know that Cita was changing her ways. A new year, a new Cita, she had thought. Now she knew better. Hesitantly opening the doors of Cita's armario, Mama Fela caught her breath. The shelves were empty. The few handmade wooden hangers were bare. Running her finger along one, taking in its nakedness, she winced as a splinter dug into her skin. For the first time in her life, Mama Fela was saddened to see such tidiness. It was then she knew it was true. Cita had left her.

"Mamá, you all right?" Roberto called.

Mama Fela spun around then, startled that her actions had been observed. Silhouetted in the doorway were her son holding his son and

Graciela cradling her baby. Mama Fela called out, "Where's mi'jita? Where's Cipriana?"

They all looked around. Roberto called, "Cipriana!" Then more gruffly, he said, "Cipriana, come out right now."

"Here, Mama Fela," a small voice called out.

Mama Fela searched the room. Deep in the shadows, Cipriana stood, her small shoulders bent. Even in the dark, Mama Fela could see her pigtails sticking out.

Mama Fela bent down and called to Cipriana. "Mi'jita, come here."

Cipriana looked over at her father.

"Go on, 'jita. Your Mama Fela wants you."

Mama Fela waited while Cipriana slowly moved toward her. "Quickly, 'jita!" Bending down, Mama Fela asked, "Did Cita say anything to you last night about where she was going?"

Cipriana shook her head.

"Are you sure, 'jita?"

Cipriana nodded.

Roberto stepped forward, the stomp of his boots echoing against the wood floor. "You sure, Cipriana?" he asked, his impatience audible. "She didn't say anything last night to make you think she was going someplace?"

Cipriana shook her head again. "No, Daddy. Really."

Mama Fela could hear the strain in her granddaughter's voice. She was on the verge of tears.

"Leave her be," Mama Fela and Graciela said in unison. Mama Fela gaped at Graciela, who was still standing in the doorway. They eyed each other until Graciela turned away.

"Leave her be, Robert," Graciela said again. "She doesn't know anything."

"I'm just trying . . ."

"Leave her be," Graciela repeated, more sternly this time. "Mama Fela, you can't stay alone tonight. Come to our house."

"No," she snapped. "Thank you, but no."

"Well, at least let Cipriana stay with you."

Mama Fela paused to consider the suggestion carefully. She recalled Cipriana's eyes not a minute before. Even though her granddaughter had been hidden in the shadows and Mama Fela could only see out of one eye, she had been able to make out her granddaughter's face. The expression she was wearing was not recognizable. It was as if Cipriana were afraid of her, afraid of what she would do to hurt her, as if that were possible. Never had she seen Cipriana look that way. But the night before, she had seen that very expression on Cita's face. Cipriana had been right. The children were always right. She did have a mean way of saying things sometimes. Especially to Cita. Especially last night. Oh, what had she done? Why had she driven Cita away? Why couldn't she understand that girl? Why?

Mama Fela felt exhausted all of a sudden. All she wanted was to go to bed. She cleared her throat and looked straight at Graciela. "No, Graciela. Not tonight. Cipriana should be in her own bed tonight." Mama Fela yawned. "Anyway, I'm very tired."

Before they left, Mama Fela could hear Roberto starting a fire in the woodstove. Without seeing them out, Mama Fela retreated to her room. Without removing her clothes or taking her daily sponge bath or brushing her hair, she removed her teeth and slipped into her sheets. She couldn't sleep. Her mind raced with thoughts of Cita. Why did she leave? With whom did she leave? When would she return? Where was she? She prayed the rosary twice, trying to numb herself into a state of sleep, but she still couldn't. Her body would not conform to her wishes.

Mama Fela emerged from bed with unexplained energy. Still in the clothes she had worn that day, she scurried from room to room in her bed slippers and a sweater wrapped around her shoulders, gathering all three lamps from each of the rooms. By the dim light of one lamp, she scrubbed their chimneys in the platón until the water was black with bits of char floating on top. Afterward, she trimmed their wicks and filled their bases with kerosene, lighting each one. She repeated the same steps until the third lamp was also clean and ready to light. From the kitchen table, where she set all three lamps, emerged a light as bright as day. By their light, she stirred the embers of the fire in the woodstove and added two more pieces of wood from the pile Roberto had left. She stood, rubbing her hands together vigorously to get warm.

The kitchen was in disarray from the night before when Mama Fela had her accident. The kitchen table was still dusted with flour, and a mound of crusted dough stood in its center. Several empanadas with crimped edges stuck to the wooden table, their raw dough glowing by the light of the oil lamp. The pot that held the bubbling-hot oil was still now, a thick solid film of *manteca* formed at the top. The only evidence of the accident were the glistening spots all around the cast-iron stovetop where the grease had splattered up a storm.

Mama Fela peered into the water jug, sure that she would need to visit the cistern to replenish it before she could begin her kitchen cleanup. Dreading the task, she was surprised when, to her delight, she saw that it was filled to the brim. Sure that Roberto had saved her from the chore, she said a little prayer for him, asking God to give him a place in heaven when it was his time.

She poured some water into a pot and placed it on the stove to heat. While it was warming, she dipped a clean estropajo into the water and began scrubbing the stovetop, trying to remove the remnants of her accident. She didn't know if she could ever do anything about her eye, but she could certainly do something about the soiled stove. She wanted no reminder of the night past.

When the water was warm enough, she poured it into the porcelain dishpan, steam rising as it cascaded over dirty dishes. While they soaked, she gathered up the dried dough and wondered if it was salvageable for biscuits or tortillas. With a little water and a little kneading, it would probably be as good as new, but she couldn't bear the idea of saving anything from her accident. She gathered it up along with the few raw empanadas and rolled them up into a soiled piece of butcher paper saved from the roast that filled the empanadas. Washing the table was hard work because it was so crusted over with dried dough. She felt a droplet of sweat sting her bad eye as she finished sweeping the last of the dried bits of flour-encrusted dough into her open hand. At least she could feel.

Once the dishes were washed and rinsed, the flour and lard put away, and the kitchen straightened out, Mama Fela swept and washed the floor on her hands and knees. At the doorway, she slowly stood, bracing herself against the door frame. Her knees were aching and her finger joints felt stiff, but despite her aches and pains, she inspected her work with satisfaction. The kitchen sparkled; she had removed all traces of the accident. Not an ounce of dough or a spoonful of apricot was in sight. She was wide awake now. Sleep would evade her tonight.

Taking an oil lamp with her into her room, Mama Fela held it up to view her unmade bed. Setting it on her nightstand, she tore the sheets from the mattress, gathered them in her arms as if she were carrying a cloud, and let them float down into the tin tub that doubled as her laundry basin. Opening up her armario, she rummaged through the few clothes she possessed, took her coat off a hanger, and wrapped herself within it. With a heave, she pulled her mattress off her bed and dragged it out of her room, through the kitchen, and to the door that led outside. The moment she opened the door, a blast of freezing air made her catch her breath. At the doorway, she had to force the mattress this way and that to fit through the opening. When at last it was free, she tugged at it some more and finally laid it against the house. With the broom covered in a clean flour sack, she pounded the mattress until it was smooth and even. She would have removed the wool and washed it, but tonight was not the night for that. She was doing what she did because she had nothing better to do. And she loved the sound of the broom against the mattress. It lulled her into a state of relaxation and helped chase away any thoughts of Cita. She watched with amusement as her puffs of breath floated away with every strike of the mattress.

At last, Mama Fela dragged the mattress back inside. If any of her neighbors had seen her at this time of night in the middle of winter fluffing her mattress, they would have thought she was crazy. Maybe she was.

From the trunk at the foot of her bed, she removed a pair of clean sheets. She was embarrassed to tell people she had an extra pair of sheets, even two. It was a luxury none of her comadres could afford and neither could she, but she spent the money anyway. She convinced herself that the purchase was fine because she used the sheets to lay out her sewing projects, to keep the dresses clean and herself organized. It was a little business expense, she told herself.

Even though these sheets were a little frayed with age, they were as white as the day she purchased them. It was wonderful what a few thimblefuls of bleach and a day of sunlight could do.

By the time Mama Fela looked up from making her bed, the first rays of morning light peeked into her window. She was exhausted and yet she wasn't a bit sleepy. For a moment, she stiffly sat at the edge of her bed, staring out the window. She didn't want to muss her newly made bed and yet she had to relieve the strain on her back and knees. From her nightstand, she took a vial of arnica and, lifting her skirt, she rubbed the salve onto her knees. Inching her skirt above her waist, she strained to rub the ointment across her lower back but could barely reach. Frustrated, she stood and slowly unbuttoned her dress. Her fingers were stiff but she was stubborn. Finally, she slipped her long dress over her head. She replaced it with her long white nightgown.

She poured the tepid water from the pitcher into the palm of her hand and lightly splashed her face. Once she placed the pitcher down, she applied pressure to her eyelids with her fingertips and held them there for several minutes. Removing the pins from her bun, she watched in the mirror as the rivulet of hair fell past her shoulders. She brushed her hair with as few strokes as possible. Her black hair was starting to fall out while the gray held staunchly to its roots. The last thing she wanted to do was to help the black along. Finally, she removed her teeth and collapsed into bed.

A whisper of sunlight caressed her cheek. Letting a sigh escape from her lips, Mama Fela thought of Gilberto, out there somewhere on the llano. She thought of Solomón and his children. Out there somewhere far away. She thought of Cita, out there, alone, in an unknown place, seeking a dream she would never find. Life didn't work that way. You were born, had babies, worked and saved, went visiting in your old age, prayed to your god, and you were content. That's all. She didn't understand Cita and she never had. She had tried to make Cita accept reality, but she had failed. She tried to make Solomón understand, but she had failed again. They were like their father, those two, seeking an unknown happiness that didn't exist.

Mama Fela had been so good at cleaning, at sewing, at praying, she forgot how to be a good mother, a good wife who passed around doses of hope at every turn. She was of no use anymore. And she wondered if she ever had been. She always managed to chase her family away along with their dreams of happiness. They always left her behind. Alone with her thoughts of mere contentment.

For several days she rested, drifting in and out of sleep. She didn't clean. She didn't sew. And she didn't pray. Every time she awoke, Graciela seemed to be there, passing in and out of her reality with a bowl of caldito or a cup of manzanilla. Cipriana was never far behind, but always in the shadows. The days seemed to pass by like the wind.

After several days, when Mama Fela refused a spoonful of tea, Graciela said, "Mama Fela, something's wrong. We should call the doctor."

Mama Fela didn't respond. Instead, she whispered, "Graciela, I'm not well. You know that, don't you?"

Graciela nodded.

"I want you to do something for me." Mama Fela licked her parched lips. She reached for Graciela's hand. In a voice barely audible, she continued. "Promise me, you'll go get Cita and bring her home." Mama Fela searched her daughter-in-law's eyes to see if there was any reaction. "Promise me, Graciela. You and Roberto. You go and get her." Mama Fela could hear her own voice grow louder, transcend her own body. "I have some money. You take it and you bring her back, do you hear me?"

"But Mama Fela . . . ," Graciela stuttered.

"You do what I say now, you hear me? You do what I say."

Graciela nodded, wiping away a tear with her fingertip.

Mama Fela gently placed her hand along the side of Graciela's face. Graciela let out a sob. "You're like my own daughter, Graciela."

Graciela nodded, kissing Mama Fela's palm.

"You know it's time, don't you Graciela?" Mama Fela gazed into Graciela's eyes with her one good eye. Graciela's face went in and out of focus. Finally, she gave Graciela two pats along her cheek and closed her eyes. "It's too late for that doctor. Now call the priest," she whispered, settling down into her pillow, letting her hand fall to her chest.

Mama Fela drifted in and out of consciousness. Far away, it seemed that she heard singing. She could barely make out the words until she realized they were in Spanish. Oh, would the heavenly angels speak Spanish? She had never thought about it before, but surely they must. Surely, heaven was a place for all, americano or not. And the lovely voices were calling her. Calling Fela Armijo Romero to her final resting place. And she was ready. More than ready. A feeling of pure joy swept over her entire being. It traveled from her toes to her fingertips. For a moment, she wondered if she deserved this. She wondered if she was worthy of heaven.

Suddenly, a hollow knocking startled Mama Fela out of her reverie. She breathed in and out, trying to recapture the tranquil space she had reached only moments ago. And then she heard voices, not those of San Pedro or God, not big booming voices as she imagined, but those that sounded familiar, sweet and soft: Graciela's and Cipriana's. And then she knew. She wasn't in heaven yet but in her own home still, in her bed with the clean white sheets. Through the slit of one eye, she saw Graciela take a candle, leaving the room with Cipriana following close behind, clutching at her mother's skirt. She wished Cipriana had stayed at her side, but Mama Fela could tell that her granddaughter was scared. She had been frightened of Mama Fela for several days now, since the night she had chased Cita away. Just as she had driven Cita and Solomón and Gilberto away from home, she had run her granddaughter off too. It was like a curse. And now God was punishing her by keeping her out of heaven. Chasing her from the place where she could finally find some peace.

All Mama Fela felt was an overwhelming desire to close her eyes and to sleep. To rest the body that felt so tired. Suddenly, she heard violent sobbing and with just a hint of movement, she turned her head to see the one child who hadn't yet abandoned her. Roberto was sobbing violently, his head bent in prayer. Every so often, a hiccup of grief was emitted from deep in his chest and she felt like getting up to comfort him, to hold him as she did when he was a boy, sick with fever, vomiting into the platón. He grasped her hand and suddenly all she could feel was her hand being squeezed like the pulp from a sweet juicy orange. Her hand felt small within his, like a child's. For a moment, she thought of telling him to quiet down, to let go of her hand, to leave her be, to give her some peace and quiet. But only for a moment. Instead, she resisted these thoughts and hung on to the only thing that connected her to this life.

Mama Fela heard singing again. She opened her eyes and through her good eye, she saw Cipriana return, bringing light into the blackened room. Graciela followed, her hands on Cipriana's shoulders. Mama Fela's comadres, Beatríz, Sulema's mamá Lupe, Sulema, Francisquita, Adela, and Carlota, trailed behind Graciela, slowly making their way into the room on bended knee, chanting the rosary. Her parents followed slowly, inching their way into the room, hand in hand, faces completely devoid of emotion. *Cry, Mamá! Cry!* Fela felt like screaming. At the tail of the procession was Father O'Grady, all in black except for the white of his collar, carrying a black case like a doctor making a call to the sick. Only she knew that deep inside the recesses of that infamous black case were not the instruments for healing, but rather, for death. She knew now this was it. It was time. She watched dreamlike as figures passed in front of her in a haze, gathering around her bed, holding hands. Roberto stood up, giving Father O'Grady his seat. Graciela whispered to Cipriana, who set the candle on the nightstand. And then, before Cipriana slipped past, she stole a glance at Mama Fela's face and Mama Fela quickly shut her good eye.

Father O'Grady sat and one by one, he revealed the tools of his trade. First, he took a single white candle and lit it, placing it on Fela's nightstand next to the one Cipriana had set down. Then, he unrolled the purple and white stole, kissed it, and placed it around his neck, amethyst face up. Removing a metal vial from his case, he unscrewed the lid, dipping his thumb into the small opening. As he mumbled in Latin incoherently, Mama Fela felt his gentle touch against her forehead and the palms of her hands. Then she felt a breeze of air as the priest lifted the sheets at the foot of her bed and touched her lightly on the feet, making the sign of the cross over her instep. It was fortunate she had changed her sheets. She would have died of embarrassment instead of old age had Father seen rumpled sheets.

At last, she felt the shock of cold water upon her cheek as the priest sprinkled holy water over her and across the faces throughout the room.

Her family and friends made the sign of the cross and then resumed holding hands. A small voice started up in song. Fela strained to recognize it. And then, she realized it was her own mother singing "Bendito, Bendito, Bendito sea Dios." She had heard this song time and time again at every wake she had attended, but she never dreamed it would be meant for her. Soon, everyone joined in, holding back sobs, wiping away tears. Fear swept over her body until she felt the gentle touch of Beatriz's fingers over her lips and heard the lilt of her friend's lisp as she whispered a final goodbye. And then, she felt Adela and Francisquita on either side of her. She would know Adela's cold hands anywhere. Adela laced Mama Fela's fingers across her bosom. No sooner had Adela kissed her cheek than Mama Fela detected Francisquita's sweet breath on the other cheek. Soon her hands were being manipulated once again, one hand moved over her heart, one hand taken down to her side. After Sulema and her mamá said goodbye, she felt the hand at her side being turned upright and a handful of glass beads filled it. As soon as she heard the voice say, "Ooh, comadre, you beat me to heaven," she knew it could belong to no other than Carlota. Her friend whispered, "You can have one of my dresses, comadre. I'll make sure of it. You don't want to meet San Pedro with your nalgas showing. Save a place for me. I'll be there soon."

Mama Fela felt so good, so full of joy and laughter and love. Her heart filled with pure gladness. This is what life should be but wasn't. She had to wait for this all her life. She had to wait until she was at heaven's gates for a glimpse of what Cita and Solomón and Gilberto sought.

When the singing stopped, Mama Fela felt compelled to open her eyes but she knew she couldn't, she shouldn't. Instead, she felt a teardrop wet her nose. And then another one. She heard Graciela's gentle voice and felt the small hands of her granddaughter try to wrap themselves around her middle. And then just as quickly as they had appeared, they were gone. Mama Fela wanted to feel her granddaughter's touch again. She wanted to wrap her measuring tape around the little waist, to make her one last toddy before bed. She wanted to hear Cipriana laugh just once more. Suddenly, it hurt to feel. It hurt to remember. She just wanted to die, to forget. She wanted the pain to stop. She wanted the loneliness to end.

All she could hear was the mumble of voices, the wail of guilty mothers, the ghostly incomprehensible voices of sons and daughters and Gilberto, always Gilberto. She felt her blood stop and suddenly she became dizzy. The voices were incoherent . . . fading . . .

The next morning, Mama Fela woke with a start, then just as suddenly, squeezed her eyelids shut. She had died last night and now it was time to meet San Pedro. She didn't think it would be anything like this. She didn't think she would remember anything about her earthly life, but she did. Her earthly life ended yesterday, her heavenly life begins today, she thought to herself. She could feel her heart beating, she could feel the blood flowing through her veins, she could feel a soaring spirit. Lacing her fingers together, she prayed a little prayer, hoping this was the heaven she had been longing for. Mustering up all the courage she thought she had, she squeezed her eyelids tightly, afraid to open them, afraid of what she would see. And then, she let them pop open. Turning her head from side to side, all she could see was the bright light streaming from every direction. Ah yes, this is how she imagined heaven. Yes indeed.

And then something blocked her vision and she cowered, shutting her eyes tight. Perhaps this was San Pedro in all his glory. But all she could hear was mumbling followed by wailing. Oh, no, she thought heaven was going to be a joyful place and the people in it a joyful lot. What had she gotten herself into? What had she wished for?

Voices were calling her name, louder and louder and more voices, calling her. She opened her eyes slowly and there, all around her, were figures in black. Black *mantillas* covered the faces of the women on their hands and knees. She could see the tops of men's heads, bent in prayer, their hats lying silently by their sides. Looking closer, trying to make out the faces underneath the mantillas, she recognized these people: they were her family, her comadres, kneeling around her, reciting the rosary. At first, she didn't believe it. Her heart seemed to stop beating momentarily and then she was overjoyed. It was not her time yet. God did not want her yet. She had more to do in this earthly life. And she was relieved.

She heard her name again. And this time, she responded, sitting up. She heard gasps all around but for the first time in her life, she didn't care what kind of impression she was making. Cipriana rushed into her arms and Mama Fela felt her strength return. This was her life.

Cipriana dropped to her knees in front of Mama Fela. Her eyes were wet with tears but they weren't fearful this time. They were curious, questioning. "We thought you left us to go to heaven, Mama Fela."

Mama Fela nodded and smiled. "I did, 'jita, but I missed you too much. Now bend your head in prayer. I'll give you la bendición." Mama Fela leaned on one elbow and made the sign of the cross with her palm outstretched over Cipriana's head. "Dios te haga una santa," she whispered, touching her granddaughter lightly with her fingertips. Without a moment's hesitation, she kissed Cipriana gently and released her once again.

❧

CHAPTER THIRTEEN

THE RECITAL

Cipriana ran to keep up with her father's long strides on their way home from church. She was hoping for his undivided attention since her mother had stayed home with Pablito, who was sick, and with the baby, who didn't have to go to Mass.

They usually accompanied Mama Fela to church and joined her in her assigned pew. However, Mama Fela confided in Cipriana that she had told God that she was too old to go to Mass until the spring when her legs thawed out from winter. Cipriana had laughed at the time but soon realized that it was lonely in the pew they had all to themselves. There would be two more weeks of winter, and Cipriana was counting the days until her Mama Fela would join them again.

Until then, their after-church Sunday visit would have to do. As she and her father approached Mama Fela's little stone house, Cipriana breathed in relief when she saw Mama Fela's hand rubbing steam from the window and waving them inside. Cipriana took the steps two at a time and popped in the door without knocking.

"I need to tell you something," Cipriana said eagerly, just now remembering what she had forgotten long ago to ask her Mama Fela.

"What, 'jita? Is something wrong?" Mama Fela asked. Her face fell and a knot of lines punctuated her forehead.

Immediately, Cipriana was sorry she had alarmed her grandmother. She hated the way Mama Fela could act when she was frightened. Too many times, she had seen Mama Fela turn mean and lash out. At these times, Cipriana learned to retreat from a grandmother she didn't want to know.

"No, Mama Fela. I just wanted to tell you that we're having a recital at school. And I need to wear my best dress. Can you make me one?"

Mama Fela's face softened. "A recital? How nice, Cipriana."

Nodding, Cipriana said, "All the parents are invited. And, you too, Mama Fela!"

"Me?"

"Yes. And Mama and Daddy. And Tía Cita and Papa Gil but I know they won't be able to come because they're away . . . Mmm. Mama Fela, it smells good in here."

"Come. Come. Eat breakfast," she said, motioning Cipriana toward the bench, pointing with her spatula. "I have your favorite, 'jita. And you can tell me more about this recital of yours. Roberto, you want some coffee?"

"Please, Mamá," he said, sitting down at the table.

"Get the Karo syrup, mi'jita. So when is this recital of yours?"

"Next Friday, Mama Fela."

"¡Ave María Purísima, Cipriana!" Mama Fela spun away from her stove to face Cipriana and her father. "You give me no time. How am I ever going to make a dress in a few days? You'll just have to wear an old one."

"But Mama Fela . . ."

"'Jita, I'm not a machine. Why didn't you tell me sooner?"

"Sorry, Mama Fela. I forgot."

"Forgot? Something so important? What is it you're going to recite, anyhow?"

"A poem. Everyone has to recite a few lines from 'The Village Blacksmith' and three kids will say the whole thing out loud in front of the school, parents, and everybody. The best one gets a trophy."

"What three children?" Cipriana's father asked.

"We don't know yet. We find out tomorrow."

"Will you be one of them, 'jita?" Robert asked.

"Oh, no, Daddy. Not me. It'll be the real smart ones like Ruby Quinn or James Forest or Mary Jane Beford. Maybe even Samuel Ployt."

"You sure, 'jita? Maybe it could be you."

"No, Daddy. Besides, you have to try out. Miss Shute's going to pick the best three from all the kids who try out."

"And you are going to try out, right?"

"No. You're supposed to know the whole poem. I only know half of it."

"Well, you better learn the other half, 'jita."

"Not all the kids have to try out, Daddy. Only the ones who want to. All the rest just have to say their six lines."

"Que six lines ni six lines. Don't you want to say the entire thing? Just think how proud you'd feel, 'jita."

"Don't force her, Roberto," Mama Fela interceded. "Cipriana will do what she can."

"I'm not forcing her, Mamá. But Cipriana can do more than she thinks she can. She's smart like her mama."

Cipriana noticed Mama Fela's eyes on her. She waited for her to say something else, anything at all. She wanted her Mama Fela to agree with her father but instead of opening her mouth to concur, she gave Cipriana another pancake. Cipriana wasn't hungry anymore but she knew that Mama Fela considered it a sin to waste food so bit by bit she dutifully spooned up the flapjack smothered in syrup. She didn't want to sin, especially in Mama Fela's house.

By the time Cipriana's father stood up to go, Cipriana was feeling sick to her stomach.

"You go on now, 'jita. There's something I have to tell your daddy." Mama Fela shooed Cipriana out the door like a summer fly. Instead of closing the door, Cipriana left it ajar, hovering near the crack, hoping to hear snatches of conversation.

"¡Mocosa! Go on now!" Mama Fela laughed, shutting the door tight.

Cipriana waited, wondering what they were talking about. Finally, she walked home alone.

The next day, she arrived at school early. When she reached her classroom, she knocked and was greeted shortly by her teacher. "May I come in early, Miss Shute?" Cipriana asked. "I'd like to study my poem."

"I'm sorry, Cipriana. You'll have to wait for the bell like the other children."

"But, Miss Shute, I just decided that I want to try to say all of the poem."

"Don't you think it's a little too late for that now, Cipriana? The other children have been studying all weekend, I'm sure."

"I already know half of it, Miss Shute. I just have to learn a little more."

"I'm sorry, dear. I can't let you in but if you really want to try out, you have until this afternoon. You can study at recess and learn as much as you can then."

"Thank you, Miss Shute. I'm going to learn it. You'll see."

Cipriana ran off to the playground to wait for her best friend, Gloria. When Cipriana spotted her, she flew over to her. "Gloria! Gloria, you've finally come."

"What's the matter, Cipriana?"

"Would you like to try out for the poem contest with me?"

"But, it's today."

"So, it's not until this afternoon. We can study at lunch."

Gloria frowned. "I could never learn all those lines, Cipriana. Six lines are hard enough."

"Yes you can, Gloria. If I can, you can too."

"What makes you so sure that you can?"

"I don't know. I just know it."

"But I don't even understand what the poem means."

"Neither do I. Not all of it, at least. Please, Gloria!"

"But why, Cipriana? Miss Shute isn't making us."

"No. But maybe we'll get extra credit if we do it."

"Do you think so?"

Cipriana didn't really know but she nodded anyway. Maybe Gloria would do it for just this reason.

"She didn't say so before, Cipriana."

"Maybe she forgot."

Gloria was quiet and Cipriana could tell she was thinking about it. She crossed her fingers behind her back and said a little prayer for Gloria to give her consent.

Finally, Gloria said, "All right."

Throughout the morning, Cipriana took every opportunity to peek at the poem. At one point, she asked Miss Shute for permission to go to the bathroom. All the way there and all the way back, Cipriana practiced the poem out loud. Finally it was time for recess but instead of heading home for lunch as was customary, she and Gloria studied the poem together.

"Quiet, Cipriana! I'm trying to concentrate."

"I didn't say anything."

"Sure you did," Gloria rebutted. "You're babbling like my crazy tío."

Cipriana laughed. "But Gloria, it helps me learn the lines quicker to say them out loud."

"Well, go ahead then, but I'm going to have to plug my ears or I'm never going to learn all these lines."

"Sure you can, Gloria. Just read one line out loud. Then close your eyes and say it to yourself over and over until you remember it all. You can peek back at the line if you have to."

"No, Cipriana, I can't do it. I'm too scared I'll mess up."

"Come on, Gloria. It doesn't matter if you mess up."

Gloria shook her head and Cipriana knew she would never be able to change her friend's mind.

"I'll help you learn your lines, though," Gloria said. Cipriana thought she sounded a little too glad.

Now Cipriana was growing more anxious by the minute and she still had two stanzas to go. Her empty stomach was doing somersaults and for the moment, she considered herself lucky that she hadn't eaten lunch. When she started to recite her lines to Gloria, they were interrupted by the raucous ringing of the bell by a teacher whose wrist whipped back and forth. All the way to class, Cipriana focused on her poem, mumbling the lines out loud.

"Hey, Cipriana, talking to yourself now?"

"Hey, Esteban, be quiet."

"No really, what are you doing?"

"I'm learning all the lines of the poem."

"No way! You can't do it. Only the smart kids can."

"Just wait and see, Esteban. I'll show you."

"¡Ándale, Güera! You're too good for us now."

Cipriana entered the classroom determined to try out. She held her head high, recalling the way Mama Fela held hers when she didn't want to argue anymore. And it worked. Esteban didn't say another word.

When the class settled, Miss Shute addressed them. "Now class, for those of you who are trying out for Friday's recital, you'll have fifteen minutes to review the poem. The rest of you, please put your heads down and give the other students some quiet."

As Cipriana scanned the classroom, a feeling of pride welled up inside of her. Her head was bobbing amongst the smart kids, reviewing their poem one last time. She looked over at Gloria, who had her head resting in the crook of her arm. "Good luck, Cipriana," Gloria whispered, waving with her pinky. "You can do it," she said.

Immediately, Cipriana felt lonely, afraid that her best friend would never know that she was smart too. She was heartened by the thought that if she were one of the finalists to recite the entire poem on Friday, her father would think she was smart. And perhaps, her mother would take off from school to come and see Cipriana. And maybe even Mama Fela would break her own rule and come out of the house before spring. Her daydreams quickly turned to alarm as she realized that the time was drawing near. She still had twelve lines to go.

Even if she didn't know every line, she longed to beat Mary Jane Beford and Ruby Quinn and Jim Forest. She was determined to win the tryout and go on to the recital on Friday. But first she had six more lines to go.

"Time's up," Miss Shute called. "I'll call you in alphabetical order. Each of you will recite what you can in your best oratory possible. Remember to pronounce each word clearly and be expressive."

Cipriana felt like she was in two worlds at once. In one, she drowned out all sound and studiously reviewed her poem one last time. In the other, she floated above the scene, observing and remembering what she saw. Mary Jane was proficient, but Cipriana knew that she would be. She always studied hard but in Cipriana's opinion, every line sounded a little like the one before it. James Forest would win because he did everything well. He didn't have any friends though. Sarah Faye Gale was awful. Cipriana had to strain to hear her at all and Cipriana figured that Miss Shute was having the same problem. "Speak up, Sarah Faye," she kept saying at intervals when Sarah seemed to pause at the end of a stanza. From long experience, Cipriana knew that Emma Parsons wouldn't win because she was just plain dumb. Surprising no one, Emma forgot half her lines too. Samuel Ployt was smart in every subject. Cipriana thought he had to be, because his father was a principal in the county schools. Taking a ratcheted breath, Cipriana realized there were two to go: she and Ruby Quinn. For the first time in her life, she was happy that her last name came at the end of the alphabet. Briefly, she returned to the world, where she was able to take in her poem one final time. Instead of air, she breathed in the black and white of the words before her.

Finally it was her turn. She could hear herself swallow. She looked over at Gloria, who smiled. Standing at the front of the class with all eyes on her, she willed herself to move her lips. Before she knew it, she could hear words gushing from her mouth as easily as water flowed from the water faucet at the Stevensons'. At one particular point, she said something that made the other children laugh. Surprised at their giggles, but driven to finish, she continued with earnestness. She surprised herself when she said the final word.

On the way back to her seat, the moment was ruined for Cipriana when Esteban whooped, "You said chore instead of choir. Even I know that word, dummy," he teased.

Cipriana wondered what Esteban meant. Sliding into her seat, she quickly scanned the poem with her finger guiding her but by the time she found the mistake, everyone was clapping for James. And then Ruby. And then Cipriana heard the teacher calling out her name. Her name! She couldn't believe it.

"Cipriana, dear. Hurry up, now. Stand at the front of the class with the other winners. You and Ruby Quinn and James Forest will represent our class on Friday and will compete for first place."

"Me, teacher?" Cipriana asked, wide-eyed.

"Yes you, dear. And you did a mighty fine job of it too. Now study hard before Friday's recital so you won't be the least bit nervous. Good luck, Cipriana." Turning to the class at large, Miss Shute said, "Now, let's give everyone a nice big round of applause."

Cipriana started to clap but her thoughts quickly escaped to a place where they seemed to be floating on air. She could see the other children clapping. Some were staring at her; Esteban was making faces. All of them were clapping, though, far far away. Cipriana started to understand what Miss Shute meant by being nervous.

When at last school was out, Cipriana ran all the way to Mama Fela's, aching to tell her the news.

"Mama Fela! I won! I won!" she yelled, bursting open the door of her grandmother's house. Mama Fela was at her sewing machine, looking up at Cipriana over the top of her spectacles.

"What? What did you win, 'jita?"

"The contest, Mama Fela. Teacher picked three kids to say the whole poem on Friday. And I was one of them."

Without saying a thing, Mama Fela got up and opened her armario. She reached up to the top shelf, standing on her tiptoes, moving her hand along like she was dusting it. Just then Cipriana had the sudden urge to tickle her grandmother's underarm, but somehow she knew now wasn't the time. To Cipriana, her Mama Fela seemed perturbed at something instead of full of joy, as Cipriana had expected. At the very least, Cipriana knew her grandmother wasn't in the mood for play. But Mama Fela's reaction puzzled her. She thought Mama Fela would be proud of her.

"What's wrong, Mama Fela?"

"Shh. Leave me to my thoughts for a moment, 'jita."

Cipriana flinched at Mama Fela's rebuff. For a brief moment, she watched as her grandmother continued to silently search the armario. Finally, she sat down at the kitchen table and took out her poem.

The impolite clop of Mama Fela's heavy black shoes alerted Cipriana to her grandmother's return. With her coat buttoned up to her neck and a scarf wrapped tightly around her head, she barked, "Come, 'jita," and Cipriana obeyed immediately. As her grandmother descended the stone steps in front of her, Cipriana caught sight of her Mama Fela's purse hanging from the crook of her arm as it often did on their summer jaunts. Her heart skipped an excited beat.

"Where are we going, Mama Fela?" Cipriana asked eagerly.

"Shh. Let's just hurry, 'jita."

"But, it's still winter, Mama Fela. Your legs? Don't they hurt?"

"Que pain ni pain, 'jita. We have something important to do."

Cipriana didn't say anything anymore because she had to run alongside Mama Fela to keep up. She had never seen her grandmother walk so fast. By the time they crossed Route 66 and stepped into the train station, Cipriana struggled to catch her breath. "Wait, Mama Fela," she huffed and puffed.

Mama Fela ignored her. Instead she walked right up to the ticket counter and waved Cipriana over.

"Tell him we want to send a message."

"To who, Mama Fela?"

"Never mind, Cipriana. Just tell him."

Mama Fela snapped her purse open. She dug through it until she found a slip of paper and snapped it shut once again. She hesitantly gave Cipriana the piece of paper as if she wasn't sure she could trust her with it. But her eyes danced.

When Cipriana read what was on that paper, she jumped up and down. She stopped long enough to translate what Mama Fela was telling her for the telegraph operator. He tapped a little machine, his finger moving so fast it was a blur. And Cipriana's heart danced just as fast.

He read the message back to them word for word. "To Cita Romero, 247 Spruce, Las Vegas, New Mexico. Stop. Cipriana best in her class. Stop. Says poem in front of school. Stop. This Friday. Stop. Six P.M. Stop. Please come. Stop. Mamá. Stop." Finally he said, "That'll be fifty cents, ma'am."

Mama Fela raised her eyebrows and Cipriana knew what her grandmother was thinking without having to ask.

"Are you sure?" Cipriana asked the man.

When he nodded, unsmiling, Mama Fela dumped everything from her coin purse and counted out two dimes, four nickels, and ten pennies. "Lucky I haven't been to church for a while," she murmured, chuckling. Cipriana proudly pushed the money across the smooth counter.

When they arrived back at the stone house, Mama Fela added wood to the fire and made coffee while Cipriana studied her poem. They both drank it black with a single teaspoon of sugar. For a brief moment, Cipriana considered adding a little more sweetness to her cup when Mama Fela wasn't looking but upon further contemplation, she decided that she didn't want to ruin her grandmother's opinion of her altogether so she restrained the impulse. Cipriana longed for Mama Fela to think that she was growing up to be just like her.

Together, they tore their tortillas into pieces, dunked them in the coffee that swirled in the saucers, and spooned them into their mouths. Mama Fela listened while Cipriana recited her lines. Each time she forgot one, Mama Fela gave her a hint. Mama Fela could no longer see out of one eye, though, and Cipriana was afraid that her one good eye would get tired after so much strain so she soon decided to put away her poem and talk to her grandmother instead. After thinking it over a little while, Cipriana decided to ask Mama Fela something that had long been on her mind.

"Mama Fela," she began hesitantly, "Mama once told me you went to heaven for a little while but didn't like it so you came back. Is that true?"

Mama Fela chuckled, not with any sound coming out of her mouth, but with her chest moving up and down. Immediately, Cipriana regretted asking the question.

"No, no, 'jita, I'm not laughing at you. It's just that what you say is so true. I couldn't have said it any better myself."

"But why didn't you like it? I thought it was supposed to be the best place anywhere."

"I thought so too, 'jita, until I went there. It wasn't at all what I expected."

"Why not, Mama Fela?" Cipriana asked.

Mama Fela remained quiet for a long time, blowing out the smoke from her tiny cigarette and tapping the ashes into her empty saucer. "I guess, mi'jita," she said slowly, "because it wasn't home. I would rather be here talking with you than with all the angels in heaven."

"But what if you got to talk to God Himself?"

Mama Fela smiled then. "Perhaps it might be tolerable then, mi'jita, but . . ." Mama Fela paused, staring at Cipriana with her good eye. "He had better speak Spanish, mi'jita, because I can tell you one thing, I'm not going to speak with a mocho to my god. I'm not going to speak English or Latin or any other language but mine."

"But, Mama Fela, what if they won't let you into heaven unless you speak English?"

"Then I'll be on this earth for a very long time, Cipriana. A very long time."

Cipriana nodded. "I hope so, Mama Fela," she said.

After she finished her cigarette, Mama Fela took a package wrapped in waxy brown tissue paper from her bed and gave it to Cipriana.

"There now, 'jita. Open it."

"What is it, Mama Fela?"

"I've been working on it a while. It's your Easter dress but it will do for your recital too."

"Oh, Mama Fela," Cipriana exclaimed, fingering the navy-blue sailor dress.

"It's a rayon piqué, 'jita. Your mama bought the gold braid and the gold buttons and stars from the catalog."

"It's beautiful, Mama Fela."

"Not yet but it will be. It still needs some work. Come . . . ," she said, standing. "Try it on while I get my pincushion."

"Will it be ready in time, Mama Fela?"

"Cipriana, for something as important as this, I'll work day and night if I have to. You do good in school. That's your job. Mine is to make you a pretty dress."

Cipriana stepped up onto a chair while Mama Fela looked over her work, sighing. "You've filled out a bit, mi'jita. You're looking more and more like that girl in the pictures. What's her name?" Mama Fela asked, winking.

"Mama Fela, you know her name!"

Mama Fela took up Cipriana's hands in hers, smoothing the skin over Cipriana's bony hands with her thumbs. "No dimples, yet, mi'jita," she told Cipriana. "Better get you fattened up some more. But not until you've worn this dress first."

Cipriana jumped down, wondering how the dress would look when it was finished. She could imagine looking just like Shirley Temple, dimples and all.

"Now you better go see if your daddy's home yet, 'jita. I have a lot of work to do still."

The days passed by but Cipriana hardly noticed because all she could think about was the poem she was to recite on Friday. The day finally arrived whether she wanted it to or not. She didn't have much say in the matter.

"Mama's not here yet," Cipriana said, looking anxiously out the window.

"She'll be here, don't worry, 'jita."

"But where is she, Daddy? You said she'd come."

"Better get ready, 'jita. We have to be at the school in twenty minutes."

"Where's Mama Fela?"

"She said she'd meet us there."

"Did Tía Cita come, Daddy?"

"Why so many questions, 'jita? You nervous?"

Cipriana nodded. Even though she knew the poem backward and forward, she was scared. The entire school was going to be there. And their parents too. "What if I mess up, Daddy?" she asked, her voice cracking.

Robert bent down then and touched Cipriana's cheek. "You're going to make us proud, 'jita. You're smart just like your mama and you've been studying so hard. No matter what happens tonight, you're already a winner in my mind. Now go get ready, Patas Largas."

Giggling, Cipriana ran to her bed. There, she slipped on her new sailor dress, breathing in Mama Fela's lavender smell. She fingered the gold braid along the cuffs of the sleeves. She touched the stars that decorated the sailor flap across her shoulders and suddenly, she felt more ready than ever to recite the poem to so many new faces. But she knew now that the faces that mattered weren't going to be there: Mama's and Tía Cita's and Papa Gil's. They just weren't, but she couldn't let their absence stop her. She was going to make herself proud. And Mama Fela. And her father too. Reciting the poem one last time, she watched herself in her mother's hand mirror. Smiling, she poked her cheek to see if any dimples had come in the night.

It was just getting dark when they set out for the school. Cipriana walked in front of her father as he pulled Pablito by the hand and carried the baby in one arm. No one said a word. Cipriana could hear her father's footsteps trailing behind her and the snap and crackle of Pablito's stuffed-up breathing. While these sounds calmed her, she said the poem to herself once again.

When they arrived at the auditorium, they squeezed in through the side door. Cipriana looked all around, searching for her class, but the grown-ups blocked her view. Finally, with her father close behind, she made her way up to the front of the auditorium where she found her class sitting cross-legged in several rows, except for Esteban, who was rocking back and forth on his heels. When Miss Shute saw Cipriana, she scurried over like a jackrabbit being chased by a coyote. The teacher shook Robert's hand quickly and then directed Cipriana toward the stage, telling her that she needed to join Ruby and James immediately. Cipriana waved to her father as he called out, "Good luck, 'jita." Just then, someone touched her shoulder.

Turning, she was astonished to see her mother standing there. Graciela's dress was dirty and she had a black smudge down the side of her cheek. It took a moment for Cipriana to register that this was her beautiful mother, who didn't quite look like herself.

"I'm sorry I'm late, 'jita," she said. "Wouldn't you know it? I had a flat tire."

"Oh, Mama, you came!" Cipriana said, hugging her mother's middle. Taking her mother in with all her senses, she thought Graciela smelled like the wind. She could feel her mother's gentle hand smoothing her hair, which made her only want to squeeze Graciela harder. Then she felt the kiss on top of her head and an instant pang of happiness coursed through her veins.

"I wouldn't have missed this for anything, Cipriana. Your daddy had Tío Juan drive him down yesterday just to tell me."

"He did?"

Graciela nodded and seeing Robert not far away, she waved. She bent down then and lifted Cipriana's chin. "You look so grown up, 'jita, in your sailor dress. You do your daddy and me proud."

As if by instinct, Cipriana suddenly spit onto her fingers and tried to rub away the smudge on her mother's face. Graciela laced her fingers through Cipriana's and whispered, "No need, Cipriana. You focus on your poem now. That's all there is right at this moment," she said, nodding toward the stage.

Cipriana took the steps up to the stage two at a time and sat beside Ruby Quinn. It was so loud in the auditorium that she felt dizzy with the whirl of sounds and faces buzzing around her. It seemed like all of Santa Lucía was there. She gave up trying to say her poem to herself because she couldn't hear her own thoughts. She scanned the crowd for her mother and father but they were swallowed up in the sea of faces she didn't recognize. She looked for Mama Fela but didn't see her either. She wondered if maybe her grandmother's eye was bothering her. Or maybe her legs were aching after their trip to the telegraph office. Or maybe Mama Fela decided to wait until spring after all, to come out of her house again. None of these possibilities were very reassuring to Cipriana.

The program began with a speech by the principal but Cipriana didn't pay any attention. The quiet had come back and so she returned to the poem inside her head. She practiced while the first and second graders sang. But before she knew it, the time had come. Cipriana, Ruby, and James stood from their chairs as their class joined them up on stage. At first, Cipriana wasn't sure if her legs were going to hold her up. They felt like they could wobble off at any moment. But when the children in her class started up their stanzas, one right after the other, Cipriana felt lucky that she would have time to get the feeling back in her legs. She shook them one at a time, squeezed them with her fingertips, and prayed, thankful to be in the back row.

After the applause stopped, their teacher introduced James, Ruby, and Cipriana. "These are three of my finest students," she said. Cipriana looked around, not really believing that Miss Shute was talking about her. "They represent the best of their class, the best that Santa Lucía

Elementary has to offer. You should be very proud of them for they have passed a rigorous test of memory and poise to get here tonight. This evening, they will compete for first place by reciting Longfellow's 'The Village Blacksmith.' Now then, let us get started."

James went first, then Ruby. Cipriana was last. As she moved to the edge of the stage, she looked out over the audience but she couldn't see anyone she knew. She cleared her throat, mimicking her father's morning ritual, and opened her mouth, but nothing would come out. She saw the lines of the poem in her head flashing one after the other but Cipriana could not force them out of her lips. All she could think about was how her parents had told her how proud they were but now their opinion would change. She could envision her mother returning to school, not even staying for the weekend because Cipriana had embarrassed her. She could feel Mama Fela ripping off the dress she made for her right in front of all her classmates, showing Cipriana's *nalgas*, and she shivered. Cipriana cleared her throat again because she knew these things didn't have to happen. She looked out into the audience, knowing she was looking for something but she didn't know what. And then, from out of nowhere, a booming voice called out, "Dame un speeche, mi'jita." And Cipriana knew that it could only belong to one person: her Papa Gil. She couldn't see him but she knew he was there watching her.

Cipriana puffed herself up like Papa Gil often instructed her to do when she was making a speech for him. He always said people would think you had something important to say if you made them believe you did. She looked out into the audience like she knew every face there. And Cipriana said the words, some soft, some loud, some drawn out and some quick, like she was telling a story. Papa Gil always said that a speech was a good story. It was about trying to convince someone of something they didn't want to believe. And so Cipriana recited her poem, every word, to every person there.

When she was done, she didn't care what people would think. She jumped off the stage and ran into the crowd as the clapping grew louder, not knowing where she was going but sure of what she would find. And there was her Papa Gil in a dirty old jacket, patches at his knee, his beard long and scraggly. He opened his arms wide and Cipriana ran into them, hugging him with all her might.

"Sorry, mi'jita," he whispered. "I didn't have time to wash up. I smell like the llano."

"It's all right, Papa Gil. I like the smell of the llano."

"You gave a good speech tonight, mi'jita."

Cipriana smiled. "But how did you know, Papa Gil? How did you know about my recital?"

"I knew," he said, chuckling.

"He knew," Mama Fela said as she walked up behind him, followed by Cipriana's mother and father, Pablito, and the baby. Cipriana still wondered if maybe Tía was on her way. Just then, Mama Fela handed her a tube. "This came for you today," she said. "I meant to give it to you before you started, but we were a little late. El viejo barbón here was taking his sweet time," she added roughly, but Cipriana could tell there was a smile behind her grandmother's words.

Cipriana pulled a roll of paper out. Graciela helped unroll it, holding onto one corner of the paper while Mama Fela grasped the other. They held it open while Cipriana looked it up and down. "It's me," she said happily. "Tía Cita drew me."

"Look at the hands," Mama Fela said, pointing. "They have dimples, mi'jita."

Cipriana smiled again. And then, looking at the faces around her, she thought maybe Mama Fela was right. Heaven is home.

❧

ACKNOWLEDGMENTS

This novel wouldn't have been possible without my mother, Marie Sierra Baca, whose gift for storytelling fascinated and sustained me after my father died when I was just twenty-one. Not only did her vignettes imbue me with a sense of history and connection at a time of great loss, but they also gave me a sense of purpose. In her accounts, I recognized the potential for fiction and my imagination began to soar where her narrative ended.

My deepest gratitude goes to my editor, Beth Hadas, who instilled hope and confidence at every turn, even in the early stages of the book. She has helped to bring a dream to fruition with her keen insight, her intuitive brushstrokes, and her grounded advice. She is a gifted steward of stories who inspires with her brilliant skill, humor, and strength.

I owe a heartfelt thank you to dear friends: Lucinda Lucero Sachs, a gifted storyteller who sustains me with her enduring friendship and encouragement. Jean Salas Reed, a jewel whose warmth, enthusiasm, and positive energy always inspire me. Eileen Spinelli, a kindred spirit who has taught me about grace by her very essence. Her gentle wisdom, generosity of spirit, and sunny correspondence nourish my soul. Jerry Spinelli, whose warmth, humor, and encouragement mean the world.

Many thanks to my teachers, past and present, who instilled a love of literature and encouraged my own creativity. To name just a few: Debra Ancich, Barbara Mraz, Sister Ruth Dolores, Tim McCorkle, Marilyn Winkler, Rebecca Marks, Jay Fliegelman, Laurie Alberts, and Monica Espinosa. Especially for Ana Castillo, who generously pointed me toward the writing path; Julia Cameron, whose book *The Right to Write* had a profound impact on me as I resurrected my manuscript; and Rudy Anaya, who encouraged me to tell these women's stories.

I am grateful to my family for their support: Jackie has been a steadfast champion of my writing life. Ken, for his interest and praise. Cathy, for helping to create my writing space, and Eugene, who bolstered my sagging confidence when he said, "I didn't know you could do that!"

Most of all, this novel would still be languishing in a box had it not been for my sister Marijo. She was my first reader and supporter extraordinaire, who encouraged, researched, and understood with tremendous empathy and insight. Running her first marathon at age fifty, she motivated me to finish my own project by modeling hard work, perseverance, and commitment. She has been my greatest inspiration.

And finally, for the women who suffered, adapted, persevered, and laughed, but most of all for their strength. To each of them, I say thank you.

❧